Praise for the Baby Ganesh Agency series

'An absolute delight. Vaseem Khan's brilliance lies in the palpable realism that he infuses his characters, man or beast, with.'
Indian Express

'*The Perplexing Theft* maintains the excellent standard of the series, and with the impressive number of plot elements there is never a dull moment.'
Crime Review

'Fans of Alexander McCall Smith will find a lot to like.'
Publishers Weekly

'Delightful and uplifting.'
The Bookseller

'A cast of intriguing characters that it will be a joy to see develop. But the greatest strength is the setting in the teeming city of Mumbai, from which the colour and atmosphere flows out of every page in this enjoyable, whimsical tale.'
Daily Express

'A sparkling debut with a zippy plot and an endearing set of characters.'
The Lady

'A charming story.'
Marie Claire

'Prepare to be completely and utterly charmed . . . While a suspicious death leads Chopra to begin an investigation, it's the descriptions of everyday life that really bring this fascinating novel to life. The baby elephant Ganesha is a star in the making.'
Lovereading

'A quirky murder mystery . . . full of colourful characters and insightful details about human motivation.'
Irish Examiner

Also by Vaseem Khan

The Unexpected Inheritance of Inspector Chopra

THE PERPLEXING THEFT OF THE JEWEL IN THE CROWN

Vaseem Khan

MULHOLLAND
BOOKS

HODDER

First published in Great Britain in 2016 by Mulholland Books
An imprint of Hodder & Stoughton
An Hachette UK company

First published in paperback in 2017

A CIP catalogue record for this title is available from the British Library

Paperback ISBN 978 1 473 61232 7
eBook ISBN 978 1 473 61229 7

Typeset by Hewer Text UK Ltd, Edinburgh
Printed and bound by CPI Group (UK) Ltd, Croydon, CR0 4YY

Hodder & Stoughton policy is to use papers that are natural, renewable
and recyclable products and made from wood grown in sustainable
forests. The logging and manufacturing processes are expected to
conform to the environmental regulations of the country of origin.

Hodder & Stoughton Ltd
Carmelite House
50 Victoria Embankment
London EC4Y 0DZ

www.hodder.co.uk

This book is dedicated to my nephews and nieces. To Safiya, Aiza, Owais, Zayan, Faris, Zakaria and Aadam; and to the team in India, Arjun, Nupur and Aman. If everyone loved animals as much as children do, wouldn't it be a better world?

A TRIP TO SEE A DIAMOND

'Arise, Sir Chopra.'

As the gleaming blade touched gently down upon his shoulder, Inspector Ashwin Chopra (Retd) found himself overcome by a jumble of conflicting emotions. Pride, undoubtedly, at this supreme moment in his life. But with pride came a boundless sense of humility. That he, the son of a schoolmaster from a poor village in the state of Maharashtra, India, could be thus honoured seemed altogether improbable.

After all, what had he really achieved?

He was an honest man who had worn the uniform of the Brihanmumbai Police with an unblemished record for over thirty years – before a traitorous heart had forced him into early retirement – and in the India of today that was something to be proud of indeed.

And yet was integrity enough of a virtue to warrant such an accolade?

Surely there were more deserving candidates . . .

What about his old friend Assistant Commissioner of Police Ajit Shinde, who even now was fighting Naxalite bandits in far-off Gadchiroli and had already lost the tip of his right ear to a sniper's bullet? Or Inspector Gopi Moolchand, who had lost a great deal more when he had selflessly dived into Vihar Lake on the outskirts of Mumbai to rescue a stricken drunk and been attacked by not one but three opportunistic crocodiles?

Chopra was overcome by a sudden sense of pathos, as if this singular occasion marked a peak in his life from which there could now only be a perilous and unwelcome descent.

He stumbled to his feet from the knighting stool and cast around at the circle of gathered luminaries in search of Poppy.

He saw that his wife, radiant in a powder-pink silk sari, was engaged in conversation with a haughty-looking white woman, a peer of the realm whose name Chopra could not recall. Standing in the lee of the old dowager was his old sub-inspector, Rangwalla, fingering the collar of his ill-fitting suit . . . and next to Rangwalla was Ganesha, the baby elephant that Chopra's mysterious Uncle Bansi had sent to him seven months previously with the intriguing missive stating 'this is no ordinary elephant' . . .

He frowned. How did Ganesha get here? Or, for that matter, Rangwalla? And did they *really* allow elephants inside Buckingham Palace?

Chopra turned back to the supreme monarch.

For the first time, he realised that she bore an uncanny resemblance to his mother-in-law, the widow Poornima Devi, right down to the black eye-patch and expression of intense dislike that Poppy's mother had reserved for him ever since she had first set eyes on him all those years ago.

The Queen's mouth opened into a yawning black hole . . . *Dee-dah dee-dah dee-dah!*

Chopra swam back to consciousness with the insistent ringing of the alarm threatening to shatter his eardrums.

He lifted his head dazedly from a carpeted floor and looked around in thorough disorientation. Confused images bobbed before him: a shattered glass display case; the recumbent bodies of numerous well-dressed men and women; bright lights reflecting off dazzling jewellery . . .

Before he could register anything else there was a flurry of movement as a horde of men in black military fatigues poured into the room.

He was hauled unceremoniously to his feet by brusque hands and then frogmarched out of the red-carpeted chamber, down two flights of marbled stairs and out through a fortified doorway into late-afternoon sunlight.

Someone pushed a glass of water into his hands; someone else wafted smelling salts under his nose, jerking him back to alertness. A stern-looking woman shone a penlight into his eyes, then asked him how he was feeling.

Chopra blinked rapidly. He was groggy, his memory slow to return.

He was sitting on a manicured lawn in front of the Prince of Wales Museum in Fort. He recalled, with a sudden rush, that he was there to visit the Grand Exhibition of the Crown Jewels of the United Kingdom. This thought instantly brought with it another: Poppy!

His wife had been with him in the jewel room. He looked around wildly for her.

He saw her standing on the grass just yards away, haranguing a matronly woman in a black uniform.

Chopra scrabbled to his feet and jogged over to his wife, who turned to fling herself at him when she spotted him approaching. 'Are you OK?' she asked, concern in her eyes.

'Yes,' he replied, raising his voice to be heard above the museum's alarm, which continued to ring out over the lawn. 'You?'

'I am fine,' she said. 'But they won't tell me what's going on.'

Chopra looked around.

Around them, black-uniformed guards were running in orderly fashion to blockade the entrances and exits to the museum. Other guards were quickly and efficiently rounding up all those present in the grounds.

On the lawn beside Chopra, his fellow visitors from the room in which he had awoken were being tended to.

And suddenly, with the clarity of a shaft of sunlight spearing a darkened room, Chopra understood what was happening. He recalled what he had seen when he had come to: the broken display case, the recumbent bodies. He believed he had a very good idea of what was going on.

Someone had attempted to steal the Crown Jewels.

Thirty minutes later Chopra and his fellow visitors were marched to the museum's swanky Visitors' Centre and told to wait in a back room. Armed guards were placed at the door to a wail of protests. They were informed, in no uncertain terms, that no one was permitted to leave. Someone would be along to question them soon.

There was nothing to do but wait.

It was another three hours before Chopra was taken to a small, brightly lit room to be interrogated by a man named Deodar Jha, who introduced himself as the commander of Mumbai's Force One Unit. The elite unit was a special anti-terrorist squad set up amidst a blaze of publicity following the 2008 Mumbai terror attacks. Since then the commandos had spent their days sitting in their Goregaon HQ idly polishing the M4 assault rifles they were wielding so impressively today.

Chopra knew that the Force One Unit had been employed to safeguard the Crown Jewels during the exhibition at the Prince of Wales Museum.

It seemed that they had failed.

Jha was a big, round-faced man with an aggressive moustache. He had an arrogant demeanour and the manner of a bully. Chopra, veteran of countless such interviews that he had himself conducted, responded to the commander's questions precisely and accurately. He knew that the faster Jha got his answers, the faster they could all leave. Behind Jha's sweating anger he sensed a growing desperation. Perhaps it was already hitting home that whatever had transpired at the museum would surely cost him his career.

There was a mystery here that would take more than the brute force methods of Force One to solve, Chopra suspected.

'Let's go over this again,' growled Jha. 'One more time: tell me precisely what happened.'

What *had* happened? Chopra tried to concentrate on everything that had occurred that day. As he did so he felt the automatic whirr of memory taking him back, back to the beginning . . .

'We're going to be late.'

Inspector Chopra (Retd) glanced at his wife, Archana – known to all as Poppy – from behind the wheel of his Tata van as she fidgeted in the passenger seat.

Chopra loved his wife dearly, but at this precise instant he was struggling to recall why.

It had been upon Poppy's insistence that they were here now, on their way to the Prince of Wales Museum. Chopra had known that traffic at this hour would be horrendous, but Poppy had been hounding him for days, ever since the exhibition had arrived in Mumbai two weeks earlier, a full ten days before Her Majesty, the Queen made her historic visit to the city.

It was the first time that the Queen had ever visited Mumbai, the first time in two decades that she had set foot on Indian soil. The newspapers had been full of little else.

Poppy, like most in the city, had quickly succumbed to the 'royal malaria', as it had been dubbed. Chopra, however, had remained aloof.

As a closet Anglophile he was secretly delighted that the Queen had chosen to visit Mumbai. But Chopra was a sober and rational man. From his father – the late Shree Premkumar Chopra – he had inherited both an admiration for the British and the progress they had brought to the subcontinent, and a healthy perspective on all that the Raj had taken from Indians. He did not see the need to gush just because Her Majesty had come calling.

Naturally, Poppy did not agree.

All her friends had already been to see the exhibit, she had complained. They talked of nothing else.

Chopra's eventual surrender was inevitable. He had rarely refused his wife anything in the twenty-four years of their marriage. Poppy was a force of nature, flighty, romantic and a devil when aroused. It was far easier to acquiesce to her occasional whims than to act the curmudgeon. And besides, he knew that in the perennial war between the sexes it behoved a husband to surrender the occasional battle.

The trick was picking the right battles to lose.

He glanced again at his wife.

A slavish follower of fashion, Poppy had styled her long, dark hair into a beehive, which seemed to be all the rage following the release of a new Bollywood movie set in the sixties. Her cheeks glowed with rouge and her slender figure was encased in a bottle-green silk sari with gold-flecked trim.

Chopra himself was dressed in his best – and only – suit, a dark affair that his wife complained made him look like an undertaker. But he had not seen the need to purchase a new suit for a simple visit to the museum. The suit had served him well for the past fifteen years; it would serve him well for a few more.

As a concession he had made an effort with the remainder of his appearance. His thick black hair – greying at the temples – was neatly combed and his brisk moustache was immaculate. His deep brown eyes sat above a Roman nose. Nothing could be done about the frown lines, however, that had recently taken up residence on his walnut-brown forehead.

Supressing a sigh, Chopra looked back out at the Horniman Circle in south Mumbai where a hapless constable was attempting to herd the gridlocked panorama of cars, trucks, motorbikes, bicycles, rickshaws, handcarts, pedestrians and stray animals.

If there *is* a hell, he thought, then it cannot be worse than this.

The queue at the ticket window stretched around the stylish new stainless-steel-plated Visitors' Centre. For once the usually riotous mob was being held in check by the presence of the severe-looking Force One commandos patrolling the grounds. A line of them stretched all the way around the museum, adding an air of intrigue to the picturesque formal gardens in which the building sat.

As the queue inched forward, Chopra took the opportunity to once again admire the recently renamed museum. It was now called the Chhatrapati Shivaji Maharaj Vastu Sangrahalaya after the warrior-king Shivaji, founder of the Maratha Empire.

But to Chopra it would always be the Prince of Wales Museum.

As he looked up at its three-storeyed façade clad in kurla stone and topped by a Mughal dome, he felt a gladness knocking on his heart. This feeling overcame him each time he thought of the treasure trove of ancient relics housed inside those walls going back as far as the Indus Valley civilisation, which scholars now claimed might be the oldest of them all.

He had been coming here for nearly three decades, ever since he had first arrived in the megalopolis as a freshly minted constable from his native village in the Maharashtrian interior, a bright-eyed seventeen-year-old with Bombay dreams in his eyes. Since then he had learned a great many lessons, the most painful of which was that all that glittered was not necessarily gold.

The relentless pace of change in the big city often dismayed him. The constant striving for the future, as if the past were a yoke that had to be cast off and trampled into the dust of history. He had found the museum a refuge from this headlong rush into the unknown, a balm for the affliction of nostalgia from which he suffered.

Chopra considered himself a historian, a guardian of the legacy of ancient India, one of a dwindling number. He knew that his country was now intoxicated by progress and the prospect of becoming a superpower. But for Chopra there was still much to be gleaned from the traditions of a culture that had persisted for more than seven thousand years. Modernity was not everything. Technology was not the answer to all problems.

They purchased their tickets and then waited patiently as they were taken inside the Visitors' Centre and thoroughly searched by the Force One guards. Security had been a major concern for the exhibition and Chopra succumbed to the search with due resignation. He had come prepared, without any of the items on the widely advertised prohibited list. Others had not been so sensible.

Chopra watched as the tall, broad-shouldered Sikh man ahead was asked to remove his ceremonial kirpan, the curved dagger that many devout Sikhs carried on their person. The man argued at first but eventually gave up the weapon. Another man insisted on taking in his gutka pouch. He was unceremoniously divested of the offending article.

At least the guards are being thorough, Chopra thought with approval.

All the visitors were asked to deposit their phones and cameras, as these were not permitted inside the exhibition.

Search completed, they were next herded towards the museum's main entrance where they queued up to pass through a metal scanner. Ahead of Chopra a woman refused to give up her gold wedding necklace. The guards inspected it and allowed her to keep it. The big Sikh man set off the scanner with the thick steel bracelet on his wrist, another core article of his faith. This time – when it seemed that he might explode – he was permitted to keep the religious artefact. A portly, aging man argued to be allowed to take in his asthma inhaler. The guards examined the object, turning it this way and that in their calloused hands, then exchanged mystified glances.

Eventually, they shrugged and handed it back.

Finally, they all stepped through the entrance and into the museum's Central Gallery.

Chopra was intrigued to note that the usual exhibits had been replaced by a collection of objects from the days of the Raj. Ordinarily, the Gallery housed pieces from all eras of India's past – a jewelled dagger from the court of Shah Jahan; a terracotta lion from the empire of Asoka the Great; a clay seal from the Harappan civilisation inscribed by that enigmatic and as yet undeciphered Indus Valley script.

Chopra's eyes came to rest on the tacky waxwork models of the British royal family that now took pride of place in the gallery. A plump, middle-aged man with sunglasses parked in his heavily oiled hair had his arm slung cosily around 'the Queen's' waist whilst his wife beamed at him. Chopra glowered.

He would have liked to linger over the Raj exhibits but Poppy was already urging him onwards and upwards.

They followed the herd as everyone jostled their way up the marble staircase, past Miniature Paintings and

Himalayan Arts, to the second floor where the Sir Ratan Tata Gallery had been commandeered for the Crown Jewels exhibit. Four more Force One guards were stationed outside the newly installed reinforced steel doors that now fronted the gallery. The guards straightened to attention as the visitors arrived, their fingers involuntarily flickering to the triggers of their assault rifles.

Chopra knew that the draconian security measures now on display had been inevitable as soon as it was announced that – for the first time in their history – the Crown Jewels would leave their native shores and travel abroad with the Queen. He remembered the fuss in the UK earlier in the year when the press had got wind of the plan. An ancient law had had to be amended just to permit the jewels to be moved.

In truth, very few pieces had been given the all-clear to go abroad. The Indian government had had to give exceptional reassurances, with the Indian Prime Minister himself offering his personal guarantee that no effort would be spared to safeguard the priceless treasures whilst they were on Indian soil.

It was still unclear exactly *why* Her Majesty had agreed to the Indian government's request for the jewels to be exhibited on the subcontinent. The Queen herself had remained tight-lipped on the matter. Chopra, for his part, had always held the monarch in high regard and considered her adherence to traditions emblematic of a bygone age, a time when discretion and good manners were paramount.

Only twenty visitors were permitted inside the Tata Gallery at any one time.

Chopra's group waited impatiently as the previous bunch filed out, buzzing with excitement.

Eventually, they all shuffled into the air-conditioned sanctum of the gallery where they were immediately greeted by two tall, broadly built white gentlemen wielding ceremonial halberds and wearing the ruffed, red and black uniform of the Tower of London guardians. Chopra had read that they were called Beefeaters, a term that had caused some consternation in India, where the bulk of the population considered the cow to be an avatar of God.

The guards stepped aside to reveal a portly Indian in an ill-fitting Nehru jacket, Nehru cap and round-framed spectacles. To Chopra he looked like a plumper version of the freedom fighter Subhash Chandra Bose.

The man welcomed the newcomers with a beaming white smile and spread his arms as if he meant to sweep them all up in an enormous embrace. 'Welcome to the Crown Jewels exhibition!'

Chopra squinted at the tour guide's nametag: ATUL KOCHAR.

Kochar was an enthusiastic man. He might have been an actor in his spare time, Chopra reflected, such was the animation with which he narrated the tour of the exhibits.

Chopra listened with only half an ear. Like most of the others in the red-carpeted room, his attention was instantly drawn to the Crown Jewels securely ensconced behind various glass display cases stationed around the gallery.

He plucked his reading spectacles from his pocket and pushed them self-consciously onto his nose. From his other pocket he removed his copy of the *Ultimate Guidebook to the Crown Jewels*, which Poppy had insisted they purchase from the Visitors' Centre for an extortionate sum.

As Kochar continued to speak, Chopra peered at the nearest display cases then leafed through the guidebook for the corresponding entries. In spite of the fact that few of the treasures had made it to India, there were, nevertheless, some breathtaking artefacts on display and the guidebook sought to provide the glamorous back story that lay behind each one.

'But how much is it all worth?'

Chopra looked up to see the plump man who had stuck his arm around the waxwork Queen accosting the tour guide with a belligerent expression.

Kochar gave a somewhat strained smile. 'No value can be placed on the Crown Jewels, sir. They are the very definition of priceless.'

'Nonsense,' barked the man bombastically. 'My family are Marwari. We are in the jewel business. There is always a price. Come now, don't be coy. Let us have it, sir.'

A chorus of agreement washed over Kochar.

As he looked on, Chopra felt a twinge of sadness. Was this all these people saw? A dragon's hoard of treasure to be weighed in dollars and rupees? What about the weight of history that lay behind each of these magnificent creations? Or the skill that had been employed to manufacture them?

'Stop your yapping, man. Did you come here to appreciate the jewels or buy them?'

Chopra turned to see the tall Sikh man from the queue glaring at the Marwari. The Sikh was a big, muscular gentleman with a fine beard, fierce, bushy eyebrows and a stupendous yellow turban. The retort that had sprung to the Marwari's lips died a quiet death. His face coloured but he said nothing.

The Sikh pointed to an eight-foot-high sandstone carving of the goddess Kali, which had presumably been left inside the gallery due to the fact that its rear was affixed to the wall. 'You are probably the sort of fool who does not appreciate even our own history.'

Chopra felt an instant affinity with the irate Sikh.

'Yes,' agreed a pretty young woman in a bright blue sari and red spectacles. 'We should all learn to appreciate our own heritage. Only then can we truly appreciate someone else's.'

The crowd swiftly saw which way the wind was blowing and galloped towards the moral high ground. There was a sudden chorus of agreement with the big Sikh. 'Indian culture is the best, no doubt about it!' 'You can keep your Crown Jewels, sir. The Mughals threw away more magnificent treasures when giving alms to the poor!' A circle widened around the Marwari, who blushed furiously.

Kochar spared the hapless man further embarrassment by smoothly drawing everyone's attention to the centrepiece of the exhibit – the Crown of Queen Elizabeth, the Queen Mother, in which was set the Koh-i-Noor diamond.

The presence of the Koh-i-Noor on Indian soil had caused quite a stir.

Ever since the legendary diamond had been 'presented' to Queen Victoria more than one hundred and fifty years earlier it had been the subject of controversy. Many in India felt that the Koh-i-Noor had been stolen by the British, and that it was high time those great colonial thieves were forced to rectify the matter. The news channels had been awash with talk of demonstrations and civic protest, particularly from the India First lobby. In an attempt to ward off potential embarrassment for the government, Mumbai's Commissioner of Police had ordered a clampdown on protests during the royal visit, an act which itself had courted controversy as it was deemed inherently unconstitutional.

Kochar gave a brisk rendition of what he called 'the dark and bloody history of the Koh-i-Noor', beamed at his rapt audience, and then abruptly announced that they had a further fifteen minutes to view the Crown Jewels before they would be requested to make way for the next party.

The crowd dispersed around the room.

Chopra bent down to take a closer look at the diamond.

'Careful, sir. Don't get too close or the sensors will go off. They are very sensitive.'

He looked up to see Kochar smiling wearily at him. He realised that another man, late-middle-aged, with greying hair and a noticeable paunch, was staring down at the crown from the opposite side of the display case. The man's brow was furrowed in consternation and Chopra could make out that he was sweating heavily even though the room was air-conditioned.

The man seemed to notice his scrutiny and looked up with a guilty start.

Chopra's own brow furrowed.

It seemed to him that he had seen this gentleman before, but before he could place him the man turned and shuffled quickly away towards one of the exhibits lining the walls of the gallery.

Chopra looked back at the crown, resplendent on its velvet cushion. His eyes were automatically drawn, once again, to the Koh-i-Noor. The display lighting had been set up so that it accentuated the legendary diamond's beauty. Truly, he thought, it deserves its name: Koh-i-Noor – 'mountain of light'.

And suddenly there was a feeling inside him, like a whispering in his blood. Here was a living tie to the ancient India that he so cherished. He wondered what it would feel like to hold that enormous jewel in his fist, just as the greatest monarchs of the subcontinent had once done. Would he sense the ghost of Babur hovering on his shoulder? Would he know Shah Jahan's misery as he looked longingly at the prize taken from him by his own flesh and blood? The Koh-i-Noor, which, for centuries, had set man against man, king against king, legion against legion . . .

A loud bang jerked him from his reverie.

Instinctively, he turned and looked for the source of the noise. He heard another bang, then another. Alarm tore through him as he saw a dense cloud of smoke swiftly expanding around the room, engulfing everything in a choking miasma of white. The world began to spin around him, the room sliding away into a gentle, sighing darkness. Another noise now, just on the edge of hearing, a thin high-pitched whine that he couldn't identify.

As he slumped to the floor and into unconsciousness, the last image that came to Inspector Chopra (Retd) was of the Koh-i-Noor diamond, spinning in the heart of a white cloud, rays of light shooting from it in all directions, incinerating everything in their path . . .

Chopra completed his account and focused on Jha.

The Force One commander had stood up and was now pacing the small, airless room. Jha had purposely left the air-conditioner off – an old and well-worn interrogative tactic – and the room was as hot as a sauna. Sweat poured down the commander's haggard face, drenching his moustache, but he made no move to wipe it away. He had more pressing concerns.

Jha whirled on Chopra and began peppering him once again with questions: what purpose did you have in coming here today? What time did you arrive? Who else did you know in the jewel room?

These were all questions that Chopra had already answered, but he knew that repetition was another key weapon in the interrogator's arsenal. Jha was trying to force Chopra into changing his account, to reveal some thread that he could use to unravel a dishonest tale. But Jha had forgotten the obvious flaw in this technique: when an interviewee told the truth, his answers would stay the same, no matter how many times you asked your questions.

As Chopra watched Jha fumbling, his mind whirled with questions of his own, questions brought about by some of the revelations that Jha had inevitably disclosed during his interrogation. How had the thieves managed to smuggle the gas canisters into the museum with which they had incapacitated Chopra and the other visitors? How had they shattered the supposedly impregnable reinforced glass of the display case? How had they then achieved the miracle of vanishing from the crowded and heavily guarded museum with their stolen treasure?

By the time Jha wearily dismissed him, Chopra had come to the private conclusion that this was a mystery that would prove beyond Jha's ability to solve, a mystery that would swiftly become a national scandal.

What would the Indian government do then?

POPPY'S BAR & RESTAURANT

Some hours later, when Chopra arrived at the restaurant after dropping Poppy back at their apartment complex, he found the place in its usual state of regimented chaos. The harrowing events of the afternoon had left him in need of a quiet hour or two with his own thoughts and so he had come to the restaurant just as he usually did at about this time each day.

The dining area, with its chequered tablecloths and glitzy chandeliers, was a cauldron of animated chatter and beguiling smells. He picked his way through the crammed tables, accepting greetings from regular patrons, many of whom were old police friends, but not stopping to converse.

Quickly, he made his way to the rear office of the establishment he had opened following his forced retirement from the police service earlier in the year.

Once inside his office, he flicked on the air-conditioner, only to hear it gurgle and wheeze to an untimely death.

Cursing, he picked up the phone and ordered a lime water and a dampened handkerchief from the kitchen.

He then slumped back in his padded chair and allowed his thoughts to return to the tumultuous events at the Prince of Wales Museum, going over the details Jha had let slip during his ham-fisted interrogation.

The robbery had been immaculate.

The thief or thieves had entered the Tata Gallery from the rear, blasting a hole through the unguarded, sealed door at the back of the gallery with a shaped explosive charge. Once inside, they had rendered the occupants of the gallery unconscious by using pressurised gas canisters. The thieves had then somehow broken through the reinforced glass of the display case housing the Crown of Queen Elizabeth, as well as shattering some of the surrounding cases. Puzzlingly, they had taken only the crown and, with this single prized possession, had fled the scene through the destroyed rear door. The door led to a passage that connected the Tata Gallery to the Jahangir Gallery in the east wing of the museum. The thieves, it was presumed, had taken the unguarded fire exit stairs, halfway along the passage, down to the ground floor . . . where they had promptly vanished into thin air.

Clearly, the ring of Force One guards stationed around the perimeter of the museum had not spotted anyone fleeing the scene. The instant that the glass display case had been shattered an alarm had gone off, placing each commando on red alert. Not even Houdini could have slipped through the net. The museum had been instantly locked down and every single person in the building had been rounded up and searched, as well as every corner of the museum premises.

Nothing.

The sound of a truck backfiring on the main road returned Chopra to the present.

He stood up and made his way through the restaurant's kitchen to the compound at the rear.

The generous space was lit by a single yellow tubelight around which a cloud of midges roiled. The compound was walled in on three sides by crumbling brick walls topped by a confetti of multicoloured shards of bottle glass. A narrow alley ran from the compound back along the side of the restaurant and out on to Guru Rabindranath Tagore Road.

The noise of late-evening traffic drifted in, punctuated by the occasional blood-curdling scream as a pedestrian came too close to the passing vehicles.

Chopra walked to the rear of the space and lowered himself into the rattan armchair that he had installed under the tubelight. The light was suspended from a line strung between the compound's single mango tree and a TV antenna on the roof of the restaurant. It swung gently in a sudden breeze that leavened the muggy December heat.

Beneath the mango tree, a grey shape stirred.

A flush of warmth moved through Chopra as Ganesha raised his trunk and gently ran the tip over his face. 'How are you, boy?' he murmured.

The moment lasted only an instant before the elephant turned away huffily and hunkered back down into the mudbath in which he had been wallowing.

Chopra knew that Ganesha was upset with him. It was just another sign of the young calf's burgeoning personality.

When he had first been sent the baby elephant by his Uncle Bansi Chopra had not known what to do with the creature. What did he, a retired police officer, know about caring for an elephant? But gradually, as Ganesha had accompanied – and then actively helped – him in solving the murder of a local boy, he had come to realise that there was something mysterious and unique about the little creature. His uncle's words, set down in the letter that had arrived with his strange gift, had come back to him then: 'remember . . . this is no ordinary elephant'.

Once a sceptic, Chopra was now a believer.

There was something improbable about Ganesha, something quite beyond Chopra's ability to slot him into the neat little boxes of rationality and logic that he had lived by his whole life. There were depths to the elephant that he had yet to fathom. And, of course, there was the mystery of the creature's past, upon which he had singularly failed to shed any further light.

Ganesha: a riddle inside an enigma wrapped inside an elephant.

Often, when he looked into Ganesha's gentle brown eyes, he would think he saw his Uncle Bansi staring back at him. The same mischievous uncle who had grown from a rascally boy into a white-bearded wandering sadhu, disappearing from their Maharashtrian village for years at a time only to return with tall tales of magical encounters in faraway lands that he would share with his callow nephew and credulous kinsmen.

Chopra knew that one day he would get to the bottom of the mystery, but for now he had barely enough time to count his blessings, as his wife took pains to regularly remind him. After all, not only had the restaurant got off to a flying start, so had the second venture that he had embarked upon following his retirement.

Chopra had been a police officer for more than thirty years. For thirty years he had awoken, put on his khaki uniform, taken the police jeep to the nearby Sahar station and settled down behind his desk knowing that he was about to embark upon his allotted duty in life. For thirty years he had been a man with a purpose, one that was perfectly suited to both his disposition and his talents.

And then, one day, following a heart attack that had dropped on him out of a clear blue sky, a doctor had told him that he was the victim of a curse called 'unstable angina' and that the next time the attack might be fatal. To his despair Chopra had been forced to leave the police service and ordered to avoid stressful activity.

This had been easier said than done.

The murder that Chopra had subsequently solved had opened a can of worms in Mumbai, implicating senior politicians and policemen in a nationwide human trafficking operation. The scandal had done wonders for the new Baby Ganesh Detective Agency and they had been inundated with cases ever since.

And yet . . . the cases that now came his way were hardly the same as those he had tackled as head of the Sahar police station.

Take the past few months. Chopra had spent endless days trailing errant husbands and delinquent children. He had tracked down missing wills. Companies engaged his services to check up on the backgrounds of dubious employees; political parties paid him to uncover potential skeletons in the closets of election hopefuls. He was even approached by worried parents wishing to discreetly verify the bona fides – and assets – of aspiring sons-in-law.

It was all steady work.

Yet the truth was that such cases did not quicken the pulse the way a solid police investigation did. There was no sense of the greater good being achieved.

Chopra had always believed in the ideal of justice. He knew that sometimes justice was a malleable notion, particularly in India where money and power often tainted the application of due process. But this did not alter his view that the books of the cosmos could only be balanced when good and evil fought and good came out on top.

He shuffled around in the rattan chair, seeking a more comfortable position. His right hip hurt from where he had slumped onto the floor at the Prince of Wales Museum.

'Come now, Ganesha, be reasonable,' he said to the elephant. 'I could hardly have taken you with me. They would never have let you into the exhibition.'

Ganesha snuffled noisily and hunched further away.

Chopra sighed. It was bad enough, he thought, to be burdened by a temperamental wife, but to also have to adjust to a temperamental one-year-old elephant was sufficient to try even the patience of a saint.

He decided that young Ganesha would be best left alone until he had overcome his fit of pique.

Pulling a sheaf of papers from the leather document folder that he had carried out into the compound with him, he excavated a calabash pipe from his pocket and set it into the corner of his mouth.

Chopra did not smoke. The calabash pipe was an affectation that he employed to promote clear thinking. He had long been a devoted fan of Sherlock Holmes – in particular the incarnation portrayed by Basil Rathbone in the 1940s – and the calabash pipe gave him an instant sense of stepping into the great detective's shoes.

He settled his spectacles onto his nose and began to read.

Soon he was engrossed in his work. A mosquito hummed by his ear and he swatted it away without lifting his eyes. Smells and sounds drifted out from the restaurant kitchen: the nose-crinkling odour of frying onions and seared garlic; the chilli haze of innumerable exotic spices; the spit and sizzle from Chef Lucknowwallah's giant copper pans; the growl of the clay tandoor.

He sneezed as a waft of ginger tickled his nose – he had always been fiercely allergic to the stuff.

The smells from the kitchen mingled with the undercurrent of elephant dung in the backyard. The odour was somewhat leavened by the sweet scent of ripe mango and jacaranda blossom floating in from the neighbouring Sahar International Cargo & Freight Company compound. The on-off breeze carried with it a raga from an old Bollywood movie playing on a nearby radio.

After a while Chopra realised that Ganesha had turned back to him and was watching him work. He peered at his young ward over his spectacles. 'Something extraordinary happened today. There was a robbery at the museum. They stole the Koh-i-Noor. It is going to be a big scandal: mark my words.'

To his credit, Ganesha did indeed seem intent on his every word. Chopra reached out and patted him on his knobbly skull.

When Ganesha had first arrived he had been undernourished, quite the frailest elephant Chopra had ever laid eyes on. In his letter, Uncle Bansi had given no clue as to where Ganesha had been born or in what circumstances he had been sent to Mumbai and to Chopra.

It had taken a long time for him to earn the little elephant's trust.

He was not by nature a sentimental man, but there was no doubt that the bond that had grown between them meant as much to him as any human relationship. In a way, Ganesha was now the child that he and Poppy had never been able to have. Poppy certainly treated their ward as if he were a member of the family, doting on him and spoiling him with treats such as the never-ending supply of bars of Cadbury's Dairy Milk chocolate that Ganesha was addicted to.

There was something universally endearing about the elephant calf. Certainly he was much loved by Chopra's friends and the staff at the restaurant, with the notable exception of Poppy's bilious mother.

He turned back to his papers. They comprised his handwritten notes on the various cases that he was currently working on as lead and only detective of the Baby Ganesh Agency. They all seemed so mundane in comparison to the theft of the Koh-i-Noor. Now *there* was a case! He felt a sudden pang of envy for the officer who would land that investigation. Envy, and sympathy, too. The whole world would be looking over the poor man's shoulder.

The rear door leading from the kitchen swung open, its fly-screen cracking vigorously against the whitewashed clapboard wall.

Chopra watched as young Irfan emerged into the moon-lit compound.

For a second the boy stood on the creaking veranda beneath the cantilevered porch roof. Below the veranda, bullfrogs chorused a late-evening dirge. The boy knelt down and lit a mosquito coil, the acrid smoke adding to the panoply of smells in the compound. Then he straightened and came trotting over the knobbly grass, the steel bucket in his hand clanking by his side.

Chopra turned as Ganesha lumbered to his feet. He couldn't help but note the sudden sparkle in the young elephant's eyes.

Ganesha greeted Irfan with an exuberant bugle.

Irfan set down the bucket and rubbed the elephant on the crown of his forehead and then tickled him behind his ears. A smile split the young boy's features. Ganesha wrapped his trunk around the boy's thigh and attempted to haul him off his feet. Irfan guffawed loudly.

Chopra watched the pair horsing around and felt happiness flower inside him. Ganesha and Irfan had become firm friends and he knew that this was good for both of them.

He recalled the day six months previously, just a week after he had opened the restaurant, when Irfan had walked into his office.

VASEEM KHAN

Chopra had been up to his neck in paperwork. Who knew that a business required such meticulous recordkeeping – an honest business, at any rate? He had looked up as the young boy, clearly a street urchin, peered at him from the far side of the desk. Irfan had seemed to him no different from a million other street children in the city of Mumbai. His only garments were a tattered vest and ancient shorts; his dark hair, streaked blond in places by constant exposure to the sun, was an unkempt mass; coloured strings – makeshift charm bracelets – were wrapped around his wrists; his hazel eyes were milky and his thin frame the product of years of malnutrition. And yet there was something about the boy, some indomitable sense of the human spirit, that shone through in his steadfast gaze and confident swagger.

Chopra reached into his pocket and removed a one-rupee coin. He held it out to the boy.

'I did not come here for baksheesh, sir.'

Chopra looked surprised. 'Then why did you come?'

'To become a waiter.'

Chopra smiled. 'You are too young to be a waiter.'

'What age do you have to be to be a waiter?'

Chopra opened his mouth and realised that the question had no answer.

'Well, how old are *you*?'

The boy shrugged. 'I don't know. But old enough to be a waiter.'

Another smile tugged at the corners of Chopra's mouth. 'Where do you live?'

The boy shrugged again. 'Everywhere. Nowhere. Whole Mumbai is my home.'

He knew then that the boy was one of the nameless, faceless masses who lived on Mumbai's overcrowded streets; beneath flyovers hurtling with traffic and in darkened alleyways smelling of human excrement; in shanty squats slapped together with discarded junk and inside the mouths of abandoned concrete sewage pipes.

'Where are your parents?'

'I have no parents.'

'Who looks after you?'

The boy prodded his chest. 'I look after me.' Then he pointed at the ceiling. 'And He, too.'

Chopra marvelled at the boy's cheerful disposition. 'What is your name?'

'Irfan, sir.'

He examined the boy, his eyes travelling the length of his undernourished physique. He noted the bruises on the boy's arms – reminiscent of the marks left behind when wooden lathis were beaten upon human skin – and the cigarette-burn scars forming a constellation of dark stars on his shoulders. He noted the crooked set of the boy's left hand, a physical deformity of birth. 'How can you be a waiter with one hand, Irfan?' he said gently.

'Sir, Gandhiji conquered the British only with his words. Why I cannot be a waiter with one hand?'

Chopra felt an unbidden lump steal into his throat. He wondered if someone had informed the boy of his fondness for Gandhi.

Inspector Ashwin Chopra (Retd) lived by Mohandas Gandhi's words and the personal example of charity and human kindness he had set forth for his countrymen to follow. He suspected that if the great statesman had been in the room at that moment he would have had a few choice things to say to him . . . Why was he hesitating? If ever a child deserved the benefit of the doubt, then surely it was this indomitable youth standing before him.

He watched now as Irfan slid the bucket beneath Ganesha's trunk. It contained Ganesha's evening ration of milk. Chopra's nostrils flared as he smelled the generous helping of coconut milk and ghee that Chef Lucknowwallah had added to the milk. The chef believed that Ganesha needed fattening up and had taken to lacing the milk with rich additives. The luxurious diet seemed to agree with Ganesha, who was filling out nicely.

'Chopra Sir, I have something for you also.' Irfan reached inside his garish pink waiter's jacket – worn, as per Poppy's instructions, above equally garish pink shorts – and handed over a sheaf of envelopes and string-tied manila folders.

Chopra felt his heart sink.

Less than a year in and his fledgling detective agency was busier than he could ever have imagined. He had always known that Mumbai was a hotbed of crime, but who knew that it was also a place of such familial intrigue? It seemed that everyone with a missing pet or errant husband was beating a path to Chopra's door. In the past months he had had to turn away case after case. There simply weren't enough hours in the day.

It was fortunate, Chopra often thought, that young Irfan had turned out to have a razor-sharp mind and a near photographic memory. Although the boy was all but illiterate – a lack that Poppy was desperately trying to convince Irfan to remedy – he had become, through sheer necessity, Chopra's de facto assistant. Irfan was now adept at managing the ever-increasing backlog of files, juggling irate customers who called demanding progress reports, and generally helping Chopra to stay on top of the spinning logs beneath his feet.

With a guilty conscience Chopra put the manila case folders to one side and instead focused on the envelopes.

Ever since he had placed an advert in the local paper he had been inundated with applicants. The fact that he had advertised for the position of 'associate private investigator', however, appeared to have completely escaped the vast majority of those who had written to him.

He knew that in a city of twenty million, finding gainful employment was no trivial matter. And yet he was continually taken aback by the singular unsuitability of the mountain of applications that he had been forced to read each evening since placing the advert. He wondered if there was something inside the human psyche that convinced people that the role of private investigator was one that anyone could turn their hand to – like writing. They said that there was a novel waiting inside everyone. Perhaps there was a private detective hiding inside everyone too, he thought cynically. After all, snooping on one's neighbours was possibly the oldest hobby in the world.

Chopra believed that people were intrinsically different. They had different talents, dispositions and motivations.

Sometimes it took a long time for a person to find out exactly what they were good at. Chance, upbringing, education, all these played a part. But there was also such a thing as karma. Fate. Destiny. Some people were simply born to play certain roles in the great story of life. And others . . . well, he had always believed that you couldn't fit a crooked peg into an honest hole, no matter how hard you tried.

'Sir, Mrs Roy called again today,' Irfan announced. 'She said, "If Chopra does not call me today I will have him arrested for fraud. Then I will have him castrated",' he added helpfully.

Chopra sighed.

Mrs Roy was the wife of the president of the local Rotary Club, a severe and uncompromising woman. Chopra had unwisely accepted a retainer from the old harridan to investigate the possibility that her husband had returned to his old drinking habits, which she had hoped that thirty years of marriage had cured him of. But he had simply not had the time to follow the old sot around. And now his wife was on the warpath.

'What did you tell her?' asked Chopra wearily.

Irfan grinned. 'Do not worry, sir. I told her you were working very hard on her case. I told her that you followed Mr Roy today and that you suspect she is correct.'

Chopra gaped at the boy. 'But that is not true!'

Irfan shrugged. 'What is truth?' he said philosophically. 'This is Mumbai, sir. Truth comes in many disguises. Why don't you call her and tell her you will follow Mr Roy again tomorrow? And then you will give her a final report. That can be the *true* truth, yes?'

Chopra tried to suppress a smile. The boy had initiative, he'd give him that. Still . . . 'Irfan, the next time you wish to give a client advice, please check with me first.'

Irfan looked crestfallen. 'Did I make a mistake, sir?'

Chopra reached out and tousled Irfan's hair. 'No. You merely learned something. Namely, that the client is not always right.'

Chopra watched the smile return to Irfan's face and found a warmth suffusing him. Just as Ganesha had grown close to Irfan, he had grown closer to the boy too, though he would not have been able to express his feelings in the obvious way that his young ward did.

He knew that he had made the right decision by taking him on. Poppy, ever the big-hearted advocate of social change, had applauded his action, though others had not been so easy to convince. Poppy's horrified mother Poornima had warned them against taking in a 'slum dog', a child 'with no name or address'. 'He has probably been lying and thieving since before he could walk,' she had muttered.

'His name is Irfan,' Chopra had said sternly. 'And whatever he was or was not before today is irrelevant. This is his home now.'

To accommodate Irfan he had purchased a charpoy and installed it on the veranda at the rear of the restaurant. This was where Irfan now slept, though it had taken a while for the boy to adjust to his new arrangements. Early on Chopra had discovered that Irfan often slept *beneath* the charpoy instead of on it. 'It is too soft, sir,' Irfan had explained. It had stung him to realise that this child had spent so much of his short life sleeping on the street that even a rope char-poy was too 'soft'.

Chopra hauled himself to his feet. 'Come, let's go and see what Chef has prepared for supper, shall we? The mice are wearing a hole in my stomach.'

ARTHUR ROAD JAIL

The next morning Chopra awoke to find that he had the apartment to himself.

It was a rare luxury.

Chopra lived with Poppy and his mother-in-law on the fifteenth floor of Poomalai Apartments, one of three identical towers that made up the Air Force Colony complex in the bustling Mumbai suburb of Sahar. The apartment was spacious and well ventilated. During the hot post-monsoon months they would leave the windows open, permitting a welcome breeze to cool the place down.

He discovered a note from Poppy on the glass coffee table that sat before the hideous new leather sofa that she had recently installed, though Chopra had seen nothing wrong with the previous one. It had lasted twenty years and he was certain that it had another decade in it, but Poppy was not to be swayed.

The apartment was being transformed on a daily basis. Sometimes a beleaguered Chopra would wake up and think he had somehow ended up in someone else's home. Poppy had been an early victim of the mall mania that had swept the country. It seemed to him that his wife intended to shoe-horn into their home every item of kitsch being recommended by those so-called doyennes of good taste that now held sway over the lives of ordinary Indians just as astrologers and snake-oil swamis had once done.

He read the note. *Have gone to work. Your idlis are in the microwaved oven. Make sure you take your pills. Poppy.*

He frowned.

Ever since Poppy had started her new job she had been a whirlwind of activity.

In all their years of marriage Poppy had never had a real job, substituting for gainful employment a never-ending catalogue of social causes and personal crusades instead, many of her own making. Chopra was used to finding his wife at home in the mornings and when he returned from work in the evenings. Her presence had long been a constant in his life, as was her attentiveness to his needs.

He found that he was, inexplicably, put out by the sudden wife-shaped hole in his life.

His brow darkened as he dwelt momentarily on the individual he blamed for this state of affairs – Sunita Shetty, middle-aged former beauty queen, whose show *Modern Indian Woman* had taken the nation's housewives by storm. The Modern Indian Woman, Ms Shetty regularly informed her audience, was mother, wife and worker. She was honest, able, hard-working and the very vision of chaste beauty. She was both traditional and modern, custodian of India's ancient family values and an icon of fashion and good taste. She was pure, virtuous and effortlessly alluring. A veritable superwoman.

Chopra pottered into the kitchen alcove and recovered his breakfast – steamed idlis with masala sambar – before sitting down in front of the TV.

The sensational robbery at the Prince of Wales Museum dominated the news channels. 'Bungling Bombay Cops' screamed one well-known commentator. 'Koh-i-Noor diamond stolen from under the noses of Mumbai's finest!' roared another tagline.

A clip showed Force One commander Deodar Jha outside the Prince of Wales Museum being hotly pursued by barking newsmen as he retreated to the sanctuary of an armoured truck. Another clip showed a grim-faced Commissioner of Police arriving at the museum in the company of the Chief Minister of Maharashtra. In Delhi the Prime Minister of India appeared on television promising swift action and appealing to the thieves to show a sense of patriotic decency and return the crown forthwith. The leader of the principal opposition party took the opportunity to suggest that the Prime Minister's face had been irredeemably blackened by the incident.

Many channels focused on the plaza outside Mumbai's Lilavati Hospital where a large crowd had gathered. A number of women in the crowd beat their breasts and wailed hysterically. 'She is like our mother,' blubbed one woman, wiping snot from her face with the tip of her sari.

It appeared that the Queen, devastated by news of the theft, had taken ill during the night and had been admitted to the hospital. Her Majesty was due to be flown home the next morning on an RAF jet.

Conspiracy theories were rife.

Fingers were being pointed at the various Indian nationalist organisations that had made such a fuss about the Koh-i-Noor diamond in the first place. A self-satisfied spokesman for India First stated that although his outfit was innocent of the crime he nevertheless fully applauded the act as no more than natural justice demanded. 'How can it be theft if you take back what was stolen from you in the first place?' he opined smugly.

Many commentators warned that the theft would strain Anglo–Indian relations.

A terse statement from the British Prime Minister had already been interpreted as laying the blame for the theft on the complacent security arrangements employed for the protection of the Crown Jewels. Chopra knew that it was only a few letters from 'complacency' to 'complicity'.

There was little doubt that the theft had put many important noses out of joint.

The stakes could not be higher.

The phone rang.

For a moment Chopra fumbled with the shiny new cordless handset his wife had purchased just days earlier and which had so many buttons on it he was thoroughly confused about how to operate the damned thing. When he did manage to answer, he was surprised to hear a voice that he had not heard in many years.

'Chopra? Is that you? It's Garewal here. Shekhar Garewal.'

'Garewal?' Chopra's tone was one of surprise. 'How are you, Garewal? It's been a long time.'

'Yes, it has.' Garewal went silent. Chopra had a sudden sense that Garewal was struggling to speak, that there was a hint of desperation behind his call. 'Look, I don't have long. They're not allowing me to see or call anyone. One of the . . . others here lent me his phone. Any second now he'll take it back . . . I need your help, Chopra. I need you to come down here and help me.'

'Look, Garewal, what is this about?'

'I'm in a big jam, old friend. I need you to come right away before they bury me in here.'

'Where are you exactly?'

'I'm in Arthur Road Jail.'

Some prisons, in enlightened countries, are designed to rehabilitate those who have gone astray. Others are engineered to provide a suitable environment to safely house those who might be a danger to others and to themselves.

In the annals of penology, Chopra reflected, there had probably never been a prison like the Arthur Road Jail.

Mumbai Central Prison – as it is officially designated – occupies two acres of prime real estate near the Seven Roads district in the southern part of the city. Almost a century old, it is Mumbai's oldest and largest prison. The prison had originally been built to house eight hundred inmates – it now served as home to almost three thousand.

The horrendous overcrowding, which he had witnessed on his not infrequent visits, was beyond comprehension to those who had not personally experienced it. Barracks designed for fifty were routinely crowded with two hundred, so that inmates were forced to sleep on top of one another or in awkward positions like somnolent yogis. Sanitation was non-existent, hygiene a dirty word. Lice were rampant. Bedbugs crawled openly over the filthy blankets that served as beds. In the canteen, rats and cockroaches conducted parade ground manoeuvres with impunity.

Chopra knew that prisoners in the jail had the highest rate of HIV in the country and were routinely abused both by their fellow inmates and the hardened guards. Murder was commonplace, the suicide rate off the scale.

Mumbai Central was also one of the few major prisons in the world to be surrounded by commercial and residential properties. A few feet from the jail's roll call of desperate criminals were ordinary Mumbaikers, rich and poor, proceeding with their daily lives in blissful ignorance of the ocean of hate and anger dammed in nearby behind just a few flimsy walls of stone and barbed wire.

Chopra parked his converted Tata Venture in one of the network of alleys that surrounded the jail. The grey van, with its darkened glass panels and reinforced frame, had been refitted to his specifications. He had wanted a means of moving Ganesha around the city and by engaging his mechanic friend Kapil Gupta to remove the van's rear seats and strengthen the chassis, he now had a vehicle capable of doing just that.

After he had made the decision to permanently adopt him, Chopra had realised that Ganesha grew listless spending all day in his compound. Elephants are emotional and highly intelligent creatures. Ganesha required more than his material needs to be considered in the matter of his upbringing. Chopra instinctively felt that the sights, sounds and smells of the city would provide his ward with the stimulation that all growing children craved.

And so he had got used to loading the elephant calf into the van each morning and taking him out on his various errands. Eventually, he began to take Ganesha along on the cases he was working on.

It soon became apparent that his inquisitive young companion possessed an innate affinity for the role of private investigator. Ganesha was a master of the art of surveillance, spending hours in the van with him while they waited for some errant husband to emerge from his secret love nest, or for a crooked businessman to furtively exit the offices of a hawala trader where he had just illegally converted black money into white.

Sometimes, in the lazy heat of the day, Chopra would find himself drifting off, only to be prodded awake by Ganesha's trunk just in time to see their quarry hustling along the street. The little elephant was tirelessly vigilant, he had discovered, and as long as he was regularly fed could stand in one position all day awaiting developments. By the end of their watch the floor of the van was usually ankle-deep in Cadbury's Dairy Milk wrappers and discarded cartons of mango juice.

Chopra patted Ganesha on the head. 'I won't be long, boy,' he said, then left the van, taking care to leave an open window.

He walked to the front entrance of the jail, with its familiar yellow and blue painted steel gate. To the side of the jail a blacksmith hammered away at a horseshoe bent over his anvil while a tongawalla fed a banana to his mare. Next door to the smithy a goat was tethered to a lamppost below a butcher's signboard. A rancid smell emanated from the open shopfront. A desperate chicken emerged from the shop, hotly pursued by a burly man in ragged shorts and a blood-stained T-shirt. As Chopra looked on, he swept the zigzagging bird up in his arms, passed a meaty forearm over his sweat-soaked brow, then retreated back into his cave.

A pair of constables armed with automatic rifles straightened as Chopra approached.

He removed his wallet from his pocket and flashed the identity card that had been issued to him following his successful cracking of the human trafficking ring earlier in the year. It was the only reward he had been willing to accept from a Chief Minister eager to distance himself from the stink of discovering that a number of his close friends were embroiled in the scandal.

As a retired police officer Chopra could no longer carry a police badge. But the new identity card proclaimed him 'Special Advisor to the Mumbai Police' and was duly stamped and signed – albeit grudgingly – by the Commissioner of Police, Mumbai. The card was invaluable as it opened many doors that would otherwise have remained closed.

On the bottom of the card was the motto of the Mumbai Police – 'To protect the good and to destroy the evil'.

The guards squinted suspiciously at it, and then made a call into the jail from a phone inside their hut.

Moments later the gates swung open and Chopra entered.

He showed his card to another set of guards and was let through a pair of arched doors into the main complex where he was met by an impatient clerk who enquired haughtily as to his business. Chopra knew that the best way to deal with such a man was to be brisk to the point of rudeness. He adopted a high-handed attitude.

'My business is confidential, sir. Did you not read my identity card? I am a "special advisor". I have been sent here to speak to Garewal. That is all you need to know.'

The clerk hesitated. 'Sir, Inspector Garewal is under special warrant. I have instructions from Warden Sahib that he is to speak to no one without Warden's express permission.'

'Is the warden higher than the Chief Minister?' roared Chopra. 'Should I go back and tell him that I have been prevented from carrying out my duties by some white-shirted flunky? By some jumped-up adminwallah?'

The clerk grinned queasily. 'Warden Sahib has gone out to a meeting. He will be back shortly. If Sir would care to wai—'

'Wait?' bellowed Chopra. 'Do you think important matters of state can wait? Have you any idea what is going on, you oaf? The Prime Minister himself is breathing down the CM's neck. The CM needs answers now, not when some dolt with four pens in his front pocket decides he should have them.'

44

The clerk paled. 'Come this way, sir.'

They moved through the whitewashed administrative building and out into the prison's main compound. Chopra squinted as the hard sun beat down against his face and onto the parched, dusty ground.

The jail was just as he remembered from his last visit.

Directly to his left was the holding cage for undertrials waiting to be transferred to the courts – a number of prisoners looked out between the bars, their expressions listless and grim. At the rear of the compound were the four large barracks that housed the bulk of the prison's inmates; white, box-like buildings that reflected the sun and shimmered with lost hope and decaying dreams. In the far right corner lay the hospital, woefully under-staffed and under-resourced. A form of relative sanctuary was afforded to a lucky few by the twin buildings set before the hospital, the canteen and laundry, where prisoners fought for work. A few yards from the canteen, Chopra's eyes alighted on the notorious Barrack No. 3, fiefdom of jailed members of the Chauhan gang.

His brow darkened.

He had dealt with Chauhan gang thugs in the past and considered them to be nothing less than vicious animals. Even Mumbai Central Prison was too good for them.

He completed his survey of the compound by looking to where the Anda Cell was located on his right, a brand-new nine-cell solitary confinement unit designed for the prison's VIP guests – the maximum-security prisoners.

Chopra followed the clerk to the Anda Cell, which was surrounded by a high, wire mesh. The interior of the unit was laid out like a giant cake with nine slices. A narrow corridor led to a circular anteroom at the very centre of the cake where a bored guard sat behind a steel desk reading a copy of the *Marathi Times*.

The clerk spoke to the guard who reluctantly rose and led them to Cell 7. The guard punched a code into the keypad installed in the steel-plated door. It swung open and Chopra entered the cell, the door shutting automatically behind him.

The cell was dimly lit and it took a few seconds for his sun-blasted eyes to adjust to the gloom.

The room was spacious and, in comparison to the rest of the prison's facilities, opulent. The floor was marbled and a generous-sized single bed was bolted against one wall. There was even provision for a private bathroom. A number of posters of Bollywood film actresses adorned the wall above the bed. Chopra suspected that they had been left behind by the previous incumbent.

He had never been inside the Anda Cell. He knew that it was where the top criminals were lodged – the dons of the underworld or those suspected of terrorist bombings. An exposé earlier in the year had revealed that through bribery and intimidation such men lived a life of ease inside the Arthur Road Jail. This image had enticed at least one man to attack the guards stationed outside the prison in the hope that he would be arrested and thus be able to enjoy the 'luxurious life of a convict instead of struggling like a beggar on the streets'. The prison's super-intendent – the warden – had been arrested on bribery charges the previous year. He had been released on bail and remained in post, awaiting a trial date that would take years to arrive.

Slumped on the bed with his head in his hands was Inspector Shekhar Garewal.

Chopra had not seen Garewal in years.

Many moons ago they had worked together on a joint taskforce hunting down the suppliers of a new designer drug that had entered the city, working its way from the fashionable southern zones to the impressionable suburbs. Ultimately the taskforce had been successful and a number of unsavoury individuals with links to organised crime had been apprehended. Major shipments of the drug had been seized, and both Chopra and Garewal had been felicitated by their seniors. But since then the two officers had lost touch. Chopra had remained at the Sahar station, content to serve in the locality where he had spent most of his adult life. Garewal had moved on to better things.

Chopra remembered him now as an intensely ambitious man, one willing to cut corners when the need arose. For this reason he had never quite thought of Garewal as a friend.

Finally Garewal lifted his head from his hands and rose to face his visitor.

My God, what has happened to him? thought Chopra.

Garewal was wearing the standard uniform of the Indian penal system — white with black chevrons. His eyes were sunken and bruises had swollen his face, which seemed far older than his years. His short, greying hair was dishevelled. Garewal had never kept a moustache but a drunkard's day-old stubble now darkened his chin.

Garewal stared at Chopra and then stepped forward to clasp him in a desperate embrace, sobbing uncontrollably into his shoulder.

Eventually the astonished Chopra found his voice. 'Get ahold of yourself, Garewal,' he said, perhaps more gruffly than he had intended. 'What exactly is going on?'

Garewal stepped back, passing a sleeve across his face.

'They've got me, Chopra. They've well and truly got me this time.'

'Start from the beginning,' said Chopra. 'Don't leave anything out.'

Garewal nodded, his eyes hollow. 'It was my own fault. If I hadn't asked my uncle . . .'

Chopra waited. 'If you hadn't asked your uncle what?'

'Six months ago when they made the announcement about the Crown Jewels I knew that whoever got the job would be set for life. The post of in-charge for the security of the jewels, I mean. I knew that if somehow I got it I could write my own ticket afterwards. So I asked my uncle – you know, the one who works for the Chief Minister? – to put in a good word for me. Of course, I promised to pay him one lakh rupees to show my gratitude. And another lakh for the CM, of course.

'The next thing I knew I was given the assignment. I thought all my Diwalis had come at once. It wasn't as if I had to do too much thinking myself, you understand. There were all sorts of security experts to advise me. And the CM himself assigned the Force One brigade to the job. All I had to do was sit back and coordinate the operation. It was a dream gig.'

Garewal turned red-rimmed eyes to Chopra. 'And now that the whole thing has blown up in my face, they're blaming me. They're saying I masterminded the whole show. That I stole the crown and with it the Koh-i-Noor!'

Chopra took a deep breath. 'Did you?'

Garewal's face was pained. 'How can you ask me that? On the life of my children, I had nothing to do with it.'

'Then why do they think you did?'

'I don't know. They say I knew all the security procedures and how to get around them. They say I asked for the job. That I've been planning this from the very beginning.' Garewal looked ready to sob. 'It's a set-up, Chopra. They need a scapegoat and I am the goat. They're going to black warrant me for this!'

'Nonsense. You're accused of theft, not murder. They can't black warrant you.'

'You don't get it, do you? This is an international scandal. They need to show that they're doing something. They'll say I'm the mastermind and then they'll arrange it so I'm silenced in here. A knife in the back. Or maybe a convenient suicide. They'll never let me out of here, never. I am a dead man walking. Unless someone finds the real culprit.'

'What makes you think *they* won't?'

'Because they've already nailed their colours to the mast. Oh, they'll *look* all right, but as each day passes the pressure will mount. Sooner or later they'll quietly drop it and announce to the world that all their enquiries have confirmed I am the one. And then I'm done for.'

'But if you didn't do it, they won't get the crown back by pinning it on you.'

'But at least they'll have a culprit. And that's why I won't make it out of here alive. Once they publicly confirm me as the thief, I'll have to be silenced. Even if they find the real thief later, they'll say I was his accomplice. You know I'm telling the truth.'

Chopra allowed Garewal's words to sink in, then said, 'Why did you call me?'

'Who else could I call? No one on the force will help me. They won't even allow me a lawyer – they say my constitutional rights have been suspended because this is a case of national security. You are the only one who can help me now, Chopra. You are a private investigator. I've gambled my life on you. Do you know I had to promise that guard outside a thousand rupees just to use his mobile phone to call you? If you don't help me, I am a dead man.'

Chopra thought Garewal would begin weeping again.

'They beat me all last night,' Garewal whispered, his eyes dropping to the floor. 'I think tonight they will use the electrodes.'

Chopra thought about what he would do in Garewal's position. He knew only too well the brutality with which his fellow officers often interrogated prisoners. And when the stakes were this high, who knew how far they would go.

He thought of Garewal's children. A boy and a girl. The boy would be ten by now and the girl nine. How would they fare if their father never came home again? How would they live under the shadow of a father accused of a crime that would never be forgotten?

'How did you know I would take the case?' he asked finally.

Hope flared in Garewal's eyes. He stepped forward and stood under the room's single light fixture. The light threw shadows across his haggard features. 'Do you remember that time we chased Arun Ganga up onto the roof of the old warehouse in SEEPZ?'

Chopra recalled the chase. In the dead of night Garewal had got a tip-off. He had roused Chopra and together they had gone into the industrial quarter known as SEEPZ, the Santacruz Electronic Export Processing Zone. The team had split up and, before Chopra knew it, he and Garewal were chasing the wanted serial murderer Ganga into a derelict warehouse.

'Do you remember, on the roof, you had Ganga in your sights? You could have shot him then and no one would have known. He was not the kind of man anyone would have shed tears over and I would never have told anyone. So why didn't you shoot him?'

Chopra was silent.

'You always do the right thing, old friend,' said Garewal. 'Well, now I need you to do the right thing by me. I need you to save my life.'

Chopra turned as the door to the cell swung open and two men barged into the room.

'Chopra! What the hell are you doing here?'

The words exploded from the short, portly man with bulging cheeks, pomfret eyes and a pencil moustache that looked as if it had been drawn on by a child. He was dressed in the khaki of an Indian police officer, though Chopra had never considered him worthy of the uniform.

Suresh Rao had once been the Assistant Commissioner of Police in charge of three suburban police stations including Sahar. For many years he had been Chopra's commanding officer; for many more years, he had been Chopra's personal nemesis.

The two men had never seen eye to eye. Rao represented everything that Chopra loathed in the Indian police service. A man who donned the uniform to serve himself rather than the public who had placed their trust in him.

Following the scandal of the human trafficking ring he had heard that Rao had been hauled off by the Criminal Bureau of Investigation as part of a thorough enquiry into all those allegedly involved. But, in the perverse way of such things in Mumbai, far from having the stars ripped from his shoulder as Chopra had felt the man deserved, Rao had ended up being promoted into that same CBI unit and given the responsibility to investigate fellow officers accused of corruption.

Only in India, Chopra had thought darkly when he had heard the news.

Behind Rao towered a white man, one of the largest he had ever seen. His broad shoulders spread the width of the doorframe and a venomous paunch extended into the room. The man's face was thick and red, and above it the great dome of his skull gave way to a short skirt of peppery brown hair around a terrific island of baldness. A bristling moustache – streaked with grey and resembling a horse brush – sat under a bulbous nose. His eyes were gemstone blue and shaded by magnificent eyebrows.

The man was dressed in brown cavalry twill trousers, black oxfords and a starched white shirt with the sleeves rolled up. A linen jacket dangled from one massive fist. A crumpled black tie stamped with a prominent red and yellow crown hung loosely around his mottled neck. Saddlebags of sweat radiated from under his arms. The man's face was flushed and lathered. In fact, he was perspiring so heavily that even his sweat seemed to be sweating.

Chopra watched as the man lifted a sodden handkerchief to dab at his forehead.

'I asked you a question, Chopra.' Rao had moved closer so that the top of his own head was now level with Chopra's chin.

'I am here to see my client,' Chopra said woodenly.

'Client? What the hell are you talking about?'

'Garewal here has requested my help.'

Rao looked from Chopra to the stricken figure of Inspector Shekhar Garewal. Chopra saw that a cloud of terror shadowed Garewal's expression. With a burst of anger he understood that it was Rao who had inflicted the punishment manifest on his former colleague's face.

Rao let out an angry laugh. 'Garewal is beyond help. And you are not a police officer any more.'

'At least I *was* a police officer, Rao. No one has ever accused you of that.'

Rao's eyes bulged and his grip tightened on the lathi stick that he had unconsciously slipped from his belt.

'I want to know why Garewal is being held here,' Chopra continued. 'Why is he accused of this crime? Why is he not permitted a lawyer?'

'By Gods, man, you haven't changed!' Rao exploded. 'Always the cockerel! Well, take a look around. This is Mumbai Central Prison. Innocent men don't end up here.

Your friend Garewal has made a big mistake and now he will pay for it. If you don't like it, take it up with the Chief Minister.'

'Perhaps I will,' said Chopra hotly.

'Who is this fellow, Rao?'

Chopra looked from ACP Rao's glowering face to the enormous white man looming behind him.

'No one,' Rao ground out.

'My name is Chopra,' Chopra said stiffly. '*Inspector* Chopra. Retired.'

He reached into his pocket and removed a business card, which he handed to the big man. The man squinted at the card, his bristling moustache dancing above his upper lip as he mouthed the words. 'The Baby Ganesh Detective Agency . . . You're a private detective?' His eyebrows came together in a V of consternation. He had somehow contrived to make the words 'private detective' sound like 'loathsome cockroach'.

'Yes. And this man is now my client. He is innocent of the crime you have accused him of. I will be investigating the incident.'

'You will do no such thing!' Rao whinnied. 'You have no jurisdiction here. What do you think this is? A kitty party? I heard about your agency. Do you know what they're saying about you on the force? You are a joke. Garewal has no rights. This is a matter of national security. The only one doing any investigating here will be me. Why don't you go back to looking for lost cats and dogs?'

Chopra stared coldly at Rao. He willed himself to control his fury. Then he turned to Garewal. 'Hang in there, Garewal. I will be in touch.'

He stalked out of the cell, barging past the two men. As he reached the door he stopped and turned to the white man. 'I didn't get your name.'

'That's none of your business,' Rao said.

'I can speak for myself,' growled the big man. 'My name is Bomberton. Detective Chief Inspector Bomberton. From New Scotland Yard. I run the Metropolitan Police's Art and Antiques Unit.'

'You are here to investigate the theft of the crown?'

'What else do you think he is doing here?' Rao blared. 'Enjoying the scenic views?'

Chopra stared at Bomberton. 'I will give you a word of advice.' He pointed at Rao. 'If you listen to this man you will never find the crown.'

He turned and walked out of the cell, Rao's furious last words echoing in his ears: 'If I see you here again I will have you arrested! Do you hear me, Chopra? I'll throw you in a hole so deep you'll never see the light of day again!'

IRFAN MAKES A DELIVERY

The drive from Poppy's Bar & Restaurant to Chopra's home ought to have taken barely fifteen minutes, but in the horrendous traffic of the lunchtime suburbs could easily take an hour. For this reason, at precisely 12.15 p.m. each day, Irfan set off on his sturdy Eastman delivery bicycle to make the journey back to the Air Force Colony complex.

Deftly leaning his red-framed cycle around corners – seemingly unhindered by the deformity of his left hand – and whistling a tune from the latest Bollywood blockbuster, Irfan would imagine that he was Assistant Commissioner of Police Jai Dixit, the hero from his favourite movie *Dhoom*, which featured a glamorous motorcycle gang.

When Irfan arrived at the complex he discovered, to his delight, the Nepalese security guard Bahadur hard at work washing Chopra's Royal Enfield Bullet.

The enormous 500cc motorbike was Chopra's pride and joy, but Irfan knew his boss was constrained from riding it as often as he would have liked by Poppy Madam's unwavering disapproval.

Eyes shining, Irfan set his bicycle against the compound's gate, removed the package containing Mrs Subramanium's lunch from the pannier and approached Bahadur, who was down on his haunches in his flip-flops and shorts, carefully rubbing down the bike's gleaming metal spokes with a yellow cloth.

'Here, let me,' said Irfan. 'That's not the way to do it.' He set down his package next to the motorbike, and took the cloth from Bahadur. 'It's all in the wrists,' he said authoritatively. During his years on the street, Irfan had found many ways to earn a living, including polishing shoes and washing cars amongst other less savoury vocations.

Bahadur stood up, pushed his cap back on his head, and watched with interest. He was sweating heavily in his tatty white vest. Yet he did not begrudge having to clean the bike. Like Irfan he held a deep fascination for the Bullet.

When the spokes had been polished to his satisfaction, Irfan handed the cloth back to the guard. 'Hold this.'

He scrabbled up onto the bike and grasped the handles. His feet couldn't quite reach the pedals, but what did that matter? He was sitting on top of a Bullet! The most powerful motorbike in the whole of India! No longer was he Irfan the delivery boy, but rather a daredevil policeman – like Chopra – chasing the dangerous head of an evil bike gang down the Western Express Highway at two hundred miles per hour!

'Irfan, what are you doing here?'

Irfan turned to see Poppy getting out of a rickshaw.

'Hello, Poppy Madam!' he said cheerily. 'I was just delivering Mrs Subramanium's lunch order.'

'Or not delivering, would be a more apt description.'

Both Poppy and Irfan turned to see Mrs Subramanium, the president of the apartment complex's Managing Committee, descending upon them.

Poppy narrowed her eyes.

Mrs Subramanium had long been her nemesis, a perennial thorn in her side. With her short grey hair and dark saris, Mrs Subramanium cut an intimidating presence in the complex, materialising when you least expected to issue dire edicts from her legendary building regulations manual. Most people were frightened witless by the aging widow, but Poppy refused to be cowed. As a consequence, the two women were frequently at loggerheads.

'Boy, you are late. Again.'

'Sorry, Mrs Subramanium Madam,' said Irfan, scrambling to get off the bike. Unfortunately, as he did so, his foot caught the bike's support stand, knocking it aside. The bike began to waver under him. As he sought to regain his balance, the bike teetered, and then toppled over, squashing the package beside it. Irfan leaped aside just in time to land in the arms of the unfortunate Poppy, who cried out in alarm, then hugged him. 'Be careful, you silly boy!'

Mrs Subramanium meanwhile had moved closer to inspect the remnants of her lunch.

The thin dahl had leaked from the sides of the package and was running towards Bahadur's feet. Bahadur stared at the approaching yellow rivulet in rapt fascination.

'This is outrageous,' said Mrs Subramanium eventually, turning to Poppy. 'I will be speaking with your mother.'

Poppy glared at the older woman. She knew that her mother and Mrs Subramanium were as thick as thieves. In hindsight, their alliance had been inevitable. Both were widows, of a similar age, and possessed equally insufferable dispositions. Both treated her as if she were still twelve years old, a girl to be bossed and bullied.

'My mother does not own the restaurant,' said Poppy icily. 'It says *Poppy's* on the signboard, in case you had not noticed.'

'Well, then, *Poppy* will have to see to my lunch,' said Mrs Subramanium haughtily. She turned on her heel, swished her sari, and walked back into the building.

'I'm sorry, Poppy Madam,' said Irfan, hanging his head.

'What are you sorry about?' said Poppy. 'That woman would complain if you served her gold bars for lunch.' She smiled at the boy. 'I have some time before I go back to work. Why don't I take you for an ice cream?'

'Poornima Madam will be very cross if I don't get back to the restaurant.'

'Oh, don't worry about her. Come on, we'll go to Natural's.'

Irfan shook his head. 'No, Poppy Madam. I am working now. I must do my job. It would not be right to go and eat ice cream when I should be working. Chopra Sir would not do that.'

Poppy stared at the boy, a faint smile playing over her lips. 'No, you are right. Chopra Sir would not do that.' She gave Irfan another hug, and tousled his bonnet of dark hair. 'You are my conscientious little man, aren't you! Go on then, off you go. And ride carefully!'

THE SCENE OF THE CRIME

The Prince of Wales Museum was a hive of activity. A convoy of official vehicles now guarded the front entrance on M.G. Road, hemmed in by dozens of mobile news trucks. Swarms of journalists and cameramen waited beyond the police barricade like mosquitoes ready to pounce at the first scent of blood. A crowd of passers-by had also gathered and, in the absence of new developments, were being endlessly interviewed for their opinions.

If there was one thing Mumbai would never be short of, Chopra thought darkly, it was passers-by.

He parked the Tata Venture on the edges of the melee. Then he went to the rear of the van, swung open the door and lowered the ramp.

Ganesha trotted out into the afternoon haze, his ears flapping gently as he greeted the sun. He blinked as he took in the raucous crowd.

A group of eunuchs had begun to sing nearby in their gravelly voices, accosting a pair of Force One guards, demanding money to go away. Itinerant peddlers of everything from twice-fried samosas to straw hats that would dissolve at the first hint of rain moved amongst the crowd. A nukkud natak – street theatre – performance was attracting a great deal of attention as the costumed actors caricatured the all-round incompetence of the Force One Unit.

Chopra gave a rueful smile. Another thing one could always expect of his fellow Mumbaikers was that they would excel themselves in making a comedy out of a tragedy.

'Come on, boy,' he muttered.

At the entrance to the museum's formal gardens they were confronted by a phalanx of Force One guards. Chopra took out his identity card. The senior-most guard stared at the card as if it were written in ancient Sanskrit. Clearly, this fell beyond his jurisdiction.

'Look,' growled Chopra, 'I am a special advisor authorised by the Chief Minister himself. He was here this morning, wasn't he?'

The man's dark face took on a look of panic. Chopra guessed that the CM had not had many good things to say to the Force One contingent. 'Do you want him to come back?'

The man looked around wildly as if the CM might appear in a ball of flames behind him at that very instant. He ushered Chopra through and did not even seem to register the fact that the former policeman was accompanied by a baby elephant.

In the museum's Central Gallery Chopra was confronted by the surreal sight of two white men in plastic crime-scene suits chatting and sipping cups of steaming tea. As Ganesha came in, they stopped talking and stared at him.

'I say, do you know there is an elephant behind you?'

Chopra nodded. 'He is with me.'

'You have a pet *elephant*?' The man seemed incredulous.

'He is not a pet.'

He left Ganesha there, examining the waxworks of the royal family, and walked up two flights of steps to the Tata Gallery.

When he had first gone to see Garewal Chopra hadn't been sure that he could help, or for that matter whether he even wished to. But the encounter with Rao had left him resolved to prove Garewal's innocence or, at the very least, to establish for himself that Garewal was guilty as charged.

ACP Suresh Rao always seemed to bring out the worst in him, he reflected.

He had decided that the first thing to do was return to the scene of the crime. He had often found, during his long career, that taking a second look at the scene the day after the crime was one of the wisest things any investigator could do.

The Tata Gallery was bustling with activity.

A half-dozen or so white-suited forensic technicians were crowded into the gallery going over the scene using a variety of arcane instruments, many that he did not recognise.

Forensic science was still an emerging discipline in India. Chopra, who had made a habit of perusing forensic text-books and international criminology journals during his police years, had often lamented the fact that much of what he read would remain a distant dream as far as the Brihanmumbai Police was concerned.

The first thing he noted was that the remaining Crown Jewels had vanished. He had expected no less.

The theft of the Koh-i-Noor had put paid to the magnificent exhibition. He had no doubt that even now the priceless collection would be under heavy military guard awaiting transport back to its home in the Tower of London. The news channels were beside themselves, but the Indian government remained resolutely tight-lipped as to the current location of the hoard.

Chopra's eyes scanned the room.

A smattering of glass particles from the shattered display case sparkled on the carpet as they caught the light from a ring of arc lamps. His wandering gaze alighted on the gaping hole in the gallery's rear door. He recalled now that the door had been sealed for the duration of the exhibition. At the time it had seemed like a sensible precaution. Reducing the number of entrances into the gallery allowed the Force One guards to concentrate their vigilance on a single one. In hindsight, it seemed an unforgiveable error to have left the rear door completely unguarded. The hole in that door – just large enough for a man to squeeze through – now served as a chastening rebuke.

'And exactly who might you be when you're at home?'

He turned to see a tall, thin figure bearing down on him. The man pulled off the white hood of his forensic boiler suit to reveal a head of spiked orange hair and a pink freckled face in which green eyes sat below red eyebrows and above a large, sunburnt nose. Chopra couldn't place the man's accent. It was English but not quite English.

'Inspector Chopra. Retired. Special Advisor to the Mumbai Police. I am investigating the theft of the Koh-i-Noor diamond.'

'Och, are ye now?' the man said, giving him an appraising look. 'Well, that would be grand, except that as far as I've been told it's a crown we're looking for.'

Chopra coloured. But the ginger-headed man broke into a grin. 'Semantics. Never had much time for them myself.' He stuck out a gloved hand. 'Duncan McTavish. I work for the Met Polis. Forensics. What can I do for you, Chopra? And where's that oaf Bomberton?'

'I am not with Detective Chief Inspector Bomberton.'

'Detective Chief Inspector. Hell's bells, Chopra, you make him sound like the Second Coming. Between you and me the man is a complete buffoon.'

'Why have they sent him here, then?'

McTavish tapped the side of his freckled nose. 'Connections, Chopra. It seems our DCI Bomberton is distantly related to the royal family. Five hundredth in line to the throne or some such guff. Pardon me for not bowing and scraping in the presence of His Majesty.'

'What about you?'

'Och, I'm a Scot, Chopra. The day they make a Scot King of England is the day I'll dance naked on the Windsor Castle lawn.'

'I meant, what are you doing here?'

McTavish waved a hand at the activity behind him. 'Can ye no' see, man? We're going over the place with a fine-tooth comb. I've brought the whole kit and caboodle with me. By the time I've finished in here I'll be able to tell you what the old professor had for breakfast last week.'

Chopra wondered which professor McTavish meant, but then guessed that the Scot was referring to the learned historian who ran the museum.

'Have you discovered anything useful to the investigation?'

'Depends what you mean by useful. Here, put these on.' McTavish pulled a pair of plastic overshoes and latex gloves from the pocket of his boiler suit. Chopra slipped them on then followed the man across the room.

McTavish led him past the shattered display case to the rear of the chamber. They stopped in front of the eight-foot-tall sandstone sculpture of Kali that Chopra had noticed the previous evening. The sculpture, which had probably been torn from the façade of one of India's numerous ancient temples, resembled a figurehead from the bowsprit of an old wooden sailing ship.

McTavish beckoned Chopra around to the side of the sculpture. 'Take a look.'

Chopra's eyes followed the curve of Kali's back as it flowed down to the gallery wall . . . and then he spotted the hole.

'My guess is they chiselled that cavity out months ago,' said McTavish matter-of-factly. 'Then they put the gas canisters inside and cemented a thin sandstone shell back over.'

'How do you know the canisters were in there?'

'Microscopic paint chips from the canisters. We found them inside the cavity.' McTavish patted Kali on the shoulder. 'Our thieves knew she wasn't going anywhere. On the day of the robbery all they had to do was break through the shell. Easily enough done with a fist.'

Chopra reflected on this. 'You are saying that this crime was planned a long time ago.'

'No flies on you, I can see,' McTavish said. 'Come on.'

He led Chopra next to the shattered display case in which the crown had been housed. 'This is reinforced ballistic glass. You can bounce bullets off it. It'd take a sledgehammer to break through it, and I'm pretty sure there's no' enough space in that hole for one of those.'

'Then how did they do it?'

'I don't know. Not yet, anyrood. To be frank I'm no' so sure they *broke* the glass.'

'What do you mean?'

'I have a theory . . . but I need to conduct more tests first. Come on.'

Chopra followed McTavish to the gallery's rear door, where a swathe of debris was being hoovered up by a forensic technician. Looking through the gaping hole in the very centre of the door Chopra saw another technician out in the corridor, similarly vacuuming the floor. Noticing his gaze, McTavish said, 'They used enough charge to blow that hole through, but not enough to damage anything else in the gallery. Standard plastic explosive, C4, packed inside a copper focuser. Detonator and blast-cap set-up. Professional work. There seems to have been a bit of blowback into the corridor.'

'Is that usual?'

McTavish shrugged. 'Well, explosions aren't my speciality, but I believe so. Something to do with shock waves and negative-pressure blast winds.' He scratched the back of his skull with a gloved finger. 'At any rate, the current thinking is that our villains came up through the fire exit stairs, into yonder corridor, blew a hole through this sealed door and ducked straight into the gallery. They recovered the gas canisters from the statue, put everyone to sleep, smashed the display case, grabbed the crown and went back the way they came. The whole caper couldn't have taken more than a few minutes from start to finish.'

Chopra looked through the gaping hole again and into the marbled corridor that stretched from the Tata Gallery to the Jahangir Gallery on the east wing. He knew that the corridor had been off limits during the exhibition, another security precaution that had backfired as it now meant that there were no witnesses. Halfway along the corridor, double doors led onto the fire exit stairwell. The media had surmised that the thieves had used these stairs both to infiltrate the corridor and then later to make their escape.

'How did they get the plastic explosive into the building past the Force One Unit and the scanners?' Chopra asked. 'And if they had a way to do that why did they need to hide the gas canisters in the statue beforehand? Why didn't they just bring them in on the day of the heist, like the explosive?'

McTavish gave a wolfish grin. 'Top marks, Chopra. Who says Indian polis cannae find their own bottoms without a map?'

Chopra frowned. 'I do not know. Who says this?'

'What?' It was McTavish's turn to frown.

'Who says this? About Indian officers and their bottoms?'

McTavish opened his mouth, then closed it. 'It's just a saying. To answer your question: we might assume they hid the plastic explosive in another part of the museum, inside another statue perhaps, one accessible outside the Tata Gallery.'

'Did they?'

'Not a chance,' replied the Scot briskly. 'We've gone over everything. Every exhibit. Every nook and cranny. No sneaky hiding places. Nothing.'

Chopra's frown deepened.

'Little things, Chopra,' continued McTavish. 'You ever read that story about the princess and the pea?'

'What has that—?'

'There was this prince,' interrupted McTavish, 'on the lookout for a princess. Only he couldnae be sure the ones he knew were the real McCoy, if you get my meaning. But then along comes this wee lassie he likes the look of. So he decides to put her to the test. Sticks a pea under her mattress. Twenty mattresses, actually. And guess what? That pea kept her up all night. That's me, right there.'

Chopra was bewildered. 'Are you saying you are a princess?'

'What?' McTavish coloured. 'No, man, I'm saying that little things like that pea bother me. That's what we have here. Lots of little peas.'

Chopra considered this. Aside from the matter of the plastic explosive there were other things bothering him too. 'How did the thieves avoid the effects of the gas?' he asked, eventually.

'Nose filters would be my guess. Either they brought them along or they were also inside that hidey-hole in the Kali statue.'

'What about prints? Did they leave them on the canisters? Or anywhere else?'

'You think they'd be so sloppy?' McTavish waggled his finger as if at a child who has got an answer wrong in class. 'They wore latex gloves, I'll wager. Either had them waiting in the statue or smuggled them in on the day of the heist. You can roll them up to practically nothing. Stick them in the heel of a shoe, or the lining of a jacket. Easy enough for those Force One ninnies to miss.'

Chopra suddenly noticed the fish-eye camera peering down at him from above McTavish's shoulder. 'What does the CCTV footage show?'

'I wondered when you'd get around to that,' said McTavish. 'The answer is: not a damned thing. It cuts out seconds before the heist. The CCTV was only installed a few weeks before the exhibition. The museum has never traditionally gone in for that sort of thing, you understand. They picked one of these modern, fully digitised systems, everything controlled by computers. As best as we can figure it, a day before the heist some sort of computer algorithm – let's call it a virus – was installed on the system. This virus was designed to kick in at a pre-planned time and shut the system down. Which is precisely what it did. We havenae any footage of the thieves before, during or after the heist.'

Chopra was not, by nature, technologically inclined. 'Is that sort of thing even possible?'

'Ever hear of the Stuxnet virus?' replied McTavish. 'Made headlines a wee while back. A virus so canny it took a year to work out what it did. And what it did was infect computerised networks running industrial programmable logic controllers – specifically those that ran Iran's nuclear centrifuges. It made the centrifuges tear themselves apart. Did a damned good job of it, too.'

'How did the thieves install this virus?'

'I'm guessing the same way they put those gas canisters inside the statue.'

Chopra arrived at the inescapable conclusion. 'They had someone on the inside.'

'For a wee long while, would be my guess. It must have taken time to scrape out that cavity.' McTavish absentmindedly tapped the sides of his thighs. 'I hate to say it, Chopra, but these guys were good. We're looking at a gang that is patient, sophisticated and well financed.'

An urgent thought that had been beckoning for attention now forced itself to the front of Chopra's mind. 'Why didn't the Force One guards stationed outside the gallery stop them?'

'Because as soon as they got inside the gallery our thieves locked the doors – from the *inside*. Those wee doors were specially installed for the exhibition. Six-inch plated steel. Once the thieves locked them our Force One friends could-nae break in. And the powers that be always assumed that any attack would come from the front of the gallery, so that even if the Force One buffoons were overpowered, the Beefeaters could batten down the hatches and wait for reinforcements. By the time they discovered the hole in the back it was too late.'

Chopra shook his head. 'They went to all this effort. And yet they stole only one item.'

'Because that was the plan, Chopra. They spent months dreaming up this caper, all with one goal in mind. To steal that crown.'

'Why?'

'You know why.'

'The Koh-i-Noor.'

McTavish nodded. 'Which leaves us with the million-dollar question . . . Where did they go once they left this room? As soon as the display case was broken the museum went into lockdown. According to Jha everyone in the museum was rounded up and searched. And every corner of the place was turned upside down with metal detectors. The man may be an idiot but I'm sure he would have found the crown if it had still been anywhere on the premises.'

'But how could they have just vanished?'

'That's the big mystery, isn't it? Maybe when we find our inside man we can ask him.'

Chopra cast his mind back to the previous evening. The motor of memory hummed, focusing in on the faces of those around him in the gallery. Recalling that only twenty visitors were allowed in at any one time, he concluded that there had been twenty-three people in the room. That included the two Beefeaters and the guide, Kochar. He remembered the bangs he had heard, and the cloud of fast-moving gas. And then nothing until he had found himself swimming back to consciousness, his face still buried in the red carpet onto which he had swooned. How he had looked around woozily and seen the at-first incomprehensible sight of the shattered display case. And then rough hands were pulling him to his feet as the Force One guards poured into the gallery from the hole in the rear doorway.

He paused his memory and then rewound from that moment.

He remembered entering the gallery, Poppy's silk sari rustling beside him, the gust of her perfume in his nose. He remembered Kochar's long-winded spiel, the bored looks on the faces of the two Beefeaters when they thought no one was paying attention. He remembered flicking through his guidebook and bending down to take a closer look at the Koh-i-Noor . . .

And suddenly there was a face in his mind, the face of the man he had thought he recognised just moments before the explosion. With the face came a name, dredged from the deepest pit of memory.

Bulbul Kanodia.

Chopra had one more call to make before he could leave the museum.

The office of the museum's director was located behind the Curator's Gallery on the first floor of the east wing. He knocked on the door and then entered without waiting for a reply.

He found Professor P. K. Patnagar sitting behind a teak desk with his head in his hands.

The desk was an apocalypse of paper. Towers of leather-bound tomes teetered at its corners. From the whitewashed walls a gallery of framed diplomas and certificates glared down. A ceiling fan rattled noisily above. A harried-looking assistant wearing spectacles on a silver chain fluttered around the professor like a distressed moth.

'But, sir, I *did* ask him. Mr Jha was most rude! He told me that if I ever showed him my face again he would arrest me and hang me upside down in a cell and beat me on the soles of my feet!'

'I told you, Gaekwad! Didn't I tell you? I said no good would come of this!'

'But, sir, I distinctly remember you saying that exhibiting the Crown Jewels would be most auspicious for the museu—'

'We are ruined, Gaekwad, ruined! Why did you ever suggest that we agree to this madness! You are a damned fool, a first-class imbecile!'

'But, sir, it was you who—'

'Gaekwad, I am getting a headache. Go fetch me a lime water.'

The harried assistant seemed about to argue and then nodded. He hurried from the room, leaving Chopra alone with the despondent academic.

Chopra coughed. 'Professor Patnagar?'

The professor looked up.

He had a long domed forehead, like a latter-day Shakespeare, over which had been combed a handful of desultory grey hairs. A limp moustache lay dying above moist lips.

Patnagar rose to his feet. His body resembled a collection of coat hangers clothed in a dark suit many sizes too big.

'Who are you?' he bristled. 'Another of Jha's goons? If so, I have nothing more to tell you. I am not one of your Chor Bazaar pickpockets, sir. I am a BA, MA, PhD, FRIS and former DG of the ASI. I am an alumnus of the University of Guwahati and an honorary professor of the Lebanese Institute of Mankind. I am a fellow of the Royal Geographical Society of London. I have written three books, sir, and one of them was even published. So do not think you can intimidate me. I have told you all I know. You cannot wring blood from a stone, my good man. And that is that.'

'Professor, I am not with Jha's Force One Unit. My name is Chopra and I am investigating the theft of the crown in my own capacity. I must ask you some questions.'

'Questions! Questions!' exploded Patnagar. 'My very existence has been reduced to questions. First, Jha's endless interrogations. And then the media! Is it open season on honest men, sir? Do you know that I cannot even set foot outside these walls? Those carrion-eaters from the press are waiting for me. They are camped outside my home. They will not rest until they have gnawed every scrap of flesh from my bones. And for what? I am a man of letters. I do not consort with jewel thieves and I do not know where your damned crown is.'

'I do not want to ask you about the crown, Professor. What I want to know is whether anyone new has entered your employ in the months since you announced that the museum would host this exhibition.'

Patnagar's glistening forehead creased with consternation. 'You suspect foul play from one of my people? An "inside man", as they say?'

Chopra nodded.

'Impossible! They were all thoroughly vetted.'

'Nevertheless . . .'

'Well, you will have to ask our personnel department for the records but we have taken on quite a few new staff recently. You see, after years of neglect, once New Delhi agreed that we would host the exhibition they could not throw enough money at us. The museum was to be the face of India, sir. A glittering vision of our ancient heritage. A veritable jewel in its own right. Prized footage for those foreign newsreels, you understand.'

'I understand, sir. Could you please authorise your personnel department to provide me with a list of all those who began work here after you announced the exhibit?'

The door opened behind Chopra and the harried assistant returned with a glass of lime water, which he handed to the professor.

Patnagar collapsed back into his seat and morosely eyed the mint leaf floating on top of the glass. 'I honestly believed this exhibition would be a shot in the arm for the museum. Youngsters these days have no respect for the past. They have no idea how venerable their heritage is, if only they could be bothered to glance up from their masala movies and their nightclubs and whatnot. And as each day passes their memories become narrower and narrower. Do you know the other day I overheard one teenaged oaf asking his friend what all the fuss was about the "little bald fellow in the bedsheet"? Is this what we have come to, sir? Is this the price of becoming a superpower? Oh, what a magnificent ship of fools!'

'Professor?'

Patnagar waved a hand at his assistant. 'Gaekwad here will get you what you need.'

Chopra arrived back in the Central Gallery to discover a crowd of McTavish's scene of crime officers gathered around Ganesha, laughing. The crowd parted as he approached.

Ganesha had settled onto the marble floor in front of the royal waxworks. Curled up in his trunk was the head of Prince Charles.

Chopra looked up and confirmed that the wax Prince of Wales had indeed been crudely decapitated.

'Ganesha!' he scolded sternly.

'Relax, Chopra, it was an accident. No need to fill your breeks.'

He turned to see McTavish bearing down on him. The ginger-haired man was sipping from a can of Coke. 'Your young beastie here was just trying to ken Bonnie Prince Charlie's face. Little bairn doesn't know his own strength.' McTavish squared up to him, his expression suddenly serious. 'By the way, I just took a shufty at the list of visitors in the Tata Gallery when it was robbed. Imagine my surprise to find one A. Chopra on that list. Why didn't you tell me you were there when it happened?'

'You didn't ask.'

McTavish grimaced. 'Chopra, I'm a straightforward man. But if you want to play silly buggers, then so can I.

For instance, I could ask our Force One friends to take another look at that identity card you showed me. Or I could ask you to hand over those papers you're holding in your hand there.'

Chopra stared at McTavish, a burst of blood colouring his cheeks. Then he nodded. 'You are correct. I should have been honest with you. I apologise.'

McTavish gave Chopra the eye, then grinned. 'Apology accepted. Now tell me something . . . I had a look at the interview transcripts from yesterday. A number of the visitors in the gallery reported hearing a high-pitched whine just before they passed out. Did you hear it, too? Only you didnae mention it in your interview with Jha.'

Chopra realised that McTavish was right. He had forgotten about the strange noise he had heard after the gas had enveloped him, a noise that had set his teeth on edge and made his palms itch. 'Yes, you are correct. I did hear such a noise. Why? Is it significant?'

'Could be. It's a theory I'm working on.'

There was a short silence as the two men evaluated each other.

'You know, Chopra, you'd make a better door than a windae, as my old da used to say,' said McTavish eventually.

Chopra's brow furrowed. 'I don't understand.'

'It means I cannae see what's inside your head, my friend.' McTavish slurped at his can. 'You ever hear of the Stone of Scone?'

Chopra shook his head.

'It was used for centuries in the coronation of Scottish kings until the English made off with it back in the thirteenth century. For nearly seven hundred years they held on to the stone. But eventually they had to give it back. I think your Koh-i-Noor has found its way home. For what it's worth, I dinnae think it will ever leave these shores again.'

THE RAREST PIGEON IN THE WORLD

Chopra drove back through the congested city, his mind carefully processing the wealth of new information he had discovered. He knew that once McTavish revealed his findings to Rao and Bomberton they would come to the same conclusion as he had. They would search for an inside man. It would not take them long to get the same list from the museum's personnel department that Chopra had obtained.

Chopra knew that if Rao employed his usual methods, then sooner or later someone would confess, whether they did it or not. And that would either lead to the true criminals or else Rao would simply coerce a confession that implicated Garewal.

ACP Rao would stop at nothing to bring glory to himself.

And there was one other thing.

Chopra was convinced that he had seen Bulbul Kanodia in the Tata Gallery. What he did not yet know was how – or even if – Kanodia was connected to the robbery.

He had good reason for suspecting that this was the case, however.

Kanodia had been arrested by Chopra more than a decade ago. At the time he ran a small jewellery shop in the industrial zone known as SEEPZ near the Sahar station. Word had reached Chopra that Kanodia had graduated from gemstone merchant to small-time fence, with an expertise in stolen jewellery. He had immediately initiated an investigation.

The subsequent arrest and prosecution of Kanodia had sent him away for two years. Since then Chopra had heard nothing of the man. Kanodia was simply another of the many criminals that he had delivered onto the stuttering conveyor belt of Indian justice.

But now, now he needed to find out everything he could about Bulbul. He was certain that Rao and Bomberton would perform background checks on all those who had been in the gallery at the time of the robbery. This would bring Kanodia's past to light. Chopra wanted to confront Kanodia before Rao got to him. He wanted to question him while he looked in the man's eyes. He believed he would be able to tell whether or not Kanodia was lying. And he hoped he would learn whether Garewal was part of the plot.

But first he needed to fill in the missing years since he had last crossed paths with the jewel merchant. He needed Kanodia's old case file and he needed information. And the best way to find that information was his old lieutenant Sub-Inspector Rangwalla.

The temperature outside the van had climbed into the early thirties. Chopra flicked on the air-conditioner, which hummed away in the background as the van slid smoothly along Barrister Nath Pai Road, swinging across from the eastern side of the city back towards its western flank.

He drove steadily through the midtown suburbs of Dadar and Matunga before whipping the sturdy Tata Venture over the Sion-Bandra Link Road and connecting with the Western Express Highway. The highway, with its many flyovers, took him back to Sahar, where he turned off onto the recently completed Sahar Elevated Road.

Chopra's fingers drummed on the steering wheel as his thoughts lingered on the case.

Ganesha's trunk reached over the front seats and dabbed at the van's dashboard. The little elephant had become very fond of the radio. In particular he enjoyed listening to the newer music channels with their constant stream of Bollywood dance numbers. Chopra knew that this was his wife's doing. Poppy was addicted to the Bombay talkies and had infected their young ward with her passion.

Chopra himself would look on in consternation as Ganesha became engrossed in the music, his eyes closing, ears flapping in time to the rhythm, and trunk tracing circles in the air as if he were conducting the raucous music like a pachyderm maestro.

Sometimes it would be all too much and Chopra would flick the radio back towards the news on All India Radio or, preferably, the cricket commentary. This rarely went down well with his young ward, who would turn around in the van, show Chopra his bottom, and enter into a protracted sulk.

They arrived at the Sahar police station just in time to see the much-abused blue police truck coughing and spluttering its way out from the station's attached garage, a number of glum-looking constables sweating in the rear. Chopra briefly wondered where they were headed.

It had been a while since he had last visited the station. He was surprised to see that change had come to Shangri-La.

The tiles of the terracotta courtyard, bleached a pale pink beneath years of merciless sun, appeared to have been recently swept. The potted palm that had stood, sentry-like, for years by the saloon-style doors and had long ago contracted some sort of chronic fungus causing it to shed most of its leaves had been replaced by a verdant display of flowering plants. The flowers – yellow gulmohars, pink bougainvillea and bright red hibiscus – added a swathe of colour to the place and filled the air with a cloying sweetness.

A wild pig that had long frequented the courtyard on the promise of scraps from post-lunch tiffin boxes stood in the courtyard staring at the flowers in consternation, as if memorising details for the authorities later on.

Chopra stepped through the saloon doors.

As always he felt a hoop of nostalgia tightening around his chest as he recalled the twenty-odd years he had spent as the in-charge of this little outpost. And an outpost was how he had always pictured it, a little island of integrity in the great sea of wickedness that Mumbai often seemed to have become.

Chopra knew that he had been a bit of a stickler, but he believed that discipline was something to be embraced, not feared. With seniority came responsibility. A police station was a reflection of the man in charge. A bad officer, a venal officer, an incompetent officer infected the men below him. They took their cue from the man at the top. Chopra had always ensured that his men had an excellent example to follow.

He stopped and looked around. Something was different. The place was gleaming. The walls had been newly white-washed and the ancient floor tiles polished to a reluctant shine. The blades of the ceiling fans had been wiped down and the thousands of dead flies in the barred window wells had been swept away. Each of the four battered old desks in the station reception had been repaired, repainted and tidied up. Not a sheet of paper was out of place. The gallery of withered posters of long-dead criminals had been stripped from the walls to be replaced with improving epistles such as 'DO NOT SPIT IN THE OFFICE. SPITTING IS A CRIME' and 'CLEANLINESS IS NEXT TO GODLINESS' and 'WE ARE HERE TO HELP PEOPLE, NOT SHOOT PEOPLE. UNLESS WE HAVE TO.'

Chopra was confronted with a bustling activity that he was unused to seeing in the post-lunch hour, when most of his officers tended to descend into a state of semi-consciousness.

'Chopra Sir!'

He turned to see young Constable Surat bearing down on him, a wide smile splitting his homely features.

Chopra corrected himself.

Surat was no longer a constable. He had recently been promoted to the rank of sub-inspector – in part thanks to

VASEEM KHAN

Chopra's human trafficking investigation, during which poor Surat had been wounded by one of the villains.

It was still disconcerting for Chopra to see Surat out of his shorts and in his new, neatly pressed khaki uniform with full trousers and peaked cap. The trousers were somewhat strained around the young man's midriff: the new sub-inspector was overweight, impressionable, and had idolised Chopra during his tenure as the station head.

'Surat, how are you?'

'Very fine, sir!'

Chopra had given up trying to convince his former constable that he needn't call him 'sir' any more. 'Surat, what is going on? What's happened to the place?'

'Operation Clean-Up, sir.'

'Operation Clean-Up? Whatever do you mean?'

'Orders of the new station in-charge, sir.'

Ah. Chopra understood.

Following his retirement earlier in the year, he had been replaced by a fellow officer from the service. Unfortunately, the new incumbent had not proven to be the man Chopra was and had been rounded up as part of the human trafficking ring investigation. Unlike Chopra's nemesis, ACP Suresh Rao, Inspector Suryavansh had had no influential connections to deliver him from the inquisitors of the CBI and had never returned to the station.

Seven months later it seemed the higher-ups had finally got round to installing a permanent replacement.

'Is the new man here? I may as well meet him.'

Surat grinned queasily. 'Not exactly, sir.'

'Well, either he is here or he is not. Which is it, Surat?'

85

The young policeman reddened.

'I think what the sub-inspector is trying to tell you is that "he" is not a "he".'

Chopra turned.

A tall, broad-shouldered woman in the khaki dress uniform of a police inspector was walking towards him. The woman had a dusky, round face with soulful brown eyes. Her thick black hair was pulled back beneath her peaked cap. A mole sat high on her right cheek, just below a deep scar that looked to Chopra as if it had been inflicted by a knife.

He flushed.

During his long career in the service he could scarcely recall coming into contact with a female inspector. Although the Brihanmumbai Police was changing, female police officers of any meaningful rank were still a rarity. Chopra had long considered this to be a lost opportunity.

'Chopra, isn't it?'

Realising that he must look foolish just standing there, gaping, Chopra coughed to cover his embarrassment. 'Yes,' he said, then, 'Ah, you seem to have had a spring clean.'

'Correct. I thought the place could use a little freshening up. Works wonders for morale, I have found.' The woman's voice had a lilting quality to it. A voice used to authority. 'How may we help you, Inspector?'

'I am no longer an inspector.'

'Correct.'

Chopra wondered if the woman was making some sort of statement. He found himself colouring again.

'I, ah, I just came in to see Surat here.'

86

'A social visit, was it?'

Chopra's collar felt suddenly hot. 'Yes. I, er, wanted to see how he was getting on in his new role.'

'He is doing fine. He will make a good inspector one day.'

Surat swelled with pride.

'Is that all?'

'Well, I . . . I also thought I'd wish Rangwalla well while I was here.'

'Rangwalla is not here.'

'Ah. He is out on an investigation, is he?'

'Sub-Inspector Rangwalla has been sacked from the service. He is no longer a police officer.'

Chopra gaped at the woman. 'What? When did this happen? Why?'

'I am afraid I am not at liberty to discuss these matters. They are police business.'

Chopra bristled. He realised that the woman was quietly putting him in his place. He realised too that his ability to come and go at the station was going to be severely curtailed, particularly if Rangwalla was no longer around.

'Well, in that case, perhaps I will take my leave.'

The woman nodded, her eyes not leaving his face.

Chopra smiled at Surat, who looked as if he had been stricken to the floor by a bolt of lightning. His moon-shaped face swung from Chopra to his new boss and back again.

'Well, Surat, carry on the good work. I know you will make us all proud.'

Surat slapped his heels together and snapped out a brisk salute. 'Yes, sir!'

'You don't have to call me "sir", Surat. As the inspector has pointed out, I am no longer a police officer.'

Surat maintained his salute, conflicting emotions squirming over his bovine features.

Chopra turned away.

'Chopra?'

He turned back.

'You didn't ask my name.'

He stared at the woman. 'What is your name, Inspector?'

'Malini Sheriwal. Inspector Malini Sheriwal.'

As he drove away from the station Chopra realised that he had heard the name before. Malini Sheriwal . . . The memory swam tantalisingly just beneath the surface of his mind, but he couldn't quite grasp it.

Rangwalla and his family lived in a two-bedroomed apartment on the seventh floor of a nine-storey tower in Marol optimistically named Little Heaven. The tower was one of a number that had been built on land released following the demolition of a sprawling shanty town some years previously.

Chopra remembered the fuss when the bulldozers had moved in.

As head of one of the local police stations he had been told to send in his men to help evict the slum dwellers and prevent violence. Each time he thought about that day he felt a knot of shame twisting inside him. He had known well enough that the slum dwellers had nowhere else to go, but the high court order was inviolable. In a city bursting at the seams space was always at a premium and the ones that suffered were always those lowest on the totem pole. As an officer of the law he had been forced to uphold the high court's edict.

But as he had overseen the sundering of those poor slum dwellers from the little patch of earth they had called home for years, he had become infected with their rage, a rage aimed at the faceless men of power who, with a careless flick of the pen, signed away the lives of those they had never met and did not care to meet.

And he understood too that some of that hatred was reserved for people like him, the enforcers of those invisible vultures.

Chopra had rarely felt uncertain of his calling, but on that day, as he had stood behind slum children huddled together in a daze as they watched their homes being bulldozed into rubble, he had felt himself grow hot with his own helplessness.

Now, as he ascended the stairs of the building that had risen from the ashes of the slum, he realised that in all the years he and Rangwalla had worked together he had never once set foot inside his deputy's home. He noticed how worn down the building looked, even though it was barely two years old. He could not help but compare it to the meticulously well-maintained tower in which he lived. Once again, he felt perturbed by the stark reality of economics in the city of Mumbai.

The young woman who opened the door to flat 303 was wearing a red headscarf and traditional shalwar kameez.

She was young, perhaps fifteen, and was chewing gum with a ferocious pounding of her jaws. She stared at him with insolent eyes.

'Yes?'

'I am here to see Rangwalla.'

'Abbu is not here.'

Abbu? Chopra stared at the girl. 'Rangwalla is your father?'

'Correct. I don't go around calling any old person "Abbu". You must be a detective.' The girl's voice was heavy with sarcasm.

'My name is Chopra.'

The girl stopped chewing. 'Chopra? Inspector Chopra? Abbu's old boss?'

'Yes.'

Her face changed instantly. 'Then you're the one responsible for what has happened to him! To all of us! I hope you are happy now, Mister Bigshot police inspector! I hope your big belly is full!'

Chopra was astounded. The girl seethed with fury.

'Because of you we are living like beggars! Because of you we will be evicted from our home! Because of you I have had to leave my school! You have ruined us!'

'Sumaira!'

The door opened wider. A middle-aged woman, also in a headscarf, pushed the girl away from the door. 'Go on. Get back to your studies.'

'What am I studying for?' the girl shouted. 'Because of him I can't go to school any more.'

'Is this how we have brought you up? To be rude to your

elders? Is this what your school is teaching you? Do you think your abbu would be proud of you now?'

The girl glared at her mother, then stormed away.

The woman turned to Chopra. 'I am sorry. She is very emotional. It is a difficult time for her.'

'What has happened?'

'It does not matter. It is not your problem.'

'Please tell me.'

She hesitated. 'Since my husband lost his job we have found things difficult. Word reached our daughter's school. The fees for next term were already overdue. Five thousand rupees. They decided we would not be in a position to pay and so they asked us to make alternative arrangements for Sumaira. It is a very good school. Competition is fierce and they wished to allocate the place to someone else.'

Chopra was aghast. 'But . . . why didn't Rangwalla say anything?'

'My husband is a proud man. He has looked after us very well.'

'Where is he now?'

'He is on the roof. I will send someone to fetch him.'

'No. I will go to him.'

The roof of the apartment tower was a flat concrete deck bordered by a low retaining wall, ornately latticed and painted the colour of sandstone. The bleached concrete reflected the harsh sun beating down from above and would have been impossible to walk across in bare feet, even for a yogi.

In the southeast corner of the terrace was a sprawling, cage-like structure, slapped together from old bits of wood and chicken-wire, which Chopra realised was a dovecote.

Rangwalla was sitting on a stool outside it, holding a pigeon across his knees. A number of other pigeons milled around him, pecking at breadcrumbs on the floor.

As Chopra approached, Rangwalla looked around. His eyes widened, and then embarrassment came into his face and he turned away.

Chopra was shocked.

In the space of a few short weeks his former sub-inspector seemed to have lost weight, his face a haunted shadow of the one Chopra had known for almost twenty years. Rangwalla's close-cropped beard was unkempt and straggled below his chin. His dark, pockmarked cheeks seemed even more haggard than usual. He wore a string vest and below that a pair of ragged shorts and worn sandals. His dark hair was uncombed beneath a yellow-ing skullcap.

As Chopra watched, Rangwalla pinned the pigeon to his knee. He then proceeded to tie a small canister to the bird's leg.

'What are you doing?' said Chopra.

'My cousin has a garment business in Pune. We both raised racing pigeons together when we were young. Now we use them to play chess. I send him a move and then he sends me one back.'

'Who is winning?'

'I have stopped playing. I am sending him a request for a job. Perhaps he needs someone to make deliveries. I can drive very well.'

Chopra took a deep breath. 'Why didn't you tell me, Rangwalla?'

Rangwalla shrugged, his back still to Chopra. 'It is not your problem.'

Chopra moved so that he could crouch down and look Rangwalla in the eye. 'We worked together for twenty years. You could have come to me. I thought we were friends.'

Rangwalla finally met Chopra's eyes. He realised that his words had struck his former sub-inspector deeply. 'It just didn't seem right. You were my boss . . .'

'And now I am simply an ordinary citizen.' Chopra stood. 'Your daughter has grown into a fine young woman. You have a son, too, don't you?'

'Abbas.'

'How old is he now?'

'Six.'

'Tell me, Rangwalla, what does he think of his father, sitting up here in his dovecote?'

'I do not know. But it is not much of a father who cannot provide for his family.'

'Stand up.'

Rangwalla looked up.

'Stand up, Sub-Inspector. That is an order.'

Rangwalla set down the pigeon and then got to his feet.

Chopra placed a hand on his bare shoulder. 'You are the finest police officer that I know. You cannot be any less of a father. Your children are proud of you. *I* am proud of you.'

Diamonds glistened in the corners of Rangwalla's eyes.

'I am in need of a man, Sub-Inspector. A very particular kind of man. You see, I have more cases than I can possibly handle at the agency. I require an associate private detective. Someone who is quick-witted, tenacious and resourceful. Someone who knows the ins and outs of the city. Someone who understands how an investigation must be conducted. Preferably someone who has had police experience. Can you think of such a person, Rangwalla?'

A lump bobbed up and down in Rangwalla's throat. 'How much would such a person expect to receive as his monthly salary?' he asked hoarsely.

'Oh, I was thinking a sum of nine thousand rupees per month would be sufficient. Plus expenses, of course. And there would be a signing-on bonus. Five thousand rupees.'

Rangwalla blinked back tears. 'I think I may know just the man.'

Chopra clapped his junior colleague on the shoulder. 'In that case, kindly send him to me at once. I will be waiting downstairs in my van. And tell him to dress appropriately. Associate private detectives do not carry out their work in string vests and shorts.'

As Chopra walked back down the stairs he reflected on how quickly a man's self-respect could be taken from him. So much of what a man *was* was tied up in what he *did*. He recalled the dark days earlier in the year when he himself had been forced to make the transition from police inspector to ordinary citizen. He fully understood Rangwalla's sense of helplessness.

At the same time he knew that the police service's loss was his gain. He could not have found a better man to help him at the agency. Rangwalla had the street smarts and dubious connections that Chopra himself could never hope to attain. Rangwalla was a man bred for police work, particularly the kind that required one to get one's hands dirty. Chopra had no doubt that under different circumstances, his former lieutenant would have made an excellent criminal.

Rangwalla was truly a rare breed of pigeon and Chopra was delighted he could help out his old colleague whilst helping himself too.

Inside the van Ganesha greeted him with a swift trumpet of recrimination.

He raised his trunk and patted his jutting lower lip. This was a sign that Ganesha was hungry. Chopra realised his own stomach was rumbling. It was well past lunchtime. Ganesha, he knew, preferred to conduct investigations on a full stomach.

Once Rangwalla had joined them, they stopped at a Punjabi dhaba.

The smell of butter chicken and tandoori roti always filled Chopra with nostalgia for his historic homeland in the state of Punjab, in spite of the fact that he had never been there. His ancestors had moved down to Maharashtra a few short generations ago and he himself had been born in the village of Jarul in the state's Aurangabad district. He was now as Marathi as the next Maharashtrian – indeed, Poppy came from a noted Marathi clan.

As they ate, Chopra asked Rangwalla how he had ended up being sacked from the service.

'ACP Rao,' Rangwalla elucidated. 'After the trafficking ring investigation, he blamed you for the CBI picking him up. As you know he used his connections to get his neck out of the noose and transfer into the CBI himself. Because you had already left the force he couldn't do anything to you. But he found out that I had helped you. And so he came after me instead. He accused me of beating a suspect to such an extent that the man ended up in hospital.'

'Did you?'

'No.'

Chopra continued to stare at Rangwalla, who had the decency to blush.

'I mean I may have beaten him a *little*, but no more than usual. Certainly not enough to put him in hospital. The man had beaten his own wife into a coma. He was drunk and resisted arrest. When I threw him in the cells he was absolutely fine. But after Rao interviewed him, the man claimed I had all but killed him. A day later a fake medical report turned up. And that was that.'

'Well, old friend, it seems that Rao continues to be a thorn in both our sides.'

Quickly Chopra brought Rangwalla up to speed on his investigation into the theft of the Crown of Queen Elizabeth and the predicament of Shekhar Garewal.

Rangwalla confessed that even in his present depressed state the case had captured his attention. It had been all over the news. The Indian government had, that very morning, announced an enormous reward for information leading to the return of the diamond. Within a few short hours hundreds of innocent people had been implicated in the crime and dozens of Koh-i-Noor diamonds had been delivered to the authorities. So far each and every one had turned out to be a fake.

Rangwalla snorted cynically. 'It's as if they don't know their fellow countrymen at all.'

'This case is a tricky one,' said Chopra, as he slopped up the last of his butter chicken. 'These thieves were exceptionally clever. They planned everything well in advance. They had access to all the right equipment. They were well financed and thoroughly professional.'

'Are you thinking what I am thinking, sir?' said Rangwalla.

'Rangwalla, even God does not know what goes on in that head of yours. But if you are thinking that this could only be the work of one of the big organised gangs, then yes, I am thinking what you are thinking.'

'Who are your likeliest suspects?'

'Take your pick,' said Chopra. 'The Rohan gang; Das's outfit; the Chauhan mob. The Koh-i-Noor is a piece of cheese the size of the moon for such rats.' Chopra shook his head. 'I hate to admit it, but this was a slick piece of work. And they have covered their tracks well.'

'They always make a mistake somewhere, sir,' said Rangwalla encouragingly.

'Yes. But if I am to save Garewal, we will have to somehow discover that mistake on our own, in double-quick time, whilst avoiding the attentions of our friend Rao. He is determined to pin this on Garewal.'

It was Rangwalla's turn to shake his head. 'How do men like Rao live with themselves? Where do they leave their consciences each morning? Sometimes it makes me think there is no hope for this country of ours.'

Chopra frowned. '"You must not lose faith in humanity. Humanity is an ocean; if a few drops of the ocean are dirty, the ocean does not become dirty."'

Rangwalla stared at him. 'I suppose Gandhiji said that.'

Chopra coloured. His obsession with the great statesman was well known to his subordinates. Not everyone, he knew, appreciated Gandhi's homespun wisdom.

His phone suddenly exploded in his pocket, sending out the rousing chorus of the national song, 'Vande Mataram'. It was a message from Poppy. *Do not forget to go to the school. The appointment with Principal Lobo is at 4 p.m. P.S. Did you take your pills?*

Chopra cursed. The appointment! He had completely forgotten. He looked at his watch. It was a quarter to four. He was going to be late.

'Come on,' he said, standing up with such haste that his napkin fluttered to the floor.

'Where are we going?'

'To the St Xavier Catholic School for Boys.'

THE MISSING HEAD

The St Xavier Catholic School for Boys, located in the posh suburb of Juhu, had only recently celebrated its centenary and in so doing consecrated a glorious legacy of pedagogical and charitable endeavour in India's most factious city. Chopra had recently become acquainted with the renowned institution's colourful history, which came back to him now as he walked through its wrought iron gates.

Exactly one hundred years ago the Bishop of Bombay had invited a band of Portuguese missionaries to the subcontinent in the hope of making headway in the divine mission of converting the heathen. Astounded by the universal poverty and suffering that confronted them, the zealous Catholics had set about building an orphanage, which had later been converted into a school. The hope was that the school might be employed to bring the Word to the masses when they were at a more malleable age, that is, an age at which they would not take umbrage at being told that their seven-thousand-year-old faith was pagan nonsense and they would burn in eternal hellfire should they not immediately see the error of their ways.

The school had swiftly become a Mumbai institution.

Now it was one of the city's most sought-after educational establishments, with parents willing to pay extortionate sums to enrol their future Tatas and Ambanis on its hallowed roster. The school continued to stay true to its roots, attempting to inculcate in each of its wards a sense of civic responsibility and charitable endeavour. One did not have to be a Christian to attend the school, but one was expected to imbibe the Christian virtues of decency, honesty and goodwill to one's fellow man.

Chopra hoped that his wife was taking notes.

When Poppy had first told him that she had taken up the post of Drama and Dance teacher at St Xavier, he had thought she was making a joke.

But Poppy had been deadly serious.

After twenty-four years she had finally decided to join the rat race, as she had put it.

Chopra knew that Poppy had struggled for years with the fact of their childlessness. It saddened him too, though he had taken care to mask his disappointment lest Poppy mistake it for recrimination. He knew too that Poppy had never understood his steadfast refusal to adopt. He was not sure if he understood it himself. But each time he thought about taking on a child that was not his own he had somehow balked. Not because he believed that he could not love a child he had not fathered himself, but because of a strange sense that the child might not believe in *him*. In his authenticity as a parent.

After all, what qualifications did he have to be a father? For thirty years he had known only how to be a policeman. How to work long hours for little pay; how to deal with rapists and murderers; with cheats and thugs; with thieves and scam-artists. In what way did these endeavours qualify him to raise a young life?

But often, in the quiet of an evening, he would reflect that perhaps he had been selfish, and that his wife had paid for his selfishness.

Poppy loved children and they loved her. This was one reason why he had not protested when she had told him about her new job.

Chopra considered himself a traditionalist, but not old-fashioned. He had no objection to Poppy working, but he worried for her. He did not think that his wife quite understood what she was letting herself in for.

When he later discovered that Poppy had had an ulterior motive in pursuing this sudden career change it had come as no surprise. Over the years he had become accustomed to her personal crusades, which, like solar flares, burst forth with predictable regularity, usually incinerating everything in their path, but just as quickly running their course.

Poppy had learned that in the one hundred years of its history the St Xavier Catholic School for Boys had never hired a woman. This single explosive fact had seemed to her to encapsulate the entrenched attitudes that conspired to hold back the Modern Indian Woman. She had decided there and then that this scandalous state of affairs could not remain unchallenged.

And so began her campaign of guerrilla warfare.

She had hounded the school's Board of Trustees for months, relentlessly haranguing them with threatening letters whilst simultaneously firing off countless articles to the local newspapers, one of which had been published under the incendiary headline 'FÊTED SCHOOL INVITES WOMEN TO SWAB ITS FLOORS BUT NOT TO INSTRUCT ITS PUPILS'. Worst of all, she had organised a *petition*.

The St Xavier trustees, a roll call of octogenarians accustomed to dozing through the annual board meeting in readiness for the eight-course banquet that marked the end of another successful year, had felt as if an invading army had arrived at the gates.

Finally, hollow-eyed with terror at the prospect of yet another visit from Poppy, they had hoisted the white flag of surrender. A resolution had been passed unanimously agreeing that it would be an excellent idea to hire a woman and why the devil hadn't anyone thought of it before?

Poppy had then proposed that *she* be considered for the position.

The trustees had exchanged looks and then fallen over each other in their haste to be the first to congratulate her.

Poppy had suggested that perhaps they should interview her first, just to ensure that she was the most deserving candidate. The trustees, a sheen of perspiration on their wrinkled brows, had assured her that no interview was necessary. They were more than impressed with her non-existent credentials . . . and by the way, what exactly would she be teaching? At this point Poppy had smiled sweetly. 'I have one or two ideas,' she had announced.

And so, after one hundred years of not realising that it needed them, St Xavier had begun to teach its cadets the essential skills of acting and Bharatanatyam dance.

And, as far as Chopra had heard, his wife had been a big hit.

He felt a sense of trepidation gathering inside his stomach as he approached the frosted glass door of the principal's office. It reminded him of his own schooling in the single-roomed village school in Jarul presided over by his father, Premkumar Chopra, who everyone affectionately called Masterji.

Back then Chopra had not been a keen student. He was easily distracted. It did not help that the tin-roofed school-room was hot as hell, that flies buzzed continuously about his head, that chickens wandered in to peck at his toes, and that the occasional bullock coming back from the river would poke its head through the open window to see what all the fuss was about.

A dark-skinned man in spectacles and a flowing white cassock was waiting for them outside the office. He introduced himself as Brother Noel Machado, assistant to the principal.

'I am so glad you have come,' Machado said. 'He has been beside himself. I shudder to think what he will do if you cannot help us.'

'We will do our best,' promised Chopra, though he still had no idea why Poppy had asked him here. She had been suspiciously close-mouthed on the subject.

They entered the office to find a tall, vulpine, elderly man also in a white cassock pacing the flagstoned floor behind a battered wooden desk. Hard grey eyes looked out from below great winged eyebrows. A beaked nose curved down towards a hard-set mouth that moved in wordless anger above a jowly chin.

Brother Augustus Lobo, principal of St Xavier, was something of a Mumbai legend.

The principal was approaching his ninetieth year but looked no older than a man in his late sixties. Lobo had once declared that he owed his enduring youth to the fact that he had, for the past fifty years, taken a daily dose of his 'own water', following in the footsteps of his hero, former Prime Minister of India Morarji Desai, who had advocated 'urine therapy' as the perfect solution for the millions of Indians who could not afford medical treatment for the panoply of ills that plagued them.

Lobo stopped pacing and swivelled to face his visitors with a glare that had turned many a future captain of Indian industry to jelly. Chopra heard Rangwalla shuffle behind him. Rangwalla's schooling, he knew, had been rudimentary. He had no doubt the former sub-inspector was reliving the many beatings he had earned as a boy, beatings that were now personified in the minatory form of Augustus Lobo.

'Hooliganism, Chopra! Damned hooliganism!'

'Sir?'

'I blame this modern culture of yours,' growled the principal. 'Disrespect is the fashion, nowadays. Loutishness is in, sir. A nation of degenerates, that is where we are headed . . . And what can we do about it? Those spineless goons in New Delhi have tied our hands. Do you know that I am no longer allowed to beat these young goondas? Do you think Father Rodrigues spared the rod when I was a boy? Why, Gandhi himself was roundly beaten as a young man, and a power of good it did him. And St Xavier positively welcomed a good thrashing from those villainous Portuguese soldiers who had turned from the faith down in Goa.'

'Sir, may I ask why you have called me here today?'

Lobo gaped at him. 'Didn't your wife tell you?'

'No, sir.'

'A heinous crime has been perpetrated, Chopra.'

'What crime, sir?'

'Think of the worst crime imaginable.'

Chopra's expression was quizzical. 'Someone has been murdered?'

'Worse!' roared Lobo.

'A crime worse than murder? Forgive me, sir, but it would be simpler if you just told me.'

'They have taken our beloved Father Gonsalves!'

'There has been a kidnapping?' Chopra was astonished. 'If this is the case, sir, then you must inform the police immediately.'

Lobo's eyebrows met like duelling caterpillars. 'It is better if I show you. Come with me.'

The school's assembly hall looked out onto the school grounds through a succession of triumphant stained-glass windows depicting pivotal scenes from the life of St Xavier, as well as images of the Blessed Virgin and the Bom Jesus. The hall was lined with a succession of worn pews, inscribed with a hundred years' worth of juvenile graffiti as young minds were subjected to the purgatory of daily Mass, Vespers and interminable speechmaking.

At least this was how Chopra viewed the depressing chamber.

Chopra was not a religious man, though he believed that everyone had the right to believe whatever he or she wished. In his experience religion and tolerance rarely went hand in hand. In the history of humankind more murders had been committed in the name of religion than in the pursuit of money, sex and power combined. This was particularly true on the subcontinent, which had seen regular convulsions and conquests in the name of one faith or another. It bothered him greatly whenever he saw the minds of children being filled with the belief that one form of connection to the Great Mystery was somehow superior to another.

They followed Principal Lobo up a flight of short steps to the stage. A pulpit-style lectern was positioned at the front. Directly behind it, at the rear of the stage, was a marble column on which stood an empty plinth.

Lobo flung a hand at the plinth. 'There!'

Chopra stared. 'There is nothing there.'

'Precisely, Chopra! The damned goondas have taken it.'

Understanding dawned. He stepped forward and kneeled down to examine the brass plaque affixed to the edge of the plinth. It read:

> FATHER ALBINO GONSALVES
>
> FOUNDER AND GUIDING LIGHT OF
> THE ST XAVIER CATHOLIC SCHOOL FOR BOYS
>
> BORN LISBON 1880
>
> TAKEN FROM US IN THE YEAR OF OUR LORD 1942

'Someone has stolen a bust?'

'Not just any bust, Chopra. The bust of our founder.'

Chopra straightened up.

He realised that to Lobo this crime was of greater conse-quence than the theft of the Koh-i-Noor diamond, which had all but put two nations at each other's throats. After thirty years on the force he knew that crimes were often this way. He had seen men kill over what at first glance seemed the most trivial of matters.

But everything was important to someone.

'You wish us to recover the bust?'

'It is imperative that you do. The very morale of our school is at stake.'

'Why didn't you call the police?'

'This matter must be solved discreetly,' growled Lobo. 'I will not allow this school to become a laughing stock. I have informed the staff and students that the bust has been sent for polishing. The only ones who know about the theft are myself, Machado here, your wife, the janitor and the school secretary Mr Banarjee. And now you.'

'And the thieves.'

'What?' Lobo glared at Rangwalla as if noticing him for the first time.

'The thieves, sir,' Rangwalla clarified queasily. 'They know about the theft.'

'Well, of course they do, man!' roared Lobo. 'They stole the thing, didn't they?'

'When did the theft take place?' Chopra asked.

Machado took up the story while Lobo glowered at Rangwalla.

'Three nights ago. The janitor discovered it in the morning, just before Mass. He swears it was there the evening before when he swept the hall after Vespers.'

'How was the theft committed?'

'The bust is kept under a glass case, as you can see. The thieves simply unscrewed the case from the plinth and removed the bust.'

'How did they get into the school?'

'They broke a window in the rear wing and climbed in.'

'You have no guards?'

'We are a school. We have never needed guards.'

Chopra looked thoughtful. 'Do you have any suspects?'

'It is D'Souza's boys,' muttered Lobo darkly. 'I'll wager on it.'

Chopra turned to Machado. 'D'Souza?'

'Principal of the St Francis Catholic School for Boys,' clarified Machado. 'Brother Lobo believes that Principal Angelus D'Souza is behind this theft.'

'Why would the principal of another Catholic school steal the bust of your founder?'

'To humiliate me, that's why!' Lobo exploded. 'D'Souza has always been jealous of me, ever since we were boys. He used to be a Jesuit, you know, before he slunk off to join those wretched Franciscans. The St Francis school has always been second to St Xavier. Second and second rate.'

'Are you suggesting the bust was stolen because of an inter-school rivalry?'

'A rivalry that St Xavier has always had the upper hand in.'

'But why now?'

'Because His Holiness the Pope will be visiting Mumbai in a few months' time,' explained Lobo. 'He will make a stop at one of the Catholic schools in the city. The only possible choices are St Xavier and St Francis. St Xavier is the clear front runner. I have it on good authority from the Vatican that His Holiness will choose us. This is a humiliation D'Souza cannot stomach. He thinks that by stealing the bust he will undermine the Vatican's faith in us. Perhaps even tilt the odds in his favour.'

'Surely the theft of one bust cannot have such dire consequences?'

'"*Malum quo communius eo peius*",' muttered Lobo.

Unlike St Xavier, Chopra's village school had not offered Latin as part of its curriculum. If it had, he would have known that Lobo had said 'the more common an evil is, the worse it is'.

'Our founder is our guiding spirit,' continued the principal. 'Indeed, his very spirit walks these halls. I often encounter him myself, late in the evening. He tells me I am doing a fine job. He tells me to fight the good fight. Today's loutish generation need the Jesuit moral code more than ever. It is the rock upon which we have built our church. Are we to turn the other cheek while our founding father is whisked away from under our very noses? Do you think His Holiness will not take note of our laxness?'

Chopra realised that it was pointless to argue. 'Very well. In that case we will do everything we can.'

'You must confront D'Souza. The man is a spineless coward. He will crack like an egg.'

'*Sir!*'

Chopra turned to see Rangwalla staring in horror through the stained-glass windows out onto the adjoining playing fields. He followed his deputy's gaze . . . just in time to see a young boy running past with a baby elephant in hot pursuit.

'It's OK, boy, it wasn't your fault.'

Chopra patted Ganesha on the top of his head, his voice soothing. The young elephant was back in the van where he had instantly collapsed to the floor with his trunk curled up under his face, eyes closed, ears flattened against his skull.

Chopra recognised the symptoms; Ganesha was deeply distressed.

Over the past months he had become an expert in reading the emotional state of his young ward – and what a range of emotions Ganesha had! He seemed capable of displaying all the feelings of a young child – happiness, sorrow, pain, petulance, anger and, above all, affection.

Like a child, Ganesha had little ability to control these feelings. He was impetuous and without guile. Sometimes Chopra feared that the little elephant had become too trusting, too willing to offer his affection to all those who approached him with a smile and a warm word.

Ganesha did not realise that in the world of humans, deceit and treachery often lay behind such a smile.

He recalled the mad panic as he and Rangwalla had dashed out into the manicured grounds of St Xavier. They had found Ganesha butting the trunk of a neem tree in which the young boy – aged no more than eleven, Chopra guessed – had wedged himself. The boy was wailing alternatively for his mother and the saints to save him.

'Out of the way, Chopra! I'll deal with this!'

Chopra had turned to find Principal Lobo bearing down on Ganesha with an antique blunderbuss under his arm.

'What the hell are you doing?'

'What does it look like I am doing? There is a rampaging elephant on the grounds! I am going to take it down before it hurts someone.'

Chopra had stood before Ganesha. 'Then you will have to shoot me first.'

After Lobo had been hauled away by Brother Machado, Chopra had quietened Ganesha down and led him back to the van.

Now, he turned as Rangwalla arrived. 'Well?'

'Ganesha wanted to play with the boys. It seems that some of them decided it would be more fun to tease him.

That young thug in the tree tied a bunch of firecrackers to his tail.'

Chopra turned back to Ganesha and saw that Rangwalla was right. The remnants of the string with which the crackers had been tied to Ganesha's tail could still be seen. The bifurcated clump of long hairs at the end of the tail had been singed and a burn mark scarred the tail itself.

A cold fury raged through him, tempered only by the realisation that he could not, in good conscience, hold the boy to account. Boys were boys. The young oaf had probably not anticipated the harm that he had inflicted. No doubt he would learn his lesson.

He recalled the arrogant threats the little villain had shouted down from his perch as Chopra had led Ganesha away. 'My father will have you arrested! Do you know how rich he is? He'll crush you and that stupid elephant! You watch! I'll get him, you see if I don't!'

The words had strangely disturbed Chopra.

Normally, he would have ignored such silliness, particularly from the mouth of a boy still in shorts, but he couldn't help but dwell on Lobo's earlier sentiments.

Truly, the world was changing.

More and more Indian children were becoming spoiled brats – goondas, as Lobo called them. It would be easy to see this as yet another result of western influence, but Chopra felt there was a deeper malaise at work. Parents were busier, with more distractions. They spent less time with their children, and when they did they gave them the wrong messages. They had lost touch with their roots, the quintessentially Indian teachings of humility and respect that men like Gandhi had both practised and preached. Now, it was fashionable to be brash and bold. It was considered trendy to flaunt your wealth and power. This culture transmitted itself to the children, who grew up believing that the world revolved around them, and that all they had to do was reach out and take what they wanted.

Chopra couldn't help but feel that the nation was breeding a lost generation. The consequences of this would, one day, be a very bitter harvest indeed.

But what if the boy had not found refuge in a tree? Would Ganesha really have hurt him?

Chopra knew that he sometimes forgot that Ganesha was not a kitten or a pet poodle. The little elephant weighed two hundred and fifty kilos and had the capacity to inflict serious physical injury on the frail humans he lived among. Ganesha had saved Chopra's life earlier in the year by hurting the human traffickers who had attempted to kill him. But could Ganesha distinguish between villains and mischief-making boys? If not, then Chopra would soon have a real problem on his hands.

He glanced at his watch. He had done all he could for Ganesha for the moment. There was other work that he must attend to.

He looked up at his hovering associate detective. 'Rangwalla, I want you to handle this case.'

'Sir.'

'I'm not as sure as Lobo seems to be that another school is behind the theft. This might just be a prank. You might be looking for an inside man. Or boy, to be more accurate.'

'Sir.'

'And talking of inside men . . .' Chopra reached into his pocket and removed the papers that he had obtained from the personnel department at the Prince of Wales Museum. 'I want you to track down these individuals. I want to know everything you can find out about them.'

'Who are they?'

'They are all staff members who joined the Prince of Wales Museum after it was announced that it would host the Crown Jewels exhibition. You need to work fast, Rangwalla. Sooner or later Rao will make the same leap.'

'Count on me, sir.'

'One last thing . . . Do you remember a man called Kanodia? Bulbul Kanodia?'

'The jewel fence?' Rangwalla's brow corrugated into a frown. 'You think he had something to do with this?'

'What if I told you he was in the gallery at the time of the robbery?' Chopra paused, momentarily thoughtful. 'I need Bulbul's old case file. And then I need to find out where he is now and what he's been doing since he got out of prison.'

'I can help you with the second part,' said Rangwalla. 'Kanodia went back to the jewellery business. Did very well by all accounts. He has a string of big jewellery stores now.'

'How in the hell did he achieve *that* after spending two years in jail?'

Rangwalla shrugged. 'I don't know. But he's managed to keep his nose clean.'

'A leopard doesn't change its spots, Rangwalla,' said Chopra sternly.

Rangwalla nodded in agreement. 'As for the old case file . . . Why don't you just pick it up from the station?'

'I can't.'

'Why not?'

'There is a new head at the station. Just arrived.'

'Well, why don't you ask him? I am sure he is a reasonable man.'

'He is not a man, Rangwalla.'

'There is a *woman* in charge of the station?' Rangwalla could not have sounded more incredulous if he had been told that a baboon had just been elected Prime Minister.

'Yes,' said Chopra. 'And a very competent one, from what I can tell. She has certainly whipped the place into shape – I've never seen the station looking so smart. And young Surat seems very impressed by her.'

'What is her name?'

'Malini Sheriwal.'

Rangwalla paled. 'Did you say Malini *Sheriwal*?'

'Yes. Why?'

'You don't mean Shoot 'Em Up Sheriwal?'

That was it!

Now Chopra knew where he had heard the name before. Shoot 'Em Up Sheriwal.

Inspector Malini Sheriwal had gained notoriety in the Brihanmumbai Police as the only female member of the so-called Encounter Squad. For years the Encounter Squad had terrorised Mumbai's underworld, earning its unique sobriquet because of the long list of gangsters the squad members had shot dead in police 'encounters'.

Chopra had read a *Times of India* article in which the Encounter Squad's most successful detectives were lionised. Malini Sheriwal had been top of the tree. In three short years she had notched up more kills than the rest of the squad put together. Sheriwal was a crack shot, winner of the service's Golden Gun tournament three years running. The word was that she was both fearless and ruthless.

But in the past year the tide of public sentiment had begun to turn. Human rights activists had begun to raise questions about these so-called 'encounter' killings. Suddenly the Encounter Squad was being portrayed as a gang of licensed vigilantes rather than heroic upholders of the law. The upper echelons of the force had sensed which way the wind was blowing and had quietly disbanded the unit and dispatched its members to relatively anonymous postings to lie low until things blew over.

This explained what Sheriwal was doing at the Sahar station. It didn't explain to Chopra how he was going to get the Kanodia case file.

Luckily Rangwalla had a solution.

'Leave it to me, sir.'

A DISCONSOLATE ELEPHANT

The starscape above the courtyard was an astrologer's dream.

Chopra had often wondered how anyone could believe that their destiny was written up there, in the random patterns made by unimaginably distant balls of burning gas. But the human mind has an infinite capacity to delude itself. And in that gap between reason and superstition, all manner of fantasies prevailed.

Then again, he thought, if the last year had taught him anything, it was that perhaps not everything that failed to meet his own stern test of logic and rationality could be consigned to the realms of mere fantasy.

He looked down from the starry heavens to where Ganesha was hunkered down in the mud below his mango tree. The little elephant continued to be uncommunicative and withdrawn, enveloped in seeming despair.

Following the visit to St Xavier, Chopra had taken Ganesha to see the vet, Dr Rohit Lala.

Lala, who had become quite attached to Chopra's ward over the past months, had examined Ganesha carefully before applying a waxy burn emollient to his tail. 'It's nothing,' he had said in his booming, jovial manner. 'The burn is superficial. Nothing to worry about.'

'Then why is he so . . .?' Chopra's voice tailed off.

'He has suffered a shock. Do not forget that he is a child. Imagine a human child that has been teased, bullied and burned. How would that child react? This, my friend, is the sort of wound that leaves deeper scars on the inside than the out.'

Chopra sensed that Lala was right.

He had brought Ganesha home and settled him back into the courtyard. He had then pulled out his twin bibles on the care and husbandry of elephants.

The first was the weighty, fact-based encyclopaedia *The Definitive Guide to the Life and Habits of the Indian Elephant* by Dr Harpal Singh.

Chopra thumbed through the glossy pages and learned that although an elephant's hide appeared to be robust, in reality there were places where that skin was as thin as paper. He discovered that elephant skin is sensitive to heat, and that elephant calves sunburn very easily, hence their tendency to hide beneath their mothers, to squirt water over themselves and slather themselves in mud at every opportunity. Dr Singh wrote that 'an elephant's skin is so sensitive that it can detect even a fly landing upon it'. These revelations made Chopra think that perhaps Dr Lala had underestimated the pain Ganesha had suffered from his injury.

Then he turned to the second book, his personal favourite.

It was a thin volume entitled *Ganesha: Ten years living with an Indian elephant*. The author was a British woman called Harriet Fortinbrass who had come to the subcontinent in the 1920s. Fortinbrass had adopted a young elephant whose mother had been shot dead by her father, a British diplomat – indeed the name she had given her ward had inspired Chopra to select Ganesha for his own charge.

Whereas Dr Singh was a font of dry facts and details, Fortinbrass's passion for her ward shone through. 'Elephants are great communicators [she wrote]. They use their heads, bodies, trunks, ears and tail as a form of language. For example, when a female elephant feels threatened, she will make herself appear larger by holding her head as high as she can and spreading her ears wide. An elephant's mood can be determined from its bodily movements. An elephant that withdraws from the tactile world is an elephant in emotional distress.'

Chopra had tried everything he could think of to bring Ganesha out of his funk, but to no avail.

In the end he had decided to leave the elephant alone while he worked in the restaurant's back office. A number of cases required documentation and a backlog of client correspondence had built into a miniature pyramid inside his filing cabinet. Irfan had done his best but there was only so much the boy could do to keep the wolves at bay. Paperwork was a chore that Chopra did not enjoy but his long years in the service had taught him the value of maintaining a meticulous paper trail. It was a strategy that had paid dividends many times over. And he had insisted on that same rigid attention to detail in his junior officers.

A nervous Sub-Inspector Surat delivered the Kanodia case file to him just as the evening restaurant crowd was beginning to swell.

'Did Rangwalla ask you to do this, Surat?' Chopra asked sternly as he took the dog-eared manila folder.

'Yes, sir.'

'Listen to me carefully. You are not to do anything like this again. You have a new commanding officer. You owe him – *her* – your loyalty. Did you stop to think what she would do if she found out you were handing over police files to non-police personnel?'

Surat paled as he thought of the consequences of upsetting Shoot 'Em Up Sheriwal.

'Never mind. What's done is done. Let me take a look at this tonight and then I want you to return it to the station first thing in the morning.'

Surat snapped off a spectacular salute. 'Yes, sir.'

'And Surat . . . you don't have to salute me.'

'Yes, sir.'

Chopra sat out under the stars and opened the file. Crickets sang a chorus above the steady rumble of traffic from Guru Rabindranath Tagore Road. The smell of cinnamon drifted from the restaurant – Chef Lucknowwallah was preparing his special cinnamon-infused rice pudding.

Chopra hoped the chef would save a plate for him; it was a particular favourite of his.

Balram Kanodia – known to friends and associates as 'Bulbul' Kanodia – had been born in the city of Rajkot in the state of Gujarat in 1959. He had moved to Mumbai in his early thirties and had set up a hole-in-the-wall gemstone business in the industrial quarter of Sahar known as SEEPZ. In time, the business had become a small jewellery operation – Kanodia was descended from a line of Gujarati jewellers and was rumoured to be an exquisite craftsman, particularly adept at designing complex gemstone jewellery.

Kanodia had come to Chopra's attention when a street informant had fingered the jeweller as a small-time fence. Bulbul had clearly decided that the razor-thin margins he made from his work were not enough to meet his needs.

Chopra had had Kanodia's operation monitored and then sent an undercover agent in. Kanodia had taken the bait and agreed to find a home for what he had been expressly informed was stolen merchandise. The entire sting had been secretly recorded and Chopra himself had slapped the cuffs on the would-be middleman.

The investigation and arrest were meticulously logged in the file, as Chopra expected them to be. He was gratified to discover, however, a wealth of additional information.

Chopra had long insisted that his men continue to make notes in case files well after an initial arrest, so that criminals who might resurface in the locality could be monitored. It had paid off numerous times, and it did again now.

A number of further entries described Kanodia's life following his arrest.

Chopra was surprised to note that although Kanodia had begun his sentence in the general barracks of the Arthur Road Jail, within a month he had been transferred to Barrack No. 3 – the barracks run by the Chauhan gang. Kanodia's time in jail seemed to have been greatly eased through his association with this band of organised criminals.

Upon his release from prison – due to an early parole that Chopra did not believe was warranted – Kanodia had gone underground for almost a year. Then, out of nowhere, he had found the capital to set up a jewellery emporium called Paramathma – meaning 'divine soul'.

So Bulbul developed a sense of irony during his time in jail, Chopra thought.

According to Rangwalla there were now at least six branches of the Paramathma chain around the city, the largest one in the affluent suburb of Bandra. The one thing that modern Indians had in common with their ancestors was a love of jewellery. From Mughal emperors to the lowliest members of the lowest caste, this pursuit of gold and gems seemed as much a part of the fabric of Indian life as spices and religion.

Business was booming for Bulbul.

Chopra put down the file and tried to impose order on to his thoughts.

Bulbul Kanodia was now his number one suspect as the mastermind behind the theft of the Crown of Queen Elizabeth.

He knew that jewellers from every corner of the country had descended upon the Prince of Wales Museum in the past weeks. After all, when would they get another chance to behold the most magnificent creations their particular brand of artifice had ever conjured up?

Kanodia, however, was a man with a track record, a man connected to Mumbai's criminal underworld. Chopra had little doubt that organised crime had financed Bulbul's chain of jewellery stores. Kanodia was a front man and Chopra believed that the jewellery stores were being used by the Chauhan gang to launder black money into white. The plot to steal the Koh-i-Noor was exactly the sort of thing the gang would consider a coup.

A metallic clanking signalled Irfan's arrival with Ganesha's evening bucket of coconut milk. Irfan salaamed his boss and then approached the little elephant.

Chopra watched the smile fade from Irfan's face. 'What is the matter with him?'

'I am afraid Ganesha has had another encounter with human nature.'

A look of confusion passed over the boy's face. He set down the bucket and then knelt down beside Ganesha. 'Hey, boy, cheer up. Don't let the world get you down.'

Ganesha remained unresponsive.

Irfan stood up and began to dance, singing a popular Bollywood number that never failed to delight Ganesha.

Nothing.

'Chopra Sir!'

Chopra turned to see the statuesque figure of Rosie Pinto, one of Chef Lucknowwallah's two assistant cooks, standing on the veranda in her white uniform and toque blanche.

Rosie was an enigma to Chopra. A Goan Catholic with a figure that reminded him of the statues of primitive mother goddesses that he sometimes saw on the Discovery Channel, Rosie had a personality as large as her figure and a booming voice that easily cut through the bustle of the restaurant when the need arose. Chopra had found himself quite intimidated at first, but Chef Lucknowwallah had been effusive in his praise for her skills in the kitchen.

Rosie seemed equally popular with the clientele. She had a saucy air about her, and it had not escaped his eagle eye how often Rosie's generous backside was slapped by overfamiliar patrons as she wiggled her way across the restaurant floor. Rosie never seemed to mind, but he had considered having a word with her about the matter. He did not wish to encourage licentious behaviour in his staff. After all, this was a family restaurant, not a ladies bar.

'What is it, Rosie?'

'Chef wishes to see you urgently. He is waiting in your office.'

Chopra's heart sank. As he reluctantly hauled himself to his feet and trudged towards the restaurant, he tried to focus on the fact that he was exceedingly fortunate to have secured the services of Chef Lucknowwallah.

Azeem Lucknowwallah, by his own admission, was a genius. He had spent a lifetime working in the kitchens of five-star hotels and 'tip-top' restaurants. He had travelled the subcontinent, imbibing recipes and techniques from the masters. Lucknowwallah had retired three years earlier, but had come out of retirement to apply for the position of head chef at Poppy's Restaurant, the post having been

recommended to him by his nephew and Chopra's neigh-
bour, ghazal troubadour Feroz Lucknowwallah.

Chef Lucknowwallah's father had been a police constable in faraway Lucknow, once renowned as the City of the
Nawabs. Lucknowwallah Senior had been killed in the line
of duty, run down by a crazed bullock during a protest
march by the Indian farmers' union campaigning against
government-set cotton prices in the early seventies. The
young Lucknowwallah had been left with the harrowing
memory of his father expiring on a dusty cornfield to the
echoes of a police lathi charge and the yelps of stricken
farm folk. Ever since that ill-fated day, he had sought for a
means to honour his late father. The opportunity offered
by Mumbai's first restaurant dedicated specifically to the
police service was too good to pass up.

Chopra had hired Lucknowwallah on the spot and
had been greatly relieved when the chef had not haggled
over his salary. He could not afford to pay the rate that
a man of Lucknowwallah's experience could command.
Lucknowwallah had dismissed his concerns with an expansive wave of his hand. 'Neither of us are here for the money,
Chopra,' he had opined.

The chef had settled in quickly and soon the restaurant's
patrons had begun to rave at the conveyor belt of magnificent dishes that emerged from his kitchen.

The problem was not the chef. Lucknowwallah was an
artist and highly strung. He could handle that. No, the
problem had been created by Chopra himself. For the
millionth time he wished that he had not caved into his
wife's demand that he 'find something for my mother to

do'. As if the old crone did not have enough to do making his life a misery at every opportunity.

But at Poppy's behest he had installed Poornima Devi as the restaurant's front-of-house manager. He had anticipated that the old woman would quickly tire of the post and leave of her own accord.

To everyone's surprise, his mother-in-law had taken to the role with an industry that unnerved all those around her.

Poornima Devi's ability to inspire terror in the waiting staff ensured a fast and efficient service in the dining area. Her grasping memory – usually employed in recalling Chopra's numerous faults – meant that nothing was forgotten in the day-to-day running of the operation. Furthermore, with Poornima supervising proceedings the number of wastrels frequenting the restaurant had swiftly dried up. Those diners who suddenly realised that they had forgotten their wallets just as swiftly found them again under her withering, single-eyed scorn.

Chopra knew, from personal experience, that an enraged Poornima Devi was a Kaliesque vision of terror.

His mother-in-law insisted on wearing the white sari of a widow, her grey bun and black eye-patch lending her once-attractive face a terrifying severity. She had steadfastly refused to don the bright pink uniform that Poppy had chosen for the restaurant's staff. 'Should I wear make-up too, like some cheap floozy?' she had sneered. 'Would you sell your mother to the Kamathipura brothels?'

It was perhaps inevitable, Chopra reflected, that a battle of wills would ensue between Chef Lucknowwallah and

Poornima Devi. The two were chalk and cheese and rarely saw eye to eye.

He sighed. Sometimes he longed for his days as a police officer, when all you had to worry about was getting shot.

He found the chef pacing the floor of his office, vibrating with indignation.

'What has she done this time, Chef?'

'That . . . that . . . *woman* . . . has ordered me – *ordered*, mind you! – to see to the over-spicing of my Shahi Chicken Korma!' The fat little man quivered with indignation. There were curry stains on his white chef's jacket, obscuring the initials AL embroidered on the breast pocket.

Lucknowwallah's round cheeks glowed red from the jungle-like heat that prevailed in his kitchen. The top of his head was covered by the white cricket umpire's cap that was his trademark, though Chopra suspected it was a gesture of vanity, a failed attempt to conceal Lucknowwallah's thinning hair.

Before Chopra could respond the chef exploded again. 'Am I a khansama now, Chopra? A two-chip cookwallah to be ordered around by a glorified waitress? I, who trained at the knee of Master Lal Bahadur Shah! I, whose forefathers served as *vasta wazas* for the courts of emperors! When Akbar lay dying after fifty years on the throne, do you know what he asked for? Not gold or concubines . . . Akbar begged for the peacock heart basted in saffron oil that was the invention of my ancestors! When General Sikander was sentenced to be crushed to death beneath an elephant's foot for daring to love Emperor Jahangir's favourite consort, do you know what his last request was? Did he ask for one final kiss from his lost love? No, sir! He asked for one last taste of the kabuli biryani that made kings of my predecessors!'

Chopra sighed and realised that his evening's travails had only just begun.

Back in the compound Irfan knelt down in the mud and patted Ganesha on the head. 'Someone hurt you today, didn't they, Ganesha?'

The little elephant remained morose, shrouded in a depressed silence.

'You must not be so sensitive. People hurt each other all the time. Like Chopra Sir says, it is in their nature. You must become tough, like me. Then it doesn't matter how much they hurt you.'

Ganesha opened his eyes. Then he unfurled his trunk and lifted it to touch the boy's face. He slid the tip of the trunk down towards Irfan's shoulder and traced the cigarette burns that had made circular scars on the skin.

'A bad man did that to me,' said Irfan, his voice suddenly low. 'He tried to break my spirit each and every day. But one day I realised that no one can break your spirit unless you let them. So I ran away. Now he cannot touch me. No one can touch me.'

In the sudden silence there was only the steady drone of traffic from the nearby road. And then Ganesha lifted his trunk once more to the boy's face and brushed away the tears that had materialised on Irfan's cheeks.

GAREWAL HITS THE HEADLINES

Christmas in Mumbai.

Inspector Chopra (Retd) had often wondered how, given the fact that less than three per cent of the population of Mumbai was Catholic, the festival could engender such hysteria. In the run-up to the big day the whole city seemed to be overcome by a frenzy that he found impossible to fathom. It was another sign of the times, another line in the sand marking the ever-rising tide of westernisation that was engulfing urban India.

As he looked around at the streams of his fellow Mumbaikers thronging the brightly lit mall, he corrected himself. Perhaps westernisation was not the right word. Retailisation. Merchandisation.

He set down the shopping bags he had been carrying and checked his watch. The watch was twenty-five years old and had been a gift from his late father on the occasion of Chopra's wedding. He remained sentimentally attached to it even though it spent more time in the repair shop than it did on his wrist.

It was already midday. He knew that he should be working on the Koh-i-Noor case – each stuttering tick of the watch's second hand was a personal rebuke – but he had made his wife a promise.

Poppy was an inveterate fanatic of festivals. It did not matter which festival, his wife loved them all. She seemed to be instantly infected by whatever happened to be going around. He did not begrudge her this happy knack – he simply wished that she would leave him out of it. But Poppy, as is the way of some people, seemed convinced that Chopra would enjoy such occasions just as much as she did *if only he would give it a chance*.

'Ho ho ho!'

He turned. Standing before him was a short, thin man clad in a Santa Claus outfit that was many sizes too big for him, giving the impression that he had lost a lot of weight very recently. The outfit seemed to be wearing the man rather than the other way around. A fake white beard was attached to his chin and fluffy eyebrows pasted on above his eyes. One of the eyebrows had tilted downwards, but he seemed unaware of this.

'Ho ho ho!' he repeated, in a thin reedy voice.

'Can I help you?' Chopra asked crossly.

The annual epidemic of Santas was another thing that bothered him. In his opinion they were not only irritating but also suffered from the crime of being inferior knock-offs. The vast majority that descended upon the city each year – in malls, in restaurants, even in the local branch of his bank – looked more like costumed hashish addicts of the type he often saw sleeping rough under the many flyovers of Mumbai.

'Sir, we have many great offers waiting for you in our menswear department!'

Chopra looked around. Poppy was busily examining a shelf full of boys' shirts. His wife had grown greatly attached to her pupils at the St Xavier school and had decided that this year she would expend her Christmas budget buying gifts for them instead of hosting her own Christmas party. 'Just imagine their little faces when they open their presents!' she had sighed.

He slipped his identity card from his wallet and waved it under Santa's nose. 'And I have a jail cell waiting for you. Now go away.'

He watched the man scurry off, hitching up his voluminous red trousers as he went.

'How do you think Irfan would look in this?' he heard Poppy ask behind him. She held up a garish yellow T-shirt stamped with the logo of Ralph Lauren.

'Poppy, I really must go.'

She put down the T-shirt and walked over to him. Her concerned eyes carefully examined his face. 'You are working too hard.'

'I feel fine.'

'Did you take your pills?'

'Yes.'

'I am glad Rangwalla will be working with you. Perhaps now you can take things a little easier. You know what the doctor said.'

Chopra did know. The doctors had told him to stop being himself; to stop being Inspector Chopra. He could not do that.

'We interrupt this broadcast with a special bulletin. We are going live now to WD-TV studios.'

Chopra looked up at the giant television screen hanging from the ceiling high above. The screens were dotted around the store, ostensibly to provide entertainment for the shoppers. However, it had not escaped his notice that the broadcasts were regularly interrupted by prolonged adverts for the store's latest and greatest offers.

A newscaster in a tailored suit appeared on the screen. His face, below a glistening bouffant hairstyle, was grave. 'Namashkar, ladies and gentlemen. We have a breaking exclusive on the stolen crown investigation brought to you exclusively by WD-TV. We go live to CBI headquarters where Assistant Commissioner of Police Suresh Rao has convened an emergency press conference.'

The picture cut to a whitewashed room lit by bright overhead lighting. Behind a long table bristling with microphones sat DCI Maxwell Bomberton and ACP Suresh Rao, flanked by a number of other important-looking policemen. Bomberton's balding head glistened under the lights. His red face was puffed with anger.

'ACP Rao, would you care to comment on the rumours that you have taken one Shekhar Garewal into custody in connection with the theft of the Koh-i-Noor?'

'I'll give you a comment,' growled Bomberton before Rao could open his mouth. 'You're damned lucky I don't arrest you right now and throw you into jail!' He leaned forward as if he fully intended to leap from the podium and accost the reporter who had dared to ask this question. 'This is an ongoing police investigation. I demand to know where you got this information!'

'So it is true?'

'Answer the question, damnit!'

'I cannot reveal my sources, sir.'

A thin nasally voice piped up. 'ACP Rao, this is Romesh Ratnagar of the *Times*. Let us stop being coy. I request you to herewith confirm that Inspector Shekhar Garewal has been placed under arrest and that even now he is in the Anda Cell of the Arthur Road Jail.'

Rao licked his lips and exchanged nervous glances with his colleagues. Their thoughts clearly mirrored Bomberton's belligerent words. How had the press got wind of Garewal? 'I am afraid I am not at liberty to confirm this information.'

'You mean you don't know?'

'What? No. I mean yes. I do know. I just cannot . . . confirm,' Rao finished lamely.

'Ah, I understand. You do not have the authority.'

Rao flushed. 'Of course I have the authority. It is simply that—'

'You require DCI Bomberton's permission before you may speak. I completely understand. I had thought the days of the Raj were over but I see that I was mistaken.' A sniggering arose from the gathered newspeople as Bomberton scowled.

Rao's face was now the colour of a beetroot. 'Look here, Ratnagar,' he spluttered, 'DCI Bomberton is a guest of the Mumbai Police. He is not running this investigation.'

'It appears then that no one is running this investigation, sir, as you do not have the authority even to confirm—'

'*I* am running this investigation.'

'Then you can confirm or deny a simple case of fact! Is Garewal in custody or not?'

Rao glared at Ratnagar. 'Yes.'

A gasp echoed around the room, followed by a nervous buzz of chatter. Bomberton turned to Rao, his face apoplectic.

Ratnagar shouted down his colleagues, pressing home his advantage. 'So the very man you saw fit to place in charge of security for the Crown Jewels is the one behind this plot?'

Rao realised that he might have put his foot in his mouth. He struggled hastily to backtrack. 'We cannot confirm any further details regarding Garewal's arrest at this time.'

'Why not? There must be some reason that you have arrested him. We have a right to know. Or is Garewal merely a scapegoat? Have you arrested an innocent man, ACP Rao, to conceal the government's incompetence? Is the real culprit out there somewhere laughing at the Indian Police Service? Were you hoping to pull the wool over our eyes, sir?'

Rao thumped the desk. The glass of water before him leaped from the podium and fell to the floor. 'Garewal is as guilty as hell!'

'How can you be so sure?' asked Ratnagar smoothly.

'Because one hour ago we recovered the Crown of Queen Elizabeth from his home!'

A RETURN VISIT TO THE JAIL

Chopra parked the van directly in front of the Arthur Road Jail, ignoring the battered NO PARKING sign that loomed by the side of the road. For a moment he sat there, glaring out at the bustling street. A cycle-courier strained by, knots of muscle prominent in his burnished calves, a cart loaded with freshly laundered linen swaying behind him. In the middle of the road an auto-rickshaw had broken down, earning the wrath of passing motorists. A pair of teenagers on a motorbike hurled abuse at the luckless driver as they roared past in a cloud of sulphurous exhaust fumes. The driver shook a fist at the departing bike, then shrank back into his vehicle as he noticed a traffic constable moving towards him, twirling his lathi stick menacingly.

Chopra knew that he needed to control the anger flooding through his system. Now was a time for him to think clearly and to act rationally; a time to—

A furious hammering erupted on the window.

Chopra turned to see a leper, dressed in a tattered blue bathrobe, brandishing a leprous hand at him. The hand was wrapped in a filthy bandage, the fingers reduced to mere stumps.

The leper, catching sight of the expression on his face, hastily backed away.

Chopra got out of the van and stalked across the road.

He thrust his identity card at the constables stationed at the main gate and ordered them briskly to place a call to the guard in the centre of the Anda Cell.

Five minutes later the man appeared and led him hurriedly back to his desk.

As soon as they entered the inner sanctum of the Anda Cell, the man pirouetted on the soles of his worn leather shoes and blurted, 'OK, let me see the money now.' His eyes flickered with unabashed greed.

Chopra grabbed the fellow by his uniform and slammed him against the wall. 'Listen to me very carefully. There is no money. I am here to talk to Garewal. You will open the door to his cell and then you will sit down quietly until I have finished. If you do not do exactly as I say I will place a call to the Commissioner. I am sure he will be very interested to know why you took a bribe from public enemy number one. Why you allowed Garewal to make a call to the outside. To me. Do we understand each other?'

The stunned guard stared at him in mute terror and then nodded dumbly.

As the cell door swung open Chopra felt another rush of fury. He closed his eyes, breathed deeply through his nostrils, then stalked into the cell.

Garewal was standing in the gloom, waiting for him.

'The guard told me Rao is claiming he found the crown at my home,' he said anxiously. 'Is it true?'

'You lied to me,' Chopra hissed. 'You used me.'

'What are you saying?' Garewal looked aghast. 'I didn't do this.'

'They found the crown! What was it doing in your house?'

'It was planted there! Surely you can see that?'

'Planted by who?'

'By the real thieves.'

'Why would the thieves steal the crown only to plant it on you?'

'Perhaps they panicked. The whole country is looking for them.'

'No one goes to that much trouble and then just gives up a prize like that.'

'Then maybe it was Rao.'

'Rao? Why would Rao do it?' Chopra shook his head. 'For Rao to plant the crown, he would have had to find it some-where else first. Where? How? The idea is preposterous.'

Garewal's eyes were filled with anguish. 'You have to believe me, Chopra. I did not steal the crown.'

Chopra turned away in disgust. 'You made a fool of me.' The set of his shoulders betrayed his anger and disappointment.

Behind him, he heard Garewal approach. 'Chopra, you are my last hope. I have children. What will happen to them if I am sent away for this crime, a crime I did not commit?'

Chopra did not turn around.

'I am asking you to trust me. I promise you on the lives of my children that I had nothing to do with this. You are the only one who can save me now.'

Finally Chopra turned. He looked at his former colleague. Garewal's bruised and battered face was twisted with a look of such pleading that he almost turned away again. How many times during his career had he stared into the eyes of criminals and made a judgement on the truth? But now he was looking into the eyes of a policeman, a man he had known and worked with . . . Something moved deep inside Garewal's eyes. It was as if a hunted animal was in there, seeking an escape.

Chopra did not think a man could fake a look like that.

'All right, Garewal. I will give you the benefit of the doubt. For now. That is the best I can do.'

Tears glistened in Garewal's eyes. 'Thank you, old friend. Thank you.'

'Let us start by looking at the facts, namely that the crown *has* been recovered, and from your home. Why would anyone steal the crown only to return it? All to frame you? A middle-ranking officer in the Brihanmumbai Police? It makes no sense.'

'I don't know why, Chopra. I only know that I did not do it.'

Chopra paused. 'Then there is something here that we are missing. Something we haven't understood. You do not mount the sort of operation it took to steal the crown just to hand it right back.'

'I agree. But what could it be?'

'I don't know. But I am going to find out.'

Poornima Devi, slumped in Chopra's rattan armchair in the courtyard of Poppy's Bar & Restaurant, peered at Ganesha with her one working eye. 'What is the matter with him?'

'He is upset,' explained Irfan, standing beside the old woman and fanning her with a bamboo fan.

The object of their scrutiny was hunkered under his mango tree, eyelids screwed shut, trunk curled under his face, the very picture of misery. A tickbird sat on his skull as if it were the captain of a seagoing vessel that had run aground.

'What has he got to be upset about?' groused Poornima. 'Sitting there getting fed all day like Emperor Akbar while I, an old woman, work my fingers to the bone.'

The rear door to the restaurant creaked opened and Rosie came panting over the veranda to hand Poornima a glass of freshly churned buttermilk. She waited anxiously while the old harridan sniffed the glass, swallowed a generous mouthful, then sighed luxuriously and sank further into the chair. Then, realising that Rosie was waiting for her approval, she reasserted her perennial scowl. 'Don't you have anything better to do than stare at my face?'

Rosie fled.

Poornima turned her attention to the steel thaali balanced on the stool in front of her. The thaali, with its many compartments, contained her lunch, a medley of Chef Lucknowwallah's best dishes direct from the kitchen. She picked up a glutinous ball of saffron rice with her fingers and stuffed it into the corner of her mouth. 'It is lucky I have a strong constitution,' she belched. 'Anyone else forced to eat that second-rate man's third-rate cooking would have long ago expired.'

Irfan suppressed a smile.

'When I lived in Jarul I ate like a queen,' Poornima continued. 'They insisted on waiting on me, hand and foot. Wouldn't let me lift a finger. Did I tell you about my son, Vikram? He is one in a million.' Irfan knew, from listening to Chopra and Poppy talk, that Vikram was a wastrel of the first order. It was why Poornima Devi had been forced to move in with her daughter. 'Of course, what would a street urchin like you know about the village?' she went on. 'Golden fields of wheat, bajra and jowar as far as the eye can see. The Sarangi river sparkling in the distance. The walls of my beautiful white house ablaze in the midday sun.' Poornima's gaze became adrift on the misty oceans of the past. 'When I was young, men came from miles around to ask for my hand. The most beautiful maiden in seven villages, they used to say! I was married to the village sarpanch, did you know that? He was a good man, but he had many foolish notions. He believed the heart should rule the head. He was always trying to *help* people. Since when has helping people ever helped anyone? Good-natured, they called him. Hah! Can you spend a good nature? Look at me

now, at the mercy of that goonda of a son-in-law of mine.'
She scooped up another ball of rice, then waved it at
Ganesha. 'As for the fool who sent that useless creature here
– a bigger loafer was never born in this country.'

From the corner of his eye Irfan noticed Ganesha perk
up. The elephant had lifted his head and was staring at
Poornima Devi.

'Bansi. What kind of name is that for a grown man?
Wandering around in half a dhoti, pretending to be some
sort of sadhu. Reading horoscopes when he could barely
read his own name on a chit. Hah! If you ask me that man
was as brainless as the silly creature he
sent— *AAAIIIEEEEEEEEE!*'

Irfan looked on in astonishment as Poornima leaped
wildly from the chair, scattering the thaali's contents over
her white widow's sari.

'Madam! What is the matter?'

And then he saw it . . . A giant Indian hornet, having
applied its sting to the cantankerous old woman, buzzed
dazedly away.

Poornima, vigorously rubbing her arm, cursed loudly,
then fell back, limbs akimbo. 'Get help!' she panted. 'Call
an ambulance! Fetch a doctor! I can feel its poison working
its way to my heart!'

'Yes, madam!' said Irfan. 'Ganesha, keep an eye on her!'

He turned and raced towards the restaurant.

Ganesha stumbled to his feet and moved cautiously
towards the old woman, who had closed her eyes and was
now massaging her chest. He prodded her delicately with
his trunk, but she only wheezed dramatically.

Chef Lucknowwallah came bounding into the courtyard, trailed by Irfan. 'Let me see,' panted the chef.

'I told you to get a doctor and you bring me this butcher!' yelped Poornima, instantly jerking back to life.

'Be quiet, woman,' growled Lucknowwallah. He unscrewed the pot of ghee he was carrying and scooped out a good dollop with his finger.

'You're not smearing that gunk on me!' screeched Poornima.

'It is the best thing for a sting,' said Lucknowwallah. 'Trust me.' He lathered the ghee, laced with turmeric and garlic, onto the angry welt while the old woman pulled expressions of excruciating agony.

Finally, he stepped back. 'Well?'

'Well, what?' said Poornima eventually.

'Is it not better?'

'I hope you are not expecting me to thank you?'

The triumph dropped out of Lucknowwallah's grin. 'No,' he scowled. 'Why in the world would I be expecting that?' He turned and trudged off back into the restaurant.

'Who the hell do you think you are, Chopra, telling me my job?'

ACP Suresh Rao rose up onto the balls of his feet and thrust his round, red face at Chopra. Angry spittle flew in all directions.

It had taken Chopra forty minutes to race from Arthur Road Jail to the CBI's Mumbai HQ at Colaba. Now he faced down a furious ACP Rao in an air-conditioned office on the sixth floor of the run-down old building.

'I am a private investigator,' said Chopra, the skin tightening around his eyes. 'Garewal is my client. He has been framed. The real culprit is still out there.'

'Framed! What are you talking about?' spluttered Rao. 'We found the crown in Garewal's house. How do you think it got there? By accident?' Rao jabbed at Chopra's chest. 'You are not always right. This time I am the clever one. It has been Garewal right from the beginning. Why do you think we arrested him? Immediately after the theft we received an anonymous tip-off. We were told to check Garewal's bank account. Do you know what we found? A transfer of one million rupees made just one hour after the theft from an offshore hawala account. Garewal's payoff for setting up the operation. And now the crown turns up in his home! There is no doubt. Garewal is guilty. He has made a fool of you. There will be a promotion in this for me.'

'Rao, you do not even deserve the stars you are wearing now.' Chopra's mind was racing. Here was another piece of the puzzle.

Rao's claim that a large sum of money had appeared in Garewal's account explained why they had arrested him so quickly. Again he felt crocodiles of doubt swimming against the tide of his own belief that Garewal was innocent.

Meanwhile, an incensed Rao continued, 'We will see just how smart you are when I get the diamond back too, Chopr—' The ACP stopped as his ears caught up with his mouth.

Chopra's eyes narrowed. 'That's it! I knew there was something you were not telling us. They've taken the Koh-i-Noor, haven't they? They dug it out of the crown and then they planted the crown in Garewal's home. They had what they wanted all along. They didn't need the crown. By planting it on Garewal they deflected suspicion on to him *and* got rid of the incriminating evidence.' Chopra snapped his fingers as another thought fell into place. 'And that's why you didn't mention the crown in your press conference until you were forced into it. If you had recovered the crown *and* the Koh-i-Noor you would have been crowing about it from the rooftops. But now you will have to tell the truth. And you will be forced to admit that Garewal is innocent.'

'You are delusional, Chopra,' growled Rao, shaking his head. 'Garewal himself must have removed the Koh-i-Noor. He has passed it on to his fellow conspirators. We don't know who they are yet, but we will soon. Garewal will crack. I will *make* Garewal crack, that I promise you.'

'These so-called conspirators are the same ones who gave you the anonymous tip-off,' said Chopra. 'They knew you would go chasing off after your own tail.'

'Are you saying they transferred one million rupees into Garewal's account just to frame him?' Rao's voice was incredulous.

'What is such a sum when set against the Koh-i-Noor diamond?' Chopra was almost shouting, but he didn't care.

'Nonsense! This time it is you who are the fool. Garewal and his gang pulled this off together. The plan was for Garewal to keep the crown at his house, remove the Koh-i-Noor and send it on, perhaps even get it out of the country and into the hands of a buyer. Maybe the crown was part of Garewal's payoff. Or perhaps Garewal tried to cheat his associates. Garewal slipped up, Chopra. It is as simple as that.'

'What about the tip-off? Doesn't it seem suspicious to you at all?'

Rao shrugged. 'Who knows? Maybe someone had an attack of conscience. Maybe Garewal's greed turned them against him. Either way, it doesn't matter. I have Garewal right where I want him. It is just a matter of time. We will find the rest of the culprits and we will recover the Koh-i-Noor. The Prime Minister himself will pin a medal to my chest. And Garewal will spend the rest of his life breaking rocks in the deepest darkest hole we can find for him.'

THE DIVINE SOUL EMPORIUM

Chopra slammed his hand on the horn. Around him a crescendo of furious trumpeting arose like the devil's own orchestra. He had once read that in some foreign countries injudicious use of the horn was prohibited by law. He wondered how Mumbai would fare if such a law was enacted in the city.

All around him, the traffic was gridlocked.

Chopra sat in his Tata Venture on Swami Vivekanand Road in Bandra West just yards from the Turner Road junction, seething with anger at Rao's pig-headedness. It seemed clear to him that there was at least the possibility of a grand conspiracy behind the theft of the Koh-i-Noor. That a very sophisticated team of criminals had carried out the heist and had then planned their escape just as carefully, including the framing of Shekhar Garewal. The transferred funds, planting the crown in Garewal's home – these acts all spoke of an outfit that was slick, professional and well financed. To Chopra this meant backing

– the sort of backing that had access to specialist skills and almost limitless resources.

In other words: organised crime.

He was convinced more than ever that Bulbul Kanodia – backed by the Chauhan gang – was behind the robbery.

With this realisation his next course of action, over which he had been fretting, became clear. It was time for him to confront Kanodia, to rattle Bulbul's cage and see what he could learn.

Having made this decision Chopra had driven directly from his unpleasant meeting with ACP Rao to the head-quarters of Kanodia's jewellery chain, the flagship Paramathma store in Bandra.

It was time to beard the former fence in his lair.

If he could actually get there.

Before Chopra was a scene of chaos, caused by a morcha – a protest march – led by a voluble group of eunuchs and social workers. The marchers, an invading army against which the authorities were powerless, had taken over the junction. The situation had been compounded by an over-turned bullock-cart, which had spilled dozens of musk melons across the junction's cratered tarmac, drawing in an opportunistic crowd of beggars and lepers.

The eunuchs were campaigning for equality.

A recent supreme court settlement had finally confirmed that the country's vast eunuch population should be classi-fied as a third gender. This had been an important first step to improving their plight. Now the eunuchs were fighting to have legislation passed that guaranteed them equality in all areas of life, particularly in employment.

Chopra wholly supported the movement. He had long ago decided that the eunuchs – many of whom had been taken at a young age and mutilated against their will – had the worst lot in a society where caste prejudice and poverty meant a life of misery for millions on the lowest rungs of the ladder. Sadly, it would take more than legislation to change millennia of prejudice. As he had learned over the years, the hearts of his fellow countrymen were not ruled by laws written by clerks locked away in distant air-conditioned offices, but by older laws, of superstition, mistrust and unthinking hatred.

He suddenly realised that he knew the eunuch boisterously demonstrating at the head of the parade. It was Anarkali, one of his many local street informants in Sahar, a strapping six-foot-tall specimen in a bright yellow sari and permanent stubble. Anarkali was waving a placard around and exhorting her fellow third genderites to make themselves heard above the din of horns. On the placard were the words: ONE DAY THE PRIME MINISTER WILL BE A EUNUCH.

A number of news crews had arrived to cover the action.

A blue police truck was parked at the edge of the melee, a line of policemen from the nearby Bandra station leaning against it, eating roast peanuts and watching the show. Chopra knew that they would not intervene unless things got ugly. No one wanted to risk being cursed by a eunuch. You never knew what they might wish upon you. A eunuch's curse was said to persist for generations.

Chopra had had enough. He removed the keys from the ignition, checked that the handbrake was on and got out of the van.

It took him five minutes to locate the Paramathma store. The jewellery emporium was sandwiched between an Italian furniture boutique and an interior design consultancy specialising in the ancient Chinese practice of feng shui, which had recently taken Mumbai by storm. To Chopra's supreme irritation Poppy had rearranged the furniture of their flat on three separate occasions in the past months as first one then another feng shui guru gained prominence.

As he approached, a liveried doorman in a golden turban bowed at the waist and swung open the gilded doors.

Chopra had never been inside a store like this. He had never worn jewellery himself and Poppy had always been content with the jewellery she had inherited from her mother and in which she had been married. Of course, if they had had a daughter he would eventually have found himself in such a place, haggling himself into an early grave as a prelude to her wedding.

The interior of the emporium was a shrine to all that glittered and was gold.

The floors and walls were coated in dazzling white Italian marble. Ornate chandeliers dangled from the ceiling. A koi-filled fountain was situated in the centre of the vast space, surrounded by a dozen gold-plated Buddhas dribbling water from their navels. Blow-up posters of demure models in saris wearing exquisite jewellery and expressions of wistful contentment were strategically placed around the room. Armed security guards lurked behind hand-tooled pillars in the form of bejewelled caryatids.

A number of display counters were dotted around, each with an attendant clutch of sales clerks and boisterous clientele.

Behind a particularly extravagant counter Chopra espied an older-looking gentleman in a dapper suit writing on a vellum notepad. The gentleman straightened as he approached, a smile of instant welcome affixing itself to his parched features. Chopra guessed him to be in his sixties, but his hair and moustache had been dyed jet black.

He took out his identity card. 'I am looking for Bulbul Kanodia.'

The man's forehead creased into a series of horizontal lines. 'I am sorry?'

Chopra realised his mistake. 'I mean Mr Balram Kanodia. The proprietor of this establishment.'

'Ah. Mr Kanodia Sir. I am afraid he is not here today. Perhaps I may be of assistance instead?'

'Yes. You can be of assistance by telling me where he is.'

'But what is this in connection with, sir?'

'It is a police matter.'

'Police?' The man paled as if Chopra had said a dirty word. 'Please lower your voice, sir. There are respectable people in the store.'

Chopra leaned forward. 'Where is Kanodia?'

The man pursed his lips. 'I am afraid that I am not at liberty to say.'

'I see. In that case I wonder if you have been watching the news?'

The man seemed perplexed by the unexpected change of direction. 'The news?'

'Yes. For instance, did you know that the eunuchs are marching just five minutes down the road?'

'Why, of course. They have been making a racket for hours. Between you and me, they are a nuisance. Quite unnatural creatures.' The man shuddered. 'If it were up to me I would round them all up and put them outside the city. Let them live in some colony far away from us normal people.'

Chopra smiled savagely. 'Is that so?'

The man rapped his knuckles on the glass of the display counter. 'Absolutely.'

'Well then, how would it be if those eunuchs decided to pay your store a visit? How would it be if they decided to camp outside your door for the next seven days?'

'What? My God, why would they do that?'

'Because the leader of the protest is a friend of mine.' Chopra glared at the man. 'How do you think your sales figures will fare then?'

The man swallowed. His hand rose involuntarily to pull at his collar, which had suddenly become very tight. 'What is it you wish to know?'

'Where can I find Kanodia?'

'He is at the circus.'

'What?' Chopra gaped. 'Did you say circus?'

'Yes. The Grand Trunk Circus. They are currently camped on Cross Maidan. Mr Kanodia wishes to contract their services.'

'Whatever for?'

'It is his daughter's sixteenth birthday tomorrow. He is hosting a lavish party at his residence on the Bandstand. He wishes to surprise her. She is very fond of the circus, it seems.'

Chopra was silent, his mind whirling with sudden possibilities.

He had come here because he believed that confronting Kanodia was now the only avenue left to him if he wished to pursue his investigation. And yet, at the same time, a nagging doubt persisted. There remained the possibility, no matter how small, that he was wrong, that Kanodia was innocent of any involvement in the theft. After all, what did he *really* have to go on? Kanodia's presence inside the Tata Gallery at the time of the robbery? A guilty expression? Chopra's own presumption that the former fence was connected to organised crime?

The plain fact was that all he really had was conjecture.

He wondered if Rao had interviewed Kanodia yet. He suspected that he had not. Rao was focused on breaking Garewal. Perhaps Kanodia did not figure in his investigation at all.

What was it someone had once said? The difference between truth and fiction is that fiction has to make sense . . .

What if Kanodia had absolutely nothing to do with the theft? What if Garewal *was* guilty? In that case, all that remained was to find Garewal's accomplices. They in turn would lead the authorities to the Koh-i-Noor diamond.

Or what if both he and Rao were wrong, and it was neither Garewal nor Kanodia, but someone else entirely?

After all, hadn't any number of nationalist organisations complained about the Koh-i-Noor being paraded under

India's nose by the British? Hadn't scores of warnings poured in from fringe radicals threatening to steal the diamond?

One thing Chopra knew well about his country was that it was large enough to house all manner of lunatics. And a lunatic with a cause was the most dangerous kind of all.

THE GRAND TRUNK CIRCUS

The public ground known as Cross Maidan in south Mumbai's New Marine Lines district had gained its name from the sixteenth-century stone crucifix erected there by Governor Nuno da Cunha, back when the city was under Portuguese rule. The cross, planted in the northern end of the five-acre common, was deemed to possess miraculous powers – supplicants journeyed from all over the country seeking fulfilment for prayers that had fallen on deaf ears elsewhere.

Chopra parked his van on Fashion Street, the strip of Mahatma Gandhi Road that ran adjacent to the Maidan near the Bombay Gymkhana.

Even at this late hour Fashion Street was alive with the clamour of furious haggling as locals and tourists alike matched wits with the owners of hundreds of stalls lining both sides of the street and selling every type of garment known to man.

Chopra threaded his way swiftly through the chorus of

pleading and wailing and gnashing of teeth and on to the Maidan proper.

The sky above was darkening and streams of commuters hurried along the shortcut called Khau Gully, connecting the Victoria and Churchgate stations via the Maidan. In spite of the gloom numerous games of cricket were still going on. More than one famous Indian cricketer had first honed his skills on the patchwork of threadbare pitches that stretched over the common. Chopra was tempted to stop and watch, but he knew that time was short.

He wanted to catch the circus before it folded up its tent for the evening.

As he walked across the Maidan he reflected that in the days before Partition, tens of thousands of his fellow countrymen had gathered here to peacefully protest the continued presence of the British. His own father, Premkumar Chopra, who had once lived in the city, had stood shoulder to shoulder with countless others and chanted pro-Independence slogans. Gandhi himself had spoken to the masses here. And one day, his whispers had become a cyclone that had blown away the British.

The circus comprised a single two-pole big top, with a bright red roof, and red and yellow stripes marching around the sides. A colourful, hand-illustrated wooden board sat above the tent's entrance depicting an exuberant virtuosity of circus acts. The board was surrounded by lightbulbs, many of which had failed. On a second board above was a painting of a grinning, bearded Sikh gentleman, a tiger, and the words: TIGER SINGH PRESENTS THE WORLD-FAMOUS GRAND TRUNK CIRCUS.

The evening show had ended. A handful of desultory visitors hung around outside the tent, smoking beedis and spitting. One man urinated onto a tent peg.

Chopra entered the big top.

The interior of the tent was lit by hanging striplights powered by a portable generator that thrummed away in the background.

Chopra found himself confronted by a compact circus ring surrounded by rows of red plastic chairs. A cleaner worked his way between them, picking up discarded chocolate wrappers, soft drink bottles, paan leaves, cigarette packets and other junk. His expression transformed into one of horrified distaste as he peeled a discarded condom from the floor and threw it into his bag. A solitary drunk who had fallen asleep in his seat snored away, a dribble of eighty-proof saliva trickling down his chin.

The ring, a dusty circle hemmed in by foot-high portable barriers of the sort used to mark the boundaries at cricket matches, was still alive with activity.

The performers were winding down, letting off steam after the evening performance.

Chopra watched as a flame-thrower in a sequinned jacket practised blowing a jet of fire at a wooden mannequin tied to a stake five metres away. Beside him a portly, blindfolded man hurled knives at the same target. He was not very good, Chopra reflected, as another knife bounced hilt-first from the wooden figure and clattered onto the dusty floor. He hoped that in the real performance a live volunteer was not employed as the target.

His eyes were drawn to a caparisoned elephant sitting in the centre of the ring on a reinforced stool, its front legs raised in the air. A hoop dangled from its upturned trunk. A slender woman with Assamese eyes hung from the hoop, her body contorted into a ring.

Suddenly the elephant sneezed. Girl and hoop landed in a heap on the floor.

A chorus of raucous laughter arose from the far side of the circus ring where half a dozen dwarves in clown outfits were lounging in a circle smoking and playing cards. 'Why don't you come and ride my trunk, Parvati?' one of them shouted. 'I promise I won't take my trunk out of your hoop until you're finished.'

More raucous laughter.

Chopra stepped over the ring barrier and walked over to the dwarves. 'I am looking for Tiger Singh,' he said.

The dwarves stopped laughing and stared at him, their jovial clown make-up re-forming into baleful expressions. The dwarf who had spoken to the contortionist spoke again: 'Are you from the AWBI?'

'Who?'

'The animal welfare people,' clarified the dwarf.

'No. I need to talk to Tiger Singh. It is a business matter.'

The dwarf turned back to his cards. 'He is in the back.'

Chopra found Tiger Singh in a straw-lined temporary paddock behind the circus tent in which were tethered a number of threadbare camels and emaciated horses. Singh was seated on a cane stool on one side of an upturned wooden crate. On the other side was an old dwarf in a tight-fitting scarlet ringmaster's jacket with gold trim. A cheap cigar stuck out of the side of his mouth as he intently focused down on Singh's hands.

Singh had three coloured balls laid out on top of the crate. As Chopra watched, his hands became a blur, moving the balls around on the crate's surface.

Suddenly, one of the balls vanished.

The dwarf looked up. He plucked the cigar from his mouth, blew a cloud of brackish smoke into the humid night air and said, 'Not bad.'

'Excuse me.'

Chopra waited for the two men to look up.

'May I help you, sir?' asked Tiger Singh eventually.

Singh had once been a big man, but seemed to have lost weight. His beard was black, with a single white stripe down the middle. His turban was a deep midnight blue and he wore a flowing black kurta pajama sashed at his waist with a bright red tasselled rope. His face was deeply lined with a map of crevices . . . and something else. A weariness that had nothing to do with age or infirmity.

Chopra flashed his identity card. 'My name is Chopra. I am investigating the disappearance of the Crown of Queen Elizabeth.'

'I thought they already found that,' said the dwarf. 'It was on the news.'

'They did. But the Koh-i-Noor had been removed.'

The dwarf raised a bottle of cheap whisky to his mouth and took a swig. 'What can we do for you?'

'It is my understanding that Bulbul Kanodia has engaged your services for a birthday party at his Bandra residence tomorrow afternoon.'

Tiger Singh's expression was curious. 'How does this concern you?'

'Please. It is important,' said Chopra.

Tiger Singh stared at him. A shadow passed over his face. 'The things we must do to survive,' he sighed eventually. 'Do you know that this circus has been running for over a hundred years? Once upon a time we toured the length and breadth of the subcontinent. We had the very best acts in the land, better than the Jumbo, the Gemini, or even the Great Royal. Thousands flocked to see us. Now, all we get are the uninterested and the drunks. I cannot blame them. What reason have children to come to the circus any more? Look at me . . . I am a Tiger Singh without a tiger. Ever since the animal welfare people tightened the regulations, our acts have been decimated. I fear for the next genera-tion. Who wants to send their children to join the circus now? Who wants to break every bone in their body learning the trapeze when they can sit in an air-conditioned office and sell sand to the Arabs? Who wants to burn their mouths hurling flame or lie down beneath an elephant's foot? The only ones we get now are the borderline criminals, the girls without dowries, and the dwarves. No offence, Vinod.'

'None taken,' said the dwarf mildly.

'Vinod is our general manager,' explained Tiger Singh. 'I do not know what I would do without him.'

'The birthday party,' said Chopra, steering the conversa-tion back to the reason for his visit.

'Ah, yes. What about it?'

'It will take you inside Kanodia's home?'

'Yes. We are not street performers, sir.'

'In that case I wish to go with you. As part of your act.'

Vinod and Tiger Singh exchanged glances.

'Sir, I know that we must not look like much,' said Singh eventually. 'But we take pride in what we do. I cannot permit an amateur into my troupe. Our private clients pay us well. I will not compromise the integrity of our performance.'

'This is a matter of life and death.'

'Each day in the circus is a matter of life and death. I am afraid I cannot help you.' Singh looked back down at his crate and began to spin the remaining two balls.

Chopra thought fast. He had to get inside Kanodia's residence. It was the only avenue of investigation he could think of.

'I have an elephant.'

Singh looked up. 'What?'

'I have a baby elephant. He is very smart. I will bring him with me. That will be my contribution to your act.'

Singh's eyes were suddenly far away. 'It has been many years since last we raised a young elephant in the traditions of the circus. Now we have only Aurangzeb, the old bull. He is very temperamental. Also I think his mind is going. He forgets his acts. I have told the mahouts not to give him drink, but they do not listen. They say without alcohol he cannot function at all.' Singh shook his head. 'It will be good to see a young one again.'

'Ganesha is no ordinary elephant,' Chopra said, repeating the words that his uncle had written.

Tiger Singh smiled. 'No elephant is ordinary, sir. They are the king of beasts.' He exchanged glances with Vinod. Something unspoken passed between them.

'Can you juggle, sir?'

Chopra resisted the temptation to lie. 'No.'

'Can you swallow a sword?'

'No.'

'A goldfish, at least?'

'No.'

'Have you ever been fired out of a cannon?'

'No.'

Singh stroked his beard thoughtfully. 'We will have to find something for you to do. Vinod?'

The dwarf blew more smoke from his cigar and sized Chopra up. 'I am sure we can manage something. Be here with your elephant early tomorrow morning. We will rehearse.'

Chopra nodded. 'I will be here. Thank you.'

He turned to leave, then looked back.

'One more thing . . . where did the ball go?'

Tiger Singh smiled thinly. 'Once upon a time I used to put my head into the mouths of tigers, but now . . . now Tiger Singh has been reduced to a mere conjuror.'

He reached up to take off his turban. Chopra realised that rather than being a long strip of cloth wound around the skull, the turban was in fact a solid mass, glued together to form a sort of hat.

This was how the illusion worked. Misdirection and sleight of hand: the twin tools of the prestidigitator.

Singh lifted the ball from his head and twirled it around his fingers. 'It is a hard life and not the one most would choose,' he said. 'But that is karma, yes?'

TWO STRANGERS IN THE RESTAURANT

The air-conditioner, newly repaired, thundered away in the corner of the office. In spite of its best efforts, the atmosphere had become decidedly heated.

'Poppy, the boy has a mind of his own,' said Chopra, who had returned to the restaurant to find his wife waiting for him, and not in the best of moods. 'You cannot tell him what to do.'

'I am not telling him what to do,' huffed Poppy. 'It is in his best interests if he attends school and learns to read and write properly.'

'I agree. But he must make the decision himself.'

'He is a child. What child wants to go to school? We are looking after him now. It is up to us to guide him.'

'We have no legal claim over him. He is free to make his own decisions.'

'You are working him too hard,' said Poppy, folding her arms.

Chopra sighed. His wife had the annoying habit of changing the subject, without *actually* changing the subject, whenever she found herself losing ground in an argument.

'I am not working him at all. Whatever he does, he does because he wishes to. He is a very hard-working and bright boy.'

There was a knock on the door and Irfan entered holding a stack of manila folders.

He beamed as he saw Poppy, whose irritated expression immediately melted away. She bent down and gave him a hug. 'Put those things down,' she said. 'I have a gift for you.'

She watched as Irfan unwrapped the shirt she had purchased for him. 'Wow!' he said, eyes shining. 'It's just like the one Shah Rukh Khan wore in *Chennai Express*.'

Poppy clapped her hands. 'But you look even more hand-some than him!'

Irfan sneezed.

An expression of alarm overcame Poppy's face. 'My goodness, you are ill!'

'It's just a sneeze, Poppy,' said Chopra.

'What would you know, Mister Slavedriver?' she snapped, rounding on her husband. 'The poor boy is clearly over-worked.' She cradled Irfan's head as he struggled to escape. 'Come, I will take you to the doctor right away.'

'But really, I am quite fine!' said Irfan, wrenching himself loose.

'Come and stay with us for a few days,' begged Poppy. 'At least until you are better.'

'I like it here,' said Irfan. 'All my friends are here. Plus Ganesha is here.' He saw that Poppy seemed crestfallen and went back to give her a hug. 'Maybe you can take me to EsselWorld next week, like you promised?'

'Of course!' said Poppy, brightening up. 'It will be a day out for us.'

After Irfan left, Chopra looked at his wife, at the softness illuminating her features.

He would have to choose his words carefully.

After twenty-four childless years Poppy's heart was over-flowing with affection for their two wards Ganesha and Irfan. It was as if a dam had burst inside her and now a great torrent of maternal love was sweeping all before it. He knew that deep within the folds of his own heart he had grown as fond of Irfan as she had. Although the thought remained unspoken there was no doubt in his mind that in Ganesha and Irfan his wife had found an outlet for her long-suppressed mothering instincts, that, in some sense, they had both circumvented Chopra's diktat against adoption.

And it was enough. For him, if not for Poppy.

'Poppy, if you smother him, you will drive him away.'

'I am not smothering him!' said Poppy indignantly.

Chopra regarded his wife, standing with arms folded and chin jutting out, an unequivocal display of hostility. He thought of all the things he could say, and then he waved his hands in surrender. 'OK, OK. I have enough on my plate as it is without fighting with you about Irfan.' He turned to leave.

'Just you wait a minute, Mister Bigshot.'

Poppy had not finished with him yet. With a sudden sinking premonition he realised what she was going to say.

'Poppy, I am tied up wi—'

'Yes, yes, I know. You have a big case for the Queen of England. Well, let me ask you this: is the Queen paying you? Did the Queen ask for your assistance? Does she even know that you exist?'

'Poppy—'

'Don't you Poppy me! Augustus Lobo is my boss. He specially requested my help. What is the point of having a private detective for a husband if he cannot locate one silly little statue?' Poppy's glare would have melted stone. 'Is it too much to ask that you spare some time for a paying client?'

'A man's life is at stake, Poppy,' Chopra said through gritted teeth.

'What man?'

He hesitated, considering the wisdom of telling his wife everything, and decided that Poppy had a right to know.

Chopra explained about Garewal.

'Well, why didn't you say so in the first place?' Poppy finally exhaled. 'Poor man. And two children, you say?' She shook her head again. And then a thought seemed to occur to her. 'And you are sure he is innocent?'

He hesitated. 'No, I am not sure. I have only my own instincts to guide me. They have served me well for thirty years. Right now, they are telling me that this is not the work of Garewal. That he is being set up. I cannot just stand by. I worked with the man – I owe it to him.'

Poppy's expression softened. She walked around the desk and laid a gentle hand on his cheek. 'Always the hero,' she sighed. 'Well, I would rather you were a hero than a villain.'

Chopra found Ganesha horsing around with Irfan in the rear courtyard.

Earlier that morning, he had made the decision to leave the elephant behind, hoping he would recover from his sombre mood. He was delighted to discover that Ganesha did indeed seem his usual self.

The little calf was playing cricket with the boy. His trunk was curled around the handle of a cricket bat. Irfan ran up and hurled a tennis ball at him with his good hand, in imitation of Irfan's favourite fast bowler. Ganesha's trunk whirled around and – *smack!* – the ball went arcing over the wall and into the neighbouring compound.

Irfan leaped up and clapped his thighs delightedly. 'Wah, Ganesha! Good shot!'

Chopra smiled. 'Indeed it was. If Ganesha keeps playing like this we will have to consider replacing Sachin Tendulkar as India's number four.'

The boy and the elephant turned to watch him approach. Irfan's face was flushed, and even Ganesha seemed happy to see him.

Chopra was aware that a special bond had sprung up between Ganesha and Irfan. Baby elephants and human children were, after all, similar in so many ways.

For one, they both grew to maturity at almost the same rate. This was not surprising given that elephants and humans had similar lifespans. Elephant calves and human children also shared the same sense of play and fun. And, as he had discovered to his occasional cost, the same sense of mischievousness.

Chopra was relieved that Ganesha had found a friend. It

sometimes bothered him that the elephant had been sundered from his own species. Elephants were extremely social animals. He often dreamed of how Ganesha might enjoy a different life if he was with his own kind out in the jungle. But orphaned male calves were not always welcomed into a strange herd. In the wild, elephant bulls were aggressive and unpredictable beasts. An outsider, even a calf such as Ganesha, might easily be shunned or even injured. He could not take that chance.

And then there was the simple fact that Ganesha was now a creature of the city, as much a Mumbaiker as Chopra. He had not been trained in the ancient jungle crafts by a caring mother and fussy aunts. He did not know the first thing about how to survive outside the *concrete* jungle.

But there was another reason that Chopra was glad that Irfan and Ganesha had become companions. He had read that any young elephant raised in a human environment ran the risk of becoming over-reliant on a single carer. There had been a calf in Africa reared by a white woman. For years the woman was the calf's sole carer, to the extent that the calf would allow no one else to feed him. And then the woman had been called away for a protracted period. Without her the calf pined, refusing to take his feed. He died shortly before the woman could make her return.

Now, when Chopra arrived at the restaurant in the early mornings to find Irfan hosing down Ganesha in the little elephant's favourite game, he would feel a gladness blooming inside him. If anything ever happened to him, there would be others who Ganesha loved and trusted and who, in return, loved him.

His stomach growled suddenly and he realised that he had hardly eaten all day. 'Irfan, can you ask Chef to prepare me a plate? I will eat in my office.'

'Yes, sir. Do you want butter chicken? Chef is also doing special mutton karahi today.'

'Did he put ginger in it?'

Irfan scratched his head. 'I will ask him.'

Chopra watched the boy scurry away.

Then he knelt down beside Ganesha and patted him on the head. 'I am so happy to see that you are feeling better.'

Ganesha blinked and swished his ears.

'I need your help, boy. An old friend of mine is in trouble. He has been accused of a crime that I do not think he committed. I am trying to clear his name. For that I will need you by my side tomorrow. Do you think you can help me?'

Chopra knew that if a stranger were to see him talking in this way to an elephant they might think that he was becoming addled. But, irrational or not, he had come to believe that Ganesha understood everything he said. And there was also that insidious voice at the back of his skull that he couldn't quite shake – the voice that told him that somewhere behind those wet elephant eyes was his Uncle Bansi.

And yet Chopra had never subscribed to the notions of rebirth and reincarnation that so many of his countrymen took for granted. He did not believe that human souls could be transmigrated into the bodies of animals once they passed from this world. He had no idea where the human soul actually went, but he was fairly certain that he was in no danger of being reborn as a cockroach.

The journey of the human soul post-death was the greatest mystery of all, and one that he intended to solve only
when he shuffled off this mortal coil.

Ganesha blinked again as if considering the request.

Then he lifted his trunk and patted Chopra's face.

'Thank you, boy.'

Rangwalla was waiting for him in the office. The room was
redolent with the fragrant aroma of mutton karahi. Chopra
eased himself into his seat and stirred the thick curry base
of spiced tomatoes and fried chillies. The karahi was one
of Chef Lucknowwallah's signature dishes and one of
Chopra's favourites. He ladled himself a generous measure
from the copper serving bowl and then ladled out another
bowl for Rangwalla, who was drooling quietly.

'Sit down and eat,' he commanded.

'That's OK, sir. I will eat at home later.'

He looked up at Rangwalla.

Rangwalla appeared as uncomfortable out of uniform as
Chopra had first felt when he had been forced to shed the
khaki. He was wearing a short black kurta with embroidered buttons, a pair of heavily starched and creased navy
blue trousers, and closed-toed black sandals. His beard had
been trimmed and his hair was pomaded with an Arabic
perfume.

'Rangwalla, let's get something straight. We are now
partners. I am your boss but I am also your friend. Perhaps

I should have said this years ago. Well, better late than never. Now sit down and share a meal with me. And besides, I cannot hear myself think over the rumbling of your belly.'

As the two men ate, Rangwalla described his day.

While Chopra visited the circus the former sub-inspector had been travelling to all corners of the city tracking down the employees of the Prince of Wales Museum from the list that his new-old boss had given him.

Rangwalla removed a sheaf of papers from his postal bag and smoothed them out on the table, instantly smearing them with curry.

Chopra gave his new associate detective a black look and then took the papers.

There were eleven people on the list. Of the eleven, one, a junior curator, had died early into his tenure at the museum, a victim of the so-called Malabar Hill leopard attacks.

The leopard had terrorised the affluent Malabar Hill area for weeks. Another refugee from the city's relentless growth, the big cat appeared to have decided that enough was enough. Its unprecedented boldness had made headlines. It had even been caught on CCTV entering the lobby of an apartment building to attack the security guard as he dozed behind his counter.

The leopard had not actually killed the young curator. It had merely chased him out of a parked taxi and into oncoming traffic. The terrified fellow had been run over by a truck.

A second employee had quit her post a month after joining, and left the state following her marriage. Rangwalla had tracked her down and phoned her in far-off

Kanyakumari. He was satisfied that she had nothing to do with the robbery.

Of the remaining nine, eight still worked at the museum.

Rangwalla, employing the arcane skills for ferreting out information that Chopra had come to rely on over the long years of their association, had obtained photocopies of personal documents for each of these individuals, as well as statements from colleagues, neighbours and family members.

Chopra quickly scanned the dossiers and realised that, superficially, at least, each of these individuals was a law-abiding citizen with no conceivable connection to the crime or to anyone capable of committing such a crime.

That left one.

Rangwalla tapped the sheet. 'This is your man.'

The sheet of paper showed a headshot of a dark-skinned man with a flat cap of oiled hair, a thin moustache and a pugnacious expression. The document, a copy of a driving licence issued by the state of Maharashtra, named the individual as one Prakash Yadav.

'What makes you so sure?'

'Because that driving licence is a fake. A very good one. The same goes for all the other documents he submitted when he applied for the position of security guard at the museum six months ago. Those documents were vetted by the security agencies and came up clean. That is how good they are. Do you remember Ragu the forger? I showed the documents to him. He said they were the best fakes he has ever seen.

'A day before the heist, Yadav took extended leave, claiming that his father had passed away back in his native village. Earlier today I spoke to the sarpanch of the village he named on his papers. No one there has ever heard of him.' Rangwalla paused to mop up the last of his curry. 'There is also the fact that as a security guard he would have had access to all areas of the museum. He was a night-shift guard which would have given him plenty of time to chisel out that hole in complete secrecy.'

Chopra was silent. Rangwalla had uncovered something of great significance. A first thread that they could use to unravel the mystery.

'So we have no idea who he really is?'

'No. And not much chance of finding him either. This man is no mastermind. He was employed for one reason – to get into the museum before the new security measures were installed and plant the gas canisters inside the Kali statue ready for the day of the heist. If what this McTavish person told you is correct then he also installed a computer virus into the CCTV system just before he vanished.' Rangwalla knuckled his jaw. 'As soon as he completed his assignment, he was no longer needed. If you ask me, he is probably lying at the bottom of Mahim Creek modelling a pair of concrete sandals.'

Rangwalla was, in all probability, correct, thought Chopra. There would be no reason for those who had orchestrated a crime of this magnitude to leave alive a walking, talking liability such as Yadav – and if this was the case the trail might end right here.

A knock on the door interrupted his thoughts.

'Come in.'

A large belly entered the room, followed by its owner, a big man in a navy blue safari suit. The man was swarthy, with a thick moustache and curly hair. He beamed at Chopra. 'Myself Pramod Kondvilkar. You are Chopra, yes?'

'What can I do for you, Mr Kondvilkar?'

Kondvilkar flashed his eyes at Rangwalla. 'In private, if you don't mind.'

When Rangwalla had left Kondvilkar lowered his bulk into the vacated seat. The wooden frame protested beneath the unaccustomed strain and Kondvilkar's fleshy arms flopped over the sides.

'Forgive me, sir, but it has been a trying day.'

'What can I do for you?' repeated Chopra, his tone clipped and to the point. He was overcome by an instant feeling of dislike. Kondvilkar emanated a palpable sense of sleazy menace. His apparent bonhomie did not fool Chopra for a second. He had seen enough sharks in his time to know when one came swimming by.

For his part, the big man continued to smile pleasantly. 'I am working for the Maharashtra Dangerous Animals Division, Chopra Sir. I have received a complaint. It seems that you are keeping one elephant here on these premises. It seems that this elephant attacked a young child yesterday. At the St Xavier school, yes?

'He did not attack the boy. He merely defended himself. The boy set fire to Ganesha's tail.'

'Ganesha? Ah, what a correct name for an elephant!' Kondvilkar continued to beam genially. 'But, Chopra Sir, you will be agreeing that when an elephant defends itself against a human it is not a fair contest, yes?'

'What is it that you want?' Chopra ground out the words.

Kondvilkar raised his hands. 'For myself, nothing, sir. No, no, goodness me. But you see, my bosses, they are saying we cannot have dangerous elephants on the loose. They are wild creatures. Why, in the villages, they are known to cause much destruction and injury to human life. My bosses wish me to take this Ganesha of yours into custody.'

Chopra's hands whitened on the arms of his chair. 'You will do no such th—!'

'Calm yourself, sir,' Kondvilkar interrupted, patting the air placatingly. 'I am on your side. Elephant is avatar of our Lord Ganesh, yes? How can he be harming anyone? I think that if I tell my bosses this, they will believe me.'

'Then why don't you do that?'

Kondvilkar's white teeth flashed once more. 'Such paper-work costs a small fee, Chopra Sir.'

'Fee?' Chopra replied warily. 'What do you mean?'

Kondvilkar's smile crept around his mouth but he said nothing.

Understanding dawned. 'You are asking me for a bribe?'

Kondvilkar looked pained. 'Who said anything about a bribe? Why to use such dirty words?'

A yawning silence stretched across the suddenly chilly expanse of Chopra's desk. 'Stand up.'

'Sir?'

'I said stand up.'

Kondvilkar stopped smiling.

Slowly, he hauled himself to his feet.

Chopra walked around the desk. Without warning he reached out and grabbed Kondvilkar by the scruff of the neck.

'Hey! What are you doing? Have you gone mad?'

Pushing Kondvilkar before him, Chopra made his way through the restaurant where a buzz of laughter erupted at the sight of the protesting official and the enraged former policeman.

'You are making a big mistake, Chopra! You will pay for this! That elephant is a menace! I will have him put down!'

Chopra heaved Kondvilkar out into the road. He tripped over the steps leading up into the restaurant and fell in a heap on the dusty street.

A rickshawwallah parked outside the restaurant erupted in a bray of laughter.

Kondvilkar rose to his feet and dusted himself off. 'You mark my words, Chopra. You have not heard the last of me.'

Chopra watched the fat man waddle off down the street.

Back inside the office, it took him some time to calm his thoughts.

Intellectually, Chopra knew that things would grind to a halt on the subcontinent if the system of bribes and kickbacks were eliminated overnight.

In one sense Kondvilkar had been correct.

Bribery permeated so much of life in his country that most people simply considered it a cost of living like any of the other taxes or surcharges the politicians dreamed up. And with government salaries so low the temptation to go along with the status quo was very strong indeed.

But it was a slippery slope. If you paid one bribe, you could not stop there. You would become known as someone who offered bribes. As a policeman, you would also be someone who *took* bribes. And if you did that then what was the point of your uniform?

There had never been a price at which Chopra was willing to sell his integrity, in or out of uniform.

He closed his eyes and leaned back in his chair. It had been a trying day. He dearly wished to rest. He did not know that the day's most unpleasant surprise was yet to come.

An hour later he stepped back out into the bustling restaurant. It had become his routine to look the place over before he headed home each night. Often he would sit for a few minutes with old colleagues or new acquaintances. It was a good way to keep up with the police grapevine. Chopra had never been the most gregarious of men, but he found this daily ritual invigorating.

Word of the restaurant had spread and, by and large, Mumbai's police fraternity had embraced his vision. It gratified him to see so many policemen in the place. It gratified him even more to see that most left their rank at the door.

And, contrary to his own expectations, he was discovering that he quite enjoyed having a circle of friends who were actually glad to see him each evening.

It was a somewhat new experience for Chopra, who had spent his career maintaining a professional distance between himself and his colleagues, particularly those he did not feel measured up to his own lofty standards of integrity. He was now beginning to realise that policemen were people too, plagued by the same desires and foibles as ordinary citizens. It was inevitable that they would occasionally succumb to the weaknesses that were part and parcel of the human condition. Some resisted better than others.

Then again, every finger was not the same, as his father would have said. But put them together and you made a fist.

It was while he was sitting with Inspector Joshi from the Marol station, congratulating the younger man on his recent promotion, that he noticed the grizzled-looking gentleman seated across the aisle. The man had a dark face but light hazel eyes. A scar ran from the lower lip to under his unshaven chin. He wore a dark kurta and a gold bracelet on his wrist. A short rolled turban covered his hair.

Chopra could not recall ever seeing the man in the restaurant before.

He was dining alone, mopping up what looked like Chef's chicken jalfrezi with a tandoori flatbread.

There was something about the coarse-looking individual that gave him pause. An aura that he had come across many times during his years in the service. The aura of a born criminal. But then again, what criminal would be foolish enough to eat *here*?

The man belched loudly, then raised his hand and called out loudly for a waiter.

Chopra turned and saw Irfan approaching, holding a jug of water. Irfan reached the man, who looked up and met his eyes.

The copper water jug clanged off the restaurant's marble flooring as Irfan froze.

The man's face split into a slow smile that sent shivers up Chopra's spine. 'Hello, Irfan,' said the man. 'At last, I have found you.'

Chopra stood and stepped across the aisle. He looked down at Irfan and saw his petrified expression. There was no doubt in his mind that the boy was terrified.

'Irfan, do you know this man?'

The man glanced up at him. Then he turned back to Irfan. 'Why don't you tell him who I am, Irfan?'

Chopra glowered at the man. 'Why don't you tell me yourself?'

The man unfurled from his seat. Chopra realised that his thin face had made him seem smaller than he was. In reality, the man was taller even than himself, with a rangy physique, muscle on bone. 'My name is Lodi. Mukhthar Lodi. And I am the boy's father.'

Chopra was astounded. Of all the things he had thought the man might say, this was the most unexpected. He felt his knees tremble.

Controlling his voice, he said, sternly, 'You are lying. Irfan is an orphan. He told me so himself.'

Lodi smiled. 'Irfan is a runaway. He is fond of telling lies and causing his father much grief. It has taken me many months to find him.'

'I do not believe you.'

'Then why do you not ask the boy?'

Chopra knelt down and took Irfan's hand. 'Irfan. Do not be afraid. No one can harm you here. Just tell me the truth. Is this man your father?'

He watched as Irfan looked up at Lodi. And then the boy closed his eyes, a shudder passing through him.

'Yes.'

A SLEEPLESS NIGHT FOR
POPPY AND CHOPRA

'But why didn't you *stop* him?'

Poppy paced the floor of their bedroom, wielding her hairbrush in one hand and her night cream in the other. Her obvious agitation sent ripples of protest through the fabric of her cotton nightgown.

'He was the boy's father,' said Chopra calmly. 'What could I do?'

'He was a liar and a villain. You said so yourself.'

'Irfan confirmed his story. The boy agreed to go with him. I couldn't stop him.'

'He is a child!' Poppy wailed. 'He was afraid. You should have asked for some proof, a birth certificate or . . . or . . . something! Anything!'

'Have you any idea how many children are born in the slums without birth certificates each year?'

Poppy turned to her husband, anguish in her eyes. 'But how can he just *go* like that?'

Chopra, seated on the bed in his shorts and T-shirt, knew that this was the question to which there was no easy answer.

How could he explain to Poppy how hard he had tried to convince Irfan not to go, to at least wait a day while Chopra investigated the matter? How could he explain the feeling of helplessness that had overcome him as he had watched Irfan walk out of the door with a stranger?

But, in the end, what hold did he have over the boy?

Irfan had arrived of his own accord and was now leaving by his own wish. The boy had repeatedly confirmed that Lodi was his father and that he was going with him willingly. Beyond that Chopra had not been able to ascertain anything, no matter how hard he tried.

The situation had left him deeply upset, not least because of how vested he himself had become in the boy's welfare.

Chopra had done everything he could for Irfan since he had entered their lives. Indeed, he did not think he could have offered Irfan more had the boy lived in his own home, had he signed documents to lay a legal claim to the child.

Chopra believed in destiny. He believed that human beings possessed the ability to change minor eddies within the great river of their fates, but not the course of that river. If he were to attempt to alter Irfan's life entirely – for instance, by enrolling him into the sort of fancy school that Poppy kept insisting the boy needed – he believed that he might upset some sort of cosmic accounting and nothing good would come of it. If Irfan himself wished to attend school, then certainly he would arrange it. But he would not force his and Poppy's own belief systems on the boy. He was confident that with just a little guidance Irfan would make something of himself one day.

His brow darkened as he privately admitted that he had seen himself as that guiding hand. A father figure to the boy. Not one to smother, but a reassuring presence who would always be there, patiently waiting for whenever he was needed . . . But now, now that harmless dream had been shattered.

'I cannot sleep,' he declared, rising from the bed.

He left his distraught wife and retreated to the relative safety of his office, where he settled into his armchair and switched on the television.

A late-night debate show was arguing over the 'legitimacy' of the theft of the Koh-i-Noor. The crowd was divided. Many felt it was an act of justifiable revanchism; others that it was a crime no matter which way you looked at it.

Chopra found himself unable to focus on the discussion. He wondered where Irfan was now. Back in the slums? Back with a man who he strongly suspected was responsible for the cigarette burns on Irfan's body, though the boy had denied it when he had taken him to his office at the restaurant and questioned him privately.

Fate. Karma. And nothing in between except the Brownian motion of human lives moving along their random paths, bouncing between moments of joy and those of trial and tribulation with only the illusion that they had control over what they were doing.

What was the point of dwelling on it?

He picked up the remote and changed the channel. On WD-TV a reporter lurked outside the apartment complex in which Shekhar Garewal lived. 'Is this the home of the mastermind behind the theft of the Koh-i-Noor?' he asked in a sombre baritone.

The complex was in a relatively affluent sector of Bandra. Chopra wondered which floor Garewal lived on. He wondered how his wife and children were coping with their father's sudden notoriety. He imagined that they were besieged, that they had turned off the phone, drawn the curtains and no longer dared to venture out into the city.

It was in his hands now to rescue them from their ordeal.

The scene shifted to live footage of the exterior of Lilavati Hospital, where the Queen had spent a night before flying back to the UK. News reports confirmed that she was still ill, despondent and upset by the loss of the Koh-i-Noor.

In spite of the Queen's absence the crowd outside the hospital had swelled. Hundreds of lit diyas glowed amongst the well-wishers. In the centre of the crowd a temporary shrine had been set up, with a blown-up photograph of Her Majesty set inside a wooden mango crate and perched on a hastily erected stand. Garlands of jasmine flowers were strung around the photograph and sticks of incense poked from the slats in the crate. A line of devotees edged up to the stand, brought their palms together in respectful greeting and offered up a prayer for the Queen.

The news item returned Chopra's thoughts to the 'dark and bloody history of the Koh-i-Noor' that had been related by the tourist guide Atul Kochar, describing how the great diamond had ended up in the Queen's possession, having fallen through the centuries trailing misfortune in its wake . . .

The first historically verifiable record of the Koh-i-Noor came from the memoirs of Mohammed Babur, descendant of Tamerlane and Genghis Khan, and founder of the Mughal Empire. Babur claimed the diamond had been gifted to him by the Pashtun sultan Ibrahim Lodi, though the truth was far bloodier. Lodi had fallen to Babur's invading army and the Koh-i-Noor had been part of the plunder claimed by the new ruler of the subcontinent.

It was at this time that the curse became widely known.

Discovered in an ancient and enigmatic Sanskrit document the curse stated: '*He who owns this diamond will own the world, but will also know all its misfortunes. Only God, or a woman, may wear it with impunity.*'

Over the coming centuries the curse had proved alarmingly accurate in its dire prediction.

Babur's son, Humayun, was the first to be eclipsed by the diamond's black shadow. His short-lived empire was overrun by the Pashtun general Sher Khan. A broken man, Humayun would later die in a freak fall from the stone steps of his court library. Sher Khan himself perished soon after when a cannon packed with gunpowder exploded during the siege of Kalinjar Fort in Uttar Pradesh.

Next came Humayun's grandson, Shah Jahan, the visionary behind the Taj Mahal, who installed the Koh-i-Noor in his magnificent Peacock Throne, and paid the price for tempting fate when he was subsequently imprisoned by his own son Aurangzeb. Legend had it that in order to torment his father Aurangzeb had the Koh-i-Noor set outside the window of his cell so that he could see the Taj only by looking at its reflection in the great stone.

In 1739 Nadir Shah, the Shah of Iran, sacked Agra and Delhi and carried off the Peacock Throne to Persia, not realising the ill fortune he was bringing upon himself. He was assassinated shortly thereafter.

The Koh-i-Noor subsequently passed through a number of hands before ending up in the treasury of Maharaja Ranjit Singh, ruling prince of the Punjab.

In 1839, following Singh's death, the British claimed the Punjab for the Empire, and the Koh-i-Noor was surrendered – through the machinations of the British East India Company – to Queen Victoria. Transported to England in 1850, it was duly presented to Her Majesty as a tribute from her 'loyal' subjects on the subcontinent. A line of female queens had safeguarded the great jewel ever since.

In this way the prophecy was said to have been fulfilled.

Irfan's face kept intruding into Chopra's thoughts. To divert himself, Chopra picked up his notebook, pushed his spectacles on to his nose, stuck his calabash pipe into his mouth, and tried to organise his thoughts about the case. His pen scritched across the paper as a moth, circling the light fixture above, threw dancing shadows over the page:

Robbery planned months ago once location of exhibit known.

Motive = theft/recovery of Koh-i-Noor.

Fake security guard inserted into museum. 'Prakash Yadav'.

Yadav left behind gas canisters and (possibly) plastic explosive. Canisters in statue. But where was explosive? If not hidden in advance then how did thieves bring it in?

Chopra paused and realised that the whole question of the plastic explosive was something that had been bothering him, like a piece of grit in his eye. He placed himself back in the gallery now, looking through the ragged hole in the sealed rear doors and out into the corridor connecting the Tata and Jahangir galleries. The hole had been blown *into* the Tata Gallery, so the thieves had to have come in from the corridor. That was the assumption. But sometimes assumptions were the very worst thing for an investigation . . . And suddenly he had it, the thing that had been bothering him. He had seen a technician vacuuming up debris in the *corridor*. McTavish had said this was probably debris from the blowback of the explosion. But Chopra felt that something was wrong with this explanation. He was no explosives expert, but it didn't sit right. An idea was circling his brain that he just couldn't latch on to.

Eventually he gave up and continued with his list.

Yadav false identity. High quality forgeries = expensive!

Yadav missing, possibly dead.

How did the thieves break into display case?

Did they temporarily hide crown in museum? If so, where?

How did they get crown *out* of museum?

Who is the mastermind? Bulbul Kanodia? How involved is the Chauhan gang? What was Bulbul doing in the museum? Why did he need to be there?

Chopra stared at the paper for a long time. He recalled Basil Rathbone as Sherlock Homes in *Terror by Night* in which a fictional diamond – the 'Star of Rhodesia' – was stolen. The culprit had eventually been identified as an old friend of Dr Watson.

He looked at his list again and wrote:

Can I trust Garewal?

He gazed at the paper, then underlined the final point. Twice.

INSPECTOR CHOPRA PERFORMS
THE HIGH WIRE ACT

'Poppy Madam! What are you doing here?'

Rangwalla gaped at the apparition of his employer's wife nonchalantly seated on the threadbare sofa of his living room sharing a cup of tea with his wife. Judging from their cosy demeanour and somewhat startled expressions, the two women appeared to have been embroiled in the depths of conspiracy.

Rangwalla had just emerged from the shower, dressed in a vest and towel. Droplets from his still-damp beard plopped onto the worn granite tiles of the floor.

Poppy placed her teacup onto the scarred surface of the coffee table. 'We have work to do, Abbas. I want to make an early start.'

Rangwalla blushed.

There were very few people in the world who used his first name. Not even his wife called him Abbas, preferring to use the universal 'ho, ji!' or the demure 'janaab' when she wished to wheedle something from him. Then again, Poppy had always treated him like a younger brother, though he suspected that they were of a not too dissimilar age.

Rangwalla pinched himself to check that he was not dreaming, then briskly rubbed his forearm as his eyes began to water. 'Work?' he echoed eventually.

'Yes,' said Poppy firmly as she rose to her feet and smoothed out her sari. 'And if we are to proceed you had better put on some clothes.'

In the rickshaw, Poppy explained. 'My husband appears to be preoccupied with this Koh-i-Noor business. However, we have a paying client who is waiting for results – and who just happens to be my employer.'

'You are referring to the missing bust case.'

'Yes.'

Rangwalla scratched his beard in an unconscious gesture of discomfort. 'I must confess, madam, that I have not had much time to devote to this investigation.'

'Well, it is high time that you made time, Abbas,' said Poppy, primly. 'You are now an associate private detective of the agency. It is time to do some detecting.'

The rickshaw struck a pothole in the road. The driver swore as he skidded into the adjacent lane, earning a torrent of horned abuse from the red BEST bus behind them, which swerved wildly on its exhausted axle-springs and sent a ripple of chaos back along the swarming traffic. Howls of rage permeated the fog of pollution that had sunk to the level of the road.

Poppy, who lived in perpetual fear of death-by-road-accident – ever since Chopra had almost killed them both on his infernal Bullet not long after their wedding – waxed wrathfully upon the unfortunate rickshaw driver, haranguing him for a good few minutes.

Rangwalla glanced at her from the corner of his eye. Finally, he decided that he must lance the boil, even if it meant attracting her ire.

'Madam, perhaps you would like to tell me what is bothering you?'

Poppy swivelled in the plastic-coated rick seat to fix him with an angry glare. He braced himself for an explosion . . . but then she turned away.

He saw her biting her lip. Eventually, she spoke. 'You are right, Abbas, something *is* bothering me.'

Ah, thought Rangwalla, now we will get to what this is really all about.

'Yesterday a strange man walked into the restaurant. He claimed to be Irfan's father. He took Irfan with him . . . You know who Irfan is, don't you?'

'Chopra Sir explained everything.'

Poppy sniffed. 'Well, did he explain why he simply let that man walk off with a helpless little boy?'

Rangwalla, sensing that he was treading on dangerous ground, thought a moment before replying.

Over the long years that he had known Chopra, he had always found his senior officer's wife a somewhat intimidating presence. She was a force of nature, of that there was little doubt. But he also knew her to be a well-intentioned woman, with a heart large enough for the city-monster that was Mumbai.

He knew, too, that Poppy and Chopra's childlessness was a delicate matter. 'Madam, what is this about?'

'I wish to locate Irfan. I wish to assure myself that he is well.'

Now Rangwalla understood why Poppy had really come to his home. He imagined the poor woman had barely slept since the boy had been taken from the restaurant.

'Chopra Sir mentioned that the boy's father had left an address.'

'Yes. I went there this morning. No one has heard of him there.'

Rangwalla fell momentarily silent. He considered his next words carefully, not wishing to reignite Poppy's wrath. 'Well, I suppose it could simply be that he did not wish to be harassed.'

'I do not want to harass him,' sniffed Poppy indignantly. 'I simply want to make sure that Irfan is being properly looked after.'

'He is the boy's father. There is not much that we can do, even if we do find him.'

'Let me worry about that when the time comes.'

Rangwalla gave in.

Poppy was a woman on a mission, as single-minded as a tigress protecting her cubs. Heaven help anyone who got in her way. 'As you wish, madam. I will make some calls. Perhaps we can pick up the trail.'

Poppy nodded firmly. 'Good. In the meantime, let us see about this missing bust business.'

'He is too tall to be a dwarf.'

The dwarf glared at Chopra with accusing eyes.

Chopra felt his face turning hot beneath the make-up. He looked once again in the full-length mirror.

A six-foot-tall clown in oversized shoes, baggy dungarees and curly ginger wig stared back at him, smiling crazily. The smile was fixed, painted onto the bone-white face in a garish smear of red. A broad-brimmed top hat jammed the wig securely to the clown's skull.

Inspector Chopra (Retd) had never felt so ludicrous in all his life.

What the hell am I doing? he thought.

A soft trumpeting behind him alerted him to the presence of his young ward. He looked around to see Ganesha staring up at him with an expression of happy innocence.

'I do not know what you are smiling at,' he muttered. 'You do not look much better yourself.'

Ganesha turned to admire himself in the mirror.

The elephant calf wore a richly coloured caparison across his back, with a Keralan-style nettipattam headdress tied over his forehead. The nettipattam stretched all the way down to the top of his trunk and was painted gold and edged with a rainbow of coloured pom-poms. White cheek spots had been painted on either side of his face, and coloured garlands and brass bells had been tied around his tail.

Unlike Chopra the little elephant was delighted with his new look. Like any child he was enormously proud of his new outfit and wished to show it off.

Realising that Chopra was not an appreciative audience, he turned away, swished his ringing tail at the glowering clown, and wandered off to examine the strange smells of the circus ring.

'There is nothing we can do about his height,' sighed Tiger Singh, passing a critical eye over Chopra.

'But he does not even know our act!' protested the dwarf, whose name, Chopra had learned, was Bhiku.

Bhiku was the acknowledged leader of the clown troupe at the Grand Trunk Circus, though he himself claimed that he was only 'first among equals – as long as the other equals do what I tell them'.

Circus dwarves, Chopra was discovering, were a notoriously factious bunch.

'What is there to know?' he said grimly. 'You fall down. You throw pies at each other.'

The dwarf glared at him. 'Oh, so you think it is easy, do you, Mister Bigshot? Have you ever fallen off a bicycle in a humorous way? Have you ever been hit in the private parts with a broom handle whilst balancing on a beach ball? Let me tell you, clowning is a serious business.'

Chopra raised his hands in surrender. 'Look, all you have to do is get me inside Kanodia's bungalow. After that, I'm on my own.'

VASEEM KHAN

A bear sidled up to Chopra and then stood on its hind legs and folded its paws across its chest. 'Well, if you ask me, you look like a very fine clown.'

He gaped at the bear. 'But you're a man!' he exclaimed.

'We can no longer afford to keep a real bear,' Tiger Singh explained wearily. 'A man in a bear suit is the next best thing. Children expect a bear. What to do?'

The St Francis Catholic School for Boys might have been a carbon copy of St Xavier. As Rangwalla and Poppy walked across the school's grounds a game of soccer was in progress. Two sets of young boys in coloured outfits were racing around the grass whilst an elderly gentleman refereed. The elderly gentleman, a stick-thin figure in a blazing white T-shirt, white shorts, tennis socks and sneakers, continually blew on a shrill whistle that bounced around his neck.

Rangwalla stopped as a pair of Franciscan brothers in white cassocks swished by. 'Excuse me, can you tell us where we might find Principal D'Souza?'

One of the two men pointed back the way they had come. 'You have just passed by him.'

The referee jogged to a halt before them. Up close he was even thinner than he had seemed at first glance, with a long, scrawny neck in which an Adam's apple rode up and down like an elevator.

'What can I do for you?' asked Principal Angelo D'Souza crossly. His hawkish face was pinched into an expression of annoyance at having been called away from his football match.

Rangwalla was instantly intimidated by the old Franciscan. He was reminded of his own school days, which, admittedly, had not lasted very long. He had spent more time playing cricket in the playground and chalking lewd images onto his slate than he had studying. A voice reached out to him from the dim mists of the past: 'Rangwalla! Pay attention, boy! Do you think Gandhi could have defeated the British if he had spent all his time in school sketching images of nude milkmaids?'

He coughed to clear his throat. 'Ah, we are here to enquire about the bust of Father Albino Gonsalves that was stolen from St Xavier three nights ago. Sir.'

'Bust? Bust? You interrupt my game to ask me about Lobo's silly statue. Why, man?'

Rangwalla glanced at Poppy. 'Er, Principal Lobo thinks . . . What I mean to say is . . . he believes that . . .'

'Well, spit it out, man, spit it out. Haven't got all day.'

'Well, it's just that . . . St Francis and St Xavier are old rivals . . .' Rangwalla's voice tailed off.

D'Souza's eyes narrowed. 'That damned Lobo is accusing *me*?' His face swelled with rage. He jabbed Rangwalla in the chest. 'Now you listen to me, you blue-footed booby. I had nothing to do with Lobo's damned bust. He who lives in a glass house should not be throwing stones. He's always had it in for me. Even when we were in seminary together, he always had to throw his weight around. Well, you can go back and tell him that Brother D'Souza isn't warming his toilet seat for him any more!'

Rangwalla frowned. 'Sir?'

But D'Souza had already turned on his heel.

Bulbul Kanodia's Bandstand bungalow was fronted by ornate gates, the ironwork sculpted into a classical image from Hindu mythology – Lord Hanuman, the monkey-headed god, chasing the sun which, as a child, he had believed to be a ripe mango.

The largest guard hitched up his black trousers beneath the pregnant swell of his stomach, unleashed a mouthful of scarlet betel fluid onto the sizzling tarmac, then tipped back his cap and stood with his hands on his hips staring, slack-jawed, at the surreal sight of the circus troupe gathered in the middle of the dusty road.

The troupe, in turn, stared up at the lavish three-storey, purpose-built, colonial-style bungalow that Bulbul Kanodia called home.

The bungalow was located on the same stretch of real estate as the homes of some of Bollywood's biggest stars – on the promenade, where, on sultry summer evenings, Mumbai's mega-rich stood on their breezy balconies drinking imported Colombian coffee and watching the sun set on the Arabian Sea. For this and other reasons the Bandstand was a popular venue for walkers and gawpers.

At the end of the kilometre-long promenade lay the Bandra Fort, built by the Portuguese in 1640 as a watchtower. Now it was employed by late-night lovers to canoodle – safely hidden from the eyes of disapproving elders – and by scores of roosting pigeons.

Chopra quelled the sudden feeling of nervousness pooling in his belly as the guards talked animatedly with Tiger Singh. Pedestrians swirled around them, a few pausing in their headlong dash along the promenade to cast curious glances at the motley crew.

Chopra knew that what he was doing might be classed as borderline criminal. He was, effectively, entering a man's home under false pretences, with the intention of conducting an illegal search. Had he still been a police officer this alone would have been grounds for instant dismissal . . . He took a deep breath and willed himself to calm.

Perhaps this was the essential difference between a police officer and a private detective.

One was bound by the law, whilst the other merely used the law as a guide.

As Chopra was quickly learning, the second way was sometimes the only way to get things done.

Eventually the guards led the troupe inside the compound, herding them through an alley that ran alongside the bungalow and out into a lavish garden. The garden had been set up with white marquees and strategically placed hors d'oeuvres tables, manned by staff in crisp, white waiters' outfits. A selection of well-heeled Mumbaikers trolled between the tables, sipping from champagne flutes. They all turned as the circus troupe was led through the garden to a specially built stage at the rear of the expansive lawn.

A round of polite applause trailed the costumed performers as they clambered onto the stage. The audience, chattering good-naturedly, settled into rows of plastic chairs set out in front of the stage.

Chopra looked down on the sea of faces before him.

He felt absurdly self-conscious.

He transferred his gaze to Kanodia's bungalow, painted in shades of powder yellow and white. A cantilevered awning extended from the back of the house, beneath which trestle tables had been laid out, crammed with food for the luncheon scheduled for after the circus show. Standing to one side of the tables, partially obscured by a water fountain, was the largest birthday cake Chopra had ever seen, a ten-foot-tall, six-tiered confection in white chocolate. The base of the cake rested on a platform fitted with castors. The intention, he assumed, was to wheel it out later for a gala cake-cutting as the grand finale to the birthday party.

At that moment a paunchy man in a gleaming white jodhpuri suit emerged from the bungalow. Affixed to his arm was a fat woman in a shimmering blue sari. They were trailed by a hefty young girl in a frilly pink dress.

An energetic round of applause burst out as Kanodia and family took their places on a leather sofa placed before the stage.

Chopra felt himself flush once again as Kanodia's gaze ran over the gathered troupe. He felt sure Bulbul would recognise him. But the former jewel fence lingered on the tall clown for only a second, and then looked away.

'Gentleladies and gentlemen,' Tiger Singh began, 'welcome, one and all, to the Grand Trunk Circus!'

As they returned to the waiting rickshaw, Rangwalla turned to Poppy. 'My instincts suggest that he is telling the truth. Chopra Sir also felt that this is most likely the work of an insider, not the St Francis school.'

Poppy looked genuinely alarmed at the possibility. 'Oh, Abbas, do you really think it could have been one of my boys? But they look like such angels.'

Rangwalla bit down on his tongue.

He wanted to tell her that the reality of the world was that all the devils he had ever encountered had, at one time, been doted upon by their mothers as their 'little angels'. But Poppy had a unique way of looking at things; she tended to believe the best of people. Rangwalla had no wish to puncture her balloon of optimism with the needle of his own cynicism.

'Do you have anyone else that you suspect?' he asked instead. 'At St Xavier, I mean. Have any of the students been acting suspiciously over the past couple of days? Going out of the way to make themselves heard? In my experience, children make very poor criminals. They need others to know how clever they have been.'

Poppy considered this, before shaking her head. 'I cannot think of anyone in particular.'

'Anything else out of the ordinary? Anything at all? Sometimes it is the smallest thing . . .'

Poppy bit her lip as she considered this. 'I cannot think of anything—' She stopped, her brow crimping into a frown.

'What is it?'

'Well, there is one thing . . . but it has nothing to do with the theft.'

'Please tell me.'

'It's Mr Banarjee, the school secretary. The morning after the theft he took a turn. He has not been in to work since.' Poppy hesitated. 'Well, the thing is . . . Mr Banarjee has not had a day off in the past forty years.'

'I am not riding that thing,' hissed Chopra.

'You do not have to ride it,' Bhiku the dwarf hissed back. 'The whole point is that you do not *know* how to ride it.'

Chopra was awash with terror.

The circus performance had proceeded well. The flame-thrower and the sword-swallower had been a hit. Then Piyush, Master of Pythons, had strolled around the audience with an enormous serpent entwined around his shoulders, encouraging the tremulous nabobs to pat the creature. Ruma, the contortionist, had curled herself into a ball and allowed herself to be rolled around the stage before being locked up inside a tiny box, from which Tiger Singh had made her vanish.

Now it was time for the clown show . . . and Chopra was suffering from an acute case of stage fright.

'What is the matter?' whispered Tiger Singh, who had come over to investigate the delay.

'First he is too tall to be a dwarf, now he does not know how *not* to ride a unicycle!'

Bhiku glared daggers at Chopra.

'Come now, Chopra,' said Tiger Singh encouragingly. 'There is literally nothing to it.' He patted the reluctant clown on the shoulder and walked away.

Beneath the white make-up Chopra's face was burning with embarrassment as he picked up the unicycle and placed one foot on the pedals. He looked around and saw that even Kanodia was watching him intently.

Chopra did not believe in prayer, but for once he wished that there *was* a god he could pray to, preferably the kind who deigned to listen once in a while. He took a deep breath and put his other foot on the other pedal whilst simultaneously flinging out his arms to steady himself. For a second he teetered like a gyroscope, and then his feet began to pump the pedals and he began to circle around the stage . . .

A wave of delight arose inside him, obliterating all other thoughts.

'I'm doing it!' he exclaimed. 'I'm doing it!'

He saw Bhiku's face flash past. The mask of clown paint was twisted into an evil grimace. 'Yes,' said the dwarf, 'but this is not funny, is it?' He stuck out a stick with a boxing glove on the end and jabbed Chopra in the back.

'Hey!'

Chopra's arms flailed as he lost control. A cry of anguish escaped him as the unicycle arced out over the edge of the stage . . .

He landed in a heap on the grass, the unicycle on top of him, its solitary wheel still spinning forlornly in the air. A round of laughter added insult to his injury until he realised that everyone believed his denouement to be part of the act.

He untangled himself and stood up, gathering together the remaining shreds of his dignity.

'Oh, Papa, the poor clown is bleeding!'

Chopra raised a hand and discovered that Kanodia's daughter was correct.

Blood was flowing from his nose.

At the same instant he saw that fate had provided him with the opening he had been looking for.

'Is there a bathroom I can use?'

For a second Kanodia stared suspiciously at him. Chopra immediately realised his mistake. The make-up disguised his features but there was no way to disguise his voice.

'Follow me, sir,' said a helpful waiter. 'I will show you.'

He felt certain that Kanodia's eyes were boring into his back as he limped stiffly away.

Mr Banarjee lived in an old colony in JB Nagar, a neighbouring enclave of Sahar. Banarjee's flat was on the fifth floor of a run-down apartment building. A hand-scrawled OUT OF ORDER sign had been jammed into the accordion-style shutters that fronted the lift, forcing Poppy and Rangwalla to trudge up the betel-stained stairs.

Arriving on the fifth floor, they knocked on the door to flat 501 – residence of one AUROBINDO BANARJEE – to which an elaborate cross had been nailed, the workman-ship of the cross leaving much to be desired.

To Rangwalla the splayed Christ seemed cross-eyed and listless.

The door swung back to reveal an elderly and obese cleaning woman holding a broom. Once they had explained their presence, she led them grumpily to the apartment's narrow balcony where Banarjee was slumped in a rattan armchair clad in a white shirt and shorts, distractedly thumbing through a book of psalms.

The old man arose with a start as they approached. His eyes swam behind bottle-bottom spectacles, and a sudden gust blew up the few hairs that he had scraped across his bald pate.

A strange shadow passed over his face as he stood there. Rangwalla recognised it immediately.

Guilt.

'Mr Banarjee,' he said, 'I am Rangwalla. I am a detective from—'

'Detective!' Banarjee ejaculated, interrupting Rangwalla. 'Oh, Mother Mary help me!' His knees buckled and he fell back into his rattan seat.

'Mr Banarjee, are you all right?' asked Poppy, leaning over her stricken colleague in concern.

'Forty years! Forty years in the service of our Lord and Saviour and now I am to break rocks in jail!'

The poor man seemed ready to faint.

'Mr Banarjee,' Rangwalla said sternly, 'kindly pull your-self together.'

They watched as the veteran administrator gradually calmed himself.

'Now, please explain yourself.'

Banarjee would not meet their eyes, preferring to stare at his sandals, the book of psalms clasped tightly in his hands. Eventually he spoke, in the tone of one confessing a mortal sin. 'I have lost this year's examination papers.'

Rangwalla gaped at him. 'What do you mean, lost?'

'The papers for the January exams were sent to us one week ago. As school secretary I am responsible for them. I locked them away inside the new safe that we had purchased just for this purpose. A safe that I had recommended. And then, two days ago, I discovered that the papers had been stolen.'

'Two days ago? You mean they were taken on the same night as the theft of the bust?'

Banarjee nodded miserably.

Rangwalla considered the old man's revelation.

From the balcony he heard the sounds of late-afternoon traffic passing five storeys below, the buzzing of rickshaws, the ringing of bicycles, the shouts of two women embroiled in an argument. It seemed to him that they had stumbled across an important turning point in the investigation. The shape of things was emerging from the fog of mystery. 'Mr Banarjee, please get dressed. We are going to the school.'

Bulbul Kanodia's office was located on the second floor of his lavish bungalow.

Chopra slipped out of the bathroom into which he had been deposited following his tumble and quietly climbed the marbled staircase to the second floor, his tread as light as a cat burglar's.

The upper floors were deserted. Everyone was preoccupied with the birthday party.

Kanodia's office was unlocked. Chopra entered and looked around.

The room, like everything else in the grand residence, was opulently furnished. In the manner of many rich men Bulbul Kanodia had allowed himself the vanity of a grand bookcase, extending across one entire wall, stuffed with volumes that he would never read. In Kanodia's case, Chopra wasn't sure the man *could* read. The remaining walls were covered in stylised paintings of Indian rural scenes that must have been purchased at inordinate expense from one of Mumbai's burgeoning art galleries. No doubt they were by noted Indian artists. The floor was polished granite and gleamed under the artfully placed spotlights. An enormous television, flanked by towering speakers, took pride of place before an imported Italian sofa.

Chopra hurried to the expansive teak desk in the centre of the room and began to riffle through the drawers.

Kanodia kept very little in them. He discovered a clutch of useless papers, a selection of jeweller's loupes, and a well-thumbed library of gemstone catalogues.

In the bottom drawer he found a slim volume entitled *The Koh-i-Noor Diamond: A Jeweller's Guide*. It was an old edition, written by an American jeweller who claimed to have examined the Koh-i-Noor in the late sixties at the invitation of Her Majesty, Queen Elizabeth II. It rehashed the history of the Koh-i-Noor and then went into meticulous technical detail about the diamond itself. The detail – elucidating on the cut and characteristics of the stone – meant nothing to Chopra.

The volume in itself didn't prove anything – after all, Kanodia was a jeweller. But Chopra felt that old tingle he got when he was on the right scent.

He finished with the desk and moved to a rosewood Regency writing bureau beside the room's French windows, which opened on to a narrow balcony.

On top of the bureau lay a number of exquisite fountain pens and pads of scented notepaper stamped with the logo of Kanodia's Paramathma jewellery brand.

Quickly, he searched inside it.

Tucked into one of the tiered letter compartments he discovered an ornate envelope, covered in gold leaf, but bearing no name. Chopra slid out a single card. His eyes scanned it:

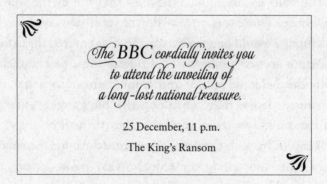

*The BBC cordially invites you
to attend the unveiling of
a long-lost national treasure.*

25 December, 11 p.m.

The King's Ransom

Chopra was astounded. His instincts were telling him that he had found the very thing he had been looking for – evidence of Kanodia's involvement in the theft of the

Koh-i-Noor diamond. After all, what else could this 'long-lost national treasure' be?

But what did the BBC have to do with this? Surely the British Broadcasting Corporation was not involved?

No. He cast the preposterous thought aside. This had nothing to do with *the* BBC. The BBC mentioned in the card was something else entirely.

A noise sounded in the corridor outside.

Chopra looked around wildly, his heart thundering in his chest. If he were discovered here, it would be a disaster. He would be unmasked in front of Kanodia. He could not afford to alert him to the fact that he had discovered this vital clue.

There was nowhere to hide inside the office . . . nowhere *inside* . . .

He flung open the French windows and walked out onto the balcony, pushing the doors shut behind him.

The balcony overlooked the alley that ran by the side of the house. There was no way down, yet if he stayed on the balcony he would be seen by anyone who entered the office.

Before second thoughts could deter him, he clambered onto the balcony railing and from there onto a narrow, decorative ledge that ran along the bungalow's exterior wall and disappeared around the edge of the house.

With his back to the wall, arms spread-eagled, he slowly inched his way along the ledge. Sweat poured from his brow, washing his clown make-up into his eyes.

Finally, he made it to the edge and turned the corner.

Now he was above the garden. He could see the stage, and the audience with their backs to him. On the stage the

Brain of Bangalore was hypnotising a short man in a bad toupee into believing that he was a langur. On cue the man dropped to his haunches and began to nibble at an imaginary mango clasped in one hand whilst scratching his behind with the other. The crowd guffawed.

Chopra had no doubt that if anyone chose this moment to look around, he would be spotted. A clown clinging grimly to a wall two storeys above the ground was not a sight you saw every day, even in Mumbai.

He looked around wildly. *What the hell did he do now?*

'There! See for yourselves.'

Banarjee stepped aside and waved a hand at the wall. Rangwalla and Poppy were standing in the secretary's office at St Xavier. The office was sparse, a single meticulously kept steel desk surrounded on all sides by a sea of metal filing cabinets. On top of the cabinets were worn ring binders with yearly dates on the spines. Rangwalla could read dates marching all the way back to 1952.

Behind the desk, on the whitewashed wall, there had been a large painting of Father Albino Gonsalves, the school's founding father, staring down at them with an expression of beatific idiocy. Banarjee had unhooked the painting and laid it to one side.

Behind it was a wall safe, but one more complicated than any Rangwalla had ever encountered. The front of the safe had no dials or turning wheels or even a keypad. All that

Rangwalla could see was a black, rectangular LCD screen and a narrow socket like the ports on a computer.

'It is a very modern safe,' explained Banarjee. 'Completely computerised. One must attach this device,' he held up something that looked like a mobile phone, 'and then one must input the correct nine-digit code.'

They watched as the old secretary plugged the device into the port on the front of the safe. Instantly the display flashed with red letters: 'PLEASE ENTER CODE'.

Banarjee pushed his spectacles further up his nose and then punched in the code on the portable device's keypad. There was a sequence of beeps and the door to the safe swung open.

Rangwalla and Poppy peered in.

'There are papers in here,' observed Rangwalla.

'Yes. They are historical papers and rare volumes from the school's early years.'

'So the thieves took only the examination papers?'

'Yes,' said Banarjee wretchedly.

Poppy considered this. 'Why can't we just request the Examination Board to send us new papers?' she said eventually. 'I mean, with new questions?'

'My dear Poppy, do you understand what a laborious process it is preparing and vetting these papers? It takes months of work on the part of the Examination Board. It is too late to change the papers.'

'But then, if someone has stolen the papers, they will be able to cheat.'

'Precisely!' Banarjee seemed ready to collapse into despair once again. 'Not to mention the scandal that will engulf the school once it becomes known that we – that *I* – have inadvertently aided that cheating. We are not like those schools in Bihar where cheating is openly encouraged. Our motto is *honestas et fides* – "honesty and faith". We will be ruined. And the Holy Father's visit . . . *ruined!*'

There was a clattering outside the office and then Principal Augustus Lobo burst in. 'What the devil is going on?' he barked. 'Banarjee? What are you doing here? I thought you were down with suspected dengue fever? Is this some sort of miraculous recovery?'

Rangwalla looked at the wretched Banarjee wringing his hands in terror.

Poppy spoke up. 'Sir, there is something you should know.'

Quickly, she explained the situation. Lobo's face expanded like a bullfrog during mating season. Rangwalla waited for the explosion, but then the principal shook his head in a gesture of sadness. 'Banarjee, how long have we worked together? Why didn't you just come to me?'

Banarjee hung his head. 'I was ashamed.'

'"A friend loveth at all times and a brother is born for adversity",' intoned Lobo. 'Take heart from the words of Solomon, Banarjee.' The principal turned to Rangwalla. 'It cannot be coincidence that the bust went missing on the same night as the examination papers.'

'No, sir,' agreed Rangwalla. 'I believe that the bust was stolen to deflect attention from the theft of the examination papers. I believe the thieves – knowing of your animosity towards the St Francis school – thought they could misdirect any investigation. At the very least they aimed to muddy the waters.'

'I still think it is possible that the bust – and the papers – were stolen by those damned Franciscans,' grumbled Lobo stubbornly.

'I do not believe so, sir. Besides, this is a very complicated safe. To break into it requires specialist expertise. It is my belief that some very intelligent young minds were behind this theft.'

'You mean students?' Lobo shook his head in disgust. 'So it has come to this. The reputation of St Xavier besmirched by some goondas with a computer.'

Rangwalla turned to Banarjee. 'Is there anyone that you suspect, sir? Any particularly bright pupils with an affinity for this computing business? Any that have been acting out of character recently?'

Banarjee's eyes narrowed behind his thick spectacles. 'Yes,' he said. 'I believe I know exactly who is behind this.'

'Oh, Papa, he is so sweet!'

Aarti Kanodia clasped her plump hands to her sixteen-year-old bosom and jumped up and down, the skirts of her pink frock bouncing around her. The source of her delight looked down from the stage, blinking modestly.

Ganesha had had a day to remember.

Firstly, he had gone to the circus and learned many new tricks in the company of a giant bull elephant, the first elephant he had encountered in his time in Mumbai. Then he had been gussied up in wonderful new clothes and brought to this interesting place where he had watched the circus troupe perform. Ganesha had particularly enjoyed the dwarf clowns. Even Chopra had made him laugh when he had ridden his unicycle over the edge of the stage.

But now it was Ganesha's own turn in the spotlight.

With the seasoned swagger of a ring veteran he trotted into the centre of the makeshift stage and, by bending his front legs and dipping his head, bowed to the audience. Then he went through the repertoire of simple tricks that he had been shown by the bull elephant and its trainer.

First he sat back on his hind legs and pretended to beg. Then he leaned forward and performed a handstand, which met with wild applause. Ganesha rolled over, once, twice, three times. More applause. He walked backwards in a circle. Then he turned around and walked backwards in the other direction.

The little elephant trotted over to the dwarf clowns and took a beach ball. He threw it up in the air with his trunk, then caught it again. Delighted claps. Then he rolled onto his back, threw the ball up and bounced it between his feet.

The crowd roared him on.

Tiger Singh leaned down to whisper into the dwarf Vinod's ears. 'He is a very clever elephant. How did he learn so much in just one morning?'

'I do not know,' said Vinod. 'We did not teach him half of those things.'

Chopra looked on in amazement from his elevated vantage point. Glued to the rear wall of the bungalow, he momentarily forgot his own predicament. He had known that Ganesha was adept at picking up tricks, but this was truly exceptional! He blinked. This was no time to think about elephants – *he had to get down!*

He surveyed the ground as it swam before his sweat-soaked eyes. The striped awning that extended from the rear wall of the bungalow was one storey beneath him. Could he jump into that and use it to break his fall?

No. The fabric was too flimsy; it would not hold his weight. He would go crashing through it and clatter into the trestle tables groaning with food that lay directly below.

He looked around.

Where the awning ended, just a few feet from where Chopra was perched, was the giant cake. Ten feet of solid cake base, coated in white chocolate. It was all but hidden by a water fountain from where the circus show was going on.

He made a decision.

Blinking droplets of sweat from his eyelashes he edged to the very corner of the ledge, then, with a final muttered curse, leaped from the wall.

He landed on the topmost tier of the cake, which collapsed downwards through the remaining layers. The hard sponge served to cushion his fall, and he ploughed to a halt having burrowed through to the very centre of the cake like a meteorite.

Chopra sat up and wiped cake from his eyes. He was sitting in the centre of a cake explosion, covered in cream, chocolate and icing sugar. A plastic cut-out of the number 16 had affixed itself to his groin.

He plucked it off and stood up on shaky legs.

No one had noticed him, but at any moment one of the serving staff might emerge from the bungalow and spot him. Then all hell would break loose.

He had to get out of here, even if it meant temporarily abandoning Ganesha. The thought filled him with guilt but he was certain that the circus troupe would take good care of his ward until he could pick him up later on.

Chopra limped along the alley to the front of the house. The TOPS guards had congregated by the gate, smoking and drinking tea from tiny glasses. They laughed as he stumbled past.

After all, what was suspicious about a clown covered in cream and cake?

'Checkmate!'

The boy tilted his head and fired a victorious sneer at his opponent whose shoulders crumpled with disappointment, Adam's apple bobbing up and down in defeat. 'Better luck next time, Rathore,' he said imperiously before striding to the adjoining table where a second opponent was desperately scanning the board.

'Four moves and you're done, Bhandari.'

The seated boy's face collapsed into panic. Tremulously he touched one of the pieces arrayed before him, then changed his mind and moved another. The standing boy smiled.

'Make that one move,' he said and plucked one of his own pieces from the board before setting it down again. 'Checkmate.'

He walked over to a third table where a portly boy was examining the board through owlish spectacles. As he saw his opponent approach, he immediately knocked over his pieces. 'I resign,' he squeaked, and sat back in relief.

The standing boy turned and grinned imperiously at the cassocked Brother seated at the head of the class. 'A new record, I think, sir,' he said.

The Brother tapped the stopclock on his desk, bringing the moving hands to a halt, then frowned. 'Do not forget your Proverbs, Wadia. "Pride comes before destruction and a haughty spirit before a fall."'

At that moment the door to the classroom opened and Rangwalla entered, Poppy and Banarjee crowding in close behind.

Rangwalla surveyed the members of the St Xavier chess club and then said, 'I am looking for Raj Wadia, Anoop Joshi, George Fonseca and Rafeeq Baig.'

Rangwalla passed a severe look over the four boys seated before him. It was instantly clear to him who the leader of the group was: Raj Wadia, a tall boy with lacquered hair, bright eyes and a permanent expression of disdain on his handsome features. Joshi, in contrast, was a thick-shoul-dered brute with a bulbous nose and fleshy lips. His simian-like upper torso strained his uniform. He seemed forever hanging on Wadia's words – Rangwalla instantly recognised a born lieutenant. The third member of the group, Fonseca, was a pudgy specimen who looked out at the world through thick glasses and an expression of constant alarm. Baig, in contrast, was exceedingly thin, as if he had been ill. His mop of thick brown hair was uncombed and looked as if a bird had built a nest on top of his head.

Rangwalla had gathered the four boys together in a classroom in the east wing of the school.

The former sub-inspector knew that, contrary to appearances, these four boys were highly intelligent. Mr Banarjee had said that they were informally known around the campus as the 'Bright Bulb Club'. He had also told Rangwalla he believed them to be behind the theft of the examination papers. He had no proof, of course, merely the strongest of suspicions. The four boys were 'as thick as thieves', he explained, and all bona fide computer geniuses, particularly Fonseca.

Furthermore, they had raised Banarjee's suspicions because, in the days following the arrival of the examination papers, they had each found different excuses to visit the old secretary's office. Wadia had casually enquired about the examination papers, not once, but on three separate occasions!

'My name is Rangwalla,' said Rangwalla sternly. 'I would like to ask you a few questio—'

'Excuse me for interrupting, sir, but who, precisely, are you? I mean, you are clearly not part of the faculty,' said

Wadia. He was slouched in his chair, legs spread-eagled insolently before him.

'I am a detective,' Rangwalla began.

'Are you out of uniform?'

Rangwalla frowned. 'I am a private detective.'

'Then you're not a real detective at all, are you, sir?' Wadia sneered. Joshi sniggered.

'I served the Mumbai police force for over twenty years,' snapped Rangwalla irritably.

'Were you sacked?'

Rangwalla gritted his teeth. 'No. I was not sacked. I retired.'

'If you are retired, why are you here?'

'I am here because of the examination papers that went missing from the office of Mr Banarjee four nights ago.'

There was a sudden silence in the room. A blush overcame Fonseca's round face and Baig's Adam's apple bobbed up and down like a piston.

'The examination papers are missing?' said Wadia eventually. 'Well, that is a shame. But what has that got to do with us, sir?'

'Mr Banarjee believes that you might know where those papers are.'

Wadia looked around innocently. 'Who? Us? How would we know, sir?'

'Because you are the ones that took them.'

Fonseca let out a little whimper of alarm. It had not escaped Rangwalla that the boy was sweating profusely even though he was seated directly below the ceiling fan. Here is the weak link, he thought.

Rangwalla walked very deliberately over to Fonseca and looked down at him with a stern expression. Fonseca suddenly found something deeply interesting in the surface of his desk.

'That is quite an accusation, sir,' Wadia said finally. 'I suppose we should be offended. Do you have any proof that we took those papers?'

'Are you denying that you took them?'

'We had absolutely nothing to do with it,' replied Wadia promptly.

Rangwalla continued to stare down at the top of Fonseca's head. Fonseca's shoulders twitched. There was something mole-like about the boy, Rangwalla thought; he certainly looked as if he wished to burrow into the ground.

'If necessary, I will find the proof.'

'Well, when you do that, sir, why don't you come back and talk to us? In the meantime . . .' Wadia scraped back his chair and stood up. 'We are late for our next class.'

Rangwalla watched the boys file out.

Wadia paused at the door and met the former policeman's glare, a knowing, arrogant smile on his face.

'Good luck catching those thieves, sir,' he said. And then he winked.

After the door had closed Poppy rushed in from the corridor where she had been anxiously wearing a hole in the floor. Rangwalla had insisted on handling the questioning alone. He had interrogated thousands of suspects in his life; it was something that required experience and patience. It was no task for an amateur.

At least Banarjee had seen the wisdom of leaving it to a professional. The chastened martinet had retired to his office. Rangwalla suspected the old man had no desire to face those responsible for his humiliation.

'Did they confess?' Poppy asked breathlessly.

'No.'

'What about Fonseca? He is a good boy at heart. I am sure if we work on him he will blurt out the truth.'

'Perhaps,' said Rangwalla. 'But I would not bet on it. Wadia is the leader of that pack. I doubt Fonseca would be willing to cross him.'

'But then what do we do? We cannot just let them get away with it.'

Rangwalla scratched thoughtfully at his beard. He was thinking about Wadia's supercilious expression and that parting wink. The boy was arrogant. Like many criminals Rangwalla had met Wadia believed he was smarter than everyone around him, too smart to ever get caught.

'I may have a plan,' he said eventually. 'I need to see Principal Lobo. We will require his help.'

The party was well underway.

As Chopra looked on from the shadows of his office, a group of uniformed policemen stood and raised a toast to a senior officer seated in their midst. A chorus of 'For he's a jolly good fellow' rose above the piped restaurant music. The man of the hour, who Chopra vaguely knew, stumbled to his feet, feigned surprise, and thanked his colleagues profusely.

The door to the kitchen swung open.

Rosie Pinto advanced on the senior officer behind a vertiginous birthday cake that wobbled enticingly atop a silver dessert trolley.

Chopra frowned. He had had enough of birthdays and birthday cakes to last him a good long while.

Following his ignominious exit from Bulbul Kanodia's bungalow he had returned home to shower and change out of his cake-splattered clown suit. Bahadur, the apartment complex's security guard, had almost fallen from his stool at the sight of Chopra in his outlandish get-up.

Having scrubbed himself to a high sheen, Chopra had dressed and then gone to fetch Ganesha.

At Cross Maidan he had discovered a despondent Tiger Singh.

It seemed that Bulbul Kanodia had been so displeased with the destruction of his daughter's cake that he had cancelled the festivities there and then, and banished the troupe from his home. Aarti Kanodia had flung herself to the lawn and thumped the grass with her fists, wailing at the ruination of her grand day. Incensed by his daughter's distress, Kanodia had refused to pay the circus performers.

The dwarves, who did not take such things lightly, had turned violent.

Furniture had been broken. Guests had been abused. Threats had been made.

Eventually the police had been called.

It had taken Chopra the rest of the day to fix the mess.

He had hurried to the Bandra police station where the dwarves had been detained. By enlisting the help of an old police contact he had engineered their prompt release. He had then written out a cheque for Tiger Singh to cover the circus's losses. Finally, he had invited the entire troupe to a complimentary meal at his restaurant, which they had declined, the dwarves having made up their mind to visit a ladies bar instead to help them recover from their bad mood.

'You are a gentleman, Chopra,' Tiger Singh had sighed, 'even if you are not much of a clown.'

Chopra walked out through the restaurant's kitchen and into the rear courtyard, where he found Ganesha hunkered down under the mango tree, investigating fallen mangoes with his trunk and picking out the best ones. He liked to line them up before popping them into his mouth one by one. It was a game, one of a number Ganesha had recently invented.

Chopra was continually amazed by how the little elephant developed in new and intriguing ways each and every day. Ganesha was still decked out in his colourful outfit, a gift from the circus troupe for his extraordinary debut.

Chopra settled into his rattan chair and considered his next course of action.

He now had in his possession what he believed to be compelling proof of Bulbul Kanodia's involvement in the theft of the Crown of Queen Elizabeth from the Prince of Wales Museum. Chopra believed that the card he had discovered was an invitation to a gathering where Kanodia would attempt to auction the Koh-i-Noor diamond to unscrupulous buyers.

Had he still been an officer of the Brihanmumbai Police Chopra would have passed the invite – along with his suspicions – to his seniors. He would have allowed those best placed in the service to deal with the matter.

But the fact was that he was no longer part of the police service.

What's more, he did not trust a man like Suresh Rao to give due consideration to any evidence that he, Chopra, had unearthed. ACP Rao was the sort to cut off his own nose to spite his face. And Rao had gone out on a limb with his own seniors by arresting Garewal – he would not change course now.

The only thing that could save Garewal was if Chopra produced the Koh-i-Noor and with it a red-handed Kanodia. The more he thought about it the more certain he felt that this was the correct course of action.

A bucket clanked in the gathering darkness.

Chopra turned, expecting to see young Irfan. But it was Rosie Pinto who came striding across the courtyard, the steel pail swinging by her side.

'Good evening, sir.'

'Good evening, Rosie.'

He watched as Ganesha stirred from his well-earned rest and lumbered to his feet to greet Irfan. Ganesha froze.

His ears flapped once. He peered behind Rosie, then, not spotting Irfan, raised his trunk and sniffed the air.

Then he turned to look at Chopra, who recognised the puzzlement on the elephant's placid features.

Chopra felt a great sadness welling inside him.

During the frenetic action of the day he had managed to avoid dwelling on Irfan's absence, clamping down on his emotions every time his thoughts drifted in that direction, but now, as he observed the distraught elephant, the realisation that Irfan would never again bring a bucket out to Ganesha landed with a thud.

He leaned forward and patted the little elephant on the head. 'I am sorry, Ganesha, but Irfan is gone. He has returned to his home.'

The elephant calf stared at him, confusion evident in his eyes.

'There was nothing I could do. We must all make the best of it.'

Chopra stood and moved towards the restaurant. As he walked away he felt Ganesha's eyes on his back. At that moment the guilt that he had suppressed ever since he had allowed Irfan to walk out of the restaurant returned with a vengeance.

Poppy was right. He had been too quick to permit the boy to leave. Children could so easily be intimidated. What if Irfan had been too afraid to tell the truth? Chopra had sensed that this man who called himself Irfan's father was a bad egg, even before he'd found out who he was. Why had he let Irfan just walk away with him? If Irfan had been his own flesh and blood would he have allowed him to leave with a man like that?

A cloud of shame arose inside him. He felt the ghost of Gandhi hovering on his shoulder, rebuking him: 'There is a higher court than courts of justice and that is the court of conscience.'

There and then he promised himself that he would track the boy down, no matter what it took. He would ensure that Irfan was in good hands. And, if not, well then he would move heaven and earth to return the boy to where he belonged – a safe and loving environment.

Rosie watched her boss disappear into the restaurant, then set down the bucket. 'Well, young man, how about some lovely coconut milk? I have put some Dairy Milk chocolate in it today.'

Ganesha swivelled his head towards the assistant chef, then looked down at the bucket. Then he turned his back on them both, collapsed onto his knees and closed his eyes, his ears folded flat against his head in the profoundest sorrow.

SEARCHING FOR IRFAN

The next afternoon, Poppy once again arrived at Rangwalla's flat with the glint of purpose in her eye. This time she was armed with a renewed sense of optimism.

A long conversation with her husband the previous evening had revealed that he had finally come around to her way of thinking, that he too had been having serious misgivings about the manner of Irfan's exit from their lives. Chopra was now firmly behind the notion that they must find Irfan and assure themselves of his wellbeing. He had even spoken with Rangwalla, who had sent all his old informants out scouring the city for the boy.

Now, as a bleary-eyed Rangwalla materialised from his bedroom, Poppy felt a bright band of hope around her heart.

'I have been up all night, hounding my people,' Rangwalla explained, somewhat embarrassed at the fact that he had only just arisen from his slumber. 'I have an address.'

'Then what are we waiting for?' said Poppy.

The ragpickers' slum was a notoriously difficult place to navigate.

Having negotiated their way through a Byzantine maze of narrow, open-sewered alleyways, Rangwalla and Poppy emerged into a tiny courtyard around which a ragtag assortment of shanty homes had been haphazardly thrown together as if by a storm. In the courtyard a single spigot provided water for the locality. A line of women bearing clay pots chattered by the tap.

A naked infant squatted to play with a dead cockroach while his mother filled her pot. Leaning in the doorway of one of the dwellings a milky-eyed old man chewed on a neem stick as he watched the water-gatherers.

The ragpickers of Mumbai were a community unto themselves, low down even in the pecking order of the city's poorest classes. The majority were children from the rural economy who had gravitated to Mumbai in search of a better life. They spent their days trawling through the waste generated by a human termite mound of twenty million, rooting for plastic, metal, glass, anything that might fetch a few rupees at one of the city's many unscrupulous scrap dealers.

The ragpickers lived a hard life of constant exposure to the dangers of untreated waste – noxious gases, medical cast-offs, hazardous chemicals. To claim a few grams of copper they scarred their lungs making bonfires of discarded electrical goods. They worked barefoot and without gloves. Often they earned barely enough for a day's meal. Some called them parasites. But the city's civic authorities understood that without these 'parasites' Mumbai would become a cesspool, drowning beneath the weight of its own accumulated rubbish.

Rangwalla moved towards the old man and spoke to him. The man gesticulated with his neem stick to a dwelling on the far side of the courtyard.

As he walked over to the bricolage home Rangwalla checked his watch. It was already 5 p.m. He had to be at St Xavier's in precisely one hour to put into motion the plan that he had hatched yesterday with Principal Lobo, the plan that would entice Raj Wadia and his gang out into the open.

It had been a busy few days for the former sub-inspector. If truth be told, he was still coming to terms with the sudden upturn in his fortunes.

Once again he felt a surge of gratitude towards Chopra for delivering him from the hell that he been in since being sacked from the police service. Now he was intent on repaying the confidence his senior officer had shown in him, starting by cracking the case of the missing bust.

He had spent the best part of the previous evening sourcing the information and materials he needed for his plan to entrap Wadia. It had taken longer than he'd anticipated to convince Lobo of the necessity of his machinations – the old principal was not enamoured of what he insisted on calling 'this new-fangled hoodoo'. The technicians Rangwalla had found worked late into the evening in Banarjee's office, beneath the principal's brooding gaze as he prowled the flagstones with his hands clasped behind his back, jowly face gummed into an expression of furious impatience. 'I should just thrash it out of them,' he kept muttering.

The technicians, unsure who the old man was referring to, were suitably unnerved.

Rangwalla rapped on the shanty home's rickety balsa-wood door. Seconds later, the door swung back to reveal a short, emaciated woman in a dull brown shalwar kameez staring out at them with a blank look. Behind her he could see milk boiling in a steel pot on a kerosene stove resting on the floor. A second woman was busily sweeping the tiny one-room dwelling with a rush broom.

She stopped as Rangwalla peered in at her, then came to the door to stand by the first woman.

'My name is Rangwalla,' said Rangwalla. 'I am looking for Mukhthar Lodi.'

'Why are you looking for him?' asked the woman with the broom. Her eyes were fish-like and her lips taut with distaste.

'You knew Mukhthar?'

'What do you mean "knew"? Is he dead?'

'No.'

'Shame,' said the woman.

'Do not say that, Nazia,' admonished the woman who had opened the door. 'Would you take my husband from me?'

'Husband!' pouted Nazia. 'Hah! He is an animal!'

'Do not call him that!'

'What else do you call a man who beats and terrorises his wife?' She turned to Rangwalla. 'That animal even put cigarettes out on her. He did—' Her eyes flickered to Poppy. 'He did many bad things. But will my sister hear a word said against him?' She rolled her eyes. 'Allah save us from martyrs.' She turned back to her sister. 'Shabnam, you are a fool.'

'He is still my husband,' muttered Shabnam stubbornly.

'Then Irfan is your son?' said Poppy quietly.

Shabnam stared at her, before shaking her head. 'No. I am Mukhthar's second wife. Irfan is not my child.'

'Ask her what happened to the first wife,' Nazia prompted belligerently.

'It is just a rumour.'

'Yes, the sort of rumour that gets up and applies hot candlewax to your breasts when you are asleep.' She leaned forward and said, in a conspiratorial voice, 'He burned her alive. Whoosh! Claimed it was an accident, but we all know the truth. I have heard of Hindu women committing sati by jumping on their husband's funeral pyres, but he made a sati out of her in advance.'

'Ugly lies!' snapped Shabnam, hot tears springing to her eyes. 'You are just jealous because you are an old maid.'

'Yes, I am jealous of your husband. A murderer, a liar and a thief. Wah wah, sister, what a prize specimen you have caught!'

'Where can we find him?' Rangwalla said, interrupting the quarrelling sisters.

'Why do you want to find him?' asked Shabnam, her expression suddenly wary.

'We are looking for Irfan,' explained Poppy.

'Why?'

'He ran away from your husband. He came to live with me. Then your husband found him and took him. I want to make sure he is well.'

'Hah!' snorted Nazia. 'If he is with Mukhthar then he will not be well, that is for sure. That man is the devil himself. Do you know he makes them all steal? The boys. And if they don't get him what he wants, he beats them – heavens above how he beats them!'

'You are exaggerating, Nazia,' scowled Shabnam.

'Oh, am I?' said Nazia. She grabbed her sister roughly by the arm and spun her around. 'Is this an exaggeration?' She pointed at a jagged knife scar running across the back of the woman's neck. 'This was his idea of an anniversary gift.'

'It was an accident,' whispered Shabnam, shaking off her sister. But her voice was miserable.

'Please tell us where we can find him,' pleaded Poppy. She reached into her purse, removed a one-hundred-rupee note and held it out to the women.

Nazia bristled. 'Just because we are poor, madam, it does not mean that we have no shame. Keep your money. If Mukhthar has Irfan then it is not a good thing. We do not know where he is but we wish you Allah's blessings in finding him. And if you do find Mukhthar . . . kill him!'

She led her stricken sister away, closing the door behind them.

Poppy was crestfallen, and Rangwalla sensed her anguish. 'I will keep searching,' he promised. 'I will find him.'

'How, Abbas?' said Poppy miserably. 'Even his own wife does not know where he is. And the city is so big! How do we find one little boy in a haystack of twenty million?' Tears lurked at the corners of her eyes.

'Perhaps we must trust in God,' suggested Rangwalla. He waited, then said, gently, 'We must go to the school. Lobo will be expecting us for this evening's assembly.'

Principal Augustus Lobo, veteran of innumerable Christmases in the city of Mumbai, reflected that in all his years he had rarely presided over a Christmas Eve Vespers such as this. Over those long years he had come to believe himself inured to the manifold pranks and mischiefs of his young wards, but recent events had convinced him that the world had indeed changed, and not for the better. He had always looked upon himself as a shepherd, tending his flock through their treacherous formative years to a profitable manhood from which both they and society might benefit.

But now he saw a blight taking hold of his young wards, the blight of modernity, where the pursuit of personal gain at any cost was all-serving, all-conquering.

He looked down now upon his gathered congregation with a stern expression. 'Students of St Xavier, it is with a heavy heart that I stand before you today. At a time usually reserved for veneration of our Saviour, I am forced instead to discuss a most unsavoury matter.' Lobo's gnarled fingers whitened around the edges of the lectern. 'Three nights ago something of great value was stolen from the office of the school secretary. I will not divulge the exact nature of the stolen goods, but the perpetrators of this deed know that of which I refer.' He punctuated this statement by thumping the lectern, startling Brother Machado who had been looking on nervously from the wings. 'I speak now to those villains, those goondas! . . . Your efforts have been in vain! I have this very day received a revised set of the stolen items, prepared in advance against this very contingency. These new items will now take precedence over those that were stolen. In short, sirs, the originals are now worthless.' Lobo washed his petrified audience with a glare of intense disapprobation. 'I have placed the new items in the exact same place from which the originals were taken. I dare the thieves to try and take them again.' Another grimace. 'If you have a shred of decency, sirs, you will hand yourselves over to me. Did you think you could hoodwink old Lobo? Hah! I have been besting the likes of you since before your fathers were born.'

At the rear of the assembly hall Poppy leaned in towards Rangwalla. 'Do you think it will work?' she whispered.

'I do not know,' replied Rangwalla. 'But if Wadia is as arrogant as I think he is, he will not be able to resist the challenge.'

'And if he takes the bait, you will catch him red-handed?'

'No,' said Rangwalla. 'If he takes the bait I will not need to. He will be caught but it will not be *red*-handed.'

LEOPOLD CAFÉ

On those rare occasions that Chopra ventured to the south Mumbai district of Colaba he usually made a point of looking in on his old friend and batchmate Inspector Girish Poolchand.

Poolchand, a shiftless sot who had scraped his way through police training school with Chopra all those years ago, had subsequently secured a plum posting in the Colaba station to which he had clung with a limpet-like tenacity for over two decades.

Chopra had long since given up trying to convert Poolchand to the ranks of the assiduous.

Poolchand was one of many in the service who swam with the prevailing currents, waiting only to be washed up on the beach of retirement nirvana with a full pension and no further responsibilities in life save the consumption of cheap whisky and the recounting of ever-taller tales from his disingenuously remembered police years.

Whenever they met, the two men would pat each other on the back and ask after each other's families, before swiftly repairing to the renowned Leopold Café where Poolchand was a fixture in the notorious upstairs bar. Here he would partake daily of a liquid lunch safely hidden from the inconvenient eyes of those dining below – which often included his seniors at the station – behind a wall of smoked glass.

Today, however, Chopra sat alone in the bustling restaurant.

For the first time in years he had not called upon his old sparring partner. His business today was a matter for himself and the party he had persuaded – with considerable effort – to meet him here.

As a wheezing ceiling fan swirled lazily above him, Chopra found a low-wattage anxiety oozing around his colon. He was not one to second-guess himself, but the coming encounter unnerved him. His only consolation was that the meeting would take place on familiar ground. After all, didn't they say that choosing the terrain was half the battle?

As he looked around at the evening rush, he reflected, not for the first time, that Leopold's – once a rutputty eat-and-go joint – was now a bona fide Mumbai institution.

Located in the bustling heart of Colaba, the café – one hundred and forty-one years old and counting – was one of the few places in the city where foreigners and locals of all ranks, faiths and backgrounds regularly congregated. In the past Leopold's had enjoyed a dubious reputation. For many years it had operated as a sort of 'free zone', profitably ignored by the authorities, a den of genteel iniquity where all manner of shady characters conducted their business, and where tourists and Mumbaikers alike came to purchase drugs or organise illicit liaisons. And this in spite of the café's indiscreet location directly opposite the Colaba police station.

Recently, however, things had changed.

Ever since the terror attacks that claimed one hundred and sixty-four lives in Mumbai, Leopold's had become something of a beacon, a symbol of the city's indomitable spirit. The restaurant had been one of the first places attacked by the gunmen – ten people had died in the café itself – but the owners, uncowed, had reopened for business within days, sending a message to all those who thought terror could dampen the exuberance of the subcontinent's greatest city.

As Chopra looked around the bustling restaurant he noted, once again, the bullet holes in the mirrored walls, left there as a mark of respect by the café's owners for those who had fallen. The bullet holes were a reminder to all who dined at Leopold's of how ephemeral life could be.

'All right, Chopra, what the devil is this all about?'

Chopra turned to find Detective Chief Inspector Maxwell Bomberton looming over him. Bomberton looked hot and bothered.

'And a good day to you too, DCI Bomberton.'

Bomberton did not seem overly impressed by the fact that it was Christmas Eve in the city of Mumbai. There was a distinct absence of Yuletide spirit emanating from his robust frame. 'Well, man, don't just sit there, spit it out!'

Chopra stiffened. 'Garewal had nothing to do with the theft of the crown,' he said woodenly.

Bomberton glared at him, then collapsed into the seat opposite. A ceiling fan ruffled the few remaining wisps of hair on his prominent pink dome, which appeared to have been recently sunburnt.

Around them the din of the evening crowd rose and fell in a dozen languages. Food smells wafted from the kitchen as red-clad waiters buzzed between the cheap tables, where menus were trapped beneath squares of ancient, pock-marked glass. An attempt had been made to add a modicum of Christmas cheer to the proceedings – tinsel had been wrapped around the ceiling fans and a Christmas tree lurked behind the juice bar. Thankfully, the owners had drawn the line at hiring a pseudo-Santa to harangue the customers.

Chopra had considered his present course of action carefully.

The card that he had found at Bulbul Kanodia's home had convinced him that at 11 p.m. the next day the 'long-lost national treasure' would be present at 'The King's Ransom'. It had not taken him long to discover that this was not, in the strictest sense, a place.

The King's Ransom was a boat.

A yacht, in fact, that belonged to one of the richest men in the country, industrialist Mohan Kartik.

This fact had bemused Chopra at first. Surely Mohan Kartik – billionaire entrepreneur and business advisor to the Indian government – could not be involved in the theft of the Koh-i-Noor diamond? And then his mood had darkened as he reflected that greed knew no boundaries and avarice was a law unto itself. There was no rule that said a billionaire could not covet something as priceless as the Koh-i-Noor. Only time would tell how dirty Mohan Kartik's hands were in this affair.

Earlier in the day Chopra had taken the time to visit another old acquaintance, Kishore Dubey, an investigative journalist at the *Mid Day*, Mumbai's daily tabloid. Dubey had all the latest celebrity gossip at his fingertips and the nose of a bloodhound. For many years he had worked for a provincial paper in the Andheri suburbs. As a consequence he had been useful to Chopra, on occasion, when he had needed the help of the local papers.

Now Dubey took the time to piece together a profile of Mohan Kartik for him. Inevitably, the former policeman had had to hold at bay his old friend's insatiable curiosity. It was too early to even hint at what he was up to, but Dubey was a veteran newsman and not about to let Chopra off without extorting a promise that if anything came of whatever it was that he was investigating, Dubey would get the exclusive.

Returning from the bustling *Mid Day* offices Chopra had realised that if he aspired to make any further progress in his investigation then he had to get on board *The King's Ransom*, a proposition that, under the best of circumstances, presented a considerable challenge. The more he had thought about the problem the more he had come to realise that he could not achieve his goal without assistance.

'OK, let's have it.' Bomberton slouched in his seat like a shaggy hound that had just returned from an unsuccessful hunt.

Chopra frowned. 'I was thinking we might *share* intelligence.'

Bomberton removed a handkerchief and mopped his face. 'Keep talking, Chopra. I haven't heard anything yet to make me want to share even this sweaty handkerchief with you.'

Chopra stared at the bellicose Englishman, then nodded stiffly. 'Very well, I will begin . . . I believe that the theft was carried out by a gang. One of the members of the gang was this man.' He set the photocopy of Prakash Yadav's driving licence that Rangwalla had given him down on to the table. 'He is the one who placed the gas canisters inside the Kali statue in the Tata Gallery.'

Bomberton squinted angrily at the photograph. 'I won't bother to ask how you cottoned on to Yadav. I suppose you went after the personnel records, same as us. We've been looking high and low for the man. Rao is determined to prove that this Yadav fellow is one of Garewal's accomplices. But the man is a ghost. He simply doesn't exist.'

'I do not think you will find him,' said Chopra. 'Whoever he really is.'

'You're probably right. If I was the mastermind behind this I wouldn't leave a loose end like Yadav alive.'

'Then there is this man . . .' Chopra now set down a photo of Bulbul Kanodia from the police file Sub-Inspector Surat had delivered to him. 'He was in the Tata Gallery when it was hit. He is a former jewel fence. Now he runs a chain of jewellery stores.'

Bomberton slowly shook his head. 'We vetted everyone in the gallery. None of the names we were given by the ticket office came back with a criminal record.'

'That is not possible. Kanodia spent two years in Mumbai Central Prison. I myself arrested him. I have his old case file.'

'He came up clean when we looked.'

Chopra was perplexed. 'How can this be? Unless . . .' He drummed his fingers on the tabletop. 'Someone has expunged his record.' The revelation should not have surprised him. It was one more brick in the case against Kanodia. How else could his sudden reversal of fortunes be explained? From convicted criminal to renowned businessman in the blink of an eye. Even in Mumbai this was no mean feat. And yet a clean chit was not difficult to obtain, not if you had the money and influence of the Chauhan gang behind you . . . At least he understood now why Rao had not brought Kanodia in for further interrogation.

'Wouldn't be hard to arrange in this country,' said Bomberton dryly, mirroring Chopra's thoughts. He mopped his brow again. 'Look, just because the man had a criminal record, doesn't mean he stole the crown. Maybe he had his record cleaned up because he didn't want the smell following him around. Not after he went straight.'

'He did not go straight,' Chopra said stiffly. 'It is my belief that Kanodia's jewellery chain is financed by organised criminals. It is my belief that they are behind the theft of the Koh-i-Noor.'

A waiter arrived and demanded an order. Bomberton bristled at the man's surly tone, but Chopra placed a restraining hand on his arm. 'The waiters here are very rude. It is part of the charm. Think of them as actors.'

Bomberton glared at the man before ordering a beer. Chopra asked for a lime water.

Around them the restaurant's patrons raised a din that spilled out into the crowded Colaba Causeway where hawkers sold all manner of kitsch – silk scarves from Shimla, ornate hookahs from the Middle East, Kashmiri carpets, alabaster deities, pirated DVDs, sequinned handbags, Kolhapuri sandals, miniature Taj Mahals, brass bugles and even antique gramophones.

'I went to Kanodia's house today,' Chopra continued. 'I found this.' He dug out the invitation and handed it to Bomberton.

The detective squinted at the card then threw it back on the table. 'This could be anything.'

'I believe this card refers to the Koh-i-Noor diamond. I believe Kanodia has invited possible buyers of the diamond to *The King's Ransom* to negotiate its sale. *The King's Ransom* is a yacht. It belongs to one of India's richest men.'

Bomberton's blue eyes evaluated Chopra. Then he picked up the card and took a second look.

Eventually he dug out a packet of cigarettes from his linen jacket and lit one. He blew a cloud of smoke over the table, then said, 'Let's say I go along with your theory. So, on the day of the theft Kanodia's accomplices break in through the rear door of the Tata Gallery using explosives they may or may not have brought with them, retrieve the gas canisters from inside the Kali statue, set them off, wait for everyone to pass out, then break into the display case—'

'Do you know how they did that?' Chopra interrupted. 'That is something I have not figured out.'

Bomberton seemed to weigh up whether or not to tell Chopra, then shrugged. 'Do you know what a resonance frequency is?'

Chopra shook his head.

'Every material has one. It is the point at which a material will achieve maximum oscillation – or vibration – when acted upon by a force. Have you ever seen an opera singer shatter a glass using her voice?'

'I thought that was just a myth.'

'It's no myth. McTavish believes that the thieves used something similar. A device that created a high-pitched sound attuned to the exact structure of the glass in that particular type of display case. An unfortunate defect that the manufacturer will no doubt live to regret.'

Chopra remembered the sound he had heard just before passing out, a sound just on the edge of hearing, a sound that had set his teeth on edge.

'So this device was also in the Kali statue?'

'Possibly. Or else the thieves brought it in with them. It could have been concealed in any small object with an in-built speaker. A mobile phone, a camera—'

'But those were taken away from us before we entered the museum.'

'Something else then.'

Chopra thought about this. And then he recalled what had happened in the queue to pass through the metal scanner to enter the museum. The individual he would later identify as Bulbul Kanodia had argued with the Force One guards. He had insisted on taking in his asthma inhaler . . . At least this explained why Kanodia was personally present in the gallery at the time of the heist. And yet there were still questions to be answered, questions about exactly how other aspects of the plot had been carried out . . .

'Have you traced the gas canisters and explosive?'

Bomberton snorted. 'Cat in hell's chance. McTavish says the chemical signatures are generic. Both the gas and the plastic explosive could have been picked up for a song from any black market in Mumbai. Rao tells me your bazaars are awash with Israeli surplus.'

'What about the funds that went into Garewal's account? Rao said one million rupees were deposited just after the robbery.'

Bomberton tapped ash into a clay bowl full of mango pickle swimming in mustard oil. 'Hawala account set up in Dubai. The account was opened with cash by an unidentified party using forged papers. That's where the trail runs cold.'

'Many Mumbai gangsters have operations in Dubai,' Chopra said. Here was one more link in the chain leading back to the Chauhan gang.

The waiter returned with their order. He handed Chopra his lime water, then slammed a frosted beer mug on to the table, spilling some onto the glass tabletop. With a last surly look he departed.

Bomberton picked up the pitcher, took a long swallow, then wiped the froth from his moustache with the back of a meaty hand.

'I think we should work together,' Chopra said, eventually. 'I have a plan.'

'Rao won't work with you.'

'I was not referring to Rao.'

Bomberton sniffed. 'Hah! What makes you think *I* want to work with you?'

'What is your opinion of Rao?'

Bomberton shot a dark look down his nose. 'Rao is the worst officer I have ever met. The man is an imbecile. I wouldn't leave him to tie his own shoelaces. When the Commissioner dropped in yesterday I thought Rao was going to do somersaults. He is convinced Garewal did it. I've watched him trying to sweat Garewal for days. To be frank, the things Rao has done to Garewal . . .' Bomberton's voice tailed off. 'But I'm an outsider here. What do I know about your methods?' His stomach suddenly gurgled. 'Sorry. Local cuisine's been playing havoc with the pipes. Bowels in uproar.' He planted his elbows on the table and leaned forward. 'Look, even though Rao is a gold-plated idiot it doesn't mean he's barking up the wrong tree with Garewal. I mean we *did* find the damned crown in his home. Now you come up with this Kanodia angle . . . I grant you, you have something interesting there. But it's a long way from interesting to conclusive.' He paused as he was overcome by a hacking cough. Chopra heard the nicotine rattling around the British policeman's lungs. When the cough had abated he drew deeply on his cigarette again, before continuing: 'Nevertheless, I am prepared to hedge my bets. Frankly speaking, our investigation hasn't turned up much. We've rounded up all the usual suspects, combed the diamond bazaars, and put the thumbscrews on every informant in the city. Nothing, not a sniff. I cannot – I will not – leave this country without the Koh-i-Noor diamond.

The crown without the Koh-i-Noor is worthless.' Bomberton looked glum. 'A busted flush, Chopra. That's all I've got.'

Chopra's face was expressionless. 'We agree on one thing, at least . . . Rao is an imbecile.' He tapped the invitation, still lying on the table between them. 'I am going to follow Kanodia to the yacht tomorrow tonight.'

Bomberton slugged his beer again before setting it down. 'Sounds like you're asking me out on a date.'

Chopra bristled. 'It is your choice. With you or without you, I will pursue my objective.'

Bomberton flicked his cigarette into his beer mug before lumbering to his feet. 'Don't get so worked up. I didn't say I wasn't coming.'

'Then I will meet you beneath the Gateway of India at 10 p.m. tomorrow. And remember to dress appropriately.'

Bomberton glowered. 'What's that supposed to mean?'

'I mean we must not look like policemen if we hope to board *The King's Ransom*.'

'You mean we're going in disguise?'

Chopra regarded the hulking Englishman. It would be quite a task disguising Bomberton, he thought. Like trying to disguise the Taj Mahal. 'Yes,' he agreed. 'Now you are getting the idea.'

THE CULPRITS ARE UNMASKED

Augustus Lobo, principal of the St Xavier Catholic School for Boys, peered down from his lectern, his brow furrowed into an expression of intense disappointment. The gathered boys stared back up at him in collective bewilderment. 'Gentlemen, it is with the profoundest sorrow that I stand before you this morning. Usually, at this time each year, it would be my singular honour to lead you in Christmas Mass.

'Alas, it is not to enjoin you in prayer that I am here today, but to deliver the most scandalous news possible. Not twenty-four hours ago I stood before you and informed you of the reprehensible actions of a group of n'er-do-wells who had seen fit to besmirch the honour of our great institution by stealing school property from the office of Mr Banarjee. I told you that I had replaced the items in question. I openly challenged these goondas to attempt to recreate their crime, not believing that anyone would be so reprehensible, so *audacious* as to actually plunge once more into the dark pool of moral turpitude.

'Alas, I was wrong. Lightning has indeed struck twice.' Lobo clutched the lectern and leaned forward, fixing his students with a baleful look. 'I now call upon the perpetrators of this outrage to recall their teachings. We are more than an institution of learning, gentlemen. We are an organisation that stands for something. Christian values. Honesty and integrity. That is what St Xavier expects from each and every one of you. I ask the guilty parties to step forward and confess. Admit your guilt and your punishment will go lightly. For forgiveness is also one of our virtues.'

A pin-drop silence echoed around the hall.

'Very well,' growled Lobo. 'Brother Machado, if you please.'

One hundred and eighty heads turned to watch Brother Noel Machado draw the thick curtains over the stained-glass windows of the assembly hall, pitching the vast room into darkness. From this darkness came the disembodied voice of the principal.

'What I have not told you, gentlemen, is that last night a trap was set. My challenge to the culprits was merely a ruse. You see, when the thieves returned to the scene of the crime, they once again broke into Banarjee's safe. However, this time, unbeknownst to them, a hidden device had been installed. When the safe swung open, this device was activated, releasing an invisible cloud of particles into the air, particles that clung to the perpetrators of the crime. These particles cannot be seen in natural light. In order to observe them, one must employ *ultraviolet* light. Permit me to demonstrate . . . Brother Machado!'

There was the sound of a switch being flicked, and suddenly, from the stage, there blazed a bank of eerie blue fluorescents. Row by row the light swept over the assembled boys who stared in puzzled astonishment from one to another . . . And then, halfway along the tenth row, the light stopped.

'Wadia! Look at your face, man!'

'What?' Raj Wadia looked around wildly. 'What about my face?'

'It's bright green! You're glowing!'

'And you too, Fonseca. And look at your hands. They're glowing too!'

'Joshi's got it too. They've all got it!'

'And look at Baig. He's practically radioactive!'

At the rear of the hall Poppy clapped her hands. 'It worked!' she exclaimed, delightedly. 'It really worked! How did you know?'

'It is a recent technique that is being employed to safeguard valuable items in the homes of the rich,' explained Rangwalla. 'Chopra told me about it a while back when orders came down that we should be on the lookout for stolen merchandise tagged by this method. Apparently it is all the rage in western countries.'

'Well, it was a very good idea. Like you said, those boys have been caught, but not *red*-handed.' Poppy sighed. 'But what happens now?'

Rangwalla shrugged. 'That is not my business. The school will have to discipline them. It is hardly a police matter.' He winced. 'Not that I am a policeman, any more.'

Poppy patted him on the shoulder. 'No,' she said. 'You are better than a policeman now. You are a private detective, and a very good one at that.'

Augustus Lobo paced agitatedly behind the desk in his office, his hands clasped behind him, his cassock swishing against the flagstones beneath his feet. 'Well, gentlemen, what have you got to say for yourselves?'

Raj Wadia, Anoop Joshi, George Fonseca and Rafeeq Baig stood to attention before the principal's desk. Joshi and Baig hung their heads, finding something of supreme interest on the floor. Fonseca blubbered quietly into his collar, a trail of snot snaking down from his nose to his upper lip. Only Wadia remained imperious, staring coldly ahead, as if apart from proceedings. At the back of the room Rangwalla and Poppy looked on.

Lobo turned abruptly, causing Fonseca to jump. 'Wadia, you are the leader of this gang. I demand an explanation.'

Wadia maintained his stony silence.

'Speak, boy! I order you to speak!'

Silence.

Lobo paced the office again, before wheeling back on them. 'By all accounts you are very bright boys. What need had you to steal those papers? Answer me!'

Further silence, broken only by another sob from Fonseca.

Lobo's eyebrows knitted themselves together in fury. 'If I do not have an explanation, you are all finished!' he thundered. 'You will be expelled, booted out, expunged! I will summon your parents and we will have it out. Do you think grand larceny is a trivial matter? Well, do you?'

Joshi and Baig exchanged glances, then shook their heads. Fonseca let out a loud wail of anguish and buried his face in his hands. Wadia's lip curled in a supercilious smile.

'Sometimes, I long for the old days,' growled Lobo. 'A good thrashing, that's what you young goondas need.'

Poppy, who had been watching the pitiable Fonseca and had found herself overcome by a sudden mist of sympathy, now spoke. 'Sir, perhaps I might talk with them for a moment?'

'What else is there to say, Mrs Chopra?' said Lobo gruffly. 'These rapscallions have desecrated the good name of St Xavier. They have undermined everything we have attempted to teach them. They are goondas – no more, no less.'

'Just a few minutes, sir.'

Lobo stared at her crossly before throwing up his hands. 'Very well. Machado, come with me.'

After the two men had left, Poppy faced the boys. 'I know that you are frightened,' she said gently. 'Even those of you who are pretending that you are not.' She stared closely at Wadia, whose cheeks flushed.

'But what I also know is that you are children. Children make mistakes. Childhood is the best time for mistakes because you can make up for them. You can learn from them. But first you have to be willing to accept that you have made an error, and you have to be willing to make amends. I will help you, if you are willing to talk to me. I promise that I will not think harshly of you. Everyone deserves a second chance. Will you talk to me?'

She watched as Joshi and Baig exchanged looks again. Fonseca stopped sniffling and wiped a sleeve across his nose, then raised his head to look at her.

And finally, even Wadia turned to stare at her.

'If I am expelled my father will kill me, madam,' sniffed Fonseca.

'My parents will die of shame,' declared Baig.

'I won't even be able to go home,' agreed Joshi.

Wadia said nothing.

'I think there is a way to stop those things from happening,' said Poppy.

Hope flared in the boys' faces.

'Do you really think so, madam?' asked Fonseca, his eyes round behind his spectacles.

'Yes,' affirmed Poppy. 'I really do.' She patted Fonseca on the arm. 'But first you will have to tell me what you have done with dear Father Gonsalves's head.'

Chopra sat in his chair in the courtyard of Poppy's restaurant. Before him, on a stool, lay a heap of manila folders, an almost empty glass of lime water, and his mobile phone, which he had just set down, his ears still ringing with Mrs Roy's dire threats.

Chopra sighed.

The backlog of work on his cases was becoming critical. Mrs Roy was not the only unhappy customer. But what could he do? Between the Koh-i-Noor case, Poppy's missing bust, and looking for Irfan, both he and Rangwalla had been completely swamped. It was not for nothing that he had prised himself away from the Koh-i-Noor investigation and spent Christmas morning catching up with some of his other cases. But the simple truth was that he would need a dozen such mornings to make much headway.

There was nothing to do but grin and bear it.

After all, he could always return the retainers he had accepted. It was not the money that bothered him, anyway. Chopra was loath not to follow through on a commitment. In that sense Mrs Roy had every right to castigate him.

He turned as Poppy and Rangwalla entered the compound.

Chopra recalled the telephone conversation he had had with his wife that morning.

He had been delighted to learn that Rangwalla had been successful in engineering the return of the missing bust. He also knew that following the successful conclusion to the case, Rangwalla and Poppy had once again set off on their quest to locate Irfan.

From his wife's crestfallen expression he realised that they had not been successful.

'No luck?' he said, rising to his feet.

Poppy shook her head, on the verge of tears. 'It is as if he has vanished.'

'You will find him,' said Chopra reassuringly. '*We* will find him.' He put his arm around her and squeezed her shoulders, realising that Poppy was struggling to come to terms with the fact that they might never see Irfan again.

Ganesha, who had been dozing beneath his mango tree, trotted towards them and rubbed his head against Chopra's thigh. 'That's a promise to you both,' said Chopra. 'We *will* find him.'

They decided to have lunch in the courtyard.

Chopra asked Chef Lucknowwallah to set out a table and chairs and to serve up a mix of dishes: aromatic lamb biriyani for Rangwalla, an exotic chicken kolhapuri for himself, and Poppy's favourite, a traditional Maharashtrian pao bhaji – buttered rolls with a spicy vegetarian curry.

The atmosphere was subdued and Poppy seemed to have little appetite. She remarked, more than once, on how miserable it felt not having Irfan around on Christmas Day, sharing lunch with them, horsing around with Ganesha instead of focusing on his food, as he was wont to do. Chopra tried to lighten the atmosphere by asking for more details of the resolution to the missing bust case. This got Poppy talking and he was glad to see a semblance of animation returning to his wife's usually boisterous demeanour.

He listened intently as she explained their efforts, focusing on Rangwalla's successful gambit and how it had flushed out the thieves of Lobo's beloved bust. He found himself shaking his head as he pictured the four boys from St Xavier's stealing the examination papers – not once, but twice! What arrogance! But perhaps that was the problem with the modern generation. They simply did not grasp that there could be consequences to their actions. They seemed to operate from a misplaced sense of invulnerability.

It was galling to Chopra that one day this brigade of louts would be running the country.

'Well done, Rangwalla,' said Chopra, eventually. He was genuinely pleased. 'I knew hiring you would be a good idea.' He reached down and picked up the stack of folders from the stool beside his chair. 'Here is your reward. You can get on with this lot. Start by following Mrs Roy's husband around. I want to know if that old duffer is drinking his lunch. When you find out, let Mrs Roy know immediately.'

'Yes, sir,' said Rangwalla.

'Excuse me, Poppy Madam, there are some people here to see you.'

The three of them turned to see Rosie Pinto leading four youths into the courtyard.

Chopra recognised the uniform of the St Xavier Catholic School for Boys. Having just heard the story of the nefarious goings-on at the school he found himself bristling at the sudden presence of these four young hooligans. But then he saw that the boys were subdued, and advanced towards them behind expressions of intense contriteness.

He wondered what they were doing here, on Christmas Day.

'Madam,' said Raj Wadia stiffly, addressing Poppy, 'we have been sent here by our parents. We wish to say something to you.' He licked his lips and exchanged glances with Fonseca, Baig and Joshi. 'We wish to thank you for saving us from expulsion and for convincing Principal Lobo to give us a second chance.'

A smile appeared on Poppy's face. 'You are all most welcome.'

Fonseca, who was hopping from foot to foot, suddenly surged forward and clasped Poppy in a hug. 'We will never do anything like that again!'

An astonished Poppy finally extricated herself from the overcome young man. 'I know that you won't,' she said. 'You will all go on and make me very proud.'

After the boys had left, Rangwalla turned to Poppy. 'What exactly did you say to Lobo to get them off?'

'I merely reminded him what it is to be young,' Poppy told him. 'We all make errors of judgement. Everyone deserves a second chance. And besides, we place too much pressure on our young people to do well in exams. Do you know how many children committed suicide last year in our country because they could not meet the expectations of their parents? We must all learn to be a little more forgiving.'

'Wise words,' agreed Rangwalla with feeling. He had never had much time for exams and recalled the many beatings his father had given him for his poor results.

Chopra reflected once again on his opinion that many of the younger generation in India were becoming afflicted by the vices of arrogance and irresponsibility. Clearly, his wife did not share his opinion. Was he being too harsh? Hadn't he been young once? After all, who was he to judge? He had made mistakes too as a young man. What gave him the right to think ill of others?

Nevertheless, he felt that there was a sense of entitlement amongst a certain type of privileged youngster that was breeding the wrong sort of brashness. Not the kind that promoted entrepreneurialism and endeavour and might benefit both individual and nation, but the sort of loutish behaviour that led to acts of foolhardiness at best and sheer irresponsibility at worst.

Little did Chopra know then that, in just a few short hours, he was to encounter the ultimate demonstration of this phenomenon.

THE ELEPHANT CATCHER

Chef Lucknowwallah snored. Each stentorian exhalation gently lifted the damp handkerchief that he had placed over his face, and then just as gently set it down again. The dinnertime rush was over and the chef, having partaken of a simple meal of aloo matar – spicy potato and peas – was enjoying a period of quiet recuperation in the restaurant's office before the late-night crowd began to filter in. The air was redolent with the odour of flue-cured Virginia tobacco, a thick cheroot of which he had smoked just before settling himself into Chopra's chair, and which he ordered by the bushel direct from his friend Anmol Mazumdar's plantation in faraway Andhra Pradesh. His doctor had forbidden him from smoking, but what did that old duffer know? The man couldn't even boil an egg.

Lucknowwallah had had a trying few days.

Not only had he been forced to work overtime in order to prepare the spectacular Christmas dinner that they had just finished serving – an undertaking grossly undermined by

Chopra's mother-in-law, causing him more than the usual heartburn – but his sous-chef, young Romesh Goel, for whom he had high hopes, had managed to all but sever a finger whilst filleting a fresh pomfret for Lucknowwallah's Goan seafood masala.

The boy seemed increasingly distracted these days.

The chef had a sneaking suspicion that this was because of Rosie Pinto, his other assistant chef. It had not escaped him how Rosie had been making goo-goo eyes at the pimply-faced young Romesh. Really, these youngsters must think he was blind!

The thought of the burgeoning romance had caused Lucknowwallah to dwell on his own wife, departed these past ten years. The late Mrs Lucknowwallah had been a fiery one, a Mangalorean princess he had swept along on his travels, beguiling her with his fried Goli bajji, against which her prickly persona had proved no defence. In choosing her Lucknowwallah had gone with his heart, refusing the arranged marriage his family had planned for him.

He had never regretted his choice.

His wife and he had fought every day of their marriage, but that was all part and parcel of the great love that they had shared. Thirty good years and two fine sons, married now and vanished abroad. And then he had watched, helplessly, as that invidious traitor cancer had eaten her away, diminishing, day by day, the person he had known and loved since his youth. But that was life. Why get worked up about what you could not control?

The door to the office slammed open, startling Lucknowwallah from his doze. The handkerchief fluttered to the floor as the chef blearily focused on the intruder. It was Rosie Pinto.

'What the devil . . .?'

'Sir! Please come quick! They are trying to steal Ganesha!'

Lucknowwallah burst onto the veranda at the rear of the restaurant just in time to see three coolies hauling Ganesha across the courtyard by a rope that they had dropped around his neck.

The three men were being bellowed at by a fat, dark-skinned man in a navy blue safari suit. Ganesha was resisting with all his might, digging in his heels. But, inexorably, he was being pulled towards the alley that led out onto the main road.

As Lucknowwallah watched, the supervisor leaned in and jabbed Ganesha in the flank with an electric cattle prod. Ganesha immediately let out a bellow of pain, his body convulsing and his hind legs spasming uncontrollably.

As his footing faltered, the men dragged him a further yard.

A curtain of red dropped over the chef's eyes. With a bellow of his own, he charged into the fray, grabbing the supervisor by the lapels of his safari suit. The man's eyes widened in fright and he dropped the cattle prod.

'I am going to teach you a lesson you will never forget!' roared Lucknowwallah, brandishing a fist.

'Don't hit me!' yelped the man. 'I am a government official! I am merely executing an order to take this elephant into detention. If you touch me you will surely go to prison!'

'What the devil are you talking about?' Lucknowwallah's face had flushed and the unusual exertion was causing his heart to gallop wildly in his chest. Out of the corner of his eye he could see Romesh and Rosie on the veranda, expressions of horrified concern pasted on their faces.

The man scrabbled in his breast pocket and pulled out a piece of paper, which he held up to Lucknowwallah's face. 'My name is Kondvilkar. This elephant assaulted a boy. I must take him to the animal detention centre in Pune. By order of the Maharashtra Dangerous Animals Division.'

'This is preposterous! Ganesha wouldn't hurt a fly!'

'That is not for me to say. He will be examined by experts. If God is willing it, he will be returned very soon.'

The chef's mouth fell open, but he realised that he had run out of arguments.

'Please, sir, could you let go of my shirt now?'

Lucknowwallah released Kondvilkar. The big man stepped back, pulled a handkerchief from his pocket, and patted his brow in relief.

'I must inform Chopra,' growled the chef.

'You may inform who you wish,' said Kondvilkar breathily. 'But still the elephant must go with me.'

Lucknowwallah bent down and picked up the electric cattle prod. 'This stays here.'

'But that is government property!'

'Then the government can come and get it.'

It took a further twenty minutes for the struggling coolies to haul Ganesha into the black truck Kondvilkar had brought with him.

As soon as the elephant calf had been manhandled aboard, Kondvilkar clanged the rear doors shut and leaned against them in relief. Ganesha immediately turned and charged the doors – but the truck had been reinforced for bigger and stronger beasts than him.

Lucknowwallah tried one more time to call Chopra. But the man was not answering.

The chef, surrounded by the restaurant's staff, could only watch helplessly as the black truck roared away, the little elephant looking out at them through the mesh grill in forlorn unhappiness.

A white Hindustan Ambassador, long the favoured vehicle of government officials on the subcontinent, honked its way through the press of bodies crowded onto the Apollo Bunder plaza, before grinding to a halt in the shadow of the Gateway of India.

The rear door flew open and Detective Chief Inspector Maxwell Bomberton unfolded his enormous frame from the vehicle's back seat.

A beggar, faster off the mark than his peers, bore down on the Ambassador with a hopeful air, but then recoiled as the hulking, red-faced foreigner turned towards him and pulled a handkerchief from the pocket of his white tuxedo as if drawing a pistol.

'Damn this infernal heat,' muttered Bomberton, mopping his brow. 'It's Christmas Day. It's not supposed to be *hot*.'

'This is India. It is always hot.'

Bomberton turned to see Inspector Ashwin Chopra (Retd) nimbly navigating his way through the late-evening tourist crowd.

'Nice outfit, Chopra,' said Bomberton acidly. 'Who are you supposed to be, exactly? Harry Houdini?'

Chopra looked down at his attire.

He was wearing a crisp white kurta pajama with a sleeve-less black button-down waistcoat. His hair was hidden beneath a grey-furred astrakhan cap. Thick black-framed spectacles covered his eyes.

Chopra had put a great deal of effort into his appearance. In order to pursue the course of action he had chosen he would require a plausible disguise. It was a new kind of policing, one that he'd had to learn since becoming a private investigator. Although initially uncomfortable with the new methods he was forced to employ, he had vowed to himself that he would do whatever it took to pursue the cause of justice. And if that meant having to endure the ignominy of the occasional costume, then so be it. After all, hadn't Basil Rathbone often disguised himself in the course of his inves-tigations as Sherlock Holmes? Why, in *The Spiderwoman*, he had even dressed up – with the aid of a turban and a little lampblack – as a retired Sikh military officer named Rajni Singh in order to ensnare the eponymous femme fatale.

Chopra regarded the Englishman's own efforts.

The white tuxedo with double-breasted waistcoat and scarlet cummerbund straining around Bomberton's ample stomach. The red bow tie. The Sandown cap disguising the bald pate. The monocle.

'Not bad,' he conceded grudgingly, wondering where on earth Bomberton had obtained the outfit.

'Remind me again, who am I supposed to be?'

'Lord Cornwallis,' declared Chopra as Bomberton tugged at his bow tie.

'Lord? Are you trying to insult me? For my sins I am acquainted with more than a few peers of the realm, Chopra, and I can tell you that the only thing they are good for is eating large dinners in the House while they hum and haw about the price of fish. And this monkey suit is making me itch.'

Chopra checked his watch. 'Let's go. And remember, stay in character at all times.'

'Aye, aye, skipper,' muttered Bomberton, giving his colleague the evil eye.

Ganesha paced the rear of the truck, his trunk swishing angrily from side to side and his ears flapping in agitation. In the front of the truck Pramod Kondvilkar twisted his bulk to look through the iron bars partitioning the driver's cabin from the rear.

'Your master should have paid me,' he said morosely. 'Then all this trouble would not be necessary.' He shook his head. 'Always there is one! Why to give everyone a black name by trying to be honest? Who does he think he is? Raja Harishchandra?'

The driver nodded in agreement, then yanked the wheel viciously to the left, skidding the truck around a corner and almost knocking over a handcart piled high with rods of sugar cane.

'Now I will have to do something I do not like,' continued Kondvilkar. 'It is not my fault, you understand. There is simply no room for an elephant in our caging facilities.' He shook his head again. 'I know you cannot understand a word I am saying but it is only fair to tell you that you are going to meet your maker. I have a pit of quicklime prepared for troublesome creatures such as you. Do not worry, you will not be alone. There are plenty of others down there. Mad bulls, stubborn camels, worn-out mules, retired circus bears and, of course, elephants. Plenty of elephants.'

The driver sniggered and glanced back at Ganesha via his mirror. The little elephant had stopped pacing the rear of the truck and was standing stock-still, his attention focused on Kondvilkar.

'It is almost as if he is listening,' said the driver.

'Oh, he is listening, that is for sure,' opined Kondvilkar. 'But he is not understanding. None of them do. Not until the last second when the ground suddenly gives way beneath them, and they realise that they have fallen into the pit of their doom. Such a shame, really. But the state only gives me a small amount to house these creatures. If I were to actually spend it on cages what would I keep for myself? I must eat too, yes?'

'We must all eat,' nodded the driver philosophically.

Kondvilkar shuffled and reached into his back pocket to dig out a battered tin tray. He plucked a pinch of snuff from the tray and inserted it violently into his nose. Then he snorted deeply, tilted his head back and closed his eyes. 'Ahhh!'

The driver glanced at his boss, then turned his eyes back to the road.

They had moved out of the crowded Sahar area and were now passing through Mahakali Caves. This was a poor enclave – the slums of the suburbs were only a little way down the road.

The driver, whose name was Namdev, knew the way to the quicklime pit. He had been there many times. It was located in a half-finished building in an area of abandoned construction. There were many such ruins blighting the city, the sad remnants of the dreams of avaricious developers who had overreached themselves or failed to placate the planning authorities with the requisite bribes.

A garland of sweet lime and chilli swung from the mirror, a good luck charm. Namdev's fingers tapped out a tune from the latest Bollywood blockbuster on the steering wheel.

Behind the humming driver a coiled grey shape snaked between the iron bars sectioning off the rear cabin. With a sudden dart Ganesha wrapped his trunk around the driver's scrawny throat and yanked back as hard as he could.

The effect was electrifying.

Namdev yelped in alarm, his hands flying from the steering wheel to his throat, his legs flailing wildly. His foot caught the accelerator and the truck bucked forward, swerving across the road. Pedestrians and animals dived for cover. A limbless beggar on a wheeled tray suddenly sprouted legs and ran for his life. A pair of tethered goats bleated in terror, snapped their ropes, and hurdled a handcart loaded with rolls of cotton. A macaque gnawing on a rotten mango by the side of the road threw the bruised fruit at the onrushing vehicle and shot up a lime tree, howling with rage.

The truck hurtled through a pyramid of straw baskets and a waist-high mound of rotting vegetation, then ploughed headlong over a concrete drainage pipe, careening into a series of rolls until it struck a solitary brick wall, the only remnant of an ancient dwelling.

Finally, it skidded to a drawn-out halt, upside down, sparks flying, its undercarriage covered in bricks from the demolished wall.

For a long instant there was only a creaking silence, then a crow, rudely dislodged from the rubbish mound, fluttered onto the truck's exhaust pipe and began to peck furiously at the rear right tyre.

A few moments later the rear doors of the truck, now hanging loose from their moorings, swung open and the tip of a trunk emerged.

Ganesha stood for a moment, trembling on unsteady legs and blinking in the glow of the evening streetlamps. Then he shook his head violently from side to side as if to clear it.

Finally, somewhat recovered from his ordeal, he proceeded to move down the road at a brisk trot.

Behind him a chorus of groans emanated from the driver's cabin of the upturned truck where Kondvilkar and Namdev were gracelessly arranged in a tangle of bruised and battered limbs.

THE KING'S RANSOM

The pigeon waddled cautiously closer, its beady eyes glittering at the crumbs of bhel puri, scattered by tourists swarming around the plaza.

'Gerroutofit!'

Bomberton's shoe struck the pigeon and it flapped awkwardly away, squawking in indignation.

Chopra turned from where he had been leaning against the seawall.

Twenty metres below, an undulating expanse of turgid water lapped against the moss-covered bricks of the wall. Carelessly discarded junk rode up on a succession of shallow wavelets sweeping in from the deep harbour where, on the far horizon, a line of oil refineries were anchored. Beyond the refineries lay the Arabian Sea, dark and unbearably exotic, stretching all the way to the coast of Africa.

On the other side of the road, beneath a line of plane trees, late-night tourists wandered along the promenade. A caparisoned tonga jangled past, a foreign couple in the back craning their necks up at the magnificent Taj Palace Hotel.

Chopra stuffed his binoculars into the pocket of his waistcoat.

They had been monitoring the harbour for almost an hour. The silhouette of *The King's Ransom* bobbed gently on the water.

'I have been watching the jetties,' Chopra announced. 'A number of private boats have sailed out to the yacht.'

'Well, do *you* have a private boat?' asked Bomberton gruffly, eyeing the pigeon, who had settled on the seawall and was glaring back at him defiantly.

'No.'

'Then what's the point of telling me?' he said crossly.

'I have a plan,' responded Chopra calmly.

'I'll bet you do,' muttered the Englishman.

DCI Bomberton was feeling distinctly ill at ease. He was a direct man, a man of action. All this cloak-and-dagger business was, to his way of thinking, simply a form of convoluted prevarication.

Bomberton came from a long line of military men. Indeed, his ancestor, the redoubtable Sir Mallory Bomberton, had distinguished the family crest at the Battle of Balaclava back in 1854, charging – together with the rest of the doomed protagonists of the Light Brigade – directly into the Russian guns with only a cavalry sword to cover his modesty.

That was the way to do things. Up and at 'em and hang the consequences! What was the point of all this skulking about?

Chopra walked through the arch of the Gateway of India, the eighty-five-foot-tall monument built to commemorate the visit of King George V a century earlier, his first visit to India as King-Emperor of the subcontinent. In the years since it had come to symbolise the city itself and was besieged day and night by locals and tourists alike.

On the far side of the Gateway he stopped and looked out over the harbour. During the day, the harbour was a bustling panorama of yachts, rowing boats, dhows, fishing vessels, tankers, cargo barges and tourist cruisers. At this time of night the ragtag armada had been berthed, and bobbed gently on the black water waiting to be called to arms once again the following morning.

A full moon shone down from the clear night sky above, its reflection smeared wide over the water.

He walked down a flight of concrete steps onto one of the five jetties that radiated out below the Gateway. From his vantage point he could see a trio of tourist boats moored close by. The nearest of the vessels was painted a gaudy sky blue, with a ring of tyres strung around the hull, and the name *Elephanta Adventurer* painted in white just below the port gunwale.

'Hello!' Chopra shouted. '*Elephanta Adventurer*! Is there anyone aboard?'

He continued to hail the vessel until, eventually, a pot-bellied man in a string vest and dhoti emerged from the wheelhouse, blearily wiping sleep from his eyes. 'Why are you making such a racket?' groused the man. 'Can't you see I am trying to sleep?'

'We require the services of your boat,' declared Chopra.

The man stopped scratching his belly and stared at him incredulously. 'You want to go to the Elephanta Caves? Do you know what time it is? Are you drunk, friend?'

'We do not wish to go to the caves,' clarified Chopra. 'We wish to be taken out into the harbour.'

'What for?' asked the man suspiciously.

'I will tell you on the way.'

The man folded his arms. 'Are you smugglers? I run a clean ship, friend.'

'Smugglers!' spluttered Bomberton. 'Why you—'

'We wish to be taken out to *The King's Ransom*,' interrupted Chopra.

The man turned and squinted at the dark silhouette of the big yacht, then looked back at Chopra with an evaluating expression. 'Five hundred rupees,' he said eventually.

'Your signboard says one hundred,' growled Bomberton, pointing at a wooden placard on the boat's mainmast upon which was painted 'AMAZING BEST ELEPHANTA TOURS ONLY RS 100/-'.

'Yes. And your face says you are up to no good,' scowled the man. 'Five hundred.'

'Now listen here—' began Bomberton.

'It is a deal,' said Chopra.

The King's Ransom was berthed deep in the harbour, well away from any other vessels.

Earlier in the day Chopra had spent some time revisiting the research dossier that his journalist friend Kishore Dubey had prepared for him. He had learned a great deal.

The yacht was one of the largest and most luxurious private boats in the world, inaugurated a year ago by billionaire Mohan Kartik at a gala ceremony attended by a clutch of celebrities including the state's Chief Minister. Almost four hundred feet in length, the opulent vessel boasted five decks, twenty cabins, a private gym, garage and helipad, as well as capacity for one hundred guests and a crew of forty.

By anyone's standards *The King's Ransom* was a veritable ocean-going palace.

As the enormous vessel hove into view he noted the dazzling array of lights that lit up the yacht's superstructure. Music drifted across the water.

A party was going on.

The *Elephanta Adventurer* chugged to a standstill at the yacht's stern, where a ship-wide staircase of shallow steps fell to a landing apron.

A number of white-liveried crew milling on the apron stared in disbelief at the tourist boat as it clanked gently alongside.

'We are coming aboard!' yelled Chopra.

The crew exchanged glances. He did not wait for them to protest. Instead, he threw the gangplank over the side of the boat and scrambled across onto the yacht, Bomberton close behind.

Chopra turned and waved at the captain of the *Elephanta Adventurer*, who was staring open-mouthed at the magnificent vessel dwarfing his own. 'You may go.'

The captain scowled, then returned to the wheelhouse.

Chopra and Bomberton watched as the little boat chugged away, a cloud of diesel fumes drifting in its wake.

'Excuse me, sirs, but this is a private party. You cannot stay.'

The two men turned. A prim-faced steward in a starched white uniform and a peaked cap was staring at them. He seemed visibly upset.

'Of course it is a private party, you buffoon,' growled Bomberton. 'Do you think I would be here if the whole world were invited?'

The steward stood his ground, weathering Bomberton's glare. 'Sir, I must request to see an invitation.'

Bomberton reached into his tuxedo and took out the card Chopra had discovered at Bulbul Kanodia's home. 'By God, man, you are an even bigger fool than you look.' He thrust the card at the harried steward. 'Now get out of my way.'

'But, sir, this is only one card. What about your colleague?'

'Colleague?' Bomberton looked around, mystified. Then his face folded into another scowl. 'This isn't my colleague, you imbecile. This is my manservant.'

'Manservant?'

'Yes. Manservant. Are you deaf?'

'But, sir, we cannot allow servants inside.'

Bomberton drew himself up to his full height and loomed over the stricken steward. 'Have you any idea who I am? Cornwallis is the name. Descendant of *the* Cornwallis, former Governor-General of India. Name ring a bell? I am an Englishman, sir, and an Englishman

272

does not go anywhere without his manservant. Do I make myself clear?'

The steward quailed beneath Bomberton's wrath. 'Yes, sir,' he mumbled, conceding defeat.

'Good. Now kindly desist from making a nuisance of yourself and make way.'

'One more thing, sir,' squeaked the steward. 'Your masks.'

'Masks?'

'Yes, sir. This is a masked event. You were not told?'

Bomberton's mouth flapped open. 'Of course I was told. I simply couldn't be bothered to bring one along.'

'Not to worry, sir,' gasped the steward desperately. 'We have made provision.'

He turned to a table behind him and extracted two black velvet eye-masks from a box.

Grumbling, Bomberton snatched one from the steward's hand, almost yanking the man over.

As Chopra pulled on his mask, he thought: of course – for something like this, masks would be both fitting and necessary.

'How do I look?' said Bomberton.

'Sir is looking most dashing!' declared the steward, eager to preserve the remaining shreds of his tattered dignity.

'Splendid!' said Bomberton, walloping the man on the shoulder. 'We will make a manservant of you yet, my good man.'

THE SLUM AT THE END OF THE WORLD

There are few cities in the world where an elephant can move along a busy thoroughfare and attract little or no attention.

Mumbai is one of them.

As Ganesha trotted down the narrow street, shopkeepers sitting cross-legged behind the counters of their hole-in-the-wall shops barely glanced up from their wares, old men smoking beedis did not look around from their games of shatranj and carrom, chattering housewives carrying earthenware jugs under their arms did not miss a beat in their bellicose conversations as they swayed past.

Occasionally, children, inherently more curious than the adults with whom they share the world, would jog beside the little elephant. The more intrepid ones attempted to scale Ganesha's flanks.

Gently, but determinedly, Ganesha discouraged his would-be mahouts.

It is a well-known fact that many animals possess senses that humans have yet to fully understand. For instance, salmon somehow find their way back through thousands of miles of ocean to the exact pond in which they were born in order to breed and die. Silverback grizzly bears can smell a carcass from almost twenty miles away. Millions of monarch butterflies fly to the same grove of trees in Mexico each year, in spite of the fact that each generation only lives for a few months. The mechanics of how this information is passed down is still not clear.

Elephants, too, have their share of unusual abilities.

It has recently been discovered that elephants are able to sense infrasounds – sounds below the level of human hearing – through their feet. This is why elephants are usually the first to sense impending earthquakes or storms, which send silent tremors through the ground. By virtue of their amazing trunks, elephants also possess a truly extraordinary sense of smell.

Had the residents of the Sunder Nagar slum been paying attention they would have noticed that the young elephant passing through their midst occasionally stopped to lift its trunk and sniff at the night air before continuing on its journey.

Ganesha was on a mission. Having escaped the clutches of the nefarious Kondvilkar he now found himself loose in the city. It had been a long time since he had been outside his courtyard at the restaurant without Chopra by his side. At first he had been afraid, but gradually his panic had subsided.

Then he had started to think about what he should do next.

He had just survived a traumatic experience. He wanted nothing more than the company of the people he trusted most in the world, Chopra and Poppy. But his beloved guardians had been very busy of late, and he did not know when they would return to the restaurant.

Ganesha was feeling confused and upset. He was in sore need of his friend, a friend who had recently vanished with no word of explanation. Chopra did not seem to have the answer to this mystery.

Which meant that Ganesha had to solve it himself.

He raised his trunk and sniffed the air again.

The great river of smells parted into individual scents; it was like a magnificent symphony splitting into its constituent notes, each one a sparkling mote twisting in the air.

Ganesha sought the note that was unique to Irfan. It was incredibly faint, but he could sense it.

He lowered his trunk and walked on.

Eventually, the slum began to peter out. Ganesha walked until he began to hear the noise of passing traffic. He had reached the Jogeshwari-Vikhroli Link Road, the JVLR. For a moment he paused, watching the wall of honking, clanking, hooting vehicles roaring by in glorious Technicolor. A truck shuddered past, belching a cloud of fumes from its exhaust. A hurled beer bottle shattered next to Ganesha's foot, startling him and eliciting a soft bugle of fright.

The little elephant flapped his ears determinedly, put his head down, and bundled across the road and into the darkness beyond, an area known as Ganesh Nagar, a barren wilderness dotted with the occasional cluster of slum dwellings or a low-end industrial complex. There were rumours that wild leopards roamed the area; that snakes and scorpions were a constant threat; and that outlaws patrolled in gangs robbing with impunity those who ventured in. Only the most fool-hardy and desperate would actually try to live here.

But in a city as crowded as Mumbai there would always be some who were just desperate enough.

Ganesha eventually entered a slum that had recently sprung up within the concrete remains of an abandoned industrial complex. Free-standing structures devoid of windows and doors and without running water or electric-ity served as homes to the truly forsaken. This was not a functioning slum of poor families such as the shanty city known as Dharavi. This was the sort of slum to which the dregs of Mumbai society gravitated, the gutter into which the very worst and most unfortunate were eventually swept. Here were the drunks, the drug addicts, the mentally impaired, the thieves and murderers who had escaped the not-so-long arm of the law. Just as the bright face of the moon has a side permanently shadowed in darkness, so did places like this slum exist in a city that shone brighter than any other on the subcontinent.

Ganesha walked through the strangely quiescent streets, his trunk wrinkling at the unfamiliar scents of opium and hashish, his ears flapping as groans of pain and disillusion-ment were carried to him on the breeze, his frightened gaze alighting on human beings collapsed into vacant doorways and around open fires, suffering in mute agony, eyes hollowed out with confusion as if they had landed in some nether hell with no rhyme or reason for their presence there.

Beyond the furthest reaches of the slum Ganesha stared up at a looming concrete superstructure set apart like an architectural leper.

Once upon a time this skeletal structure had possibly dreamed of being a magnificent modern edifice, a leviathan of steel, concrete and glass. But that grand vision had barely got beyond the architect's drawing board. The reality had stopped at these naked walls of grey, weather-ravaged cinderblock, walls with gaping hollows where windows, doors and even whole wall sections should have been. Rusted steel rebar poked out of crumbling columns like the ribs of desert-dried skeletons.

A wind howled through the uppermost floors, which were open to the elements. A fire flickered on the top floor.

Ganesha trotted into the building.

Inside, he stopped and looked around. Between the mouldering twelve-foot-high walls, rusted I-beams and broken sections of concrete pipe were haphazardly strewn. Rubble and fallen masonry made little pyramids in darkened corners.

Ganesha sniffed the air again. Then, following his nose, he turned and walked up a flight of shallow concrete steps to the floor above.

He continued until he had reached the third floor. Here he paused and surveyed the scene.

More grey columns rose up around him, holding up a temporary roof fashioned from corroded sheets of corrugated iron.

And now there were the first signs of human habitation.

The fire that he had seen from the ground was constrained inside a pit of bricks, the edges of the pit lined with the stumps of charred logs. The fire flickered in a cross-breeze that cut across the floor, which was open to the elements on all sides. Motes of red ash danced in the wind.

A sudden blur of movement jerked Ganesha's head around. He was just in time to see the shape of a small boy in ragged shorts and vest sprint through an open doorway into darkness.

Ganesha trotted after him.

He paused in the open doorway. Then he unfurled his trunk and sniffed. He could not see into the dark, but he could sense that a room lay ahead of him, one of the few intact rooms in the whole edifice. He sensed that Irfan had been there not long ago.

He walked into the room.

For a moment he stood in the gloom, allowing his eyes to adjust. And then he saw the rope, dangling down from a ragged hole in the far corner of the room's crumbling ceiling. The rope was still swaying.

Ganesha realised that the boy had shimmied up the rope and disappeared, but why?

The little elephant turned in alarm . . . too late.

The door clanged shut, and he heard a rusted steel bolt slide into place.

For the second time that day, he was trapped.

THE BBC REVEALED

Chopra had once read a book by a noted Mughal scholar which suggested that until the Mughal emperors arrived on the subcontinent the word opulence held no meaning. The Persian descendants of the Timurid dynasty had redefined how royal incontinence was measured, cowing visitors to their imperial courts with stunning exhibitions of wealth and grandeur that, even by the standards of the day, elevated ostentation to new heights. This approach had culminated in the practice, first consecrated by Emperor Akbar, of distributing the grand mughal's bodyweight in gold as alms to the poor each year.

As they were led through the yacht Chopra could not help but think that in some ways the past was always to be found reflected in the present.

The modern-day successors to the Mughal overlords – the great tycoons of globalised, industrialised India – remained faithful to the principles of their distant ancestors. After all, there was no point in being rich if you could not flaunt it.

And yet, in spite of himself, Chopra could not help but marvel at the splendour of the floating palace within which he now found himself. Limitless vulgarity seemed to be the order of the day. Imported marble, walnut veneer, hand-tooled leather, Venetian crystal, priceless treasures from the art world – there seemed to be no end to the expense that had been lavished on *The King's Ransom*.

He wondered briefly what Gandhi would have made of it.

While millions starved on the streets of India's greatest city, there were some who could not live without a hundred-thousand-dollar bathroom suite.

Eventually they entered a red-carpeted ballroom at one end of which was a bar stocked with an array of fine liquors. A barman in a white tuxedo served the forty or so male guests milling about the room. As Chopra looked around he saw that the face of each man was indeed partially concealed beneath a mask.

A waiter materialised bearing a tray of drinks.

Bomberton deftly plucked a champagne flute from the silver platter, threw it back in one go and remarked, 'Château Lafite. Nothing but the best for this sort of skull-duggery, eh, Chopra?'

'Do not use my name,' muttered Chopra. 'Remember, we are in character.'

'Damned nonsense,' Bomberton growled. 'We should just arrest the bloody lot of them. Hold them upside down by the ankles until the diamond drops out. If it's actually here, of course.'

Chopra ignored him.

His eyes worked their way around the ballroom.

Although the faces of the individuals were hidden, he believed that he recognised some of the men in the room. For instance, this gentleman with the silver-topped cane and the red-hennaed hair – surely that was the noted media magnate who had recently built a thirty-storey skyscraper as his private residence down in Cuffe Parade? And over there, the gentleman with the trademark black-and-white beard? Wasn't that the Keralan steel tycoon now rumoured to be the seventh richest man in the world?

'Knew a cat burglar once,' continued Bomberton, cracking his knuckles savagely. 'Had a fetish for diamond tiaras. I tracked him down to a little cottage in the Pyrenees. He had a bunch locked away in a safe. Took them out once a week so he could parade around in them wearing a dress. Just goes to show, you can never tell about people.'

A sudden hush descended on the room.

Chopra turned to see two men entering the ballroom, the first a tall, broad-shouldered figure in a black tuxedo, the second a portly gentleman with grey hair carrying a small strongbox handcuffed to his wrist. Both men wore masks yet Chopra felt the immediate hum of recognition as he watched the older man make his way across the carpet. Bulbul Kanodia!

And there was something familiar too about the younger figure leading Kanodia into the room. The imposing physique; the square, cleft chin; the swarthy, pouting lips; the swept-back dark hair ... Chopra couldn't quite place him, but he was sure that he had seen this young man before.

Eventually, the newcomers reached the bar, whereupon the taller of the two turned and held up his hands. He waited as the last murmurs of conversation died away and the serving staff melted from the room, closing the doors behind them.

'Welcome, friends, welcome,' boomed the man. 'Let me begin by thanking you all for attending tonight's gathering at such short notice. As I look around I see many old friends, and others who I am certain must be trusted acquaintances for, let us not forget, we are all brothers here today. What befalls one, befalls all.' He paused to allow this not-so-concealed warning to sink in. 'But let us not dwell on such trivialities. Let us instead talk about *why* we are here.

'Tonight, gentlemen, we are gathered, we like-minded souls, to celebrate the latest and greatest achievement of the Bombay Billionaires Club. For those of you who are new to us, permit me to explain.

'When I was a boy my favourite subject was history. It gave me the greatest pleasure to hear how the world that we know today was shaped. What struck me then was that history is not a matter of dates and dry facts. The history of the world is a living, breathing testament to the greatness of individuals.

'What do I mean by this? A moment's thought and it will become obvious. The history of the world *is the history of great men.* Those men who have, through their actions, through their influence, through their sheer force of will, shaped the future.

'Of course, you all know the type I mean. The great kings of the past, the military strategists, the thinkers. Those who refuse to be shackled by the ordinariness that binds lesser men. After all, it is a simple truth that most people are cowards, doomed to live and die without making the slightest mark on the world. Why, you only have to look around at our own dear country to see a multitude of them. They are there in every government office, on every street corner, in every gully and village of our land. And yet there are others, like all of you here, who have chosen not to accept such ignominy. Many years ago I too made that choice.'

The tall youth paused momentarily, as if to allow his grandiose words to sink in.

'Of all the great men of history my personal favourite is Alexander the Great. The boy-general who conquered the known world, even making it as far as our very own India. It will not surprise you to learn that Alexander's success was founded on one simple trait of character – boldness! He took the risks that others balked at. And by so doing he achieved what others believed impossible.' Another pause. 'This, gentlemen, is the ethos of the Bombay Billionaires Club. We have shown that even the impossible is nothing if you have the courage to determine your own destiny.'

The man turned and waved a hand at Bulbul Kanodia. 'If you please.'

Chopra felt his insides tighten. His hands clenched and unclenched anxiously as Kanodia set the strongbox on the bar, then removed a key from his pocket. He inserted the key into the strongbox, then waited as the taller man took a second key from his own tuxedo and inserted it into a lock on the opposite side of the box. The two men looked at each other before turning both keys simultaneously. The top of the strongbox split into two halves, each half swinging back to reveal an interior lined with red velvet.

And there, nestled within a moulded compartment, something glittered beneath the ballroom chandeliers.

The taller man reached into the box. With great reverence he took out the glittering object, then held it up triumphantly. 'Ladies and gentlemen, I present to you ... the Mountain of Light, the Koh-i-Noor!'

A collective gasp was pulled from the throats of the rapt audience and then a wave of spontaneous applause swept around the room. A flush of exultation moved over the visible lower half of the speaker's face.

As the applause died down another immaculately dressed young man with slicked-back hair and a lantern jaw stepped forward from the crowd.

'Well, Sunny, I have to take my hat off to you. I said it couldn't be done, but you have made me eat my words.' He reached into the breast pocket of his tuxedo with a manicured hand and fumbled out a leather wallet. 'As per our wager, gentlemen, I will now hand over to my esteemed colleague, my childhood friend, and undisputed leader of the Bombay Billionaires Club, the princely sum of ... one rupee!'

He raised the crisp new banknote for everyone's inspection and then handed it with great ceremony to the man he had addressed as 'Sunny'. Then he performed a short bow with the theatrical flourish of a court dandy and retreated to the edges of the circle.

And suddenly, in a flash, things came crashing together.

Chopra now knew the identity of the young man holding the Koh-i-Noor. He had been wrestling with his memory ever since the youth had swaggered into the ballroom, but with the name 'Sunny' everything fell into place. The man holding the Koh-i-Noor must be Sunil 'Sunny' Kartik, only son of industrialist Mohan Kartik, billionaire owner of *The King's Ransom*.

Sunny Kartik seemed to be a permanent fixture on Mumbai's celebrity scene, the subject of much scandalous gossip, a young man widely considered to be a wastrel of the first order. The prodigal fruit of Mohan Kartik's loins, the junior Kartik spent more time on the front pages of the tabloids than in the boardroom of his father's company. He was notorious for his profligate ways and his intermittent run-ins with the law, from which he was invariably rescued by the long reach of his father's chequebook. Mohan Kartik appeared to dote on his only child. The consequences of such behaviour had always seemed clear to Chopra.

Spare the rod and spoil the child – hadn't he just seen an example of this very thing in the four would-be exam cheats at Poppy's school?

As he dwelt on Sunny Kartik's career of well-heeled villainy, he realised that his memory had also subconsciously identified the youth who had presented Kartik with the one-rupee note – Faisal Hussain, another scion of a noted, wealthy Mumbai family, another young man known for his prodigal bent.

The two were inseparable, the scourge of Mumbai's jet set.

He dwelt now on Faisal's words: 'the Bombay Billionaires Club' . . . So, the riddle of the 'BBC' had been solved. But what exactly *was* the Bombay Billionaires Club? What was its purpose?

Sunny Kartik turned to the bar, picked up a champagne flute, drained it, then flung it against the wall. 'Salut!' he shouted, an extravagant smile appearing below his mask. 'And now, gentlemen, the moment you have been waiting for. It is time for the evening's business to begin.'

'Let us not be so hasty,' growled a very fat man to Chopra's left who had been scowling as Sunny and Faisal performed their double act. 'I for one would like to be reassured of the authenticity of the, ah, object before we proceed.'

A chorus of 'hear! hear!'s circled the room.

'You do not trust me?' Kartik said, raising an eyebrow.

'I did not make my fortune by trusting people, sir,' asserted the fat man pompously.

Kartik pointed at Bulbul Kanodia. 'My man here is a jewellery aficionado. He has certified the diamond.'

'As you rightly say, sir, he is *your* man. Forgive me if I do not rush to touch his feet in gratitude.'

There was a round of gentle laughter.

'Then what do you suggest?'

The fat man clicked his fingers and a much leaner gentleman in an oversized tuxedo materialised from behind him as if summoned forth by magic. The man blinked owlishly, putting those watching in mind of a creature of the dark suddenly exposed to the light.

'I have taken the liberty of inviting my own expert along,' declared the fat man. 'Let us say that his name is Hirachand.

He is one of the foremost diamond assessors in the Zhaveri Bazaar. I assume you have no objection . . .?'

Kartik smiled menacingly. 'Not at all.'

The gaunt-faced assessor removed a jeweller's loupe from his pocket and carefully screwed it into the right eyehole of his mask. He approached the bar, then held out his hand. Kartik made as if to hand over the diamond, then snatched it back. The predatory smile widened. Then he dropped the Koh-i-Noor into Hirachand's palm.

Hirachand held the diamond up to the light as he examined it. Then he unbuckled a tool-belt from beneath his jacket and placed it reverentially onto the bar. From this he extracted a pair of Vernier calipers and an electronic gemstone gauge before setting to work.

Five minutes later, he returned the diamond to the strongbox.

'Well?' barked the fat man.

'The cut, colour and clarity are consistent with descriptions of the Koh-i-Noor,' declared Hirachand. 'The diamond weighs 21.6 grams and has a carat weight of 105.6 metric carats. Both these measurements are in line with the known dimensions of the Koh-i-Noor.' He paused, and then, in a dry, flat tone, said, 'Gentlemen, it is my considered opinion that this piece is authentic. It is the Koh-i-Noor.'

Another round of spontaneous applause engulfed the room.

'Of course it is genuine,' said Bulbul Kanodia crossly. 'Did you take me for an amateur?' He glared at the rival expert, took a handkerchief from his pocket and picked up the diamond, cradling it gently in the palm of his hand. He proceeded to buff it extravagantly before holding it up to the light. Satisfied with his efforts, he returned it to the strongbox.

'Well then,' said Sunny Kartik, sweeping the gathered notables with an imperious look, 'let us not waste any more time. Gentlemen . . . where shall we start the bidding?'

'I bid ten million US,' barked the fat man immediately. Chopra noted that sweat had pooled on his upper lip in spite of the ballroom's fierce air-conditioning. Naked greed makes men hot, he thought. In the presence of that which they covet, their internal fires work overtime.

'Ten million?' someone shouted out. 'For the Koh-i-Noor? Have you lost your marbles? Sunny, I'll write you a bearer cheque for twenty right now.'

This declaration of war set off a feeding frenzy as various bids, each more outlandish than the last, were thrown into the fray.

Kartik listened, an amused smile on his face. Then he held up both hands, demanding silence. 'Gentlemen, gentlemen, calm yourselves. Your offers, though generous, are also worthless. Have you forgotten our creed? None of us here are in need of more gold to pour into our ample coffers. I formed the Bombay Billionaires Club so that I might bring excitement to my life, not more wealth. Remember our manifesto! Like the nawabs of old, we stalwarts of the BBC constantly challenge each other with ever more inventive wagers. In this manner we keep things interesting. Stealing the Koh-i-Noor is merely the latest and greatest in our catalogue of achievements. Frankly, I would have preferred to retain the diamond as a souvenir, but I think that would be a little too tempting of fate, even for me. But please understand – it is not your money I am after. What I covet is something that I cannot attain for myself. Now, do any of you have such a prize? If not, you are wasting my time.'

There was a thoughtful silence as the gathered moguls looked at each other in consternation.

And then a tall man spoke up. 'Last year I purchased a medieval castle set high in the Bavarian Alps. It is like something out of a fairy tale. There is no other castle like it in the world. It is yours in exchange for the Koh-i-Noor.'

Kartik smiled. 'Now that is more like it!'

The fat man scowled at the taller gentleman, then said, 'My garage houses the world's finest collection of Rolls-Royces, over one hundred. Just tell me where to deliver them.'

A short bald man who had been scratching his jowls whilst puffing furiously on a Cuban cigar now piped up. 'I own the most coveted stable of Arabian stallions in Asia. Say the word, Sunny, and this year you will surely sit in the winner's box at the Indian derby.'

Kartik moved from individual to individual, listening to the ever more inventive offers being hurled his way. Finally his eyes alighted on Maxwell Bomberton. His forehead creased into a frown. 'I am sorry, sir, but I do not believe that I have your acquaintance.'

'Too damned right, you don't,' growled Bomberton.

Standing beside the Englishman, Chopra tensed himself for an explosion. He had felt Bomberton struggling to reign in his fury as Kartik had shamelessly displayed the Koh-i-Noor and boasted of his complicity in its theft.

The frown on Kartik's brow deepened. Clearly, he had not expected such a bellicose response. He seemed momentarily nonplussed.

He shot a glance at Bulbul Kanodia as if to ask *Who is this man, and what is he doing here?* then said, 'Perhaps you would care to tell me what you have to offer?'

Bomberton reached into his pocket. He removed a handgun and pointed it at Kartik. With his other hand he swept off his mask. 'How about twenty years in a maximum-security prison? Bed and board included.' The Englishman's face was red with rage. 'My name is Detective Chief Inspector Maxwell Bomberton and by virtue of the authority vested in me by both the British and the Indian governments I hereby place you all under arrest.'

A stunned silence greeted these words. And then the fat tycoon who had queried the Koh-i-Noor's authenticity squealed, 'Hai, Ram!' and fainted.

The others in the ballroom regarded the plump body as it lay spread-eagled on the floor . . . and then pandemonium ensued.

Bellows of panic filled the air as the gathered gentry stampeded for the exits. Those that fell were trampled underhoof. Chopra saw a veteran tycoon hurl himself over the bar, scattering rare vintages and bottles of premium Scotch. Another white-haired gentleman who had been wheeled into the ballroom trailing a tank of oxygen, now collapsed in his wheelchair, wheezing as he clutched despairingly at his chest.

Chopra's head flashed around just in time to see Kartik disappearing through a door at the rear of the ballroom.

He stepped towards the strongbox.

It was empty.

'You grab Kanodia, I'm going after Kartik.' Without waiting for Bomberton to reply, Chopra raced after his quarry.

THE GREAT ESCAPE

Ganesha stirred in the darkness. He had lost track of time, but he knew that many hours had passed since he had been imprisoned in the concrete room. He had attempted to charge the door but although he had made some impressive dents, the grim portal would not yield.

Finally, exhausted and emotionally spent, he had slumped into a corner, curled his trunk under his face, and fallen into a troubled sleep.

But now a noise had brought him up from the well of slumber.

He listened intently as the rusted steel bolt scraped back. The door swung open, and then a dark shape slipped inside. Ganesha stumbled to his feet, his every muscle tensed.

'Shhh, don't make any noise or he will hear us.'

Ganesha's ears flapped happily and then he raised his trunk and held it up to Irfan's face, a gust of affection for his friend washing over him. His delight was apparent.

Irfan patted Ganesha on the head. 'You shouldn't have come, boy.'

The tip of Ganesha's trunk froze as it reached the fresh bruise that had swollen Irfan's right eye. His ears stopped flapping.

'It's OK, boy,' mumbled Irfan. 'It's OK. I am sorry I had to leave you, but I had no choice. If I had stayed, that evil man might have hurt Poppy and Chopra. I know him too well. He would have stopped at nothing. I couldn't take the chance that they would be hurt because of me. You understand, don't you?'

For a brief moment they stood together in silence, and then Irfan stirred. 'Come on, let's go.'

With Irfan leading the way, they left the room and headed stealthily for the concrete steps to the floor below.

They had made it halfway there when a tall shape stepped out from behind a column on the very edge of the open expanse. The man held a flaming torch, the sulphurous yellow light throwing a spectral halo over his grizzled features.

Mukhthar Lodi looked down at the fugitives. And then a cold smile spread over the shadows that made up his face.

Behind him the night was dark, punctuated by strange noises. The clicking of cicadas. The whoop of a hyena. A solitary scream from the nearby slum, cut off at its zenith. A bat flew past, chittering in the moonlight.

'It seems that you have not learned your lesson, Irfan. Perhaps this time I must teach you properly.'

Ganesha snorted angrily and moved in front of the boy.

Lodi reached into the sash around his black kurta. The light from the torch now reflected from the burnished barrel of an antique revolver. 'Perhaps your friend needs to learn a lesson too.'

Ganesha did not hesitate. He lowered his head and charged.

Lodi's eyes widened. He had not been expecting this. For a second he stood there, frozen, and then his finger tightened on the trigger.

The bang of the revolver was abnormally loud inside the abandoned building.

Ganesha ploughed into Lodi, sending him careening backwards and over the side, the torch flying from his hand.

The little elephant's momentum carried him forward until he bundled headlong into the column Lodi had hidden behind. He bounced off the concrete pillar, spun backwards and then collapsed onto the floor.

'Ganesha!'

Irfan rushed to the stricken elephant and knelt down beside him.

For a moment Ganesha did not respond.

'Come on, boy!' sobbed Irfan, his face dissolving into tears.

And then Ganesha shook his head from side to side. He reached up with his trunk to pat either side of his skull. Then he flapped his ears forward. At the bottom of his right ear, where the membrane was thinnest, a small round hole was rimmed with blood. Ganesha touched the hole with the tip of his trunk. A shudder passed through him.

Irfan placed his arms around the elephant's neck. 'You could have been killed, boy.'

A piercing shout drew them both from their huddle.

Groggily, Ganesha got to his feet. Then, together, they moved to the edge of the floor.

Below them, clinging on with one hand, was Mukhthar Lodi.

He was dangling some two floors above the ground. Directly below his feet was a moving river of sludge, a six-foot-wide stream of cancerous sewage that flowed from nearby industrial plants all the way to the Mithi River at Krishna Nagar.

As they watched, Lodi tried to reach up and grasp the edge with his other hand, but his shoulder was unnaturally twisted, and as he rotated the dislocated joint a scream of pain escaped him. The arm fell limply by his side.

'Help me!'

Irfan stared down with round eyes at the man who had controlled his life since the day he had been born.

'I am your father, boy! Now help me!'

Slowly, as if walking in a dream, Irfan advanced to the very edge.

'That's it, boy! Reach out and pull me up!'

Irfan extended a tentative arm . . . and then stopped, his hand frozen mid-reach.

'What are you waiting for? Pull me up!'

Irfan stepped back.

Ganesha looked up at the boy, at the fear and uncertainty passing like storm clouds over his bruised and battered face.

Then the elephant moved forward.

He reached out with his trunk. He would pull the man up, and then they would leave. Lodi was in no shape to stop them now.

Ganesha turned at the sound of bare feet slapping on concrete.

Behind him were ranged a dozen young boys of Irfan's age. They all wore ragged shorts and vests or T-shirts. Some were bare-chested. All displayed bruises, cigarette burns and razor cuts, testaments to Lodi's brutality.

There was a moment of breathless silence in which only the wind could be heard howling between the columns of the concrete floor.

And then, acting as one, the boys swarmed forward.

For thousands of years Indians have believed that justice is a universal constant of nature, shaped by the concept of dharma – the principle of right conduct. The obligation of each individual to behave in a moral and righteous manner towards his fellow man. Thus when a man betrays the code of dharma he brings his own fate down upon his head.

Before Ganesha could move, the urchins had clawed Lodi's fingers from the edge of the floor.

Lodi fell swiftly, a scream rising from his throat. With a loud spludge he struck the ooze and immediately sank in up to his waist.

The arch thief began to thrash around but was hampered by his dislocated arm. The harder he struggled the further he sank into the sewage, which sucked at him greedily like quicksand. Soon only his shoulders were visible.

As he sank Lodi hurled curses up at the watching boys, interspersed with pitiable entreaties to come to his aid. But the boys may as well have been a succession of statues arrayed on the lip of the concrete floor.

Finally, only his head was visible.

Irfan drew closer to Ganesha. He shivered as he watched the slime creep up his father's neck. Ganesha reached out his trunk and entwined it around the boy's hand.

Lodi spluttered as the ooze found his mouth. 'The devil take you all!' he cursed and then the sludge entered his mouth and he could say no more.

The sound of choking gradually died away as the sewage rose to engulf Lodi's face.

With a final plop, he vanished completely beneath the river of black.

A SHOWDOWN IN MUMBAI HARBOUR

Chopra hurtled through the interior of the yacht, hot on the heels of Sunil Kartik. Though he prided himself on his fitness Kartik was younger, leaner and in better condition. Kartik had the added advantage of knowing the layout of his pleasure boat intimately.

As Chopra skidded around another corner he caught a flash of Kartik's handmade brogues as they disappeared down a stairwell. He halted a second, wheezing, then leaped back into the chase.

As Kartik ran he threw obstacles into his pursuer's path: a bust of his hero Alexander the Great, a gold-plated statue of Shiva in his aspect as destroyer, a priceless Oriental vase that shattered on the marble floor and scattered porcelain shards under Chopra's feet.

'Stop!' he panted. 'There is nowhere to go!'

Kartik ran on.

Chopra thundered down a passageway that ran past the galley. At that precise moment a white-suited chef chose to step out from the galley doors holding a punchbowl. 'Out of the way!' roared Chopra, but it was too late. He barrelled into the man, whose eyebrows had shot up towards his jauntily angled toque blanche.

Both men hit the deck in a tangle of limbs.

The punchbowl completed a somersault in the air, dumping its contents over Chopra and drenching him in rum and fruit. The bowl landed on the chef's head.

Chopra lay on the tiled floor staring up at the ceiling. A bright white light coalesced above his head. All noises seemed to have become muted, and then he heard a steady thundering like an approaching steam train . . . He realised that it was his heart, flailing wildly against his ribs. *Dammit! Not again! Not now!*

Chopra willed himself to calm.

In the past few months, his heart had been remarkably well behaved. This had been partly due to Chopra's own self-enforced avoidance of stressful activity, and partly thanks to Poppy's stern vigilance. But now, now he was back in the fray, and the old bomb ticking away in the centre of his chest was reminding him that it had merely gone quiescent for a while; it had not been defused.

He struggled to his feet, rubbing his breastbone with the heel of his hand. He heaved in a deep lungful of air, then continued on his way.

He reached the stern of the yacht just in time to see Sunny Kartik scrambling around inside a speedboat bobbing beside the landing apron.

He raced down the shallow stairs leading down to the apron, taking three steps at a time. Just as he bounded onto the apron, Kartik threw off the boat's moorings, gunned the motor and leaped to the wheel. In a fury of thrashing seawater, it began to pull away.

Chopra did not hesitate.

He raced across the landing apron and leaped after the departing boat, falling against the side of it with a heavy thud. His arms hooked themselves around the starboard gunnel, while his legs plunged into the water.

Chopra was dragged along by the speeding motorboat, clinging on for dear life. The roar of the motor was deafening; backwash from the wake splashed over him in a furious torrent. Each time he attempted to scrabble up, he would lose his footing and slip back down again. If he had not been so preoccupied with survival, he would have been numb with terror.

Chopra could not swim.

If he lost his grip, he would drown. It was that simple. There would be no one to save him, not this far out into the harbour, not at this time of night.

Suddenly, he sensed the boat turning.

Kartik was swinging the speedboat in a wide arc back towards the mainland. The mechanics of the turn lifted the boat's starboard hull out of the water, dragging Chopra with it. With a monumental effort, he scissored his legs up and over the side of the hull.

He collapsed into the motorboat's bilge, a froth of seawater spluttering from his mouth, his body drenched from head to toe. Finally, having regained a semblance of composure, he lifted himself onto his haunches.

Kartik, intent on the wheel, had clearly not sensed his presence. The billionaire playboy was focused on guiding the speedboat back towards the distant lights of Apollo Bunder.

Chopra raised his voice above the roar of the outboard motor. 'Stop the boat!'

At first Kartik did not hear him.

Chopra shouted again, then again.

Finally Kartik turned. Astonishment flashed across his features. Then he turned back, flipped the boat onto automatic pilot and leaned under the dashboard. When he straightened, he was holding a fishing gaff in his hand.

Kartik advanced.

Steadying himself against the motion of the boat, Chopra got to his feet. Then he reached into the pocket of his waistcoat and took out the gun he had snatched from Bomberton as he ran from the ballroom.

'Stop the boat!' he ordered.

Kartik's eyes narrowed. His arms fell to his sides. He dropped his gaze to the handgun as if judging whether or not to charge. But Chopra's arm did not waver.

Finally, Kartik stepped backwards and cut the motor. The boat drifted to a standstill.

'Sunil Kartik, I am making a citizen's arrest. I arrest you for the crime of stealing the Crown of Queen Elizabeth.'

Kartik frowned. 'Citizen's arrest? Aren't you a policeman?' Then his eyes narrowed. 'Wait a minute. I recognise you. You were in the Tata Gallery when I—' He stopped.

Chopra nodded. 'Yes. My name is Chopra. It took me a while to place you, but now I have it. You were the Sikh gentleman, weren't you?'

Kartik gave a thin smile. 'A rather convincing disguise, even if I do say so myself.'

'That's how you got the crown out,' continued Chopra. And in his mind's eye was an image of the circus owner Tiger Singh performing the three-ball trick, making the ball vanish beneath his improvised turban. He now knew that the big Sikh in the Tata Gallery – Sunny Kartik – had executed a similar sleight-of-hand.

The whole plan shimmered in Chopra's mind now, each detail laid out in blinding clarity.

Months ago Sunny Kartik had installed his man Prakash Yadav in the Prince of Wales Museum to plant the gas canisters and plastic explosive inside the Kali statue. And Chopra was now certain that the explosive had not been brought in on the day of the heist – it had been there all along, left there by Yadav. Chopra thought that he now understood exactly how the explosive had been employed in the heist. He believed that it had been used from *inside* the jewel room. To his mind, it was the only way to explain the debris that had been found in the corridor, a detail that had bothered him since the very beginning.

A day before the heist, just before he vanished, Yadav had installed a programmed virus into the museum's new CCTV system, probably using something as simple as a USB stick.

On the day of the robbery Bulbul Kanodia and Sunny Kartik had entered the museum together, Kartik disguised as a Sikh. The metal scanner detected his Sikh kara, his steel bracelet, but Kartik had made such a fuss – claiming that he could not remove the bracelet even if he wished to – that the guards had let it through. This would be vital to the plan later on. Kanodia, for his part, had brought in an asthma inhaler into which had been built the resonance generator that they would subsequently use to crack the display case.

At the pre-planned moment the CCTV cameras were disabled by the computer virus. Kartik and Kanodia had been monitoring the daily queues, knowing that each group of twenty was only permitted to stay inside the jewel room for a set time. They knew roughly when they could expect to enter the museum and had set a window for the start of the CCTV blackout accordingly.

Once inside the gallery Kartik leaped into action.

He quickly recovered the pressurised gas canisters, the plastic explosive, and nose filters and latex gloves for himself and Kanodia from the Kali statue. Employing the gas canisters, they swiftly rendered everyone in the room unconscious.

While Kanodia used the resonance generator to smash the display case, Kartik put into effect the ingenious plan they had come up with to throw those who would ultimately investigate the theft off the scent.

Using a minute amount of plastic explosive he blasted a small hole in the sealed rear door of the gallery, just enough to put his arm through and place a much larger quantity of plastic explosive on the *outside* of the door. The second explosion would blow a bigger hole, enough to obliterate signs of the first. In this way the authorities might be fooled into believing that the thieves had entered the gallery *from* the corridor. There was nothing Kartik could do about the small amount of debris deposited in the corridor from the first explosion – he had simply relied on the forensics experts assuming this to be blowback. At least for long enough to muddy the initial investigation.

Having set the explosive outside of the door Kartik had then taken the crown from Kanodia and placed it beneath his fake turban before securing the turban back on his head. Chopra guessed that he must have also taken the nose filters from himself and Kanodia – together with their latex gloves – and pushed them into the plastic explosive in an attempt to obliterate this incriminating evidence. He now had only to light the detonation fuse.

Then he and Kanodia had lain down in the gallery and waited for the explosion, just two more innocent victims of the heist.

When the Force One team had hustled them out of the museum just minutes later, Kartik – the crown concealed beneath his turban – would have set off the metal scanner. But he had simply pointed to his kara. The guards already knew that he had taken it in with him. They had not bothered to look further.

It was a very clever plan. All that was left was to frame Shekhar Garewal.

'You and Kanodia planned this together, didn't you?' said Chopra. 'Backed by the Chauhan gang.'

'Kanodia?' Kartik sneered. 'Kanodia wouldn't have the brains or the guts to pull off something this big. As for the Chauhan gang . . .' He laughed. 'This was my caper, Chopra. I merely brought Kanodia in to authenticate the diamond and remove it from the crown without damaging it. I knew of his past record. I knew he would keep his mouth shut.'

'But why? Why did you do it? You have everything. It makes no sense.'

'You wouldn't understand,' said Kartik.

'Try me.'

Kartik hesitated before speaking: 'Have you any idea what it's like, being the man who has everything? From the moment I was born there was nothing that I had to work for, nothing to strive for. My every whim was taken care of. I had only to crook my little finger and Daddy would take out his cheque-book. Everyone around me was there to do my bidding. I was never allowed to achieve a single thing for myself.'

'Millions would kill for such a life.'

'But where is the challenge, Chopra? What made Alexander conquer nation after nation? Why did he lie down and die when his men forced him to turn homewards? Without challenge, life has no meaning.' Kartik's face was shadowed in the marine night. 'My father expects me to follow in his footsteps. To take over the empire he has built. But I have no interest in an empire I had no hand in fashioning. I created the Bombay Billionaires Club so that I would have something that was mine; something that belonged to *me*. It is that simple.' Suddenly, Kartik's voice was feverish with excitement. 'You cannot imagine the rush! To plan something that pushes your abilities to the limit, that requires daring and courage and carries with it the genuine risk of danger. To then execute that plan to perfection. Let me tell you, there is no thrill like the thrill of besting fate.'

'You are a thief,' said Chopra flatly. 'And a killer.'

'Killer?' Kartik's face radiated confusion. 'What are you talking about?'

'Prakash Yadav. The man you sent into the museum to plant the gas canisters and the plastic explosive.'

Kartik laughed, the noise echoing over the moonlit water. 'Yadav – as you call him – is very much alive. His real name is Naresh Gadkar. He was my bodyguard, and a very sharp chap for all that. Now there was a man who understood challenge! He performed his role perfectly. And once he had done so, he understood that he could not hang around. He is thousands of miles away from here, back in his native village in the south. A wealthy man for the rest of his days. Gadkar understands that wealth and health do not always go together. He will never return to Mumbai and he will never open his mouth. He took a risk and it has paid off for him. He is content. And very much alive.'

'What about Garewal? Your actions have sentenced him to a living death.'

Kartik shrugged. 'One cannot make an omelette without breaking eggs. Besides, Garewal is a cop. No one is going to miss one more cop in Mumbai. They are all as crooked as the day is long. The things they do each day make my crime pale by comparison.'

'I was a cop for thirty years,' said Chopra stiffly.

Kartik stared at him. 'Now I remember where I have seen you before. You are the one who cracked that trafficking ring. "The one honest cop in Mumbai." Isn't that what the papers called you? It seems to me as if you are taking your press a bit too seriously, my friend.' Kartik leaned forward and began to speak more quickly. 'Look, this does not have to end here. I will return the diamond. You can take it back, be the big hero. Earn yourself some more headlines. All you need to do is look the other way. By tomorrow I will be on another continent. I am thinking South America, one of those hot and humid countries with no extradition treaties. Fast women and samba music. Loud shirts and beach parties till dawn. What do you think?'

'Garewal has a family. You would have let him rot in jail, just so that you could have your challenge.'

'When you steal a wallet, you can get away with it. But when you steal the Koh-i-Noor diamond, someone must pay. They won't just let it go. I am afraid Garewal simply drew the short straw.'

Chopra's face was suffused with rage. 'That's all you have to say? "Garewal drew the short straw"?' He cocked the revolver. 'I am taking you in, Kartik. You will answer for your crimes. Let us see how *you* like it in Arthur Road Jail.'

Kartik reached into the pocket of his tuxedo. He held out his arm and opened his fist. In the centre of his palm lay the Koh-i-Noor diamond.

'This is what they want, Chopra. Not me.' With a flick of the wrist he flung the diamond across the boat. Instinctively Chopra made a grab for the jewel . . . From the corner of his eye he saw Kartik lunging towards him. He turned back, one hand grasping for the diamond, the other attempting to keep the gun trained on his assailant. He failed on both counts.

The diamond bounced off his sleeve and spun away until it was perched on the very rim of the boat, just beside the outboard motor. At the same instant Kartik steamed into him, carrying them both to the floor.

Chopra's finger tightened around the handgun's trigger. The gun bucked in his hand, the shot echoing harmlessly over the silent waters.

The two men grappled in the bottom of the boat. Chopra struggled furiously, but Kartik was bigger and stronger. Eventually Kartik landed a solid blow that knocked the wind out of him.

The younger man staggered to his feet as Chopra wheezed beneath him. Stars swam before his eyes, adding new constellations to the ones visible behind Kartik's shoulder.

Kartik reached down and plucked the gun from the bilge.

'I'm really sorry to have to do this, but you leave me no choice. I tried being reasonable, but some people just won't listen to reason.' He levelled the weapon at Chopra's leg. 'Don't worry. I am not going to kill you. As I have said I am no murderer. I am merely going to incapacitate you long enough to escape. I am afraid I have nothing with which to tie you up, and I cannot pilot the boat and keep an eye on you at the same time . . . Now, which leg would you prefer to be shot in?'

'Neither,' wheezed Chopra and lashed out with a foot, catching Kartik squarely in the groin. With a howl of pain, the younger man doubled up.

His finger tightened on the trigger and the gun went off. By a whim of fate the bullet struck the Koh-i-Noor, pinging it over the edge of the boat and into the water.

For a brief second it bobbed on a wave lapping against the boat's hull and then sank into the inky darkness.

Chopra struggled to his feet.

He leaned down and took the gun from Kartik's unresisting grip. 'You do not need ropes to incapacitate a man,' he said. 'I have always found that a well-placed boot is just as effective.'

Kartik remained curled up on the floor of the boat, the occasional mewling sound the only message from the particular circle of hell into which he had descended.

Chopra turned to the boat's stern. His dark eyes scanned the swirling seawater beyond the hull. But there was no sign of the diamond.

A tremendous disappointment roared through him. The harbour was deep out here and the currents unpredictable. The chances were that the diamond would never be recovered, no matter how many men and how much money the governments of Britain and India threw into the search. It was not the resolution that he had hoped for.

In one sense he had failed.

But then again, his duty was to his client, to Shekhar Garewal, and he had succeeded in proving Garewal's innocence.

And that was good enough.

He turned to the front of the boat.

Scanning the simple set of controls, he managed to switch on the motor. The boat roared to life.

Chopra grabbed the wheel and steered the speedboat back towards *The King's Ransom*. Behind him, twinkling like a thousand fireflies in the night, were the lights of the city that he had guarded for more years than he cared to remember.

His city.

Mumbai.

A CELEBRATION AT POPPY'S

The three policemen from the Railway Protection Force, with their distinctive blue berets, looked around as the accordion-player strained the notes of a bittersweet melody from his instrument. One, moved by the song's lament, raised a beer to the young man and flung a rupee in his direction, the spinning coin deftly plucked from the air by the black-faced langur perched on the youth's shoulder. The monkey stuffed it into the jingling bag of coins clutched in its paws, then looked up expectantly for more.

The youth turned and almost walked into Chopra, who had just entered the restaurant.

On another day he would have dismissed the young man – he did not wish to encourage troubadours and beggars in his place of business – but tonight he had much on his mind.

Head down, he barrelled past the accordion-player and stormed into his office, where he discovered Poppy and Rangwalla waiting for him.

Having greeted them both, he slumped into his seat behind the desk. Poppy, who had summoned a plate of Hyderabadi egg curry and steamed basmati rice from the kitchen in anticipation of her husband's arrival, lifted the bamboo cover from the tray. Chopra's nostrils twitched at the smell, but recent events had deprived him of his appetite.

It had been a night of furious activity.

Having returned to *The King's Ransom* with a subdued Sunil Kartik he had waited with DCI Bomberton for the forces of law and order to arrive.

The wait had been anything but orderly.

The detained crowd included some of the richest and most powerful men in India – who were not about to be cowed by an Englishman and a private detective. Before the cavalry could arrive many had slipped away on hastily summoned launches, even as Bomberton did his best to corral them in the ballroom. From those who remained came a constant stream of invective, dire threats and wild-eyed oaths. Mobile phones grew hot beneath the fury of the nabobs.

Chopra had advised Bomberton to ferry those left behind to the nearby Colaba station. He had called Poolchand and asked the station's holding pens to be cleared to make room for their grandiose new visitors. Bomberton had reluctantly agreed to the plan, but before they could get within a mile of the place a pack of ravenous lawyers had descended, nonplussing the station in-charge and making him regret the fact that he had chosen to work on Christmas Day.

Thus began the machinations that would ultimately end with not a single one of those present for the Koh-i-Noor's 'auction' remanded on charges. Chopra, weary with exhaustion, had grown hoarse in his attempts to convince his seniors that these men were as guilty as Sunny Kartik and Bulbul Kanodia.

He should have known better.

He remembered the words of ACP Suresh Rao, who had been incandescent with fury to discover that Chopra had stolen his thunder. 'You may think you have won, Chopra, but you are wrong. You have made enemies of some of the most powerful men in the country. Worse, you have made them look foolish. They will not forget. And they will never forgive.'

The Commissioner of Police and the state's Chief Minister had been equally scathing.

'What exactly are we to charge them with?' asked the Commissioner acidly. 'Attending a masked ball? Their lawyers will make mincemeat of us. That is if they don't tie us up in red tape for the next ten years. You do not even have the diamond. All you have is Kartik and Kanodia, and Kartik's father will move heaven and earth for his son. Circumstantial evidence won't hold up in court, Chopra.' He had relented long enough to offer the former policeman a few words of grudging praise. 'Be content with what you have achieved. Do not try to bite off more than you can chew.'

What *had* he achieved? Well, at least he could take consolation from the fact that he had made good on his promise to prove Shekhar Garewal's innocence.

Garewal had been released an hour earlier amidst a blaze of publicity. Yet, instead of issuing an apology, the authorities claimed that Garewal's arrest was a ruse designed to flush out the real culprits, and that Garewal had been helping them with the investigation all along.

Garewal himself remained tight-lipped. It was obvious that a deal had been struck.

As he drove Garewal home, his former colleague had choked back tears of gratitude. 'Chopra, you have given me back my life. Without you, I was a dead man.'

'I should never have doubted you.'

'You didn't,' said Garewal. 'Not where it mattered. Here.' And he had touched his chest.

Garewal had asked Chopra to stay for a celebratory drink but he had declined. He knew that what his old colleague needed most was time with his family, time to sit back in his own home and reflect on his narrow escape. How that escape would shape the remainder of his life was a question that only Garewal could answer.

Chopra realised that Poppy was speaking. He concentrated now as she explained to him exactly what had been going on in his absence.

Poppy told him that Irfan had returned to the restaurant late the night before, at about the same time that Chopra had been on the yacht with Bomberton. He had been accompanied by Ganesha who, Chopra was horrified to learn, had been abducted by Pramod Kondvilkar from the Maharashtra Dangerous Animals Division.

No one seemed to know how Ganesha had escaped from Kondvilkar's clutches or, for that matter, how he had ended up with Irfan. From the boy there came only a simple explanation. 'Ganesha found me and brought me home. If you will permit me to stay, I will never leave again.'

Poppy had broken down in tears when she discovered the two of them back where they belonged, safe and sound. Chopra listened as she painted a picture for him of their happy reunion . . .

Following their dramatic escape, the two fugitives, weary and battle-scarred, had made their way back to the restaurant. Here they had been greeted with cries of delight by all the staff and an overwhelmed Poppy, who had come in looking for her errant husband, displeased that he had pulled another of his vanishing acts.

'Where have you been, you naughty boy?' she had said crossly, simultaneously hugging Irfan and scolding him. 'Who gave you permission to go?' She held him at arm's length and inspected him. 'You have lost weight! And look at those bruises! Why did you go with that man? Was he really your father? Oh, if only that villain was in front of me now!'

'You do not have to worry about him,' said Irfan, glancing at Ganesha. 'He has gone away and will not be coming back.'

Poppy squinted at him suspiciously. Then her face broadened into a smile. 'Well, if he ever comes looking for you again, he will find me here. And heaven help him then!'

She hugged them both again, then looked them over with a practised eye, her nose crinkling. 'You two need a bath.'

A look of intense worry alighted on both Irfan and Ganesha's faces. It was not that they disliked bathing; it was simply that Poppy's idea of a bath differed greatly from their own. They liked to roll around in the mud and then use a hosepipe to rinse themselves clean. A bath orchestrated by Poppy meant soap, lotions, talcum powder, loofahs, moisturiser and a veritable alchemist's cupboard of oils that left them smelling oddly for days.

'Ah, I see you are back. Had enough of lazing about, have you?' Poornima Devi hobbled into view. 'Well, instead of standing around why don't you fetch my tea? I am not paying you to gawp at the walls.'

'Mummyji, the poor boy has been through enough!' said Poppy sternly.

'Nonsense!' said Poornima. 'When he is my age and must live with pain each and every waking moment, when he is surrounded by ingrates and buffoons, when he is thrown to the mercy of a boorish son-in-law, then he can say he has had enough.'

'One chai coming up, Poornima Madam,' said Irfan brightly. He gave Poppy a last hug, then skipped from the room, Ganesha trotting close behind, a bright moon of happiness rising inside him.

Irfan could never tell Poppy and Chopra how much it had pained him to leave them, that he had only done so to protect them from his evil father. The word 'family' had been an alien concept in his life. But for the first time, he was beginning to understand what other children took for granted. He prayed that he would never be away from them again, even for a single day.

In spite of his grim mood Chopra found himself smiling as he listened to the tale. He had not had the opportunity to return to the restaurant before now, having spent the entire night at CBI headquarters with Bomberton and the senior echelons of the Brihanmumbai Police. Halfway through the night he had been asked to accompany a police diving team into the harbour to try and pinpoint exactly where the Koh-i-Noor had gone down. As he had suspected, the search had so far proved to be a fruitless task.

Finally, having been thoroughly debriefed by the Commissioner and the Chief Minister, a weary Chopra had been released, along with Garewal.

As if by divine providence a knock sounded on the door at that very moment, and Irfan entered, drawing Chopra from his moribund thoughts.

The boy's gaze alighted on Chopra. He hesitated, then ran forward and flung his arms around him. At first stunned, Chopra finally felt his own arms moving to embrace the boy. A knot of emotion bobbed in his throat.

'How are you, boy?' he said, finally.

Irfan wiped his eyes with the curved back of his malformed left hand. 'I am not crying,' he said. 'I have been cutting onions for Chef.'

Chopra smiled. 'Is Ganesha asleep?'

Irfan shook his head. 'No. He is waiting for you.'

'Then let us not keep him waiting.'

Ganesha was standing under his mango tree playing with a series of red balls that jangled as he moved them about with his trunk. Chopra recognised them as the ones used by blind cricket players.

The elephant turned as Chopra approached, then trotted forward and butted him in the midriff, almost knocking him off his feet. Having recovered from this violent demonstration of affection, Chopra knelt down and looked the little elephant squarely in the eye. 'I am very sorry that I was not there to protect you,' he said. 'It will never happen again.'

In this Chopra was merely stating a fact. It was one of the concessions he had wrung from the Chief Minister in return for his cooperation in the expansive exercise of backside-covering that was now underway in the halls of Mumbai's civic administration.

There would be no more visits from Pramod Kondvilkar or his ilk, of that he could be certain.

Ganesha bugled his understanding, then turned back to his game.

Rangwalla coughed behind Chopra. 'So what happens now? With the Koh-i-Noor case, I mean?'

'Now? Now they will search the harbour until they either find the diamond or give up.'

'They will never give up. The British won't allow it.'

'Maybe not. In the meantime, Kartik has been released on bail. He is confined to his home. His lawyers are already claiming that he is the victim of a conspiracy. Without the diamond it is going to be an uphill struggle to convict him.'

'What about Kanodia?'

'Kanodia is in big trouble. Kartik has blamed everything on him. The Commissioner's informants are saying that

even the Chauhan gang has disowned him. I think Kanodia
will end up taking the fall. It does not matter that Bomberton
and I have testified against Kartik as the real mastermind
behind the plot. Everyone wants Kanodia to be the scapegoat. Everyone *needs* him to be the scapegoat.' Chopra's
expression was morose.

'Well, at least he got to hold the Koh-i-Noor,' said
Rangwalla, his tone bordering on the wistful.

'Yes,' said Chopra, recalling how lovingly Kanodia had
cradled the Koh-i—

He froze. A thought burst into his mind like a new sun
igniting inside a nebula.

'Rangwalla, get the van. We are going to Seven Roads.'

'But what about your supper?' said Poppy.

'It will have to wait.'

BULBUL KANODIA COMES CLEAN

'The door is open, sir. You may go inside.'

Chopra gave the guard a stern look. It was the same man that he had threatened when he had come here in a rage, certain that Garewal had lied to him. The guard grinned queasily. Word had obviously been passed down from on high that he should extend every courtesy to his visitor. The guard was probably wondering if Chopra would use his newfound influence to have him removed from his post.

It was, after all, his third visit to Mumbai Central Prison in the space of a few days.

Bulbul Kanodia did not rise from the hard contours of his bunk to greet him. Dark-circled eyes looked out from a slack face at the bare ceiling above. His arms lay flat by the sides of his large belly. In his white prison suit, he looked like a corpse laid out for holy cremation.

'What do you want?' he finally asked.

'I need to ask you a question,' replied Chopra.

'Haven't you done enough? Because of you I am ruined.'

Chopra had heard this lament many times during his career. A captured criminal laying the blame for his predicament on the men who had brought him to justice.

'Why did you do it?' asked Chopra. 'You are a wealthy man. You are not chasing excitement like Kartik and his friends. So why?'

'You could not possibly understand.'

Chopra fell silent, waiting. He sensed that Kanodia had a wish to talk, a wish to confide in someone, even the man who had brought him down.

Kanodia shifted his vacant stare to his feet. 'It was the diamond. I wanted to touch the diamond. To hold it in my hand. Since before I could walk I have worked with precious stones. My family come from a long line of gemworkers. The Koh-i-Noor is a legend to us. I never thought that I would have the opportunity to see it with my own eyes, let alone touch it.'

Chopra's mouth lifted in the tightest of smiles. 'Is that why you stole it?'

A heartbeat of time ticked away.

'I did not steal it. Sunny Kartik stole it.'

'And then *you* stole it from *him*.'

Finally, Kanodia looked at Chopra. 'What are you talking about?'

'I have come for the diamond, Bulbul. I know that you have it.'

Kanodia's eyes narrowed. 'You are mistaken. The Koh-i-Noor is lying at the bottom of Mumbai harbour. It may never be found again.'

'You are right, Bulbul. *That* Koh-i-Noor will never be found. Even if it is, it will be worthless. Because you and I both know that it is a fake.'

'I believe you were present when it was authenticated by an *expert*.'

'I was,' agreed Chopra. 'Which is why I saw you reach into your pocket for a handkerchief to clean it after he had touched it. That was when you made the switch. You never had any intention of letting Kartik sell the diamond. From the moment he brought you into his plan, you knew what you were going to do.'

Kanodia swung his legs down from the bunk and heaved himself to his feet. His eyes seemed to glitter in the dim light of the cell. 'You are fantasising, Chopra. You caught the thieves, but lost the diamond. Be content with that.'

'I cannot. Not while I know you have it.' Chopra stepped forward until he was standing only inches from Kanodia. 'You have a child. You have a wife. You have a life that you can return to. If you give back the diamond and testify against Kartik you will receive a very light sentence. If you do not they will lock you up and throw away the key.'

Kanodia was silent. Chopra could see conflicting emotions warring in the jeweller's haggard face.

'It is just a diamond.'

'It is the Koh-i-Noor,' whispered Kanodia.

'Is it worth the rest of your life?'

Kanodia stared at Chopra and then he turned away. He paced the cell in agitation, and then stood with his back to Chopra, staring at the bleak wall. Finally, he spoke: 'I hid the diamond on the yacht.'

'Then it must still be there,' said Chopra. 'The yacht has been impounded since we arrested you. It is moored in the Indira dock, strictly off limits.'

Kanodia unleashed a bray of laughter. 'That does not mean it is inaccessible. The guards you have placed on the yacht are no more honest than the next man.'

'Are you saying that you have had the diamond removed from *The King's Ransom*?' Chopra grimaced. 'Did you give it to the Chauhan gang?'

Kanodia bared his teeth. 'You have no idea, do you?' He shook his head. 'Have you ever met Chauhan? He is no fool. His men befriended me in prison – on his orders. He saved my life. Why do you think he did that? It was because he saw potential in me.'

'So I was right in thinking that Chauhan bankrolled your jewellery stores.'

'He is an investor just like any other. Where his capital comes from is his business, not mine. I am a jeweller. That is what I do.'

'Was Chauhan the real mastermind behind the theft of the Koh-i-Noor?'

'Didn't you hear what I said? The Koh-i-Noor is a poisoned chalice. Chauhan is too smart to drink from it. Why do you think he has yet to see the inside of a jail cell?'

Chopra's brow furrowed in confusion. 'Then how is the gang involved?'

'Sunny Kartik has many friends in low places. He put the word out that he was looking for professional help, the sort of help that a man like Chauhan could provide. He made contact with Chauhan through an intermediary. He explained what he was planning. It wasn't that Chauhan hadn't dreamed of stealing the Koh-i-Noor; no doubt every criminal in the country has had delusions of grandeur since the exhibition was announced. But he was not so stupid as to throw in his lot with Sunny. Chauhan thought Kartik was a rich fool on a fool's errand. And yet he didn't refuse him, either. He wanted to see if Kartik would actually try to do what he had said he would. In some ways Sunny fascinates a man like Chauhan.'

'So Chauhan had his eyes on the diamond all along. He just didn't want to get his own hands dirty.'

'You're not getting me, Chopra,' said Bulbul irritably. 'Chauhan wanted nothing to do with the Koh-i-Noor. He knew that if the diamond *was* stolen, he would be one of the first people the authorities would look at. If a single rumour spread that he was holding the Koh-i-Noor his whole organisation would be in jeopardy. He couldn't bribe or bully his way out of something like that. Kartik, on the other hand – by virtue of his father's political connections – might just slip through the net. No, Chauhan never wanted the diamond.'

'You expect me to believe Chauhan helped Kartik out of the goodness of his heart?'

'Of course not. He is a practical man. He asked for his price. A "consultancy fee", he called it. One million dollars, U.S. In return he helped source the things Kartik needed – from an appropriate distance, of course. The gas canisters, the explosives, the computer virus. He hired professionals from down south to plant the crown in Garewal's home, moved funds into his account through the gang's overseas hawala operation. And, of course, he provided *me*. Aside from authenticating the diamond, I was also to keep tabs on Kartik. To make sure he didn't do something foolish that implicated Chauhan.'

'Whose idea was the auction?'

'Sunny's. Chauhan was very unhappy about that. He never expected Kartik to actually pull off the robbery. Once he did, he wanted Sunny to return the diamond immediately. That way the heat would come off. There would be no chance of any of this coming back to him. Of course, as soon as Sunny told me about the auction I got the idea to take the Koh-i-Noor for myself.'

'You intended to cheat *both* Kartik and Chauhan,' said Chopra matter-of-factly. 'A double double-cross.'

Bulbul shrugged. 'Sunny deserved everything he got. As for Chauhan . . . Like I said, he wanted us to return the diamond.'

'But you did not return it, did you?'

Another yawning silence. 'It is the Koh-i-Noor,' Kanodia said softly. 'I could not.'

'Tell me where it is, Bulbul. Let me help you.'

Kanodia turned and looked at Chopra, his eyes heavy with a strange sadness. It wasn't greed, thought Chopra. It was something else; a madness, a crazed sort of love, for an idea. The *idea* of the Koh-i-Noor.

Then Kanodia reached out and gripped Chopra's forearm. 'Promise me! Promise me that you will get me out of here.'

'I can make no promises.'

'You have to promise me!'

Chopra hesitated. 'I promise that I will do the best that I can. I will speak on your behalf. I will ask for clemency. That is all I can do.'

Kanodia turned away. He was silent for a long time. Finally, he said, 'Before the police unit arrived on the yacht, I asked the English detective if I could use the facilities. There is a toilet at the rear of the ballroom. I hid the Koh-i-Noor inside the cistern. I knew they would not search the yacht, not once they discovered Kartik had already fled with the diamond.'

Chopra nodded grimly. 'Thank you.'

'Go,' said Kanodia. 'And may God go with you.'

A PRIVATE AUDIENCE FOR GANESHA

As the lift whirred to a halt Chopra was overcome by a sudden quiver of anxiety. The anxiety had churned inside his stomach since that morning when the unexpected phone call had invited him to the British High Commission in Mumbai. The caller, a senior factotum of some description, had been tight-lipped, refusing to divulge the exact nature of the summons whilst simultaneously impressing upon Chopra the necessity of his attendance. He had revealed only that the British High Commissioner was hosting a New Year's dinner and that Chopra was invited *en famille*.

Chopra glanced at his wife, standing beside him in a flutter of nervous energy. 'Do I look OK?' she asked him for the umpteenth time.

Chopra nodded reassuringly.

Poppy was resplendent in a brand-new sari, a spectacular maroon affair with silver trim and imprinted with whorls reminiscent of spiral galaxies. Her dark hair, newly sculpted into a modern, shoulder-length style – the result of an emergency visit to Laila Beg's Beauty Emporium – was immaculate.

Chopra was once again wearing his only suit.

Poppy had harangued him to purchase a new one, but he had refused. 'This suit has been good enough for every important occasion in the past fifteen years,' he had said sternly. 'It will be good enough for today.'

But now, as he stared at the back of the security officer who had led them through the imposing glass skyscraper in the elite Bandra-Kurla Complex where the High Commission offices were located, he wondered if, perhaps, for once, he should have listened to his wife.

The doors of the lift slid open and the officer, a tall, white male with a blond military haircut, leaped out into the corridor, brandishing his automatic pistol. He spun in both directions, as if he were in a Bollywood blockbuster, then straightened and spoke into his earpiece, the coiled white cable of which Chopra could see disappearing beneath his collar. 'This is Rogers to Station 1. Corridor is clear. Over.'

A tinny voice came back. 'Roger, Rogers. You are cleared to proceed. Over.'

Rogers turned and ushered them briskly into the deserted corridor.

They trotted after him towards a set of double doors, outside which were stationed two armed security officers in black military fatigues. Behind the doors, a babble of conversation and music could be heard.

A brief exchange followed and the guards stepped aside.

The first thing Chopra saw was the sweating presence of Detective Chief Inspector Maxwell Bomberton standing beneath a colossal Christmas tree with a glass of what looked like whisky in his enormous fist. He was wearing a brand-new but ill-fitting suit with a tie that seemed halfway to strangling him. His face gleamed as if it had been newly scrubbed and his few wisps of remaining hair had been neatly lacquered over his shining pate. His gruff moustache lifted into the ghost of a smile as he spotted Chopra.

Chopra's eyes fell on the man Bomberton had been speaking to, a tall, thin gentleman in an immaculate pinstriped suit with a head of distinguished grey hair and avuncular features. He looked vaguely familiar, though Chopra couldn't quite place him.

Around the room sixty or seventy people in evening finery milled around drinking champagne and eating canapés, whilst an orchestral band played 'Carol of the Bells'.

Bomberton's companion spotted them and waved enthusiastically. 'Chopra! Delighted that you could make it. Robert Mallory at your service. Please step this way.'

Mallory, Mallory . . . Now Chopra knew who he was: the new British High Commissioner to India.

But why had Mallory invited them here this evening?

They followed the High Commissioner in mystification as he led them through the throng of urbane revellers and into an oak-panelled office.

Inside the office a short white man was busily organising manila folders on the gargantuan desk behind which a portrait of Queen Elizabeth II had been artfully hung.

'Reginald, it is New Year's Eve,' said Mallory. 'You should be out there getting drunk, not fiddling with files.'

'I don't drink, sir,' said Reginald calmly.

'Well, I order you to go and have some fun, man.'

'I had some fun last year,' said Reginald.

Mallory shook his head in mock exasperation, then turned to Chopra and Poppy.

'And this must be your lovely wife?'

Chopra's mouth opened, but he could not think of a suitable beginning. He turned to his wife.

For the first time in living memory, however, Poppy was utterly lost for words.

'What is your name, my dear?'

Eventually Poppy cleared her throat. 'Poppy, sir.'

'Poppy? I once had a nanny called Poppy. Well, that wasn't her name, but that's what we christened her. She always had one in her buttonhole, you see – a poppy, that is. Lost her young man in the Great War. Never remarried ... Of course, *she* did not own such a splendid garment as the one you are wearing. Goodness, what a lovely sari. One is almost tempted to drape the old ball and chain in one.'

Poppy smiled uncertainly, wondering exactly what the Commissioner meant by 'ball and chain'. She glanced at Chopra for inspiration.

'Come and sit down,' Mallory continued. 'Have a cup of chai with me. You too, Chopra.'

'I prefer to stand, sir.'

The Commissioner nodded. 'I thought you might. I couldn't persuade young Bomberton here to sit down either.'

Poppy flung her husband another anxious look before advancing to the desk. She gently lowered herself into the Edwardian leather armchair. A silver serving trolley stood by the desk on which was arrayed a sumptuous tea.

'Pour me another cup of that lovely cardamom tea, will you, Poppy? And perhaps I will have another of those delicious, er, what are they called, Reginald?'

'I believe they are commonly referred to as "masala idlis", sir.'

'Ah, yes. Masala idlis. I must confess one is becoming quite addicted to them.' Mallory turned to Chopra. 'Well, Chopra, young Bomberton here advises me that we owe you a debt of gratitude. For recovering the Koh-i-Noor, I mean.'

'I was merely doing my duty, sir,' said Chopra gruffly, relieved to discover that his initial guess as to the motive behind this summons had been correct, and that there was nothing more sinister behind the unexpected invite.

'From what I understand, you went quite above and beyond the call,' said Mallory. 'You are to be commended.'

Chopra looked uncomfortable. He threw a glance at Bomberton who was staring ahead, standing ramrod straight with his hands by his sides. Chopra wondered how long he would be able to keep his stomach sucked in before he was suddenly forced to exhale and send the buttons flying off his waistcoat. The man looked as if he was on the verge of a hernia.

'I am afraid this whole exhibition imbroglio has caused quite the kerfuffle.'

Chopra spent a moment deciphering this sentence before shaking his head. 'Whatever happened was unfortunate, but no one is to blame apart from the thief.'

'No. I suppose not.' Mallory drummed his fingers on the desk, then continued, 'Nevertheless, I am curious about one thing. What do *you* think of all this fuss being made about returning the Koh-i-Noor to your country? One has been led to understand that there has been considerable debate on the matter.'

Chopra opened his mouth to reply and then stopped. He frowned. Poppy had warned him not to embarrass their household. But Chopra had spent his whole life speaking the truth regardless of who it might offend. He was not about to abandon his principles now. 'I believe the Koh-i-Noor is a simple stone, not worth a thing except the value we humans ascribe to it. I believe there are things in this world that are infinitely more valuable – the happiness of a child, the miracle of love, the beauty of a generous spirit – but we are not yet mature enough to recognise this. And so, for now, the Koh-i-Noor is a symbol. It is a symbol of our past weakness because it was taken from our country at a time when we were not able to prevent that from happening. But the world has changed. *We* have changed. So now . . . now I believe that it is time for the Koh-i-Noor to return to the land of its birth.'

Mallory stared at him with an evaluating gaze. From the corner of his eye Chopra saw Bomberton turn a deeper shade of red. He glanced at Poppy and saw that an expression of mortification had overcome her.

'Well said,' the Commissioner eventually murmured. 'A man who speaks his mind. Sometimes one wishes there were more like you around. However, I must confess that I do not share your opinion. You say that the Koh-i-Noor represents a time when India was weak. I believe it is more than that. It represents the shared history that Britain and India have experienced. Both good and bad. By incorporating the Koh-i-Noor into the Crown Jewels the British monarchy understands the debt it owes to India and is reminded too of some of the mistakes we have made in the past. It is important that we never forget those mistakes. That is why we cannot return the Koh-i-Noor yet. But do not be disheartened. I firmly believe that one day it will come home. That is why we agreed to your government's request to exhibit the Crown Jewels here. This was an important first step on that road, the unfortunate theft notwithstanding. You are correct when you say that the Koh-i-Noor is a symbol. And a symbol will endure no matter where it resides.'

Chopra considered the Commissioner's words carefully, then conceded defeat. 'Very well, sir.'

Mallory lifted his teacup and sipped at it, little finger extended. Poppy watched carefully and then lifted her own cup and followed his example, resisting the urge to pour the tea into a saucer and slurp at it, as was her usual wont.

'At any rate, it is my understanding that there is another party to whom one is indebted. Reginald, where is the little fellow?'

'I believe we have him waiting in the other lift, sir,' replied Reginald briskly.

'Well, do bring him in, there's a good chap.'

They waited as the aide left the room.

He returned a few minutes later, flanked by Rogers and the armed security guards who proceeded to hold open the door. Between them, blinking in the bright light, trotted Ganesha.

The little elephant entered the room, spotted Chopra and surged forward, coming to a halt beside him, his trunk reaching out for Chopra's hand. Chopra understood that his young ward was presently overcome by the same nervousness and anxiety that he himself had been feeling. He had transmitted those emotions to Ganesha on the ride over in the van.

He understood now why Ganesha had been invited along with them to the High Commission. At the time the strange request had confused him. But now he recalled that after recovering the Koh-i-Noor he had told Bomberton how Ganesha had helped him in the search of Bulbul Kanodia's home. Bomberton had found the story infinitely amusing, particularly the part where Chopra, dressed as a clown, had fallen off the stage.

Looking at Ganesha now, Chopra felt a surge of pride. The little elephant certainly deserved his share of the credit.

'Don't worry, boy,' he whispered. 'There's nothing to be nervous about.'

'Well,' said the Commissioner, looking at the new arrival. 'You are a handsome devil, aren't you? What is his name again, Chopra?'

'Ganesha, sir.'

'Please step forward, Ganesha. Let me get a better look at you.'

'Sir, I must advise against any closer contact with the, er, pachyderm,' said Reginald. 'I have it on good authority that they can be quite temperamental.'

'Nonsense, Reginald. He's an absolute ace. You can see it in his eyes.'

'Go on, boy,' said Chopra, patting Ganesha on the head. The elephant looked up at him uncertainly, then turned and advanced shyly towards the desk. As he reached the tea trolley, his nostrils suddenly flared. His ears flapped, revealing the little bullet hole that was the legacy of Mukhthar Lodi's demise. Then he reached out with his trunk and deftly lifted an idli from the trolley and popped it into his mouth.

There was a stunned silence. Then the Commissioner burst out a loud guffaw. 'You see, Chopra. Not everyone is so eager to stand on ceremony.'

Mallory reached out and patted Ganesha on the top of his knobbly skull. 'You know, I spoke with the Queen just this morning. Over the years she has been presented with a great many creatures. Cheetahs, giraffes, sloths, bears, even giant turtles from the Seychelles. But the one animal she recalls most fondly is the elephant given to her by the president of Cameroon. His name was Jumbo. The elephant, I mean, not the president. What a lovely, gentle creature he was. The president, I mean, not the elephant. Jumbo himself was a bull and quite a churlish fellow, at first. Until she got to know him. I suppose if one were abducted from one's home and sent halfway around the world as a gift for some nabob or other one would doubtless be exceedingly put out. She told me she would have preferred to send poor Jumbo right back, but protocol can be a very tricky business. Don't you agree, Reginald?'

'Yes, sir,' said the aide.

Mallory rested his gentle eyes on Ganesha who was munching away on another idli, oblivious to his audience. There was a wistful expression on his face, as if he had been transported to another time when, as a boy, he enjoyed a life free of cares and responsibility. Then he looked up.

'Well, Chopra, it is customary to recognise such enterprise as you have displayed with some manner of reward. Young Bomberton here will receive his accolades back home. What may England do for you?'

'I require no reward, sir.'

'Nevertheless, one wishes to show one's appreciation. As India is now a republic the Queen cannot name you in her New Year's Honours list. However, there is something that she wishes to offer you.'

The Commissioner slid open a drawer in his desk and took out a small ornate box. He fiddled with a catch and popped open the lid, then turned the box around.

Inside, nestled in folds of red velvet, was a medal.

Gold-plated and oval-shaped, with the Royal Cipher on one side and the words 'Kaisar-i-Hind for Public Service in India' on the other, the medal was neatly suspended from a dark blue ribbon, also trimmed with gold.

Chopra knew that 'Kaisar-i-Hind' meant 'Empress of India'.

'Queen Victoria instituted this medal in 1900,' explained Mallory. 'It has been awarded many times to deserving citizens of your country. Although we stopped handing these out once India became independent it has not actually been discontinued.'

Chopra cleared his throat. 'I cannot accept this medal, sir.'

A trio of lines appeared on the Commissioner's brow. 'Now, why did I know you were going to say that?'

'I intend no insult. But I cannot accept a medal that is named for an empress of India, for we have no empress.'

There was an awkward silence, into which Chopra heard Bomberton hiss, 'Have you lost your marbles, man?'

'Oh, it's quite all right, Bomberton,' said the Commissioner eventually. He cupped his chin and stared at Chopra. 'Well, you are a man who knows his own mind. And I suppose your refusal puts you in good company. Did you know that a certain gentleman by the name of Mohandas K. Gandhi also turned down this medal?'

'Yes, sir, I was aware of this.'

Mallory sighed. And then Ganesha, ever the curious child, reached out with his trunk and curled it around the box with its glittering toy. He trotted back towards Chopra lest the Commissioner decide to take back his gift.

Mallory laughed genteelly. 'Well, Chopra, it seems as if the choice has been made for you.'

Chopra's face was troubled.

'Think of it as a gift,' said the Commissioner gently. 'A trinket from a friend to show her appreciation. Not only for the return of something very precious to her, but for the love and warmth that you and your countrymen have shown to Her Majesty during her time here. I assure you, your principles will not be compromised by accepting it.'

Chopra hesitated. Eventually, he smiled. 'You are very persuasive, sir. I accept. Thank you.'

'Splendid,' said the Commissioner, clapping his hands. 'Now, how about we get back to the party so you can tell me all about how you recovered the Koh-i-Noor? One does so love a good mystery!'

GLOSSARY

Aam junta – the general public / the ordinary masses

Abbu – Islamic term for Father

Astrakhan hat – hat with dark curly fleece of young karakul lambs from central Asia

Bajra – black millet

Beedi – thin Indian rolled cigarette

Betel nut – areca nut

Bhel puri – Mumbai's signature street food dish of puffed rice, onions, tomatoes, spices, and hot chutney and served with a tiny deep fried bread called 'puri'

Boondi raita – savoury dip of yogurt, spices and tiny gram-flour pearls

Brinjal – aubergine

Carrom – 'strike and pocket' table game akin to table shuffleboard

Dahl – lentil dish

Dhaba – a motorway curry house diner

Dhoti – traditional men's garment wrapped around legs and knotted at the waist

Diwali – Hindu festival of lights

Diya – cup-shaped terracotta oil lamp traditionally lit on Diwali

Duffer – an incompetent or stupid person

Eidi – gift for festival of Eid e.g. money, presents or flowers

Ghazal – poetic form consisting of rhyming couplets and a refrain

Goonda – thug or bully

Hajji – Muslim person who has successfully completed the Hajj to Mecca

Hapoos – Alphonso mango, considered 'king of mangoes'

Hawala – illegal method of transferring money outside of traditional banking systems

Jagirdar – feudal landowner or landlord

Jowar – sorghum flour

Kabuli Biryani – traditional chickpea biryani dish from Hyderabad

Kameez – long tunic worn by many people from South Asia, typically with a salwar

Khansama – male cook, who often also assumes the role of house steward

Kurta – loose collarless shirt worn usually with a salwar or pyjama

Lakh – One hundred thousand

Lathi – a stick / baton

Makhani – a Hindi word meaning 'with butter' or butter sauce

Masala movie – a movie embodying a blend of genres

Masala sambar – spicy lentil-based vegetable stew

Maya – 'that which is not' (i.e. illusion)

Mawali – Mumbai slang for lowest class of male street ruffians

Morcha – organized march or rally

Neem – Indian tree used for its antiseptic properties

Nukkud natak – Indian street Play

Pajama – a pair of loose trousers tied by a drawstring around the waist

Panchayat – a village council in rural India

Pomfret – popular fish found in Indian restaurants

Ram ram – a common Hindi greeting meaning hello

Salwar – a pair of light, loose, pleated trousers, usually tapering to a tight fit around the ankles, worn by women with a kameez (the two together being a Sadhu – a religious ascetic or holy person)

Sarpanch – elected head of the village council (the panchayat) in India

Shatranj – old form of chess from which modern chess developed

Shree – polite form of address equivalent to the English 'Mr'

Swami – holy ascetic initiated into a specific religious order

Thaali – Indian steel platter with individual sections to serve a variety of dishes

Vasta waza – Kashmiri term for a head chef

Vedji – traditional Indian Ayurvedic medical practitioner

Yaar – informal address, akin to addressing someone as 'mate'

ACKNOWLEDGEMENTS

Once again this book represents a collective endeavor. So thank you, first and foremost, to my agent Euan Thorneycroft at A.M. Heath and to my tirelessly enthusiastic editor Ruth Tross at Mulholland. As I see the series move from success to success their faith now seems prophetic. A big thank you to Kerry Hood at Hodder, who has worked miracles to catapult me into mags, newspapers, radio and TV – a veritable one-woman publicity machine.

I am grateful too to others who helped improve the original manuscript. Thomas Abraham and Poulomi Chatterjee at Hachette India; Amber Burlinson, copy-editor, and Justine Taylor, in the role of proofreader.

I would also like to thank Ruth's team at Mulholland, Naomi Berwin in marketing, Laura Oliver in production, Dom Gribben in audiobooks, and Ruth's assistant Cicely Aspinall. In the US thanks go to Devi Pillai, Ellen Wright, Laura Fitzgerald and Lindsey Hall, and also Jason Bartholomew at Hodder. Similar thanks go to Euan's assistant Pippa McCarthy, and the others at A.M. Heath working hard to sprinkle the magic of this series far and wide. A thank you to Satish Garewal for voicing the audiobook.

Yet more kudos to Anna Woodbine who designed and illustrated the novel's cover, once again bringing the story to life with a flourish of her wand.

Lastly, I'd like to thank those who have helped me research this work. My wife Nirupama Khan, my friends from Mumbai, and my colleagues at UCL who not only crack me over the knuckles when I make a mistake in Chopra's crime-solving methods but have been unflagging in their support for the whole endeavor. A special thank you to my colleague Kati Carter who baked me an Inspector Chopra cake complete with icing sugar Ganesha (though his ears have subsequently fallen off – sorry, Kati!) Lastly a mention for Khurram Khan, who many years ago, when a rabid computer had swallowed an entire manuscript of an early novel – engendering in me suicidal thoughts of quitting this writing business altogether – typed up the paper draft, so that I could, and would, carry on.

MURDER ON ELEPHANTA ISLAND

A Baby Ganesh Detective Agency short mystery

Vaseem Khan

MULHOLLAND
BOOKS
HODDER

Elephanta Island: a lonely stub of tide-tormented rock lying ten kilometres out in Mumbai harbour, dominated by mango and tamarind tree covered hills. Named by the Portuguese for a colossal stone elephant found there in the early sixteenth century, the island is a favourite tourist haunt thanks to the enigmatic cave temples cut into these hills.

The last time Inspector Ashwin Chopra (Retd) had set foot on the island, it had been under very different circumstances: a day out with his beloved wife Poppy, a genuinely pleasant time exploring the ancient India that he adored and which, he often felt, was being eroded by the myriad onslaughts of the modern world.

As he stepped from the chartered launch onto the island's western jetty, he looked back across the bay to Mumbai. The metropolis whose citizens he had sworn to protect and serve was a cannibal's stew of twenty million souls living cheek to jowl in the 'city of dreams', a city of slums and skyscrapers, a smelly, polluted, clamorous and impossibly crowded place where dreams and nightmares co-existed.

Chopra knew this better than most. He had spent three decades observing the city through his policeman's eyes, before an ailing heart had forced him into early retirement. The retirement had, ultimately, brought with it new opportunities, such as the detective agency he now ran.

'You're late.'

Chopra turned to see a pale, redheaded woman in safari shorts marching down the jetty towards him, accompanied by a balding Indian male struggling to keep pace. The woman, Chopra knew, was Hannah Troon, daughter of noted British archaeologist Henry Troon.

Two days earlier Henry had fallen to his death from a local peak known as Cannon Hill. A cursory police investigation had labelled his demise a suicide. Unhappy with this verdict, Troon's daughter had decided to conduct her own investigation, and had called in Chopra.

Hannah braked to a sudden halt, staring past Chopra to the second party disembarking from the launch. 'Why do you have an elephant with you?'

It was the question Chopra always dreaded. What answer could he give? That a year ago his long-lost uncle Bansi had sent him a one-year-old baby elephant, and tasked him to care for it? That there was much more to his little ward than met the eye? That, in some ways, Ganesha had become his 'partner' in the agency?

He sighed. 'It's a long story. Shall we get to the camp? I'd like to talk to the others.'

The camp – a collection of whitewashed brick cabins built into the hillside a half-kilometre from the island's main cave temple complex – was home to the archaeological team working on Elephanta. Chopra had asked Hannah to summon everyone to the canteen.

Just as he entered the long, low-roofed building, he felt the first warm drops of rain strike his cheek. It was monsoon season – the only time Elephanta was closed to tourists, and thus open to archaeologists – and the weather lay over the island like a damp towel.

In the canteen Chopra discovered three individuals, two foreigners – an aging, attractive blonde woman, and a greying, patrician-looking gentleman – and a young Indian male, smoking furiously in one corner.

The woman, he guessed, was Elizabeth Troon, wife of the deceased. The man consoling her must be Professor Perry Noble, an American archaeologist and longtime associate of the late Professor Henry Troon. The Indian, he suspected, was Ankit Gupta, who, Hannah had informed him, had worked directly under her father's instruction.

'I would like to ask you all some questions about Professor Troon's last movements,' Chopra began. He was interrupted by Elizabeth Troon breaking into sobs.

'Do we have to go over this again?' asked Noble. 'Henry killed himself. It's tragic, but that's all there is to it.'

'My father would never have done that,' said Hannah, eyes flashing. 'He had no reason for doing that.'

Noble hesitated. 'I didn't want to say this in front of your mother, but Henry had been deeply despondent of late. He was worried that with the end of the monsoon just a month away he would never finish his work in the caves. The local government has made it clear we will not be allowed to continue once tourist season returns.'

'That's no reason for him to kill himself!'

'Henry needed this more than you know. He has been under intense financial pressure. I'm afraid he made some bad investments over the past few years. To be frank, he's mired in debt, with the sort of people who don't take kindly to defaulters. Cataloguing his discovery would have opened all sorts of doors for him, given him a chance. But increasingly he believed that chance was slipping away.'

'What exactly is his discovery?' asked Chopra.

'Why, Henry found a new complex of caves,' replied Noble. 'An astonishing find! There are statues and reliefs in them even older than those in the present cave systems – thousands of years older. It'll make both of us household names once we publish. Or would have done.'

'What exactly is your role here?'

'I am his collaborator. Henry called me in a month ago when he realized just how much work was involved. We've known each other since our Cambridge days.'

'When did you last see Professor Troon?'

'The evening of his death. Our routine was to work in the caves from dawn till an hour before dusk. Then we would return here for supper, before retiring. I visited Henry in his room after supper. He was terribly down. I tried to buck him up, but there was no talking to him.'

'What about you, Mrs Troon?'

Elizabeth Troon lifted her haggard face. 'I was down in the village,' she said. 'The last time I saw Henry was that morning. I agree he seemed down, but I never suspected this.' She hovered on the verge of tears again.

'And you?' said Chopra, turning to the young Indian. 'Ankit Gupta, I presume?'

'Yes,' the youth replied, puffing violently on his distinctively coloured cheroot. Chopra's nostrils twitched at the pungent odour. 'I am Professor Troon's PhD student. He is a visiting professor at Mumbai University where I am completing my thesis. I have been working on Elephanta with him from the beginning of our excavations here.'

Chopra evaluated the boy's thin face, the trace of a moustache, the darting eyes. Something in his manner rang hollow. 'When did you last see him?'

'In the canteen, at supper.'

'What did you do after that?'

'I was in my cabin working on my thesis.'

Finally, Chopra turned to the man who had accompanied Hannah to the jetty.

Short, round, and balding, this was Krishnamachari

Iyengar, head curator of the Elephanta caves. 'And you, sir, when did you last see Troon?'

'I live on the mainland,' said Iyengar. 'It is my routine to join Professor Troon for supper so that he can update me on his progress. After that I left for Mumbai on a boat.'

'And who found the body?'

'Villagers,' replied Hannah bitterly. 'They're the ones you should be questioning. *They* killed my father!'

'What makes you say that?'

'The headman, a guy named Raj, came in here the day before my father died, threatening him.'

'Why?'

Noble explained. 'The current caves are dominated by statues of Lord Shiva, whom the villagers worship devoutly. The new cave system is altogether different. It is devoted to the dark goddess, Kali. The villagers are terrified of her; they fear her wrath. They wanted Henry to stop his excavations, and close the caves. They do not want Kali unleashed on their island.' He shrugged. 'They're a superstitious bunch.'

Having searched the deceased man's room Chopra discovered only one anomaly – a bedside drawer, the lock of which appeared to have been forced.

He sat down on the bed and looked at the autopsy sheet detailing the items that had been recovered from Troon's body: a bottle of sleeping pills, a mobile phone, a key. Chopra had the key with him. He inserted it into the lock.

It turned perfectly.

So, someone had broken into the drawer. What had they taken? What had Troon been keeping under lock and key?

The autopsy list had been given to Chopra by the pathologist at the Apollo Spectra hospital in south Mumbai where Troon's corpse had been taken. The autopsy had been a quick affair, death-by-suicide a convenient verdict the pathologist had been only too happy to set his seal to. Any other verdict – even death-by-misadventure – would have cast the local authorities in a negative light, and potentially damaged foreign tourism to the island.

In the end the almighty rupee had held sway.

But Chopra had been puzzled by the four round bruises on Troon's upper chest. He had seen similar bruises before, and did not think they were consistent with a fall, as the pathologist claimed them to be . . .

Yet the morning at the hospital had not proved altogether fruitless. Having viewed Troon's body, his handsome face arrogant even in death, Chopra had visited the nearby Mumbai University. Here he discovered that Troon was ill liked, a temperamental and insensitive man, respected in his field, but not admired. He seemed to have a history of rubbing people the wrong way.

In the village of Gharapuri, at Elephanta Island's southern tip, Chopra confronted the headman Jamna Raj in his dilapidated hut, with its faded yellow paintwork, and monkeys shrieking from the roof. 'I had nothing to do with his death,' protested Raj in Hindi. 'Yes, I threatened him. But the threat was not from me. I told him Kali would exact a heavy price if he unleashed her. I was right.'

Chopra knew the islanders lived a precarious existence. For eight months of the year they survived on tourism; during the monsoon they eked out a living from fishing and rice cultivation. A single failed crop could mean ruin. In the evenings life came to a standstill for the island's twelve hundred inhabitants – in spite of annual promises, the government had failed to supply electricity to the village.

'Where were you when he died?'

'Out on my boat,' replied Raj. 'If you want to know what happened to the foreigner you must ask Iyengar.'

'Iyengar? Why him?'

'Not him. *Her*.' And he would say no more.

As Hannah Troon led him up the slopes of Cannon Hill, Chopra wondered what the village headman had meant. He would have to ask Iyengar later. For now . . .

Perched at the top of a steep climb were two seventeenth-century cannon, each mounted on a circular iron dais capable of turning full circle to give a 360 degree field of attack. The space under the dais – once used for storing shells – now provided a natural shelter from the elements.

On one side of the cannon, the hill fell away sharply from a stone ledge. This was the place where Troon had supposedly leapt to his death, rolling down the rocky slope and breaking his neck.

What were you doing here? Chopra thought. His wife and colleagues claimed he was in the habit of going for walks in the evening. But Chopra had checked the weather reports. It had rained grimly that night. Why would Troon have come up here in the near dark, in treacherous monsoon weather?

He heard Ganesha shuffling around behind him. 'What is it boy?' he said. 'Are you hungry?' The little elephant became anxious if he wasn't fed on a regular basis. Chopra hunted in his pocket and gave him one of the Dairy Milk chocolate bars to which Ganesha was addicted. Having gobbled the chocolate Ganesha raised his trunk and sniffed the air. An elephant's trunk, Chopra knew, was an amazing sensory organ, one of the most powerful on the planet. He watched as Ganesha trotted to a nearby rock, and tapped his trunk against a small opening below it. It looked like a snake-hole to Chopra.

He got on his hands and knees and peered inside. 'Are you sure, boy?'

Ganesha peered at him intently. It was at such moments that Chopra was forced to re-examine the strange fact that his 'partner' was an elephant. Not that he ever said that aloud. Who would believe him if he did? But ever since Bansi had sent him the little elephant to look after – with the enigmatic note stating 'This is no ordinary elephant' – he had come to realise that, indeed, there was something altogether inexplicable about his ward. Ganesha possessed a genuine intelligence and instincts that had inspired him to come to Chopra's aid on numerous occasions during the past year. Ultimately Chopra had decided to trust his *own* instincts – he now made a habit of taking the elephant with him when he went out on his investigations. He had yet to regret his decision.

He reached into the hole, drawing out a discarded crisps packet, a Coca Cola bottle . . . and the stub of a rolled-up cigarette. Peering at it, Chopra realized that its distinctive colour looked familiar. Borrowing a lighter from Hannah he lit the soggy dog-end, and took a sniff of the damply pungent smoke . . . 'Got you!' he muttered.

'I admit I went after him,' said Ankit Gupta, his brown cheeks reddening. 'I was furious.'

'Why?' asked Chopra. He had discovered Gupta in his cabin, working on his laptop, puffing furiously on another of his distinctive rollups.

'He stole my discovery, that's why!' exploded the youth bitterly. '*I* found those new caves, as part of my thesis research on the island. I was so excited when I called him to tell him – he was my PhD supervisor, after all. He told me not to tell anyone else until he could verify the discovery. He didn't want me to make a fool of myself. I trusted him. He repaid me by holding a press conference and claiming *he* had made the big find. He told me to keep my mouth shut or he would fail my PhD. His voice carries weight – he is a world authority on Indian rock-cut temples. He's been coming here for twenty years. His text on the Ellora caves is standard reading.'

'Did you push him?'

'No. I mean, we came to blows, and I hit him. I missed his face and struck his chest. He fell to the floor, but that's how I left him. Alive.'

Well, thought Chopra, that explained the distinctive bruising – the marks left by the knuckles of Ankit Gupta's swinging fist. But was Gupta a killer?

Chopra's phone rang. It was Rangwalla, his associate investigator. He listened intently, then shut the phone, and walked determinedly towards the cabin of Professor Perry Noble.

In the cabin he discovered Noble and Elizabeth Troon consoling themselves with a bottle of Scotch. 'Tell me,' said Chopra, 'did you know about Professor Troon's book deal? His TV series?'

Noble sat down heavily. 'How did you find out about that?'

'I obtained the call log from Troon's mobile phone, then had my associate chase down each number. Troon has been in daily conversation with a big British production house for a TV series on Indian temples. He has signed a major book deal, with a huge advance. He is setting himself up as a modern day Howard Carter. It all appears to be very lucrative. The only problem is that his agent claims that Troon had no intention of sharing this new wealth with his *collaborators.* He was worried that you would cause him problems.'

Noble sighed. 'You know, he's always been a backstabbing scoundrel. He borrowed money from me years ago. A lot of money. Never paid me back. Then he calls me out of the blue. Says he'll make up for it by bringing me in on this incredible new find on Elephanta. That we'll write a book together, then go on the celebrity talk show circuit. Live out our days in splendour. Hah! I fell for it once again. When I overheard him on the phone talking to his agent about the deal, I confronted him. The pig actually admitted he was going to cut me out. He said it couldn't be helped; there simply wasn't enough to go around!' Noble reached out and took Elizabeth Troon's hands in his own. 'I could have killed him, but I didn't. Aside from anything else, the man was a philanderer.'

'You two are having an affair, aren't you?' said Chopra. 'And with Troon out of the way you would have been able to step into his shoes. To the victor the spoils.'

'I would have divorced Henry after this trip,' Elizabeth said. 'I've had enough.'

'Frankly,' said Noble, 'I don't know where he gets the energy. A man of his age.'

A man of his age. These words circled in Chopra's thoughts as he tracked Krishnamachari Iyengar down in the main Elephanta cave complex. The words had ignited a new line of enquiry. Why had Troon gone for a walk each evening, even in pouring rain? What had Jamna Raj meant by 'Not him. *Her*'. Working on a hunch, Chopra had gone back to quiz the headman, then placed a call to the mainland, to the Apollo hospital, making a very specific request.

Now, he had his answers.

He found Iyengar on a scaffold beside the twenty-foot-high *trimurti* – the three-headed bust of Shiva in his roles of destroyer, preserver and creator. A lantern swung by the curator's elbow as he patiently worked on a crumbling spot beside one of Lord Shiva's ears.

'The Portuguese used them for target practice,' Iyengar said. 'And now the tourists tramp through here with their cameras and snack bars without the slightest idea of what such antiquity implies. This is proof positive that man has a soul. That man shrugs aside the chains of his brute animal nature and contemplates the unfathomable mysteries of the cosmos. In these gods and goddesses we reveal our innermost hopes and fears.'

'And what is it that you fear most?' Chopra asked. 'The corruption of your only child? Your daughter? The sole remaining memory of your departed wife?'

Iyengar put down his pick and climbed down from the scaffold to face Chopra.

Behind him Ganesha shuffled his feet in the dim cave, squinting up at a pint-sized relief of elephant-headed Lord Ganesha. He seemed fascinated by the pot-bellied little god.

'How did you find out?' Iyengar asked.

'The villagers,' Chopra replied. 'Plus it always bothered me that sleeping pills were found on Troon – his daughter told me he slept the sleep of the dead. So I had them tested. What does an aging man with a young lover do to ensure he is up to the vigorous demands of romance? . . . He enlists the help of modern medicine. For the sake of simplicity let us call the pills that Troon was taking "Viagra". Of course, he couldn't risk his wife accidentally discovering them so he took the precaution of putting them in a pill-bottle marked "sleeping tablets".'

Iyengar sighed. 'I thought it would be good for my daughter's future if she served as secretary to the renowned archaeologist Professor Henry Troon. I was wrong. He seduced her. She was young and innocent. Their trysts took place up on Cannon Hill, beneath the shelter of the eastern cannon. Each evening, as regular as clockwork, right under my nose. Making me the fool of a father who merrily ran after the man corrupting his daughter. Like a faithful lapdog. How he must have laughed at me.'

'And that is why you killed him?'

Iyengar pushed his spectacles back up his nose. 'I *wanted* to kill him. But I did not. That is the truth.'

'I don't believe you. You followed him up to Cannon Hill on the evening of his death. Admit it.'

'I admit I planned to do just that. I had already spoken with my daughter. I knew they were due to meet that evening. But I had locked her up in her room back home on the mainland and taken away her phone. I knew he would be waiting up there, like a spider. But as I made to leave I saw someone else headed up the trail after him. I knew I couldn't go through with it then, not with a potential witness around.'

'Who did you see headed up the hill?'

'You lied to me,' said Chopra, facing Elizabeth Troon in the camp canteen. 'You confronted your husband on Cannon Hill on the day of his death.'

'If I lied it was a lie of omission,' said Elizabeth calmly. 'It's what he deserved.'

'So you admit you killed him?'

'Of course not. I didn't go up there to kill him, only to tell him I was leaving him. That's the reason I flew out here two weeks ago. Percy told me what Henry was up to – with the girl, I mean. He wanted me to wait before breaking it off, until their excavations were done, but I just couldn't. We've been all but estranged this past year, anyway. Frankly, I've hated having to share a cabin with him out here, keeping up the pretence. I'd see Henry going out each evening with a smug grin on his face. He must have thought I was so stupid. Well, I finally snapped and went up to confront him. Do you know, that wretched man laughed at me? He said that a divorce would do me no good. I wouldn't get a penny from him. He was leaving me the sinking ship of debts he'd accumulated back in England, while he and his new princess would live abroad off his newfound wealth. He said he had even made a new will cutting me out and naming her as his sole beneficiary. He stood there on a rock staring out to sea in the rain as if he was Nelson on the prow of *HMS Victory*. I could have pushed him down the hill. God knows I wanted to. But I didn't.'

On the way back to the camp Chopra whirled the possibilities around his mind. The rain had started again, and Ganesha, who loved the mud that the rain brought with it, lifted his trunk happily to the heavens as fat monsoon droplets pinged off his hide.

His guardian was oblivious, even as his hair, clothes, shoes, and even his moustache became waterlogged.

Who was the killer? Chopra thought. Each had his or her motive: Ankit Gupta, whose career-making discovery had been stolen from him. Curator Iyengar whose daughter had been sullied by the lecherous old professor. Troon's hapless would-be collaborator Perry Noble, hoodwinked once again by a consummate scoundrel. Or the dead man's long-suffering wife, Elizabeth, who had, long ago, been cut out of his affections, and was now cut out of his will.

Chopra's thoughts lingered on the will. When had Troon changed it? Based on Elizabeth Troon's testimony, it must have been recently, during Troon's time on the island. If so, where had he kept the new will? A man like Troon would have wanted it close. Chopra's thoughts flashed to the forced drawer in Troon's bedroom. Perhaps that was what the intruder had been looking for.

Who could it be? Elizabeth Troon? Possibly. After all, she had the most to lose. But something else was nagging at him. Something Rangwalla had uncovered in his investigations.

He took out his phone and dialled his associate investigator.

'Rangwalla,' he said, 'you mentioned that there was a call from a life insurance agency in the UK on Troon's phone. He had a policy with them, a substantial one. I want you to phone them back and find out who was paying the premiums. Do it now.'

Chopra waited in the canteen for Rangwalla to call back, watching Ganesha as he happily slurped up milk from a large copper bowl. His phone rang. As Rangwalla spoke, Chopra began to formulate a hypothesis. He finally had an idea of who might have been behind Henry Troon's death.

'What the hell are you doing in my room?'

Chopra turned to see a strident Hannah Troon, hands on hips, framed in the doorway of her cabin. Rainwater sparkled from her bare arms and shins, and ran in rivulets down her face.

'I am conducting a search,' said Chopra.

'What the devil for?'

'This,' said Chopra, and held up a sheaf of papers.

Hannah paled. 'You can't just come in here and take that.

You need a-a search warrant or something. That's private property.'

'This cabin belongs to the Archaeological Survey of India and I have Iyengar's permission to search it. And this document – the last will and testament of Henry Troon – does not belong to you. You stole it after you killed your father. You took it from his locked bedside drawer.'

'That's ridiculous. If I had killed my father why in the hell would I call you in to investigate his death?'

'Because insurance companies do not usually pay out for suicides. And your father had a sizeable life insurance policy. Once I had all the facts, *that* bothered me. According to Professor Noble your father was in debt – why would he take out a policy to help his wife after his death, a woman he was leaving for another? How could he even afford it? Yes, it was a real puzzle . . . until the life insurance agency confirmed that *you* had taken out the policy on his behalf, and that *you* were making the payments on it. Had been doing so for years.'

Hannah's arms fell. The fight seemed to go out of her. 'I just wanted my mother to have something in case he died. Something more than a lifetime of bad memories.'

'Why did you kill him?'

'I never meant to. I came out here to see him because I knew they were having problems. I wanted to persuade him not to give up on their marriage. But then I overheard him talking to his lawyer, about the new will he'd had made, cutting us both out. He was going to check it over and sign it next week – then hand it to my mother on her birthday. He was a vindictive man, my father, even when he didn't need to be.' She sighed. 'I followed him up to Cannon Hill, after my mother had been up to talk to him. At first I hid in the bushes, watching him. I saw Ankit march past. The two of them quarrelled; Ankit knocked him to the floor, then left. I burst out of the trees, and started helping him to his feet. That's when he snarled at me. "You're as stupid as your mother".' Before I knew what I was doing I had pushed him over the slope. It was as easy as that. After that I stumbled around in a blind panic. I wanted to confess but somehow I couldn't. And when the police came and immediately labelled it a suicide, I was elated. Yes, I took the new will from his drawer. I didn't want his secret girlfriend to inherit a penny. Everything my father had should have gone to my mother. Then I found out about the debt. There was nothing to inherit. That's when I remembered the life insurance policy. But when I called them they told me flatly they don't pay out on suicides. So I had to call you in.'

As Chopra rode back to the mainland on the launch later that evening he dwelt on Hannah's words. *It was as easy as that.* How often had he heard that sentiment in the myriad crimes he had investigated! 'People are the ultimate mystery, aren't they, Ganesha?' he murmured, reflecting on the young woman whose life was now ruined. In some cosmic accounting, a man like Troon deserved the fate that had befallen him, Chopra felt, whereas Hannah and her mother . . . deserved better.

The little elephant, peering over the gunwale at the steadily dwindling island behind them, trumpeted softly, then reached out to wrap his trunk around Chopra's hand.

'Perhaps in the next life I'll be born an elephant,' Chopra smiled, 'and *you* will be in *my* shoes. I wish you all the luck. You'll need it, my little friend.'